"PLEASE GOD, MAKE KATHLEEN GO AWAY," CERISE WHISPERED.

She squinched her eyes shut and said the words over and over. She had prayed that her step-grandmother wouldn't be at the picnic—and it worked. Maybe God would find a way to make her sister disappear.

She watched as Kathleen toddled up to the edge of the water. She was clapping her hands together and jabbering at the ducks. If Kathleen didn't go away, Cerise would be late for the races. She might not get any ice cream.

Kathleen stepped off the path into the water. Mud bubbled up around the top of her shoes.

Cerise darted forward. It took only one good shove with her hand. Cerise raced up the trail.

She had to get away before Kathleen started screaming. . . .

TERROR LIVES!

THE SHADOW MAN   (1946, $3.95)
by Stephen Gresham
The Shadow Man could hide anywhere—under the bed, in the closet, behind the mirror . . . even in the sophisticated circuitry of little Joey's computer. And the Shadow Man could make Joey do things that no little boy should ever do!

SIGHT UNSEEN   (2038, $3.95)
by Andrew Neiderman
David was always right. Always. But now that he was growing up, his gift was turning into a power. The power to know things—terrible things—that he didn't want to know. Like who would live . . . and who would die!

MIDNIGHT BOY   (2065, $3.95)
by Stephen Gresham
Something horrible is stalking the town's children. For one of its most trusted citizens possesses the twisted need and cunning of a psychopathic killer. Now Town Creek's only hope lies in the horrific, blood-soaked visions of the MIDNIGHT BOY!

TEACHER'S PET   (1927, $3.95)
by Andrew Neiderman
All the children loved their teacher Mr. Lucy. It was astonishing to see how they all seemed to begin to resemble Mr. Lucy. And act like Mr. Lucy. And kill like Mr. Lucy!

DEW CLAWS   (1808, $3.50)
by Stephen Gresham
Jonathan's terrifying memories of watching his three brothers and their uncle sucked into the fetid mud at Night Horse Swamp were just beginning to fade. But the dank odor of decay all around him reminded Jonathan that the nightmare wasn't over yet. The horror had taken everything Jonathan loved. And now it had come back for him!

Available wherever paperbacks are sold, or order direct from the Publisher. Send cover price plus 50¢ per copy for mailing and handling to Zebra Books, Dept. 2841, 475 Park Avenue South, New York, N.Y. 10016. Residents of New York, New Jersey and Pennsylvania must include sales tax. DO NOT SEND CASH.

AFTERNOON OF THE GOSLING

MARLYS HUFFMAN

ZEBRA BOOKS
KENSINGTON PUBLISHING CORP.

Any resemblance to actual persons, living or dead, is coincidental.

ZEBRA BOOKS

are published by

Kensington Publishing Corp.
475 Park Avenue South
New York, NY 10016

First printing: December, 1989

Printed in the United States of America

Chapter One

It came at him from the left. Out of a clump of wild blackberry vines . . . a small white blur . . . a dull thump. Phil's stomach muscles twisted and jerked into spasms when he felt the impact.

The momentum of the car whirled the tiny body into the air. It flashed briefly in front of the windshield, then flipped end over end. A shrill squeal pierced the air. The squeal mingled with the screech of tires to bring the green Pinto skidding to a spine-shaking stop.

Phil Thayer pulled himself up from the seat and peered across the car over Wilma's shoulder. He kept the brake pedal forced down against the floorboard until a tremor ran through his leg and the tendons in his ankle ached.

Like a punctured concertina, the body lay folded in the roadside ditch. With one last high-pitched whimper, the dog's mouth gaped and spewed blood onto the curled sprigs of bracken. The furry white body heaved once, expelled one final trickle of blood, and froze in death.

In the tangled blackberry vines, a bluejay screamed obscenely and soared into the air. A blue flash dipped low over the car and disappeared over a swaying fir. The

Oregon country road settled back into silence.

Phil eased himself down onto the seat. His long fingers gripped the steering wheel and tried to shake it from the column. He shook it with an inner fury, as if the wheel could pump air back into the animal's lifeless body.

"Oh, no. . . ." His voice trailed off, cracking in the depths of his throat. He swallowed hard and released his grip. If only he could dislodge the mixture of horror and anger surging through his chest. . . .

Anger at the owner who had let the dog run loose. Horror at realizing three-year-old Cerise was confronted with death. It wasn't the image he wanted implanted in her mind. Her new stepfather—the dog killer. Didn't most children love dogs?

He wasn't on firm ground with Cerise, not yet. He was not sure she accepted him. She looked at him with a sober, wary expression. She called him "Daddy Phil," but she hardly ever smiled at his attempts to amuse her.

Phil glanced once at his wife before he turned toward the backseat. Wilma's crystal-blue eyes were wide and glazed. For once, her mouth was open without a sound emerging. She stared trancelike out the car window, stared at the little ditch, gaped in shock. The skin pulled tightly across her cheekbones had taken on a pallor, leaving red blotches on her face.

The blotches looked suspiciously like cosmetics. Blush? Was Wilma wearing blush? She was adept with makeup. Phil clenched his fists on the wheel. He'd explained how narrow-minded his mother was, but Wilma had to have everything spelled out to her.

His fingers relaxed, and he looked away. It probably wouldn't make any difference. His mother wasn't going to accept Wilma as a daughter-in-law, not willingly. At least Wilma could have tried to make the situation easier.

6

She could have skipped the blue eye shadow and the eye liner for one afternoon.

Cerise emitted a piercing screech that made him wince. The screech reverberated in the compact sedan and sawed through his already stretched-out nerves.

"Cerise?" He turned and leaned over the back of the seat. "Cerise, are you all right?"

The little girl stood on the seat, bouncing gleefully up and down onto her toes and then onto her heels. The tiered ruffles of her pink dotted dress rippled in playful excitement. The delicate blonde hair swirled with every jump. One strand slithered from its barrette. Her green eyes glistened from under skimpy colorless lashes.

"Make the noise again, Daddy Phil!" A delighted giggle bubbled in her throat. She clapped her small hands together and hopped ecstatically around, making an improvised trampoline of the car seat.

"Doggie made a funny noise." She squealed and continued to jump. A wide smile showed the sharp, shining baby teeth. "Make him do it again."

Phil's spine shuddered at the penetrating sound of her voice. She was attempting to imitate the dog's final squeal of agony.

"Cerise! The dog is dead! He can't do it again." Phil Thayer stared at his stepdaughter and then turned back to his wife. His mouth fell open as he turned his head.

"Wilma, she's . . ." He continued to move his head from side to side and groped for the words. "I don't understand how she could laugh about a thing like this. Wilma?" He reached across the car, digging his fingers into his wife's arm and shaking it when his words failed to penetrate and interrupt her horrified stare.

"Wilma!"

Her head turned toward him. She looked directly into his face, but her eyes were blank.

"What?"

"Your daughter . . . Cerise . . . She's laughing."

Wilma turned slowly toward the backseat. Her eyes were clouded and confused. She gazed at Cerise for a moment and then looked back at him.

"Well, she's a happy child." Wilma's shoulders twitched in a so-what shrug.

"Happy? I've just killed a dog and she laughs. What kind of daughter do you have, anyway? She's not normal."

Wilma's mouth twisted at the corners and opened soundlessly. The expression on her face became more bewildered. She kept staring at him with an uncomprehending wideness of her eyes.

"She doesn't know what happened, Phil. She's only three. You're gonna have to get used to being a father."

"Going, Wilma."

"What?" Her eyes opened to their fullest extent, and the dark eyebrows arched upward.

"You must learn to say *going*. Not *gonna*. The word is *going*."

"Oh." Her voice drifted off into a faint whisper. She dropped her eyelids, submitting to his correction without argument.

Phil noticed the tight lines around her full lips and reached over to pat her knee. She was so petite and so naive. He had wanted to change her life from the first moment he had seen her floundering, trying to add a restaurant meal check. He had added the column of figures for her and been appalled at her handwriting, but most of all he had wanted to hold her in his arms.

"Don't be upset, Wilma." He gave her hand a gentle squeeze. "You can learn. I promise you. It's not your fault. Lots of girls have to quit school when they get pregnant."

8

"I dunno about it, Phil." Her eyes closed for a second, and he felt a wave of sympathy at the flicker of her long lashes. "You know I flunked two grades in school," she admitted. "I don't learn things too good."

"Who could, being raised in foster homes? I'll be teaching you now. It'll be different." He slid one hand under her chin and watched her frown disappear. He decided to ease up on the grammar corrections . . . today wasn't the day for it. She wasn't stupid, but it would take time and patience.

Phil patted her shoulder and glanced back at Cerise once more. The child continued to bounce up and down with a radiance of total happiness. When her eyes met his, she wrinkled her nose playfully.

"The doggie's dead. The doggie's dead," she chanted in a singsong voice.

He shook his head again. "I know I don't understand being a father, Wilma, but I do understand you. You aren't firm enough with her. She's going to grow up thinking everything is a game — even death. It's not right. We're going to have trouble with her, I can feel it."

He frowned. "She's supposed to have her seat belt on. Why didn't you strap her in?"

"I did." Wilma's voice was flat. "She unbuckles it."

"You have to make her mind." He turned to Cerise and snapped, "Sit down on the seat. You can't jump around. Not when we're driving. And fasten your seat belt around you."

Cerise gave one last springing leap and bounced into a sitting position. She wiggled and kicked at the back of the seat with one foot before she leaned back against the cushions. A faint smile crossed her face. She drew the seat belt around her and fastened the ends together with sober deliberation. With one last defiant glare, she folded her hands primly in her lap, waiting for the car to move.

Phil's hand twisted the ignition key with a quick, angry movement. The engine caught and roared when he tromped viciously on the gas pedal.

"Aren't you going to do anything about the dog?" Wilma asked.

"What do you expect me to do? I can't do anything for it. The animal is dead."

"Aren't you supposed to find an owner or something?"

He slid the car into gear and pulled back into the road, picking up speed to get away from the site.

"Look around you, Wilma. See any houses here? I'd have to go down side roads and hunt for hours. We don't have time enough to do anything about the dog."

He pushed down on the accelerator, sending the car into a burst of speed, more anxious than ever to put the area out of his line of vision.

"We could have buried it or something."

"Oh, sure. With what? The next thing I know, you'll be asking me to preach a sermon for the creature."

Wilma opened her mouth. A nervous giggle tumbled out, stabbed at his eardrums, and mounted into a quick intake of air. It produced the melodic effect of a starving donkey.

"Well, why not? You're a minister, aren't you?" The words sent her into another spasm of snorting laughter until Phil clenched his teeth.

"Stop it, Wilma!"

With one last choked-off snort, Wilma subsided into chewing on the flesh of her thumb while he increased the car's speed. Stark Street was straight at this point. They would soon be approaching the curves that led down to the river, and he wouldn't be able to sustain any speed on the serpentine route. He knew the road to his mother's as well as he knew the curves on Wilma's body. It wasn't possible to make up any time on the old highway into Springdale.

"I told mother we'd be there by one, and it's almost one now. She doesn't like it when people are late."

"Isn't she ever late for anything?"

"Of course not." He scowled as the road twisted sharply and he eased back on the accelerator. "She arrives five minutes early for everything. When she says one o'clock, she means *exactly* one."

He didn't bother to add that if his mother was ten minutes early, she would sit in her car until the proper time. Wilma would never understand his mother's precision in dealing with life.

The road began dipping down toward the river. Rockwork guard rails of gray boulders lined the edges of the winding street. A dense growth of alders overhanging the pavement allowed occasional patches of sunlight to flash across the car windows and made him squint his eyes in rapid adjustment to the light changes.

The summer air cooled in the tunnel of shade. Phil concentrated on manipulating the downward curves until the Pinto broke into full sunlight at the bridge.

"What if we meet a car?" Wilma's voice rose in anxiety as they approached the outdated narrow structure.

"I know how to drive, Wilma. It's wide enough for two cars," he answered curtly.

"It doesn't look it," Wilma protested. Her eyes rolled with alarm, watching the metal railing. The white strips of steel appeared to be almost touching the car as Phil sped across the two-lane span. The tires chattered over the pockmarked pavement, forcing him to keep a tight grip on the wheel.

Below the bridge, the Sandy River had shrunk to a small channel shimmering with glaring reflections that struck his eyes. At the end of the bridge he swung the

11

car into a sharp right turn . . . too sharp. Metal scraped against the retaining wall of rock. He ground his molars together, sending his square jaw jutting forward, and heard Wilma expel a sigh of relief when the car resumed a normal, smooth trajectory up the highway.

"I don't understand how your mother can live so far out here all alone, Phil. We haven't seen a house for miles."

"Some people like the country. You can't expect farmers to live in the city," he answered with a sarcastic tone in his voice. The back of his seat was surging in and out against his spine. "Anyhow, there's a small town nearby — at least a place for groceries."

"But where does she go shopping? I mean for clothes and fun things."

"Not everyone gets their enjoyment out of life buying clothes the way you do." His comment was cut short when the seat jolted violently, making him straighten and bump his rib cage against the steering wheel.

"Cerise!" His eyes turned to his wife, and his words were clipped in commanding annoyance. "Make Cerise stop pushing against the back of the seat."

Wilma gave him a startled glance. She turned and leaned over the cushions, looking down at Cerise.

Phil adjusted the mirror until the backseat became visible. The little girl was lying on the seat, her shoes braced against the back of his seat, pushing in and out on the fabric. Her mouth was partially open in curious fascination as she watched the material ripple in and out under the pressure of her feet. She had undone the seat belt again. He stiffened against the seat and glared at his wife.

"Cerise, baby, please stop. It bothers Daddy Phil's driving." She reached over and patted Cerise's leg. "Please, baby."

12

The girl's eyes met Phil's in the mirror and clouded. Her smile vanished into a thin-lipped silence. She gave one last emphatic push that jarred Phil into an exhaled grunt. Her pale lashes fluttered, then Cerise rolled herself up onto the cushions. She smoothed her dress over her lap and folded her hands together. She gazed at the back of Phil's head with a cool, emotionless expression.

Phil glared at Cerise in the rearview mirror and growled in Wilma's direction.

"You should simply tell her to stop. You're her mother. There's no reason for you to keep begging her to behave. Tell her. Don't baby her."

Wilma settled back in her seat and tugged at her skirt.

"Maybe I should have left her with the sitter until after we visit your mother."

"She's been with a sitter too much now. Maybe you should have taught her to mind."

He slowed the car and turned into a narrow graveled road. Stones crunched beneath the tires with a rumbling noise that forced Wilma to raise her voice.

"She's not really bad, Phil. It's been a long ride. She's getting tired. We should have waited to bring her out here. Of course your mother might like having a grandchild. Lots of women like . . ."

"Wilma, quit babbling!" Phil cut her off abruptly and eased the car through a yawning washed-out strip in the road. The car jolted and picked up speed. "And don't talk so much around my mother."

Her face turned pale at the reproof, and the red blotches reappeared on her cheeks. She licked at her lips and rubbed them anxiously together.

"Maybe I shouldn't have come either," she said at last.

Phil tapped the steering wheel with his fingertips. He gave her a speculative look before he turned his eyes back to the road.

"It's not going to be easy, Wilma. Mother's going to have a lot of questions, and you're not clever enough to avoid giving her the wrong answers."

"What's wrong with the truth?"

"Ordinarily, nothing." He dropped his voice into a deep, comforting tone. "Mother's extremely old-fashioned."

"What's that mean?"

Even if her voice hadn't climbed to a tense squeak, Phil could see the confusion in Wilma's quivering lower lip.

"It means she's not going to welcome you to the family with enthusiasm, and when you start babbling, you tell everything you know." His lip twisted at one corner as his own thoughts made him smile. "Which isn't much, I admit, but there are some things my mother shouldn't be told—like about Cerise not having a father."

"If you feel that way, why did you bring me out here to meet her? Maybe I should stay in the car. Why did you marry me if . . ."

"Wilma, stop it!" He let the car slow down to a crawl and glanced at her face. Wilma's wide blue eyes glistened with dampness, and the tip of her nose was growing pink. She was only a few seconds from a shower of tears, and when Wilma cried, her face became a swollen disaster. She certainly wouldn't be able to hide it from his mother.

"Honey, I married you because I wanted to." He eased the car to a stop and reached over to pat her shoulder with a gentle caress. He slid his index finger up and tickled the lobe of her ear with a coaxing smile.

He felt the physical need for her as strongly as he had the first day he'd seen her. It had been an overwhelming desire, a desire he hadn't wanted to conquer. No matter

14

what his ambitions, the need to hold Wilma and make love to her couldn't be prayed away. He had tried and tried, but he never finished a prayer without an image of her slender, perfectly shaped body.

In the darkness of the dormitory, he had fought an erection, prayed until he was driven to slipping out of bed and fleeing to the bathroom. In the privacy of the last stall, he jacked off in shamed solitude. He knew other men resorted to masturbation, but his mother's raging lectures on the evils of the practice had left him with no recourse . . . only prayer. With Wilma, prayer hadn't helped.

Only when the world went on as usual the next day was he able to accept his own sensuality. He hadn't gone blind. No accuser called him to account. Life was undisturbed, even though he had committed a sin. A sin he repeated until in the end he married her. Wilma created the physical urge, and only Wilma could assuage it. The need hadn't gone away. It only intensified every time he made love to her. Even now, he could feel an erection beginning to stir.

His hand slid down and caught hers with a quick squeeze, and her lip stopped trembling.

"Cheer up, honey. You're my wife and *I* want you. For better or worse — remember?"

She nodded and groped in her pocket for a tissue. She dabbed gently at her eyes, blotting the dampness away without a trace of streaked mascara. Phil watched and smiled with approval. He gave her hand one more pat and then turned to ease the car back into motion.

"I hope we aren't going to stay long," she said. "I know something's going to go wrong. I feel crummy."

"The worst thing you can do is talk too much," Phil answered.

He slowed the car at the approach to a long driveway

and eased it into a turn beside a large sign bearing the black lettering, "Thayer's Layers." The sign was further embellished by the black outline of a chicken.

"Mother raises chickens," Phil said in answer to the question in Wilma's eyes. There was a bewildered look on her face as she clenched and unclenched her fists. She fumbled in her purse for a mirror and checked her hair.

"Don't worry, Wilma, you look great. It's one fault you don't have. I've never seen you look anything except perfect. Even when you wake up, your hair is always in place."

A dimple appeared in her left cheek, and she flashed a row of even white teeth.

"I was lucky," she said, brushing at her hair with one hand. She glanced toward the backseat. "Too bad Cerise didn't have my luck."

Phil nodded and smiled at her as he pulled the car up in front of the white two-story frame house. She had relaxed again. The tears were forestalled. Now if he could keep her from talking, the afternoon might go better than he'd hoped.

He inhaled a long breath and glanced at his watch. Only fifteen minutes late.

His hand reached for the door and swung it open just as Cerise aimed a kick at the back of the seat. He turned around angrily, but the little girl's face beamed with delight and a playful giggle halted his outburst.

"Okay, Cerise," he sighed, "let's get out and exercise those overactive feet of yours."

"Phillip! I thought you'd never get here."

At the sound of the woman's voice, Phil looked toward the porch. A wide grin flowed from the corners of his mouth at the glimpse of his mother.

He halted Cerise's exit from the car with an abrupt, "Get out on your mother's side," then slammed the door

16

shut and with his arms outstretched, started toward the tall, sandy-haired woman.

"Mom!" He broke into a half-run, leaving Wilma and Cerise to struggle out of the car and stand waiting. He darted toward his mother with an eagerness that surprised even himself. He grabbed her shoulders in a big hug and held on tightly, forgetting everything except being home again.

An easterly breeze rippled through the short brown curls of Wilma's hair when she stepped from the car. In spite of the warm June sun, she shivered and hugged herself. The breeze sent the ties of her green chiffon blouse swirling in the air and flattened them across her mouth. She tugged at the bows, pulling them tightly to shorten the ends, and scowled as she looked at the smudge of lipstick on the fabric. With a quick twist, she turned the material to hide the glaring red stain.

Cerise dawdled her way across the cushions of the back seat, dragging one foot and then the other. Finally, she thumped to the floor and made a lengthy task of crawling between the seat and the car door.

For once, Wilma felt no impulse to hurry the girl. Instead, she watched her husband greet his mother. The embrace seemed to go on and on. She knew Phil hadn't been home for at least two years, but the display of affection struck her as too lavish.

Of course, she thought to herself, how could she judge? Her memory of her real parents was short. They never hugged anyone—even each other. The foster homes which replaced them were hardly examples to be trusted. Maybe this was how it should be. She studied her new mother-in-law with curiosity.

Phil was six feet tall, and the skinny woman holding his face with both her hands was easily as tall as her son. Wilma glanced down at her own feet. At least she had

17

worn her highest heels, although nothing helped much when you were only five foot two. Wilma was accustomed to the world towering above her, but it gave her a little more confidence when she added the few extra inches to her height. Today she needed every inch.

"Come on, Baby." She caught Cerise's hand and reached for a barrette. "Hold still. Let's fix this."

She pinned Cerise's hair back with one quick, deft movement and fluffed the girl's skirt in a last swift inspection.

Phil had finally broken the embrace and turned, motioning to her with one hand.

Clara Thayer appraised them with an emotionless face. Wilma could feel no indication of welcome in the woman's features . . . in fact, no indication of any feeling.

There was only the pair of dark brown eyes, amazingly like her son's — wide and dark lashed. The woman's face was tanned but fleshless. The skin appeared to be stretched over her skull. Even the arms protruding from a plain short-sleeved white blouse were scrawny and browned.

Wilma moved up the sidewalk, holding Cerise's hand with a firm grip. Cerise trotted to match Wilma's pace, and the little girl almost stumbled as the nervous quickness of Wilma's steps carried her tiny frame hurtling forward.

"Mother, this is Wilma and her daughter Cerise." Phil's bass voice rumbled in the open air with a practiced resonance.

Wilma gave him an inquiring look and wondered if he hadn't emphasized the words "her daughter" a bit too much. She could see no sign of reaction on Phil's face either, only a placid and handsome serenity. He could have been a model posing for a magazine ad. If he hadn't been so dead set against smoking, Wilma could imagine Phil in a magazine ad for cigarettes. Like the Marlboro man. He was totally male and outdoorsy. It had amazed her to discover he was a minister. Of course, she had never known a minister before, but he wasn't at all what she expected.

She stepped forward and paused at the bottom of the steps leading to the wide porch. An immaculate porch, with terra-cotta pots of pink geraniums and three carefully placed wicker chairs, each gleaming in absolute whiteness, each with its own blue striped cushion. The porch floor shone as if it had been waxed and polished. Not even a trace of a footprint marred the forest-green enameled surface. It should be a pleasant place to sit on a hot day — yet everything appeared untouched.

Clara Thayer looked at her impersonally. Her lips parted in a smile, but the eyes were solemn and alert. Wilma struggled to fight back a tense giggle and felt her hands begin to tremble. She shifted her stance and gripped Cerise's hand so hard that the little girl looked up at her with a quizzical twist at one corner of her mouth.

Phil clasped his mother's shoulder and gave her a wide smile, displaying a single gold crown on his lower bicuspid. The smile broke Clara Thayer's silence.

She nodded to Wilma, still without visible reaction, and said, "Come on in. I've been waiting lunch." She turned to her son and this time the brown eyes sparkled when she spoke. "I made your favorite — scalloped potatoes and pork chops."

The door opened into a cool hallway with photographs of Phil. Wilma tried not to stare as she moved past the pictures of Phil in a cap and gown, Phil on horseback. There were several enlarged snapshots of Phil beside a tall, plain-looking girl. Wilma looked up at her husband,

19

but he was intent on herding Cerise down the hall without letting her touch the wallpaper.

Cerise clawed at the air, trying to snatch the purple flowers from the wall with a determination that kept Phil busy yanking her away. To a child who had never seen wallpaper, the flowers created a magnetic attraction. After the fourth lunge, Phil snatched Cerise up and carried her into the dining room, holding her firmly in spite of her squirming.

Wilma gasped at the sight of the table and swung toward her husband with a sensation of panic.

She expected a farm kitchen, simple and comfortable. Not this. Not a dining room with a white tablecloth dangling almost to the floor at the corners. Candles in the middle of the day. Lights reflecting on crystal goblets and glistening silver stretching on both sides of every plate.

To Wilma, it was already a nightmare. Which fork was she supposed to use? What if Cerise spilled something on the tablecloth? She glanced hastily about the table and gulped when she noticed there was no highchair or any concession made to Cerise's young age and size.

Even worse, the chairs were upholstered with gold velour. Cerise would spill something. Wilma could feel it.

"Phil . . ." She looked up at him with a queasy sensation building in her stomach. Would he understand what she was worrying about?

"What's the problem?" Clara Thayer's voice was flat and disinterested, as if she were asking the question out of routine politeness.

"Cerise . . ." Wilma fought to keep her voice from squeaking. "I guess I could hold her on my lap." She let her voice trail off meekly.

The only expression on Phil's face was one of confusion. Wilma clutched the back of a chair with one hand

and felt a nervous tremor running up one arm. They should have become better acquainted as a family before they visited his mother, or they should have come without Cerise.

Phil didn't understand how careless a three-year-old could be with food. How much would be spilled and stain the white linen tablecloth? A bowl of cranberries—those stains would never come out. The heavy crystal goblets at every place were going to be hard for her to handle herself. She'd seen goblets only in movies. Did you hold them by the stem? What if Cerise snatched at one? There would be water all over the table.

Wilma looked up at her husband and tried to plead with her eyes. He seemed to know everything. Why couldn't he understand what a problem feeding Cerise was going to be?

But it was Clara Thayer who grasped the situation, not Phil.

"Don't worry. We'll put her on a stack of books." The older woman's gaze slid toward her son with a brief flash of accusation. She touched Wilma's arm lightly with her fingertips and then withdrew her hand as if body contact was to be minimized.

"I'm sorry. Phillip never explained how young your child was. I assumed he married someone closer to his own age—that your child was older. You hardly look old enough to be a mother."

Mrs. Thayer's mouth closed in a firm, disapproving line.

"I'm old enough," Wilma felt her voice slip upward and quiver.

"Obviously," Mrs. Thayer answered in a flat monotone.

Wilma sensed her cheeks growing warm with embarrassment. Mrs. Thayer quickly removed the gold-edged china plate from the table and vanished through a door. The white enameled door swung freely back and forth until Clara reappeared carrying a small earthenware plate and a plastic glass.

"Phillip!" she snapped with an abrupt and commanding tone. "Get the unabridged dictionary from the library. The child can sit on that."

Phil muttered a low, "Yes, ma'am," slid Cerise into Wilma's arms, and hurried from the room as if accustomed to instantly obeying his mother's commands.

Cerise flung her arms around Wilma's neck and clutched her mother's shoulders with a fierce, unrelenting strength.

Wilma's arms ached. Cerise's tenacious fingers were beginning to hurt her. They waited in silence for Phil's return. Mrs. Thayer made no attempt to start a conversation. She seemed to be trying to suspend time while Phil was out of the room.

The woman stood behind her chair at the head of the table. Her long skin-and-bone fingers curved over the back of the chair like the talons of a roosting bird. She stood without a trace of emotion, gazing across the length of the table and out the window at the clustered rhododendron bushes with their profusion of colors. The lawn appeared dwarfed, the grass engulfed by the mountainous bushes.

"You sure got lots of flowers." Wilma struggled to find something to stop the silence in the room. "I never seen so many."

For a second, the corners of Clara Thayer's mouth drew back as if aggravated by an offending noise.

Wilma bit her lower lip. Phil had said she was to let him do all the talking, but she couldn't stand here like a dummy. She wasn't sure what she had said, but something didn't seem right in her mother-in-law's expression.

Maybe the woman didn't like flowers, but if she didn't, why did she have so many?

"Chickens." Mrs. Thayer announced.

Wilma tilted her head, peering at the woman and wondering if she had heard right. It was an odd answer.

"Chicken manure," Clara said, drawing the words out slowly as if she were explaining to Cerise. "It makes everything grow." Her head turned toward the door and her eyes lit up. "Oh, there you are, Phillip."

She motioned to the chair at the far end of the table. "Put the child there. Dinner has waited long enough."

Wilma sat staring at the confusion before her. The little plate with a miniature knife laid across one side—what was it for? She looked across the table at Phil in a silent appeal for help, but his eyes were fixed attentively on his mother's face.

"Phillip, this is quite an occasion for me. Today when you say grace, it will be the first time you will say it in this house as an ordained minister." She was breathing the words in hushed tones, as if the honor was almost too much for her. "I have never been so happy and proud. My son is now a minister."

The woman's eyes filled with moisture. She folded her hands quickly and bowed her head to conceal the display of emotion.

Wilma bent her head. She had learned that much in the short week of their marriage, but her mind was too confused. She couldn't follow Phil's words. There were so many she didn't understand. "Dedication." "Consecration." They were only long words to her. She had so much to learn, but the table in front of her was a bigger problem.

She peeked up at Phil, but his eyes were closed. His voice had a deep rolling sound. Thankfully, he was unaware of her wandering attention.

Wilma's glance slid toward Cerise. The girl was staring at Phil with her mouth open and her attention riveted on his face. At least she wasn't squirming. Cerise would have to be taught about saying grace before meals, but for today, the novelty of Phil's voice was keeping her entranced.

The loud "Amen" from Clara Thayer startled Wilma. She lifted her head reluctantly. With the prayer over, she would be forced into using all these forks. If she made a mistake, Phil would be embarrassed.

She watched and tried it not to show her mounting alarm when Clara reached for the platter and started to pass it. How much was a polite amount to take? To her relief, Phil spoke, making Mrs. Thayer hesitate.

"Why don't we pass things my way first, Mother?"

"We pass to the right, Phillip."

"I know, but it's time I started learning how to be a father. If we make an exception, I can help Cerise." His eyes twinkled with mischief as he added, "Of course, it's an excuse to give me first chance at the food."

Mrs. Thayer's disapproving frown vanished. She turned to Wilma and beamed. "I hope you're a good cook. Phillip always likes to eat, and pork chops with scalloped potatoes are his favorite meal."

"He didn't never say what he liked best." She struggled to keep the quivering out of her voice. Once again the scowl appeared on Clara Thayer's face. Wilma tried to think. What on earth had she said this time? She looked desperately at Phil. His mouth twitched impishly before he winked at her.

"Wilma's an excellent cook, Mother. I don't think I'll starve."

He doled out a small portion to Cerise before passing the platter across to Wilma. She glanced quickly at Phil's plate and carefully placed her food in the identical

24

position on the dish in front of her.

She watched every movement Phil made. The small plate was for the rolls and the butter. She would have to ask Phil how he knew what to do so perfectly. One more thing she would have to learn, but only when they ate out. She'd never set a table in her house so fancy. It was a lot of extra work, and the food didn't taste any better. In fact, the pork chops were greasy, and the potatoes needed salt. All these fancy dishes must be to hide the fact that Clara Thayer was a lousy cook.

By the time they reached the dessert, Wilma found it easier to relax. She smiled quietly while Phil and his mother caught up on all the news about neighbors and the chicken farming business.

"Ginny was over yesterday and brought the strawberry pie." Clara Thayer turned to Wilma with her first attempt to make her a part of the conversation. "Ginny is a girl Phillip went to high school with."

"Mother, she was three years behind me." Phil gave Wilma an impish smile. "Ginny was a little pest who lived next door. Mother thought she was cute. I thought she was a pain in the neck."

Clara scowled at him. "I didn't say she was cute, Phillip. She's a sweet girl." She turned her attention back to Wilma. "Ginny plays the organ at our church. Lovely girl . . . I've almost come to think of her as my own daughter. In fact, I expected—"

Her voice stopped abruptly, and she cleared her throat at the frown on Phil's face.

Wilma wondered if Ginny was the plain-looking girl whose pictures were displayed in the hall, but her thoughts were interrupted by Mrs. Thayer's next question.

"Phillip never explained how the two of you met. Was it in church?"

She had a pleasant enough smile as she waited for Wilma's answer, but the brown eyes were cold and hard.

"Now, Mom, you can't expect us to tell you all the romantic details."

She pulled her gaze away from Wilma at the sound of Phil's voice and looked at him with a surprised arch to her brows.

"Well, why not? I hope she's a good Christian girl."

"I converted her myself, Mother. My first soul brought to God. And if we count Cerise, it will be two souls. Not a bad accomplishment for a man who has been ordained only a month. Two new converts brought to the service of the Lord, and a wife and daughter."

Wilma chewed at her lip as he took on what she called his preaching look, and she bent her head to avoid meeting Mrs. Thayer's piercing eyes. She couldn't escape the sharp disapproval in Clara's voice.

"But married by a justice of the peace—it's hardly a proper marriage. You should have had a minister. Didn't you learn anything in seminary?"

Wilma fixed her attention on the gold-edged plate. It was her fault . . . she had wanted it private and simple. Phil had said it didn't make any difference.

"Mother, we're married. It's all that's important." He chuckled, and Wilma raised her head. "Just think, Mother, you're a grandmother now."

Clara Thayer pulled her shoulders up, her back stiff against her chair. She looked across the length of the table at Cerise. She stared at the girl for a long time and was met by an answering stare from Cerise's eyes. The two were silent—evaluating, challenging each other. It was Clara Thayer who looked away.

"She's not a real grandchild, Phillip."

"Now, Mother . . ."

"Be patient, Phillip." Her eyes scanned Wilma's face

and slid past her. She gave Cerise another study and sighed. "I'll get used to the idea, I suppose, but she's so—so blonde." Her gaze came back to Wilma, and the tone was accusing. "She certainly doesn't look like you at all."

Wilma twisted her hands together under the table and murmured, "No, ma'am," while hoping Phil would find a way to get his mother's attention on another subject.

"We've never had any blondes in our family," Mrs. Thayer stated.

"We do now, Mother," Phil retorted.

Clara Thayer took a deep breath and closed her eyes. She remained silent for a long time—so long that Wilma glanced across the table at her husband for some indication of what was going on.

Phil only raised one hand and shook his head.

At last Clara Thayer opened her eyes and pushed her chair back from the table.

"The Lord says I must accept the situation, Phillip. He doesn't say I must like it."

She stood up with one swift motion and placed her napkin beside the plate. One skinny hand lifted toward her son as if to silence any further discussion.

"I want to show you my new project, Phillip." She turned toward Wilma. "The child may enjoy this. Most children enjoy baby animals."

Her glance went immediately back to her son. "You know how much I always wanted a flock of geese. Don't ask me why, when I have all these chickens. Used to make excuses that it was to keep the bugs down, but anyway, I finally got myself a start. Fourteen baby goslings."

Wilma wiped quickly at Cerise's face and hands as Phil stood up. She breathed a little easier. By some miracle, the tablecloth had come through the meal without a spot.

Cerise wiggled herself off the chair and looked soberly up at Phil. He reached and caught her hand.

"The dishes . . ." Wilma hesitated. She should offer to help, but she was suddenly terrified of breaking one. They looked fragile and expensive.

Clara Thayer shrugged. "Don't worry about them. Bess is coming in to clean up." Her hand reached out and clutched Phil's arm as they went down the hall and out into the sun.

Wilma trailed along behind them, almost glad to be ignored.

"Who's Bess?" Phil asked. "The only Bess I remember is Bess Lawson, but she's only a little kid."

"*Was* a little kid, Phillip. She's fifteen now, and not a child at all. Be lucky if she doesn't turn out like her sister. I wouldn't have her at all if I could have found anyone else."

She stopped and peered at a rosebush, turned the leaves back and forth, and frowned. "Not doing well. Hope it doesn't get aphids."

Her fingers clutched Phil's sleeve, and they turned toward a large complex of white buildings.

"Told Bess the truth," Mrs. Thayer continued. "She could work for a couple hours, but she couldn't bring that kid along."

"Bess has a child?" Phil's voice sounded astonished.

"Good heavens, no," Mrs. Thayer answered. "It's her sister's, but Bess babysits. She brought it along one day when she was supposed to clean house for me.

"Well, I can tell you, I sent her straight home. Told her I wasn't having any bastard children on the place. Born in sin—never get rid of the taint."

Wilma's lungs felt as if they were shriveling up and sinking into her stomach. She wanted to run up and snatch Cerise's hand, to pull the child back away from Clara and Phil. Snatch her up—hold her where she was safe. Phil had said his mother was old-fashioned, but she was worse. The woman was . . . Wilma searched her mind and wished she knew a word for the hatred she was feeling. The only word she could think of was one Phil didn't like her to use, but it fit. As far as she was concerned, Clara Thayer was a bitch.

Phil could preach and tell her that hatred was wrong, but Wilma didn't give a damn. He couldn't know what she was thinking. She hated the bag of bones he had for a mother. Maybe her thoughts would send her to hell, but she wasn't going to go wherever his mother was going.

She came out of her private world to hear Phil lecturing his mother. Wilma felt like screaming at the him for wasting his time. The woman was impossible. All Wilma wanted to do was get this visit over and leave.

"Nonsense, Phillip," Mrs. Thayer snapped. "Times haven't changed what's right and what's wrong."

"Why blame the child, Mother? It's hardly the child's fault. After all the child didn't ask to be born."

"I'm not going to argue with you, Phillip. You always were too weak and forgiving. There's no way to remove that sort of sin. There's only one word for a child born out of wedlock. It's a bastard."

"Bastard?" Cerise's voice rose in an imitative question.

"Now see what you've done, Mother," Phil's voice was between a laugh and a rebuke. "You've taught Cerise a bad word."

He bent to whisper in Cerise's ear. The older woman's hand flew up to cover her mouth. Her eyes held a stricken look as she mumbled something that resembled an apology.

A waft of air swept up the path and caught Wilma's

hair. The breeze carried with it an odd acrid smell, a rank odor that made her wrinkle her nose in disgust.

"Oh, stinky!" Cerise squealed.

"What is that smell?" Wilma asked, thinking with revulsion that Cerise had described it perfectly.

"Chickens." Clara Thayer reestablished her authority with a single word. "They aren't the best-smelling of crops, but this is a farm, and I raise chickens. Come on."

Clara pushed at the door. The metal scraping of the rollers started a flurry of squawked responses. The sound swelled into a chorus of discord accompanied by rattling metal. Clara motioned them into the shaded interior with an impassive face.

They stepped inside and Wilma blinked her eyes to adjust to the dimness. The sound grew to deafening proportions. Tiers and tiers of wire cages rose above their heads. Row after row of cages containing screeching white-feathered hens, each in its own wire prison . . . wire pens that gave the chicken little room to move except to beat its wings in fury at the intrusion of human beings.

The squawks and screeches pierced Wilma's eardrums, and she was assailed with an accompanying stench of chicken manure. The rattling of the wires increased and merged with the squawking chorus.

A chicken darted its beak through the wire and snatched the tempting greenness of Wilma's blouse. She jerked the material away and shrank back from the cages.

Phil caught Cerise up in his arms and held her up by one of the enclosures.

"Chickens, Cerise. They lay eggs. The eggs . . ." His explanation stopped in mid-sentence when Cerise laid her hand against the cage. The feathered occupant teetered a moment on its spindly legs, tipped its head, and aimed a vicious peck at the tiny fingers.

Cerise let out a howl and turned toward her mother. Her eyes were panic-stricken and rolling with fear. She wrenched herself back in Phil's arms until he let her slide to the floor.

She darted to Wilma and dug her fingers into Wilma's legs, clawing up toward her mother's arms.

Wilma hugged Cerise tightly against her own body and shouted at Phil above the resurging uproar of the chickens, "She's scared, Phil, and so am I."

"Nothing to be scared of," Mrs. Thayer snorted. "They just make a lot of noise whenever there's someone strange around."

"Let me take her outside." Wilma looked up at Phil with a desperate hope that he would end this nightmare of an afternoon soon. Still holding Cerise with a fierce protectiveness, she headed for the door.

Phil caught up with her and slid it open before she could readjust Cerise's weight and reach for the handle. His hand rested on the back of her neck and rubbed gently.

"We'll be out in a few minutes."

All she could do was nod and stumble out into the fresh air without answering. Her eyes stung as she continued to hold Cerise. The child's fine blond hair floated about in the soft breeze, and slowly her tense body began to relax. The tiny fingers eased their desperate grip on Wilma's blouse. Cerise pushed against Wilma's chest and started to squirm.

Wilma eased her down to the ground and stood basking in the peace of the open countryside. Cerise began to clamber up a stack of wooden crates. The ruffled dress blew up, exposing the pink underpants with lace edges. She struggled belly-first over the first wooden mound of the hill.

When Phil and his mother emerged from the building, Wilma managed to force a smile—at least for her husband. Cerise had happily forgotten the ordeal.

Phil gave her a quick hug, and Wilma slid her arm around his waist. She leaned her head against his chest and rubbed her cheek on his shirt. Mrs. Thayer sniffed and cleared her throat, turning her head away from the display of affection.

"Come, child, let me show you the baby geese."

Cerise halted in her climb, looked upward to the top of the stack of crates, and turned. Her climb had put her on eye level with Clara Thayer. This time she looked directly into the woman's eyes.

There was no smile on either face. Cerise maintained a long, sober study of the woman's eyes, ignoring the outstretched hand. Still unsmiling, Cerise turned and slid down from the stack of crates, one thump at a time, until her feet dangled over the last crate and found solid footing.

She shook her ruffled skirts, dusted her hands, and reached solemnly for Clara Thayer's grasp. Still without a smile on either face, they moved away from the large buildings and wound down a narrow dirt path toward the sound of running water. Sword-shaped ferns brushed at Wilma's skirt. Sun flickered as the evergreen trees moved gently back and forth above their heads.

The goslings were caged inside a fence beside a creek. Water rippled over moss-covered boulders and gurgled through the fencing stretched across the waterway.

"Goslings have to have fresh water," Clara sniffed. Her bony hands manipulated the gate latch, and one hand waggled for them to enter the fenced enclosure.

"Are you sure?" Wilma hung back, but Phil's hand caught her elbow as he chuckled.

"There are only fourteen of these fellows, Wilma, and

they're all babies."

"Aren't they the cutest things?" Clara Thayer's face glowed with pride. A dappled gray ball of fluff with faint spots of ecru across his back stirred from his sunbath. The gosling stretched its tiny wings in the air and flapped them before waddling toward the newcomers, his soft, fat belly scraping the grass.

"They're not flighty birds at all," Clara announced. "They're real pets." She looked down at the birds with a proud smile. "Goslings are funny. If they don't see their natural mother in the first ten hours of life, they adopt the first animal they see."

She swept her hand in a half circle. "Hatched these eggs in an incubator so I was sure I was the first thing they saw, and it worked. They adopted me just like a mother. Had to pen them up, or they'd follow me right into the house."

Around the fenced enclosure, other yellow spotted birds began to rouse and stretch. The wings fluttered. They each stretched one webbed foot and then the other, bobbing their heads up and down, stirring themselves awake.

"Come on, babies." Clara stooped, and a radiant smile came across her face. She snapped her fingers, and the web-footed creatures began swaying across the ground toward the noise. The big brown feet showed the beginnings of faint orange hues as they air-paddled their way across the pen.

"Didn't I tell you they were cute?" she said. "They'll be all white when they're full-grown. Their feet and bills will turn orange. Never knew I could get so attached to a bunch of birds."

Wilma looked anxiously at Cerise. The girl was watching the goslings with a strange tenseness in her stance.

33

"Phil, you'd better pick Cerise up." She tugged at his sleeve. "She's not used to animals."

"Oh, she'll be all right. What can frighten her? They're too little to frighten anyone."

He patted her hand and turned back to watch the goslings tumble and roll in their awkward attempts to reach the sound emanating from Clara's fingers.

Cerise continued to watch the approaching goslings with a tense concentration. Her body was rigid and her mouth half open, mesmerized by the awkwardness of their movements.

A gosling stopped, tipped his head to one side, and scrutinized the small pink tennis shoe. He darted his flat, ebony-hued bill forward, snagged one dangling shoelace, and tugged.

Cerise let out a shriek. She began stomping her feet in a wild frenzy. One pink barrette slithered free from her hair and was snatched up in the bill of another curious ball of feathers.

"Mommy!" The scream was frantic, and the child's foot began beating the earth in an increasing tempo of panic. She stomped a foot down on the back of one small bird. An airless squeak emerged as the gosling died.

Clara Thayer was frozen in her stooped position. Her mouth opened, and a row of uneven teeth gaped in horror.

Cerise jumped into the air with another shriek. This time she landed with one foot held firmly on the head of another gosling. She stood watching the webbed feet beating wildly in the air. Then she brought her other foot down on the twitching body, stomping again and again until the wings fluttered weakly and folded limply to the ground.

With an uproar of frightened hisses and the clacking

of small black bills, the goslings fled and huddled in a far corner of the enclosure. They hissed and pushed the wire until the metal creaked and twanged in protest.

Clara Thayer reached out with one shaking hand and touched the first dead gosling with the tips of her fingers. A tear trickled down her cheek. Her eyes lifted to Cerise's face, and a long moaning "ohh" croaked from the back of her throat.

Wilma bit into her fingertips. It had happened so fast she hadn't realized she had put both hands to her mouth and was holding her breath.

Cerise was watching Mrs. Thayer with an unwavering stare. Her eyes were only half open. The pale eyelashes shielded the glowing greenness of her eyes. She turned her head slowly to look up at Phil with the same defiant and watchful gaze. Her eyes opened when she tilted her head upward, and the pupils contracted. The expression in her eyes was strangely mature and challenging.

Wilma tore her hands away from her mouth and reached out for the girl. Phil appeared to be as frozen in his reactions as his mother.

"Phil, I told you she wasn't used to animals."

Wilma swept Cerise up into her arms and pulled her tightly against her chest. She felt the girl's rigid body relax against her shoulder.

"I . . ." Phil acted stunned. He stood gazing down at the dead goslings, a bewildered uncertainty in his eyes. He caught his mother's elbow, pulled her to her feet, then reached down and scooped up the two dead birds with the other hand.

Wilma hugged Cerise so tightly she could feel the child's heart pounding against her breast. She headed up the pathway to the car, carrying her child away. Away from the chickens, and the goslings, and away from Clara Thayer.

The car was the only refuge. They could stay in the car until Phil was ready to leave. Phil should have understood. He shouldn't have let this happen.

She rocked Cerise back and forth in her arms, murmuring into the child's hair, "It's all over, baby. It's okay."

Cerise rubbed her eyes and pushed herself upright with a yawn. "I'm tired."

Wilma brushed the child's hair back from her pale forehead and looked at Cerise's delicate face. The fear was completely gone. A placid sleepiness had replaced the tenseness. Cerise yawned again, and Wilma gave her one more affectionate hug.

"All right, get into the backseat and lie down."

She boosted the little girl over the back of the seat and tucked her own sweater over the child. For a few seconds Wilma watched Cerise's eyelashes flutter, and then she turned and sagged against the seat.

It had all gone wrong. Everything had gone so wrong. She didn't want to go back in the house, didn't want to stay here any longer. She especially never wanted to see another chicken or a goose in her whole life, unless it was cooked and on a plate.

She straightened and watched the path, dreading Phil's anger. He was bound to blame her for Cerise's action, but he should have picked Cerise up. It wasn't Cerise's fault.

Cerise rubbed her eyes. The seat was making squeaky sounds whenever her mother moved.

She rubbed Wilma's soft, knitted sweater back and forth against her nose and smiled to herself.

With one finger, she probed at the funny red spot on the side of her tennis shoe. Then, turning her foot sideways, she frowned and pulled a gray feather loose from the rubber sole of her shoe.

Her foot dropped limply to the cushions. She examined the feather, smelled it, rubbed it in circles around the tip of her nose and smiled.

She yawned once more and closed her eyes. The feather drifted lazily to the floor of the car.

Clara Thayer felt her son's hand on her arm and she rose with a sourness in the bottom of her stomach. It wasn't the death of the two goslings — it was the look on the child's face.

Those eyes . . . cat eyes. Like the wild tomcat that had attacked her chickens. It had glared at her even while she threw rocks at the animal, stood and defied her until she had to get a neighbor to shoot it.

What kind of child had Phillip brought into her house?

She held onto his arm and let him lead her out of the gosling pen and up toward the house.

"Phillip, the child . . ." Her chest ached as if she'd hurried too fast. She stopped and gulped in a lungful of fresh air.

"Mother, it's partly my fault. Wilma told me I should pick her up."

"Nonsense. She's an odd child, Phillip. Did you see the look on her face? Hatred . . . sheer hatred."

"Cerise is only three. She's too young to know about hate. She was frightened."

He was nudging her elbow with a gentle force as if to push her forward, but Clara held her ground. She knew it was stubbornness, but she couldn't dismiss the look in Cerise's eyes.

It hadn't been fear.

"Phillip, how can you concentrate on your ministry? The child will cause you problems — and the mother . . ."

37

Clara hesitated. She must choose her words carefully. She had to make Phillip understand. The child was evil. The mother was unacceptable.

"Mother, Wilma is my wife. I want you to like her." Philip had a fierceness in his voice she had never heard before. Clara found an uneasy tenseness swelling in her chest.

In all the years of raising her son alone, Clara had never said a word to him about his father's shortcomings. She had told Phillip his father was returning from a church conference when the car accident happened. She'd never mentioned the woman—the petite, dainty woman George Thayer had sneaked into Portland to visit.

The woman so much like this wife of Phillip's. It had been a mistake. Raising him in a God-fearing home hadn't erased all the sins of the father. Lust went into the blood.

She began to move along the path, choosing her words in her mind before she voiced them aloud.

"I know, Phillip, and what God joins together . . ." Her voice failed, and she paused a few minutes. "How can you expect her to be a help to you in your work? She uses such terrible grammar. How can she talk to people or entertain?

"I watched her gawking at the table. She's never learned etiquette. She used her bread to clean her plate. And the makeup, Phillip. Lipstick and powder should be enough."

She could feel his hand tighten on her elbow and kept her eyes on the path. The damage was done. Phillip had married the girl. She would have to accept the marriage, but it was all wrong. The girl was wrong for Phillip.

"I'm sorry." She found the words difficult. "I suppose no mother ever approves of the woman her son marries, but a minister's wife should be more socially acceptable."

She hoped her emphasis on the words "socially acceptable" would make it clear to Phillip what her objections were without alienating him. She wasn't going to lose her son's affection over some young strumpet.

He slid his hand from her elbow up to her shoulders and pulled her against him. She could hear the rumble of a laugh in his chest.

"Wilma is my wife, Mother, not the property of the church. I don't intend to be a small church minister with my wife entertaining the local ladies' club. At least not for long. I have other things in mind."

"What other things?"

"Evangelism, Mother. Oh, it will take me awhile, but I want to hold gospel meetings. Old-time revival meetings. I want to bring hundreds into the fold. Someday, my own gospel center and a school. It will take time, time and money."

He turned to her, and the sparkle in his eyes was a vital, glowing energy. Clara caught her breath. His energy surged and transmitted itself through his arm into her body. He had a magnetic way of making her want to believe all he said could happen.

"But Wilma," she said, "where does she fit into your plans? What can she do?"

Phillip stopped gazing at the top of the fir trees and looked at her with a sudden blankness to his face.

"I don't see why you expect her to fit into anything, Mother. All she has to be is my wife, nothing else."

He glanced ahead of them at the path and then pulled her forward in hurried steps.

"Come on, Mother. Quit worrying. I don't need Wilma to help me. People who believe in me and my work—it will happen."

As they approached the house, Phillip lifted the lid of

the garbage can and dropped the two goslings inside. With a clang of the lid, he paused and wiped his hand across the side of his slacks. Clara hung her head and stared at the sprigs of grass protruding from under the edge of the garbage can.

"Phillip, I'd like to bury them."

"Oh, come on, Mother. I've seen you throw away dead chickens without burying them."

"But these were pets."

She couldn't stand the mental image of her two babies lying in the can with potato peelings and coffee grounds. She had waited so long to get her pets. It didn't seem right. They would be carted off in the mechanical monster with its motors compressing the tiny feathered creatures into so much compacted waste. She had to bury them.

Phillip hugged her and laughed. "You're getting silly in your old age, Mother. Anyhow, I think I'd better get back to the car. Wilma will be upset, and we have a long drive to Maupin tomorrow. I'm anxious to get started in my first parish. Not much of a spot, but it's only the beginning."

"Phillip, be careful."

"That's an odd remark." He smiled at her as they reached the corner of the house. "What can happen to me?"

Clara stood looking at him and shook her head. "The child . . ."

He tossed his head back and laughed. "Don't be silly. You'll get used to the idea of being a grandmother one of these days, and then you'll deny you ever said anything but praise."

Clara put her hand over his and withdrew it quickly when she felt the slight tremor in her fingers. She inhaled and dragged the words, staring at the ground as she talked. She couldn't look into Phillip's eyes or she would never be able to finish.

"I'll help you all I can, Phillip. Certainly, I haven't begrudged putting you through school or buying the car for you, but I won't—I won't give you one penny if it goes to help support your wife and child."

"Mother . . ."

"Don't interrupt, Phillip. You should have waited until you were established to get married, and you should have married someone more suitable. If it's help for your church, I'll give it, but never for your own . . ." She paused, and then, because she could think of no other word, she finally said it in a half-whisper: "Your own lust."

She felt Phillip's fingers tighten on her arm, but the outburst she expected was only a chuckling in his throat.

"You never change, do you, Mother?" His voice had an amused sound. Clara saw a flash of his smile from the corner of her eye.

She stiffened her shoulders. Let him be amused. He'd find out there was more to marriage than the physical side of it. Wait until the girl's atrocious grammar embarrassed him.

She felt a weariness at the thought. It made her want to find a chair and sink into the cushions.

"Someday, Phillip, when I'm a real grandmother, I'll feel differently. But that one will never be my grandchild. I can accept your marriage, but not the child."

"Okay, Mom, but I think you'll change your mind. You'll have to come visit us in Maupin when we get settled."

"Perhaps I will, but I doubt it."

She waved as he half walked, half sprinted toward the car. She watched them pull out of the driveway. Her eyes followed the dust trail behind the car up the long

41

graveled drive to the road. Then she sighed and walked back down the path to the toolshed.

The shovel was heavier than she remembered. Her arms ached with every push. She placed the two birds gently into the hole. Dirt spilled over the feathered sides, and she cried. She wasn't crying for the dead pets. She cried for her son. She shivered and turned toward the house. She was afraid. Afraid for her son and the cat-eyed child.

Chapter Two

The dust was as oppressive as the heat. Dust on the lawn chairs. Dust coated her feet. She could even feel a film of dust when she ran her tongue across her teeth.

Wilma leaned back in the lounge chair and propped her swollen feet up on the footrest. The house perched a hundred yards from the riverbank. Below her she could hear the rushing of the Deschutes River tumbling over rugged boulders. Behind her the sound of the neighbor's shovel scraped against the multitude of rocks that riddled the eastern Oregon soil.

The afternoon heat was beginning to subside, and the residents of Maupin were starting the more strenuous of their outdoor labors. Labor like the extra room Lyle Bailey was adding onto his house.

Every evening Lyle dug a little more, preparing to pour the foundation. Every evening Wilma listened to the sound and clenched her teeth to keep from screaming at each metallic rasp of the shovel.

She squinted up at the hill. A paintless farm truck crept like a wounded animal up the steep, winding grade that led out of town. The faltering engine echoed down into the canyon, into the hollow bowl of the townsite, then slowly faded as the truck followed another bend in the highway.

Wilma grunted with the discomfort of her ballooned stomach. It lurched and twisted with the activity of its occupant. The combination of the August heat and the pregnancy was making her waver between being crabby and not caring about anything. *Languid*, Phil called it. She said the word to herself and made a face. It sounded phony. *Pooped* was a better word—even if Phil didn't like it. She felt pooped and ready to yell at someone.

Life wasn't fair. Lyle Bailey could build onto his house when the Baileys didn't need the extra room. The Thayers had to accept what was furnished them by the congregation of the First Brotherhood Church. The church people hadn't been generous with the living quarters, no matter what Phil said about the Sunday collections.

A parsonage? The place was only a one-bedroom shack—and that was a kindhearted description.

If any house needed to be enlarged, it was the parsonage, but Phil could always manage to discover other causes the church members found more exciting. Causes like the new hymnals. They'd coughed up for those. Phil had even interested six other churches in them. Why couldn't he use his fancy talk to get the church to build them an extra bedroom?

Cerise had to sleep on a lumpy studio couch with its sagging middle. The baby would have to be shoved in one corner of the bedroom. The crib—a hand-me-down affair from the lady's circle—took up all the extra space, space she wanted for a sewing machine. Now the sewing machine was pushed into the closet.

Might as well be there, she thought. It was too hot to sew. The fabric stuck to the sweat on her arms. The bedroom was too stuffy for sewing or sleeping.

She closed her eyes and tried to block out the sounds of Lyle's shovel. The metallic grating noise made her head ache. Everything seemed to make her head ache this week. Even Cerise running across the porch had made her snappy and annoyed.

Cerise? Where was Cerise?

She tilted her head and listened. Mingled with the sounds of Lyle's digging, she could hear a childish giggle.

Evidently Cerise was tagging Lyle around and capturing angleworms again. The girl had developed a fascination with the wriggly creatures. Or was it with the pennies she got from Phil whenever he wanted some of them for his fishing?

Whatever the reason, Cerise was amused and not bothering her.

Amused and grubby. There wasn't any way she could keep Cerise clean in the ever-present dust. Her blonde hair would be so filled with dust, the scalp would be black. Her clothes would join the growing mountain of laundry on the back porch.

Wilma wiped the perspiration from her forehead and groaned. The laundry would have to be done in the morning, before the heat became too intense. Delivery day was getting too close. She didn't want to come home with a new baby and face a stack of mildewed clothes. She'd have to leave enough clean clothes for Cerise.

The sounds of the shovel ceased. The pleasant lilt of Joan Bailey's laughter rippled in the stillness before the digging started once more.

"You look boiled." Joan's voice surprised Wilma into opening her eyes.

"I sure picked a lousy month to have this kid," Wilma grumbled. She attempted to shift her position, and the

45

plastic lounge chair slurped as it clung to the sweat on her calves.

"Cheer up. I have a little something to help." Joan grinned and produced a thermos and two glasses from behind her back. "My special lemonade."

Wilma smiled with relief. "I don't think I could have made it through this summer without your lemonade."

"Let's hope Phil never decides to taste it." Joan giggled as she shook the lawn chair free of dust.

"He won't. He hates lemonade. Says his mother never strained the seeds out of it, and he almost choked on one." Wilma sipped the ice-filled liquid and watched Joan sweeping the last of the dust from the chair with one hand.

Joan Bailey's shorts crawled up her thighs when she settled into the canvas deck chair. The white terrycloth accented the pecan-brown of Joan's tanned legs. She looked so slender and healthy. Her radiance made Wilma feel bloated and useless.

"Well, here's to secrets." Joan lifted her glass in a mock toast. "May the vodka hold out until the heat wave is over."

"Shh, Joan, don't." Wilma glanced over her shoulder and around the yard. "You're going to say something around Cerise, and she's bound to ask Phil what the word *vodka* means."

She took another sip of the mixture and wiped a drop of sweat from the tip of her nose.

"Cerise asks so many questions, and Phil always wants to know where she got the idea. As if *I* know what goes on inside her head."

Joan leaned back and put her feet up on the end of Wilma's lounge chair.

"I don't think I could stand being married to a

preacher, even one as good-looking as Phil. It's been tough living next door to the parsonage, but at least you're a good egg. I don't have to watch my damn language around you."

"Only around Phil." Wilma felt a hint of a breeze and pushed her hair back from her forehead to let it sweep across her skin.

"Oh, Phil never makes a big deal of it. Clears his throat kinda loud when I let loose with a 'son-of-a-bitch.' But he doesn't preach at me."

"At least he's gorgeous to look at, and he's not a meddler, like the last character they had here. His wife was worse . . . always running around doing good deeds, trying to make me feel guilty. At least you don't preach to me."

"Phil says he's the minister, not me."

"When's the Lord's servant coming home?" Joan was frowning at Wilma's puffy ankles. "Seems like he should stick around when you're so close to popping that load."

The breeze died, and Wilma held the cold glass on the shelf of her stomach.

"He'll be back late tonight," she answered, aware of the dullness in her voice. Nothing really mattered when it was so hot. "He thought he'd better visit his mother before the baby arrives. He tries to get there every other month, if he can."

"You should have gone with him and gotten out of the heat."

Wilma shook her head. "It's Phil she wants to see, not me—and especially not Cerise."

She glanced down at her misshapen body. "Maybe it'll be different after this one is born. She can't say this one isn't a real grandchild."

The shadow of the house began to stretch across the

yard. Joan reached for the thermos and refilled the glasses. The liquid gurgled out of the container.

"Wilma, you have to admit Cerise can be a stinker at times."

. "It's not her fault. First she had to get used to Phil and having a father. Then a new home and going to church. We never went to church until I met Phil." Wilma groaned as her back started to ache. "Now she's going to have another problem — she'll probably be jealous of the baby. Especially if Phil pays more attention to the baby than to her."

"Happens to all kids. God, I hated my kid sister," Joan said. "Don't make a big deal of it, and she'll get over it."

"But this will be Phil's child, and maybe he'll make a big fuss. Sometimes Cerise acts as if she owns Phil. She doesn't like it when Phil hugs me in front of her. She gets real quiet, and her eyes look hateful."

"Tough shit! You're too softhearted, Wilma. The kid needs a good swat on the fanny."

Wilma stared into her drink and shook her head. "You sound like Phil. He has two solutions for everything . . . spanking and praying." She giggled. "He prays so much that whenever Cerise does something wrong, she puts her hands together and bows her head before he can do anything."

"She's outsmarted you both. The kid's a stinker, but she's no dummy."

Joan's voice had a dry, sarcastic tone Wilma found irritating. She took another swallow of lemonade and decided it was only the heat. There was no real reason for being annoyed with Joan — especially when Joan had agreed to keep Cerise while Wilma was in the hospital.

"Mommy." Cerise tugged at her arm. Wilma cringed at

the dirt on the girl's hands.

The breeze returned, carrying the juniper scent from the hills down across the yard. Wilma felt as if she was being mercifully fanned into a slight degree of comfort.

"Mommy!" This time the tug was hard and jolting.

"What?" she snapped, and yanked her arm away. She rubbed at the dirt clinging to her sweat-dampened arm.

"Look!" Cerise dangled a long angleworm in the air. "It's the longest one I ever found."

"Ugh." Wilma stuck her tongue out in disgust. "Go put it away. I'm talking to Joan."

"But I want you to see my worm." Cerise's voice was shrill. She stomped one foot and wiggled the worm in front of her mother's face. "Look at it, Mommy."

"Please, baby, not now. I want to talk to Joan." Wilma clutched at her stomach. The sight of the repulsive worm dangling so close to her nose made her jerk away. The movement stirred another sharp pain in the small of her back. She winced and rubbed at the offending twinge with her free hand.

"Cerise, leave your mother alone." Joan barked the command. "The heat's making her sick."

Cerise swung around. Her blonde pigtails flew about her neck. She glared at the offensive tone in Joan Bailey's voice, then lowered her eyelashes and drew her lips together in a rigid line. For a few seconds she stared defiantly at Joan, then a faint smile crossed her face.

She hurled the worm into Joan's lap. "You look at him."

There was a flashing glint in her eyes before she darted away and scurried around the corner of the house.

"Damn!" Joan tossed the worm into the bushes and looked anxiously at Wilma. "Are you okay? You look miserable."

Wilma didn't feel like any more than a nod of her head. The light was gradually fading, and the sound of Lyle's shovel had stopped. The quiet was too pleasant to ruin with words.

Even the angry wail of a cat didn't really reach Wilma. She let the air current sweep across her body and evaporate the sweat.

"Oh, boy, Cerise has found Old Bessie again. I can't seem to convince her that Bessie is trying to hide her kittens." Joan got up and brushed at her shorts as if trying to erase the traces of the angleworm.

Wilma watched her with a weary feeling. She knew she should get up and go after Cerise, but the movement of air felt so good she didn't want to budge. If only she could sleep out here.

"Look, you sit here and enjoy the air," Joan said. "I'll find Cerise, give her a bath, and put her to bed. By then you'll be cooled off."

"Do you think Cerise will let you?"

"Don't worry. I'm bigger than she is." Joan's grin was barely visible in the growing darkness.

Wilma suddenly didn't care if Cerise screamed or not. The offer was too inviting, the air too comforting. She closed her eyes and dozed until a door slammed and the sound of Joan's footsteps rustled the dry grass of the lawn.

"You look better," Joan commented. "Want to help finish this off before I head for home?"

She held up the thermos with a tempting shake. Wilma groped beside the chair for her glass and held it out toward Joan in answer to the invitation.

"Cerise give you any trouble?" she asked.

"Not a bit," Joan said. She drained the last of the lemonade into the two glasses and flopped into the deck chair. "You know it's hot when a kid thinks a bath is a treat. Anyhow, I guess she wasn't after the cat at all. Bessie seems to have one kitten missing, and she's yowling for it. I suppose something must have gotten it . . . a dog or a tomcat, probably."

"That's awful," Wilma shuddered.

"Hey, she still has four. Like Lyle says, it's one less we have to get rid of later."

Wilma heard the plaintive wail of the cat and scowled. It was almost as if the animal was listening to their conversation and objecting.

"I hope she doesn't yowl like that all night," she said. "I have enough trouble trying to sleep with this extra baggage." She patted at her stomach and then began inching her legs over the edge of the chair. She had reached the stage of pregnancy where getting to her feet required two or three lurching attempts.

Joan's strong hand caught her elbow, and Wilma panted to regain her breath when she got to her feet.

"You get a good night's sleep," Joan urged. "I'll toss old Bessie some raw hamburger. She'll be so greedy, she'll forget her missing kitten."

"Poor cat. It must be terrifying to lose a child and not know what happened to it."

"Oh, Wilma, it's only a kitten."

"I know, but cats must feel the same way people do. I think I'd howl worse than Bessie if I lost a child." Wilma stopped and eyed the back steps with loathing. Steps were another problem. The weight had to be shifted, back and forth, like an elephant's. She grunted her way upward, step by step.

Joan laughed lightly and waited until Wilma reached the porch floor, then she waved a glass and disappeared into the shadows.

Phil eased the car into the driveway, letting it idle its way to a stop. The darkness of the house meant Wilma and Cerise were asleep or trying to sleep. The night air was warm and sticky. His shirt stuck to his back, and his fingers were moist against the wheel.

He reached in the backseat and picked up two of the packages. It would take him at least two trips to unload. He moved quietly, opening the door with a slow turn of the knob.

Cerise stirred and kicked one foot out from under the sheet when he stepped into the living room.

He tiptoed across the floor and placed his packages on the table. Wilma would appreciate the electric fan, even more when he told her it was a gift from his mother.

Clara Thayer was softening. The closer the birth of her own grandchild, the more she inquired about Wilma's health.

He made the second trip, taking a few extra minutes to sniff the hint of sage in the night air.

The small town was silent. Almost everyone was long asleep at this hour of the night. The river whispered in the darkness, while a few scattered lights indicated there were some restless people stirring.

A light flashed on at the Bailey's, and Joan's nude body was illuminated through the dining room window. Phil could see the white patches where her skin had been protected from the sun. She was too skinny and flat-chested for his taste. Wilma's curvacious body still held more interest for him—or it would after the baby was born.

Joan walked back through the room, showing the whiteness of her bottom, and the light went out.

Too flat. Wilma was better to look at — she had a backside with curves. He shifted his packages and started up the steps, moving carefully to avoid the one loose and creaking board.

Cerise groaned in her sleep. Her pale eyelashes flickered and fell back against her cheeks. She rolled over onto her stomach and yawned. In a few minutes her breathing settled back into a rhythmic pattern.

Phil bent and kissed her forehead, then tucked the damp pigtail behind her neck. He picked up the largest carton, sidestepped the improvised dollhouse Wilma had constructed from an orange crate, and tiptoed into the bedroom.

He stood in the darkness listening to the sound of Wilma's breathing in the stillness. She moaned in her sleep, and the bedsprings creaked with the shift of position. Although all the windows were open, the house had captured most of the day's heat within the walls and wasn't releasing it. The air in the river-bottom town was unmoving and humid, laden with river moisture.

"Phil."

The bed creaked again, and the soft light of the lamp beside the bed went on. Wilma blinked, her eyes adjusting to the light, and tugged the sheet up over her bulging stomach.

In the softness of the lamp's pink light, Wilma's cheeks were glowing. The sight of her wide, eager eyes gave Phil a surge of desire. Even pregnant, Wilma had more gentle feminine appeal than the athletic body of Joan Bailey.

He tugged at the box in his hand until the end came loose and pulled out the electric fan.

"Surprise!"

Wilma's head rose from the pillow. Her eyes and

mouth both opened at once, then her mouth widened into a delighted grin. He placed the fan on the dresser, aimed it at the bed, and began groping behind the dresser to find the electrical outlet.

"Oh, Phil, thank you." She laid her head back on the pillow, letting the moving air stir her dark curls. She looked at him with her eyes half-closed, a contented smile on her face. The fan whirred and circulated the air about the cramped bedroom.

"Don't thank me," Phil said, keeping his voice hushed. No point in waking Cerise. "Mother sent it."

"Your mother?" Wilma's face showed her amazement in a sudden alertness.

Phil pulled off his sweat-soaked shirt and nodded. "I think it's a sign she's getting a little mellow. Said she still remembered how miserable she was in the summer."

Wilma attempted to roll over on her side. Her fingers clawed at the sheet until she flopped back with a sigh.

"It's more work than it's worth to turn," she groaned. Her lips drew into a puckered frown. "Phil, it's your birthday tomorrow, and it's too hot to make you a cake."

He eased himself onto the edge of the bed, trying to avoid jostling her as much as possible.

"Don't worry about the cake, honey. Mother sent one. It's out on the table."

Wilma's eyebrows pulled together. "What got into her? A fan and a cake too. It ain't like her."

"*Isn't*, Wilma. Not *ain't — isn't*."

She drew her lips together and pouted. "Well, it isn't, then."

Phil bent and began unlacing his shoes.

"Mother can see she has to start being friendly if she expects to see the new baby very often. She's excited. Kept saying she hoped it was a boy."

54

He yanked off his shoes and pulled off his socks. They were moist with sweat, and he hurled them across the room in the direction of his discarded shirt.

Wilma ran her hand up his bare arm and smiled when he leaned across the bed to kiss her. His lips brushed hers, gently at first, then passionately. The kiss built in intensity until he pushed himself away and took a deep breath.

"Wilma . . ." His voice rasped in the stillness. He held his head down and closed his eyes, praying for the emotion to subside — at least for a while. It wouldn't be much longer.

Wilma's hand remained on his arm. When he opened his eyes, she was watching him with a serene smile of contentment. The fan roiled the air and created ripples across the sheet. Air delicately caressed the heat-damp-ened curls at her neck.

He took another breath. "I almost forgot. There's another surprise."

He slipped out of the bedroom, feeling his feet stick to the bare wood floor, and came back with the large pink striped box.

"Phil!" This time Wilma managed to roll herself onto her side and push herself to a sitting position. Her eyes gleamed with excitement, and her hands reached eagerly for the package.

"You got me something! It's clothes. I can tell by the box."

Her fingers tore at the tape and whisked the top from the box. Then she reached into it, pushed the tissue paper aside, and began stroking the satin fabric, using only the tips of her fingers to feel the luxurious softness. Her eyes glistened with tears as she ran her fingers up and across the velvet lapels.

"Phil, take it out." She whispered in a hushed tone. "Hold it up so I can see it. Please?"

He grasped the bathrobe by the shoulders and pulled it free. He gave it a quick shake so she could see the ice-blue satin and run her hands down the length of the material.

"I bought it to match your eyes," he said and watched her face shine with pleasure. "You need a new robe to take to the hospital."

"It must have cost a lot. Can we afford it?"

He reached over and tucked the robe back into the box. "We can," was all he said. No reason to try explaining to Wilma about the commission checks from the sale of the hymnals. It was a sound business arrangement, but there was no point in having Wilma brag about his deals to everyone she knew. They were good hymnals, large print and easy to read, but some people might think he was only interested in the commissions.

Her face was still glowing with delight when she turned out the lamp. Her hand rested on his shoulder with an affectionate caress. It mingled with the moving air of the fan, and Phil closed his eyes. As he relaxed, he thought in one last fleeting moment that he hadn't said a real prayer—at least a devout one—before getting into bed. He hadn't told Wilma all of the good news. He stretched, and the chugging labor of the washing machine was the next sound he heard.

Daylight filled the bedroom, and Wilma's half of the bed was empty. Her voice had a high-pitched edginess. It pierced through the thin walls of the house.

"Cerise, leave that alone."

Phil rolled out of bed, knelt with closed eyes for a few minutes, then rose and went to the closet. He stretched around the waiting crib and dragged out the most lightweight slacks and shirt. They caught with stubbornness on the adjoining hangers, and he had to tug to pull them free. One hanger clattered onto the closet floor. Wilma was right: the place was too small.

He smiled to himself. It would be nice to tell Wilma about the Pleasant Home offer, but she talked too much. The deal wouldn't be certain until after he held the gospel meetings there next month.

The Pleasant Home church board had decided to hold a week-long series of gospel meetings. If he brought them new members — if the congregation liked him — they had put up a lot of conditions, but they had promised him half of the collections.

Phil glanced about the bedroom. The parsonage at Pleasant Home had two large bedrooms, with an extra room at the rear of the house he could use as an office.

No point in telling Wilma . . . not yet. If the Maupin church board suspected he was leaving, they'd be searching for a new minister. They might find one before he was ready to move. He couldn't be sure Wilma wouldn't babble about the offer. She'd whisper it to Joan Bailey, and Joan would tell Lyle.

When the deal was certain, he'd tell her . . . not before.

Half the collections. He grinned. He knew how much his smile appealed to women. The collections would be good.

After the baby was born, he would take Wilma on a shopping spree — somewhere. The Dalles, maybe. Her eyes would sparkle as they had at the sight of the new bathrobe. Phil flexed his muscles and adjusted his shorts. The idea had stirred a tingling sensation in his groin.

"Cerise!"

This time Wilma's voice went soaring upward in exasperation. The smack of flesh against flesh and a protesting wail meant Cerise had pushed things too far.

When he stepped out of the bedroom, Cerise was balanced on the edge of a kitchen chair. Her face was flushed with anger. The flaming imprint of Wilma's hand was silhouetted on Cerise's arm. The color gradually ebbed, and Cerise's mouth clamped itself into a set line.

She looked from the cake Phil had brought home to Wilma. Her pale eyelashes lowered. Her eyes were half-closed in contemplation.

A furrow in the frosting was evidence of Cerise's sampling.

Cerise turned and looked up at Phil. For a second her eyes held a lustrous glint, then she slid out of the chair and ran to him, hugging his knees and rubbing her cheek against his thighs.

"Daddy Phil kissed me first when he came home."

She glared at Wilma and tossed her head, sending one pigtail swinging across her mouth. She shrugged and brushed it back with one hand. Her face turned up toward Phil with a possessive smile, and she squeezed his leg hard.

"All because I wouldn't let her have cake for breakfast," Wilma sighed.

Phil patted Cerise's head and pried her fingers from his leg. "We'll have the cake for lunch, and you can help me light the candles."

He looked down into her face and became aware of a coldness, an evaluation as cold as a bank loan-officer's. He frowned and wondered what was going on behind the sober expression on her face.

"I want to light a candle now." Cerise raised one foot, ready to stomp angrily, then hesitated and lowered it back to the floor.

She tilted her head to one side. The baby teeth flashed in a cajoling smile.

"Please, Daddy Phil. Light one. Only one."

Phil studied the eager excitement on her small face and had to relent. "Oh, what can it hurt?" he said.

Cerise hopped up and down while he brought the box of wooden matches from the shelf above the refrigerator. He put one candle in the center of the cake, took a match from the box, and looked at her with a serious, questioning gaze.

"You think you can blow this out?"

Her eyes glistened, and the pigtails bobbed at the nod of her head. She scrambled up onto the chair and suddenly reached for the match.

"Let me light it, Daddy Phil."

"Matches are dangerous, Cerise. I'll light it and you can blow."

"Please?" The small face turned into pucker-lipped pleading. She grabbed his hand and begged, "You can watch me. Please?"

Phil inhaled and handed her the match. "I suppose I'll never get a cup of coffee if I don't get this over with." He held the box in front of her.

"Now do it carefully, Cerise." He tucked her braids back behind her head. "Strike the match on the box, and then light the candle before it burns down and gets to your fingers."

She jiggled happily as she gripped the match and scraped it along the sandy surface. The match snapped in two and her lower lip clamped itself over the upper one with a determined frustration.

"Try again, Cerise, and this time hold it straight." He tilted the match at the right angle, and Cerise struck the match against the rough striking panel in a quick movement. The flame ignited. Her eyes opened wide in astonishment.

"Ohh," she squealed, holding the match and staring at the flame.

She squinted up at him with the beginning of a frown, but held the match to the candle wick as she was told. The wick flared and caught fire just as the match burned down. Cerise jerked and dropped the match to the floor with a howl of pain.

With a quick movement of his foot, Phil extinguished the fire and said, "I told you it would happen, Cerise. Matches aren't playthings."

He felt a twinge of pity watching her suck on the singed finger. "Blow out the candle and go play while I get my coffee. It'll quit hurting in a few seconds."

She sucked in a chestful of air and blew. The flame wavered, died, and then burst back into full fire. This time she leaned forward and blew directly onto the flame until the fire died and smoke curled up from the wick.

Phil walked to the stove and poured himself a cup of coffee. "Okay, Cerise," he said over his shoulder. "You go play."

He stepped out onto the back porch, where the ancient washer was whirling another load of clothes behind its circular window. Wilma was folding towels, building a stack of clean laundry across the top of the dryer. When she raised her head, he could see the bluish-gray circles underlining her eyes.

One hand went to the small of her back and rubbed back and forth. The loose sack of a dress pulled itself into the niche between her swollen breasts and the protruding stomach where it clung to the moisture of her body.

"You feeling all right?"

He looked at her over the rim of his cup. Beads of perspiration dotted her forehead behind a curtain of dark curls. Her feet swelled around the thong straps and her milk-engorged breasts heaved when she caught her breath.

"No, I don't think so," she groaned. "This may be the big day."

He lowered the cup and bit his lip while he thought hurriedly through his schedule.

"Are you sure?"

"How can I be sure?" she snapped the words out. "This pain in my back—it seems to come every two hours."

"In your back? It can't be a labor pain, can it?" He felt suddenly uneducated and unsure of himself. This was a portion of the world he had never wondered about. He'd said a few comforting words to a worried mother, praised motherhood from the pulpit, but what actually was happening? He looked at Wilma with confused thoughts. She must know the answers. She'd been through this before.

"It could mean it's getting close." She folded and refolded the same towel. At last, she dropped it on the stack, shook a dress of Cerise's, scrutinized it, and nodded with approval. It went directly to a hanger, then she reached for socks, matching them almost automatically and making new stacks on the dryer.

"Let me get you a cup of coffee." He floundered and searched for the right words. What was he supposed to do now? For once, Wilma was making the decisions, and he would have to follow her blindly. How was he supposed to act?

He turned and stepped back into the house, gulping the last of his own coffee. It sank into his stomach and lodged there, leaving an acid taste in his mouth.

The smell assailed him first, then the grayness of the air.

"Cerise!"

He hurled his cup in the direction of the cupboard and heard a shattering crack as he darted into the living room. Flames were shooting up from the wooden crate of a dollhouse. The room was heavily fogged with smoke.

Cerise stood leaning against the living room door with a confident smirk. She watched the flames with a fascinated rapture. The carton of matches rested on the floor by her foot.

He snatched up a throw rug and flung it over the makeshift dollhouse, beating at the flames.

"Cerise, get some water!" He shouted at her with a mounting fury in his chest. She merely stood and watched him with a cold stare. The smirk disappeared, but her eyes glowed with an intense animosity. She was challenging him to put out the fire!

He dropped the rug and dashed to the kitchen sink, turning the water on full blast. He grabbed a pan and ran, scurrying back and forth, refilling the pan.

Wilma started through the door and halted. Her eyes widened. She froze, sniffed the air, and gaped at Phil's frantic racing back and forth. Her hand clung to the door casing, and her skin paled.

Phil hurled one last panful of water on the smoldering wood and panted for breath. The house reeked with the stench of charcoal. He glanced at Wilma with reassurance.

"It's okay. I got it out."

Wilma stared at the dollhouse and then at Cerise. Her shoulder sagged against the door casing. Tears glistened and trickled down her cheek.

"The place could have burned down." She choked and turned away. "How could she. . . ." The rest of the words became murmurings, lost as Wilma walked out onto the porch.

Phil turned to Cerise and clamped his back teeth together. Control . . . he had to get control. The urge—it was wrong; hitting her was wrong. He groped for some words of prayer to staunch the anger that was making him want to strike out violently.

Cerise reached down and picked up the box of matches. Her face composed and uncontrite, she held the carton out toward him.

"You forgot to put them away, Daddy Phil."

He looked at the carton and then at her face. Her eyes were narrowed, and the green intensity of her stare made him gulp for air. His hands clenched into fists. He forced himself to relax, to open his hand and reach for the box.

"Cerise, you could have burned the house down. Don't you understand?"

He heard his own voice shaking and fought the impulse to slap the cold smugness off her face. It was the defiance that irritated him. The rigidness of her spine, the way she stared at him . . . as if the fire was his fault for leaving the matches out.

Her lips drew back, and she gave him the half smile. Then she slowly knelt, looked up at him, and placed the palms of her hands tightly together.

"Should I say a prayer because I was bad?"

Her eyelashes dropped, and Phil wondered if he was being mocked. There was something insincere—something taunting in the way she looked up at him. The half smile hovered about her lips. He let his shoulders droop. It was his imagination. Her face was too serene.

He took a deep breath and bent to gather up the charred bits of wood with the blackened scatter rug.

"Yes, Cerise," he sighed. "You'd better pray. But you will also not have any birthday cake. We won't have candles on it now. There's been enough fire in the house for one day."

He shoved the carton of matches into his pocket, straightened, and gave one backward glance before he went out the door.

Her smile had disappeared. Her eyes were closed. Her hands remained in an attitude of prayer, but her lip was extended in a pout.

Phil carried the dampened remains to the incinerator, feeling a sense of satisfaction. For once he had chosen a punishment Cerise would understand and remember.

He stood looking down at the burned pieces of orange crate and wondered about Cerise. Would his own child be so difficult? He didn't believe heredity made people bad. No matter what his mother preached, Cerise wasn't bad simply because she was illegitimate.

His glance moved to Wilma's bulky figure wedged in the canvas deck chair. She sat awkwardly, with her feet apart, her shoulders slumped. As he walked toward her, the puffiness of her eyelids told him she'd been crying.

"It's okay, hon. The fire's out, and the only damage is a slightly burned floor and an orange crate destroyed." He found himself chuckling over the cleverness of his punishment. "Cerise is forbidden to have any of the birthday cake."

"Oh, Phil, she'll be upset." Wilma looked up at him with a sad twist in the corner of her mouth.

"Wilma!" He softened the anger as quickly as he snapped the word out. "It wouldn't do any good to spank her. She'll learn more by not having the cake. And what if she is upset? I'm upset now. If the parsonage burned down, where would we live? We might even be asked to leave the church."

He frowned down at the grass. "Worse yet, Cerise could have burned with it. The humidity—the dryness—this heat makes everything burn like paper. We're lucky we caught it when we did."

"Oh, Phil!" Her voice rose into a scratchy wail. "I keep worrying about her. She's such a handful. She's really awful sometimes. Last night she threw a worm right into Joan's lap. I really don't know what we're going to do. What if she doesn't like the baby? What am I going . . ."

"Wilma, stop it." He interrupted when the tone of her voice rose and started to squeak. She was starting into one of her nervous babblings. He patted her hand and held it until she swallowed and subsided into quiet sniffling.

"Daddy Phil, can I play now? Please?"

He glanced over his shoulder. Cerise stood on the porch with her hands folded together. Her face was primly sedate while she waited for his answer.

"Yes." Phil nodded and turned back to Wilma. Her hand suddenly clamped down on his with an alarming strength.

"Uh-oh." She took a long breath and her hand relaxed. "I think we'd better head for the Dalles. That was a real honest-to-goodness labor pain."

She pushed awkwardly against the arms of the deck chair and looked up at him with a grateful smile when he caught her elbow and helped her to her feet.

"What do I do now?" He clutched at her arm and hoped she didn't feel the trembling in his fingers. "I'll get the car. I'll, oh gosh—Cerise! What do we do with Cerise?"

This time it was Wilma who was patting his hand. Motherly—patting his hand and murmuring words with a peaceful calmness. How could she be so placid and unworried?

"You go tell Joan," she said. "She's going to watch Cerise. Give her the house key while I get my bag." She patted his arm once more, speaking slowly, as if to an infant. "Calm down, Phil. We have plenty of time."

She walked stiffly toward the house, leaving him staring at her lumbering, swaying gait. He finally shook himself into action and hurried toward the Baileys', passing Cerise, who was busy digging in the mound of dirt. When he left the Baileys', he stopped and bent to kiss her lightly on the forehead.

"You mind Joan," he said. The innocence of her dirt-smudged face when she looked up into his stirred a twinge of remorse for his anger at her. "We're going to the hospital. When we come back, we'll bring you a brother or sister."

Cerise shrugged her shoulders and bent to dig another hole in the pile of earth.

"Bring a brother. I don't want a sister."

He tugged affectionately at a pigtail before he rose.

"We'll have to take what God gives us, Cerise."

She wrinkled her nose and delved into the hole with one hand.

"He'd better send a brother."

Phil rubbed at his chin and watched her, but she was intently inspecting the cavity she had created in the dirt. He scowled and trudged back to the parsonage. It was a long trip to the hospital. Wilma said they had time. What would he do if they didn't? He should have taken time—should have been interested in becoming a father.

He broke into a run and bounded up the steps. His

mind concentrated on getting Wilma to the hospital. Forget the prayer meeting tonight . . . the congregation would understand. He would call Miss Simms from the hospital. She would take over.

He kept his thoughts on the task of getting Wilma into the car. Take it step by step: get the car moving, keep moving, don't get disturbed. Even when he heard Wilma's short, panting groan, he kept his concentration on the road ahead of him. He started praying to himself: pray, steer, corner ahead, slow, speed up. He sensed Wilma relaxing against the seat beside him, and his own panic subsided.

It was all in God's hands now. He flexed his fingers, eased his grip on the wheel, and gave her an encouraging smile. He would be able to handle it. She propped one elbow on the edge of the open car window and smiled back. Her composure made him feel ridiculous. If she could go through this without getting a case of the jitters, why couldn't he?

He kept praying to himself until he turned into the hospital parking lot. Now he could say "Amen." It was up to Wilma now, Wilma and the doctors. Doctors who looked at him with a condescending patience.

Phil stumbled to the nearest chair in the waiting room and collapsed onto the cool plastic surface. Why were so many things happening in one day? He'd be glad when it was over.

"I never knew a day could be so long." Joan Bailey stepped out of the house carrying two cans of beer. "I wasn't cut out to be a mother. Guess it's a good thing I can't be."

Lyle Bailey threw another shovelful of dirt on the

67

growing mound with a grunt of exertion. He jammed the shovel into the ground, letting the handle point skyward, and walked toward the steps. With one hand he took one of the beer cans and tore the tab open, smiling at the resounding hiss of escaping air.

"She's a funny kid." He flopped his flabby haunches down on the step and winced at the pain of his belt buckle digging into the fat of his stomach.

Joan settled herself on the step beside him and took a slow drag of the cold liquid.

"Some days she's a pain in the ass. Thank God, she was good this afternoon. I don't think I could take it if she got bratty. Not in all this heat."

"Bratty? Hell, all the kid does is dig in the dirt for worms. Never says a damn word to me. Digs and chucks a worm in that fruit jar she drags around. Giggles now and then. Maybe the worms tickle."

Joan took another sip of beer and looked at the growing pile of dirt.

"Wonder what she'll do for worms when you get through digging?" She squinted at her husband in the growing dusk.

Sweat trickled down Lyle's forehead and soaked the back of his denim shirt. She had hoped he would sweat off some of his extra pounds, but Lyle had only increased his beer consumption.

"I am through digging," he grunted. "Tomorrow night I start building forms. Be ready to pour the foundation by next week."

The gurgling in his throat ended with the beer can being mashed in his hand.

"Get me another, will ya, sexy?" He grinned at her and swatted her on the fanny when she returned.

"You ought to gauge your time by the cans — not the

hour," she grumbled good-naturedly.

"Hell, this is a two-keg job, not a case." He grinned.

The plaintive wail of a cat rose from under the porch. Joan felt a shiver run up her spine at the sound of misery.

"Damn. Old Bessie again. You'd think she'd settle for four kittens and quit fussing because one's missing," she muttered.

Lyle swallowed. "You mean settle for three."

"Three? But there were four kittens last night. I looked."

"Only three left tonight. This time I looked." He rubbed the sweat from his forehead with his sleeve and burped.

Joan scowled in the darkness. "What do you suppose is getting them, Lyle?"

"Who knows? Some tomcat, most likely." He heaved his shoulders back and forth. The dampness of his shirt pulled against his body and clung to the roll of fat above his belt. "Don't worry about it, for Christ's sake. We'd only have to find homes for the damned things. I doubt if there's anyone left in town who'd take one."

He swallowed the last of the beer and reached for her with one arm.

"Your shirt's wet. You're sweating as bad as I am." He gave her a hug and pulled his arm away.

"It's not sweat," she said. "Cerise splashed water all over me when I was washing her hair."

She leaned her head against his shoulder. "Lyle, is there something wrong with me? I don't like the kid." She dropped her voice into a whisper. How could she explain the odd feeling Cerise gave her when she stared back from under those pale eyelashes? The kid was so colorless — except for the eyes.

69

Cerise made her feel watched . . . something about the child made her feel as if she was being watched by old Bessie. The look in Cerise's eyes when she waited for dinner was exactly like old Bessie when she waited for her cat food.

"Hell, don't let her get to you. I told you she's a funny kid. Preacher's kid. Who in hell would want to grow up as a preacher's kid? Bound to make her a little weird."

"Phil's not a bad sort," Joan argued. "He doesn't get on our case because we don't go to church."

"Humph . . ." Lyle scratched at his stomach and snorted. "Why should he? He's made all the old biddies in town think he's guaranteed them a special seat on the bus to heaven. He don't need us. He's got all he can handle keeping the old ladies convinced he's saving their souls. The man can't save everybody."

"You think he gave up on us?" Joan giggled and leaned closer to him. "Maybe he's heard some of our noisy lovemaking. We're going to have to close the windows."

Lyle caught her with one arm and leaned her back against the floor of the porch. A laugh rumbled in the back of his throat.

"Well, he can't be no purist." He bit at her neck and laughed again. "It's his old lady that's up in the Dalles having a kid. He knows a good-looking broad when he sees one."

Lyle's mouth descended over hers before she could answer. His tongue explored her lips and delved into her mouth. One hand went to the opening of her blouse.

Joan moaned and twisted to allow his hands to pull the blouse down off her shoulder. Her arms went around his neck. With one finger she traced the outline of his ear.

70

"Hey, we'll shock the hell out of the preacher," he muttered into her neck. "Fucking on the back porch while his kid's sleeping here."

"Mmm." She licked at his ear with her tongue, enjoying the saltiness of his skin. "He said he wouldn't drive back until tomorrow."

"In that case," he bent and blew on her neck, "there's no one to see us but old Bessie, and she's busy counting her kittens."

At the bedroom window, Cerise braced her chin on her hands and watched the dim outline of the figures on the porch. She could see the flash of Joan Bailey's breasts before Lyle's head bent over his wife's form. She raised up on her knees trying to see what he was doing.

She heard Joan Bailey's giggle and peered through the darkness, trying to hear what they were saying. Why hadn't Mrs. Bailey left the window open?

Mr. Bailey stood up, carrying his wife as easily as Daddy Phil carried a box of hymnals. Joan Bailey's blouse fell to the porch floor and was kicked away by her husband's foot.

Cerise ducked back from the window when they moved across the porch. She flopped back onto the bed and listened to the sounds of Joan Bailey's laughter while Mr. Bailey's footsteps thumped down the hall.

The bedroom door slammed and Cerise scowled into the darkness. She had never heard Daddy Phil and her mother making noises like the Baileys'. She knew the bed in Mommy's room squeaked just as bad as the one in the Baileys', but Mommy never squealed like Mrs. Bailey.

She rubbed at her eyes and wondered if Daddy Phil ever pulled her mommy's blouse off like Mr. Bailey had

71

done to Joan.

The cat wailed, a long, high-pitched howl that slowly ebbed away. Cerise smiled sleepily. It was a funny sound. She tried to keep her eyes open, listening for the cat to yowl again, but the night grew quiet. Not even the Baileys were making noises. The river gushing sounded faraway and whispery.

Her eyelids grew heavier and she yawned one last big yawn.

The morning noises were different. Mr. Bailey's truck belched and roared outside the window. Gravel crackled, and the engine faded into the sounds of Joan Bailey's bare feet splatting across the floor.

Cerise closed her eyes when the flesh-sounding steps came to her bedroom door. She heard the knob squeak as it turned, and she kept her eyelids shut. When the door made a clicking sound, Cerise peeked through her eyelashes. Mrs. Bailey was gone. She could stay in the big bed a little longer, roll on it without falling off and throw her arms out without banging into a wall.

She stroked the smooth ribbon edges of the blanket with her fingers and then rubbed it against her cheek. It felt soft, like one of the new baby blankets her mommy had put in the crib. The blue one with the white rabbits. She caressed her nose with the blanket and listened to the floor creaking as Joan Bailey walked around the house.

There was an odd scraping noise, the murmur of voices, and the wail of the cat. The wail rose in a sad cry and faded away.

Cerise rolled over and crawled across the bed to the window. The yowling noise came up from under the porch floor in a protesting wail.

"Yeeowl." Her face contorted in an attempt to imitate

the cat's distressed sound. She tried to make the noise in her throat, but only a thin squeak emerged.

The opening of the bedroom door behind her startled Cerise into wide-eyed silence.

"I thought I heard you moving around," Joan Bailey laughed. "Your daddy's here." She pointed at a stack of clothes on the chair beside the bed before she stepped back into the hall. "You can have breakfast as soon as you're dressed. Your daddy's having coffee."

Cerise nodded and rolled across the bed to slide down to the floor. She could hear Joan Bailey laughing in the kitchen and tried to imitate the sound. Mrs. Bailey laughed so differently from her mother.

Mommy had a scratchy laugh. It made her ears hurt sometimes, but Mrs. Bailey's laugh was fun to hear. It was almost as nice to listen to as Daddy Phil's. She tugged the pink T-shirt over her head and tried to laugh, but the sound wasn't right. It didn't sound like Mrs. Bailey at all. But it sounded better than Mommy. She forced the sound back into her throat. It came out lower—much better. She grinned proudly to herself, finished getting her clothes on, and hurried to the kitchen.

Daddy Phil put down his coffee cup and swung her up into his lap.

"You got your wish, Cerise. It's a baby brother."

His arm went around her and hugged her against his chest. Cerise pushed her head tightly against him and smelled the spicy scent of his shaving lotion. She rubbed her cheek across his shirt, listening to his voice rumble in his chest while he answered Joan Bailey.

"We named him Mathew John. Wilma left the choice up to me, since he was my birthday present. I chose names he'd be proud of."

His laugh boomed in Cerise's ear. She ran her hand

down the buttons of his shirt and peeked at Joan Bailey from under her eyelashes.

Mrs. Bailey was looking at Daddy Phil with her mouth partly opened. She looked like one of Daddy Phil's church ladies, the ones who called him "Reverend" and hung onto his hand for so long. They were the ones that pinched her cheeks and made clacking sounds with their teeth.

She pouted and snuggled even more tightly against him. She wrapped her arms around him as far as she could reach and squeezed hard.

His hand moved down and patted her bare thigh, rubbing it gently. She rolled with the movement of his body when he reached for a slice of toast and held it out toward her. She shook her head. She didn't want to release her hold. Daddy Phil had never held her in his lap at breakfast time. It must be because Mommy was gone. She liked the hardness of his body.

"Come on, Cerise. You have to eat before your Daddy takes you home."

She lifted her eyelashes and looked carefully at Joan Bailey. The church-lady look was gone. Now she had the frowning lines like Mommy had when she said, "Don't dawdle, Cerise."

"Joan's right. Eat your breakfast. You'll have to tag along with me for the next couple of days. Until your mother and brother come home, at least."

"You can leave her with me if you want to, Phil."

Cerise looked up at Joan and held her breath, but Daddy Phil's chuckling response made her let the air loose.

"No, I'd better take my gosling with me."

"Gosling?"

Phil's laugh was deep inside his chest. "Goslings adopt

74

almost anything—cat, dog, or human, if they don't have a natural mother. Tag after it everywhere. Wasn't sure when Wilma and I first got married, but when Cerise did decide to accept me, she went overboard. I'm afraid this one is my gosling."

Cerise cuddled against him, wondering what a gosling was until Phil gave her thigh a gentle pat and slid her off his lap. She climbed into the chair next to his and reached for the glass of milk.

It was cold and Mrs. Bailey had put it in a glass painted with purple flowers. She gulped it hurriedly and started on her toast. If Mommy wasn't going to be home, maybe Daddy Phil would hold her in his lap again. She ate quickly, scooping up huge spoonfuls of cornflakes, bigger than Mommy let her take at one time. Some of them fell off the side of the spoon and onto the checked tablecloth. Cerise glanced hastily from Mrs. Bailey to Daddy Phil, but neither of them was watching her. She scraped the cereal off the tablecloth with her spoon and dumped it back into the bowl before they could see the mess she was making.

They weren't talking about anything important. Mrs. Bailey was jabbering about cement and building the new room. She kept tugging at her shorts and fingering the collar of her blouse.

Cerise scraped the bottom of the bowl with her spoon and wiped her mouth with the back of her hand.

"I'm done, Daddy Phil."

He gave her a grin and pushed his cup aside. "Then get your pajamas, and we'll go home."

"Oh, I'll bring them over later, Phil," Joan said. She stood up, still pulling at her shorts. "I'll wash up her dirty clothes from yesterday for you."

"Thanks, Joan. She does get dirty playing in all Lyle's

diggings."

"Well, he's finished the digging. Now he'll have to shovel it all back when the foundation's poured. Cerise will have to hunt for worms somewhere else, I'm afraid."

Cerise bit her upper lip and tugged at Daddy Phil's hand. She didn't understand the laughter in Joan Bailey's voice, but Mrs. Bailey was looking down at her when she laughed. Cerise kicked at the floor with one foot and scowled. She pulled toward the door, but Daddy Phil continued to talk.

"Bring a plate when you come over. I'm stuck with a birthday cake that's going to get stale. Cerise and I can't eat all of it."

Cerise held her head down and walked ahead of them to the porch. Daddy Phil had forgotten about not letting her have any birthday cake. Why was he going to give part of it to Mrs. Bailey? It wasn't fair to give birthday cake to Mrs. Bailey. She wasn't part of their family.

Her eyes narrowed at the sight of old Bessie. The cat crawled out from under the porch, blinked at the sunlight, and meowed twice.

"Poor thing. She wants to be fed." Joan bent and picked up the cat's yellow bowl. "Sometimes I forget she's around when she's not yowling."

The grass crunched under Cerise's feet, making dry popping noises. She took long running steps trying to stay close to Daddy Phil, but he gave her hand a shake and dropped it.

"You'd better play outside, Cerise. I have to finish the washing and then write a sermon."

"I'll help." She trotted to keep beside him. "Then can we have some cake?"

Phil shook his head. "I can do it faster without you, Cerise. The cake has to wait until lunchtime. Now find

76

something to do."

Cerise stopped. He wasn't looking at her at all. The long steps he took meant he didn't want her to keep up. When he wanted her, he took short steps and waited.

She stood and watched him. He yanked the clothes out of the washer and hurled them into the dryer, the clothes Mommy was washing when she went to get the baby brother. She wiggled from one foot to the other and listened to the grass snap under her shoes. Daddy Phil wasn't looking at her at all, and lunchtime was a long time away.

She turned and scuffed her feet across the crunching grass until she reached Mr. Bailey's pile of dirt. The corners of her mouth turned up. She flopped onto the soft earth and began to scoop out another hole.

The gray-black cat padded across the porch, settled on the step, and began licking her paws. She froze to scrutinize Cerise. The black whiskers twitched twice, then she returned to working her paws back to whiteness with her tongue.

Cerise squinted up into the sun, then turned back to the mound of earth. The hole had to be a lot deeper. She took both hands and scooped deep into the earth.

Lyle Bailey picked up his shovel. Might as well get the dirt out of the way before he worked on the rest of the new addition. He'd made a lot of progress in the last two weeks.

The purple grayness of the cloud worried him. It moved steadily toward the town. The cloud and the humid stillness of the air held threats of an approaching rainstorm.

He'd have to shovel it back now, fill the cavity around

the foundation before the whole yard became a soggy expanse of mud.

He heaved the first shovelful of dirt into place. The cat stirred and lifted her ears. She had been dozing on the braided rug Joan used for a doormat, but the sound of Lyle's shoveling startled her into a protesting meow.

"It's okay, Bessie," Lyle said. He pitched the second shovelful toward the base of the concrete wall. "Go on back to sleep."

The cat's ears twitched back and forth. She blinked her eyes as if agreeing to his command, but she continued to watch his movements. Like a foreman on a city road crew, she kept surveillance of his manual labor.

He worked at a coordinated, steady pace, feeling the air grow cooler as the cloud moved closer, his rhythm broken only by the sound of the cat's mournful wail. The sound made his arm jerk and dirt spill across the toe of his boot.

"Damn it, Bessie, stop it."

He stopped, shook the dirt off his boots, and leaned on the shovel. "Hey, sexy, get me a beer, will ya?"

As he waited for a response from inside the house, the cat clawed at the rug with her white paws and emitted another long, sad wail.

"Why don't you feed her?" he grumbled when Joan appeared in the doorway. "She's getting on my nerves."

Joan looked down and nudged the cat gently with one foot, but old Bessie only twitched the end of her tail and clawed at the rug once more.

"She's not hungry," Joan answered. "She keeps yowling for her kittens."

"God, you'd think she'd have gotten over that by now. Hell, it's been almost two weeks since the last one disappeared."

He took the can of beer from her hand and drained half of it in one long continuous gulp, then handed it back and picked up the shovel.

"Thanks."

Joan shrugged, took a sip from the can, and stood watching him dig. "You want me to stand here and hold this," she asked, "or can I go now?"

He continued to move the dirt in a steady, unrelenting pattern of motion. "You got something better to do?" he grunted.

"Yeah, wise one, I do," she answered. "I promised Wilma I'd stay with the baby while she walks up to the store for some groceries and to get Cerise some new shoes."

Lyle swung the shovel and felt the dampness of sweat between his shoulder blades. He squinted up at the sky. The cloud was still a good distance away. He had time.

"Where's the preacher? Or doesn't he babysit?" he asked.

"Out of town for the week. I told you about it . . . he's holding revival meetings at some little burg near Portland."

"Going big time now."

"Oh, I don't think so. Wilma seemed to think it was some country town—close to his mom's, I think."

"Doesn't she mind him taking off when the baby's still so young?" Lyle asked. "Haven't seen her out much since she got home. Wondered if she was feeling okay."

Joan erupted in a hearty laugh. "Nothing wrong with her health. She has a sexy new bathrobe and hates to get dressed." The laugh subsided into a giggle. "And Phil told her if the meetings go well, he'll take her to the Dalles to buy a new outfit." She looked down at her own cut-offs and scratched her head. "Wilma's crazy about clothes. Why, I don't know, but she goes ape over the thought of a new dress."

Lyle looked down at the exposed dirt and frowned. He glanced at his wife, then dragged the shovel casually over the surface.

"Well, they'll probably be leaving us before long."

"What makes you say that?" She was looking at him with her eyebrows drawn together. "Did Phil say anything?"

He rubbed at the back of his neck and shook his head. "No, he didn't say a word. It's easy to see he wouldn't be satisfied with sticking around a hick town like this. Talks about wanting to have revival meetings—thinks he's a future Billy Graham. Guy like him isn't going to stick around Maupin for long, especially if he has a wife with an eye for fancy duds. Nowhere around here for her to wear anything but jeans."

He moved the shovel over a couple feet and dug into the mound of earth. "Anyhow, you better hope they do move on, sexy, or you'll be doing a lot of baby-sitting, and you're not exactly the motherly type."

"I don't mind now and then, Lyle, especially the baby." She looked at him with a broad smile. "He's so adorable with those big eyes, and already he has lots of dark hair."

Lyle stopped digging and reached for the can of beer. "Okay, in that case, I'll finish this off." The liquid was still cold as it went down, quenching the last of his thirst. "How long you going to be over there?"

"Not long. How long can it take to get a gallon of milk and a pair of shoes?"

"Who knows, with that kid? Take her an hour to size up the store and another hour to say what she liked."

Joan's voice held the light, teasing laughter of indulgence. She tossed her hair back from her neck with one hand and said, "Cerise is different, I admit, but she's crazy about the baby. She'll probably take the first thing Wilma puts on her feet so she can get home and take care of her new brother."

"Thought everyone was worried about the kid being jealous."

"You know how kids are," she answered. "They never do what you expect. Cerise acts as if they had the child just for her. Calls him 'my baby.'" Joan giggled. "Wilma had a hell of a time talking her into leaving the baby. Can you imagine, Cerise didn't like the idea of me holding him."

She shoved her blouse under the waistband of her shorts and glanced at the pile of earth. "At the rate you're going, I'll be back before you get this mess cleaned up."

"You're on!" He grinned and watched the sway of her narrow hips as she moved across the yard to the back door of the parsonage.

A cold gust of wind created a miniature dust-devil that swirled down the driveway and disintegrated. He looked up at the sky. The clouds were spreading. The western skyline was filled with the darkening threat of rain. The heat wave would be at an end when this storm arrived.

He moved the shovel back a couple feet and probed lightly, tossing out the decaying form of the dead kitten. He scowled, then scooped up another shovelful of dirt and reinterred it along the edge of the foundation. Too long dead to try to figure out what killed it. Must have been a dog. A dog would bury it like a bone.

He continued to shovel more rapidly as the clouds moved closer.

He uncovered two more rotting forms and decided to

say nothing about it to Joan. Hell, it wouldn't make any difference.

The mound of earth was shrinking. He could see the end of the pile . . . the end of the pile and the empty fruit jar Cerise used to gather angleworms. He bent to toss it out of the way. The outline of the jar's base was stamped again and again into the dirt, circle after circle in the dirt. Cerise had tamped down and smoothed the surface of the dirt with the jar.

The fruit jar rolled across the grass and stopped just as Lyle pushed the shovel down into the center of the smoothed area. Even the imprint of Cerise's hand showed her efforts to flatten the spot.

The shovel turned slightly and Lyle stared down at the bodies of the last two kittens. He stepped back and scratched at the odd prickling of his spine.

It wasn't a dog's burial. It was the kid—the funny, untalkative kid. Sitting out here. Picking off old Bessie's kittens one by one and burying them.

The prickling went on down his spine, creeping one vertebra at a time. He stared down at the two dirt-caked wads of gray hair and rubbed his backbone.

Hell, the kid was weird. He'd said that much to Joan already. She'd make a big fuss if he said anything else. The kid had only saved him a job getting rid of the kittens. Hell, his old man used to drown kittens. Nothing so bad about getting rid of the things . . . but a kid doing it?

He lifted the shovel, scooped up the last two bodies, and carried them to join the others. Better not talk about it. Not to Joan, not to anyone. Even worse to the scratchy-voiced preacher's wife.

They wouldn't be around long. The preacher was fixing to move on. Lyle could feel it coming, and if he was wrong—well, he'd keep an eye on the kid.

She'd have to be watched. Or would she? Lyle remembered his own first .22. He'd shot every bird in sight and even the neighbor's cat. Hell, he hadn't been able to sit down for a week after his old man found out. Could be there wasn't anything to worry about.

He worked feverishly at the mountain of dirt, racing the rain and erasing the ideas bouncing through his head. When he stopped, the clouds were directly overhead. Darker, lower, and close to spilling their contents.

He could hear Wilma's voice shrieking at Cerise to hurry. The screen door at the parsonage squeaked, then banged. Joan ran across the yard and stepped onto the back porch beside him only a minute ahead of the large drops of rain, huge drops that splattered the dry earth and sent puffy clouds of dust into the air with each landing.

Lyle put his arms around his wife and hugged her. The heat wave was over. They watched the water come down in a vengeful attack against the land.

He heard the sound of the Thayer baby crying before a window slammed. When he looked across the yard at the Thayer house, he saw the colorless face of Cerise at the window. She stared at the space where the dirt had been piled.

She remained at the window, staring out. Lyle swallowed a dryness in his throat. She was only a damn kid. Why the hell was he feeling like he was being inspected? His arm tightened around Joan and pulled her toward the door.

Old Bessie stretched and looked up at him. Her unblinking eyes narrowed into slits. She yawned and exposed her white teeth against the pink tongue. Lyle felt gooseflesh popping up across his back.

He glanced at the Thayers' window once more before he stepped into the house. Cerise's mouth appeared to be partially open in a smile. Her hand lifted as if she was going to wave and then dropped to the windowsill. He could see the flash of her childish teeth before she turned away from the glass.

Lyle pushed the door closed behind him and hoped Phil Thayer had a successful revival meeting. With a kid like Cerise, Phil would need an inside track to heaven.

Chapter Three

The rough surface of the basement stairs grated under Cerise's feet. She stopped halfway up, grabbed the handrails, and hoisted her body into the air. She swung her feet back and forth, like on the monkey bars at school.

Should she go out the door at the top of the concrete steps, or turn and take the small wooden stairs to the entry hall with the two sets of folding doors?

This church had so many stairways. There were two from the basement—one that led up to the Sunday school rooms, and this one. If she slipped into the church, there was a stairway to the bell tower room, and then if you opened the closet, there was a skinny steep stairway—almost like climbing a ladder—that led up into the bell tower itself. She liked to sit alone in the bell tower and feel the wind blow through the louvered openings.

If she climbed to the bell tower, she could watch the cars going by on the road. The cars hardly ever stopped. Daddy Phil said it was because Pleasant Home wasn't a real town—only a wide spot in the road. But the road didn't look any wider to her. She could see all the way up the hill to the store or all the way behind the church to the back of the cemetery. When she stood on tiptoe, she could even see over the fence and down to the creek behind the cemetery. It was the only place in the whole church where anyone could see the back corner of the cemetery.

She dashed up the last of the steps and shoved the door open. A car was slowing, pulling into a parking space. Cerise accelerated into a full run before she could be stopped and patted on the head.

Her feet pounded across the grass until she was around the corner and behind the church. The cemetery was the only place where she never hurried. She liked to amble along, touching the markers and trying to read all the words carved into the stones.

She ran her fingers over the reddish-brown marble. The smooth polished surface of the marker had a cool feeling even in the warm June sun. It was the marker that made this one of her favorite graves in the cemetery. This one had the prettiest colors in the marble headstone. The reddish-brown had tiny sparkles and dashes of black. On one corner where a piece had been chipped off, there was a long streak of white. It wasn't smooth, like the rest of the stone. It felt rough and scratchy under her fingertips.

The name was too long for her to read. She could still only read the simple ones, but the numbers were plain enough. *1801-1849*. Daddy Phil said the graves were all so old, no one knew the people who were buried here.

Her hands stroked the marker, and she looked over her shoulder toward the church. The fat lady who played the piano was going in the side door to the basement. Choir practice . . . it meant Daddy Phil would be inside for a long time.

She squinted up at the oak trees along the edge of the graveyard. Through the leaves she spotted a bird's nest wedged in one of the forked tree limbs. She dusted off her hands and scrambled up the trunk of the tree, climbing carefully and ignoring the screeching of the birds at her intrusion into their world.

By bracing her feet on the gnarled limb and clinging to the trunk with one hand, she could lean forward and see into the mass of twigs. The eggs had hatched. Three open mouths gaped up at her from the nest. From above her head, a bird squawked and wings beat furiously. Leaves drifted down on Cerise's head.

It took only one swift grab, and the bird was in her hand. She squeezed it in her fist and lowered herself to the ground branch by branch. The warm wad of feathers squirmed and became still.

She skipped down the sloping hillside to the lower part of the cemetery, clutching the bird in both hands. Her favorite grave was in the back corner—out of sight of the church, all by itself, close to the fence. This part of the cemetery was untended. The granite marker towered over her head. Four carved angels looked down at the gravesite. She settled on the grass beside the marker, mashing the unmown grass into a green cavern. The long blades of grass bent and curved over her shoulders, hiding her from everyone.

Cerise opened her hand and stroked the tiny bunch of feathers. She poked at the open beak until she finally closed it by pinching it between her thumb and forefinger. There was no one around the cemetery. She could inspect the bird without anyone asking her a lot of questions. She continued to run her finger over the feathers and stretch the spidery feet out in her hand until she could remember the song.

The tune stirred in her mind and she began to hum softly to herself. She probed into the dirt with her fingers until she hollowed out a space large enough to hold the bird's body. She covered it carefully, patted down the earth, and started to sing: "Be still my soul, the Lord is on thy side."

For some reason, she couldn't remember any more of the words, so she sat humming the same line over and over and watching a bumblebee light on the head of a dingy gray angel. It wasn't a funeral service like Daddy Phil preached. Mommy hadn't wanted him to take her to the church that day, but Matt had to go to the doctor.

Funerals were nicer than regular church. There were so many flowers. Flowers hung on the walls. Long ribbons draped across the flowers with big gold letters on them. There were even flowers on top of the coffin. The church smelled like roses and Mommy's perfume. The fat lady had played a lot of pretty music on the piano, not loud thumping music like she played in church. Even the animal lady, the one with the funny fur collar, had sounded good when she sang, not squeaky like she did in church.

There were people crying, too, but Cerise didn't feel like crying. Daddy Phil hadn't cried.

Cerise patted the ground and looked up at the granite angels. The stone wasn't as pretty as the red marble, but it was the only marker in the whole graveyard that had angels carved on it. All the angels were looking down, almost as if their eyes were closed. They should have their eyes open so they could watch all the graves.

She got to her feet and wandered back up the hill to the grave with the iron fence. Daddy Phil said the fence was to keep people from walking on the grave, but what difference did it make if they were dead? Cerise looked around the graveyard and back up the hill. No one could see her from the church. She bit her lip and climbed over the fence, stomping on the ground when she landed.

Her finger traced the outline of the name on the gravestone. *C-L-A-R-A.* Daddy Phil said it was the same name as his mother's. She sat cross-legged, staring at the letters, and then spat on the marker. The saliva clung to the letter A and slowly dribbled down the face of the stone. She got up and jumped up and down, mashing the grass under her feet into a beaten snarl of green spears. One last stomp of her foot and she climbed back over the fence and headed to the oak tree.

Music was coming from the basement of the church. The fat lady was thumping the piano again. It meant Daddy Phil would be listening to the choir practice for a while longer. She looked at the oak tree and tapped her foot in time to the music. She didn't want to go into the basement because the fat lady would hug her and tell Daddy Phil how tall she was getting.

The lady always smashed Cerise's face into her pillow-like breasts until Cerise had trouble breathing. All the time she hugged Cerise, she would be looking at Daddy Phil.

Cerise didn't like the church ladies. They only hugged her when Daddy Phil was around. The rest of the time they told her to go wash her hands or not play on the church steps.

She nodded to herself and headed for the front steps. If they were all in the basement, she could slide up and down the banisters without anyone telling her to stop. Daddy Phil never told her to stop, and it was his church. Not only could she slide, but she could listen to the music without the fat lady hugging her.

When she darted around the corner to the front of the church, she stopped abruptly and looked at the man. She hadn't expected to find anyone sitting on the steps.

The man looked at her with a kind smile. He had a lot of white hair, so he must be an old man, but his eyes were glistening blue. When he spoke to her, his voice was soft and he kept his smile. He wasn't like the church ladies, who quit smiling when they talked.

"Hello, you must be Reverend Thayer's little girl."

Cerise looked him over carefully before she answered. He wasn't dressed like Daddy Phil. The man had on overalls and a plain blue shirt . . . the kind her mommy called a work shirt. He seemed nice, but maybe he wouldn't like it if she slid down the banister. Maybe he'd tell her to go play somewhere else.

She clung to the railing and inched her way up the steps. He must be one of Daddy Phil's church people, but why wasn't he inside?

"Who are you?" she blurted out the question and shifted from one foot to the other while she waited for the answer.

"Mr. Parker. My wife plays the piano for the choir. I'm waiting for her to finish practice."

Cerise tossed her braids back over her shoulder. He was the fat lady's husband, but *he* wasn't fat. He was skinny and tired looking.

"Do you know my wife?"

Cerise nodded and moved up the last step to the top of the banister.

"Is your mother inside?" he asked.

Cerise shook her head. "No. She's home taking care of my baby brother."

She swung one leg over the railing and sat poised at the top, wondering if she should slide down.

The man chuckled deep in his throat. "Going to have a trip down the railing, are you? Don't blame you. Used to do it myself when I was a kid."

She watched his face. He talked softly, without either smiling or frowning. She decided he meant what he said. He wasn't going to tell her to stop or go away. It was easy to give herself a quick push and the slide down was fast. She bounced onto the ground and started back up the steps. The man chuckled to himself again.

"Used to fall off the end sometimes when I was little," he laughed.

Cerise sat down on the steps and peered at him through her eyelashes. "Why do you wait out here?"

He lifted his eyebrows, but he kept the slight smile. "Not much for all the singing. Only be in the way there."

"Did they tell you to go play somewhere else?" Cerise asked.

He laughed, but it was a gentle, understanding laugh. "I guess you could call it that. Janie—that's my wife—she likes to do all her church stuff. Me, I'm only a farmer. Never did take much to dressing up. She don't like it when I come after her in my work clothes, so I sit here and wait for her. That way I don't embarrass her."

"What's embarrass?" Cerise liked the quiet way he talked.

"Making someone feel ashamed of you. Guess I don't make Janie very proud. She thinks I should dress up each time I leave the farm—even if I'm going right back."

Cerise heard the piano thumping in the basement and the sound of a lady singing. The piano was too loud. She couldn't understand the words of the song.

"Do you play the piano?" she asked the man.

He shook his head. "No. Never learned anything but farming. Janie, now, *she's* the one with the learning. Her folks taught her how to play the piano, and she even taught school for a few years. Guess I was lucky she even looked at a plain old farmer like me."

Cerise chewed on her lip. Why was it so special to play the piano? The fat lady wasn't the only one in the church who could play the piano. Daddy Phil had said there were lots of ladies who could play better and it was a shame they had to put up with her.

91

Daddy Phil said it was because the fat lady was a big contributor, but Mommy didn't know what the word meant. Mommy never seemed to know what Daddy Phil's big words meant.

She looked at the tired man. "Do you know what a contributor is?"

"Can see you're a preacher's kid, all right," he chuckled. "It's someone who gives a lot of money to something. Like to the church."

"Oh." Cerise looked at the man and wondered why the fat lady gave so much money to the church and didn't even give her husband any. If he was *her* husband, she'd give him enough money for a new shirt. He had a big hole in the sleeve, and two of the buttons were missing in the front.

He got up and scratched his head. "Think I'll walk up to the store, young'n. Sounds like it will be awhile before Janie is ready to go."

He smiled at her again. "Careful when you slide down. Don't go too fast and fly off the end. You can land pretty hard."

Cerise perched on the top of the railing and watched the man walk up the street. He walked with his head down and his shoulders drooped like he was tired.

She looked down at the shiny white paint of the railing and listened to the music rising from the basement. This time she could hear the people singing, but it wasn't one of the church songs she liked. She pushed herself off and flew down the banister, landing solidly on both feet.

The music was louder than before, and she scowled. Some of the voices were singing different words. The piano stopped, and a man's voice protested, "No. No! It's all wrong."

A bird flew overhead and screeched, dipping dangerously close to her head. Her face twisted into a gleeful smile. Her eyes sparkled with excitement. She headed back for the oak tree and the bird's nest. There were still two baby birds. She could have two more funerals.

Matt toddled through the kitchen door carrying the huge calico cat he had adopted. The cat swayed limply in his arms. Its orange and black tail and white legs dragged across the shiny green linoleum. The yellow eyes blinked as they looked up into the boy's face with complacent tolerance.

The little boy stopped, tried to gather the cat's back legs up in his arms, and found himself holding the hind legs and tail while the cat's head and forelegs slithered to the floor in total relaxation.

Matt struggled once more to lift the entire cat, only to have another failure when the cat's limp form thwarted him again. This time he clutched the cat's head and front legs with the tail sweeping a wide swath across his feet. Without thinking, Wilma burst into laughter.

The cat's ears twitched at the harsh eruption of noise from Wilma's mouth. It let out a protesting howl and abandoned the spaghetti act with a bolt toward the front room.

Wilma's hand went to her mouth, then dropped. She let the laughter roll out. Phil was at church. He couldn't hear her. She would laugh all she wanted to. The dumb cat could find some other place to live if it didn't like the sound.

Matt disappeared behind the davenport in a crawling pursuit of his favorite plaything. Wilma snorted in amusement when the cat appeared on the back of the davenport. It coiled its tail neatly around its feet and sat looking down into the crawl space below. The cat wasn't really so dumb. It always managed to stay a few paces ahead of the active two-year-old. Even when captured, it resorted to the limpness defense instead of fighting Matt with its claws.

Wilma moved leisurely around the kitchen to inspect her own work. A final wipe of the refrigerator handle. A quick finger around the surface of the sink. Thank goodness, no grease.

She hung the dish towel on the rack and smoothed it into neat folds. She wasn't going to leave anything out of place when she left for the hospital to have this baby . . . not when Clara Thayer was going to be staying with the children.

Phil might think it was generous of the old witch to offer, but Wilma had her own opinion of Clara's sudden helpfulness. She wasn't going to leave one thing for Clara Thayer to criticize. The old hag could look all she wanted, there would be nothing she could tell Wilma—for her own good. Not this time.

Everything about Pleasant Home was so much better than Maupin. The parsonage was three doors down the street from the church. Some days she could even forget it was church property and imagine it was her own home. It was huge, compared to the Maupin house. Two bedrooms—large enough to divide after the new baby came—and an office for Phil. Wilma had been able to set up her sewing machine. There was room—plenty of room. But there was also Clara Thayer only a twenty-minute drive away. And Clara Thayer drove it too often.

Clara was now a regular member of Phil's congregation. She made the drive every Sunday and stayed for dinner after the services. Stayed for dinner and pampered Matt.

Oh, well, it made Cerise closer to Phil. Every time Grandma Thayer hugged Matt, Phil managed to pay attention to Cerise. A teasing tug at her braids, an extra slice of dessert, offset Clara Thayer's deliberate disregard of the little girl.

"Yoo-hoo! Anybody home?" The front door opened, and a head poked through the doorway.

Matt looked up at the woman, whose glance was darting about the living room, and he rolled off the davenport with a wail of fright. He toddled across the floor and clutched Wilma's knees with a fierce grip.

"Mommy, they bite me."

"My goodness, did I frighten the poor little fellow?" Without waiting for Wilma's reply, the woman pushed the door open and stepped into the house. One of the drawbacks of living in the parsonage was the intrusion of church members who treated it as if it were part of the church and open to everyone.

Wilma sighed and patted Matt's head. "It's your fur collar that frightens him, Miss Wilford."

The woman looked down at her draped foxes, each dead victim clutching another tail in its mouth. The foxes' glassy eyes glittered when she moved. Wilma wondered if the woman had any idea the collar was as outdated as the thick braids encircling the crown of her head. No wonder Cerise called Miss Wilford the animal lady and refused to get within reach of the patting hands.

"What a ridiculous thing to frighten him. He must be a timid child." Miss Wilford stroked the collar with one hand and adjusted it over the bodice of her flowered jersey dress. "It was my mother's, you know. She was so proud of it, and I loved it when I was a little girl. I can't imagine any child being afraid of it."

She continued to stroke the collar and raised her chin, looking at Wilma through her lower bifocals. "Is the dear reverend on the premises?"

Wilma bit her tongue as she tried to figure out what the word premises meant.

"I don't understand," she finally admitted. Why did Phil let these women wander in and out of the house as if they owned the place? Especially this one. Loretta Wilford always used words Wilma never completely understood.

Miss Wilford gave a small sigh. "I mean, is he here?"

"No," Wilma answered. "It's choir practice this afternoon. He's at the church."

"Of course. I had forgotten. I suppose they can muddle through without me. It's not as if I need to practice, like most of them do." The woman slumped disconsolately. The jersey fabric crept into wrinkles of purple at her waistline. "I did so wish to have a discussion with him. A private rapport, you know. Reverend Thayer is one of the first members of the clergy to comprehend the intricacies of bringing culture and enlightenment to our community."

She hesitated and looked at Wilma with a strange glitter in her eyes. "I am sorry, my dear, I can see you don't understand what I'm talking about."

Wilma shook her head in bewildered admission of the truth. She really didn't understand what the lady was driving at — except that she wanted to talk to Phil alone.

"You could go up to the church," Wilma said. She had little hope that her suggestion would do any good. Loretta Wilford was eyeing the davenport like a hitchhiker who had spotted a slowing car.

"I suppose I could," the woman said hesitantly. "But I'd have to explain being late. I think I'll simply wait here. You don't mind, do you, dear?"

She sank onto the cushions as she said the words, apparently not caring whether Wilma minded or not.

Wilma pried Matt's fingers from her knees and, grabbing his arm, swung him up into the nearest chair.

"My dear, should you be doing that?" Miss Wilford clucked her tongue against her teeth. "You must be—well, goodness, your condition!" She stammered and her cheeks flared pink with embarrassment. Her eyes focused briefly on Wilma's abdomen and then moved quickly away while she did a fingering inspection of the fox skins about her neck.

"Probably not," Wilma shrugged. "I'm almost due to go in. Next week, if it's on time. Might hurry things along." She leaned against the back of Matt's chair. Miss Wilford might know a lot of big words, but she was plainly uncomfortable talking about Wilma's pregnancy.

"Next week?" Miss Wilford rubbed her lips together and looked at Wilma with the corners of her mouth sagging like the jersey of her dress.

"But you'll miss the potluck, and we were counting on you to bring something special—like the lemon pies you baked for the last one. You're the best cook we've ever had at the parsonage." She clutched at her purse and thumped it on her knees to emphasize her sincerity. "You're a culinary artist, my dear."

Wilma ran her fingers through her hair. Culinary wasn't a word she knew, but from the rest of Miss Wilford's statement, it must have something to do with cooking. Whatever it meant, it was a compliment, and Wilma smiled with pleasure.

"Who knows? I may still be here," she said. "If I'm not, Phil's mother will be coming to take care of the children. I'm sure she will make something for the potluck."

Miss Wilford's eyes brightened. "How considerate of Clara. But if she's going to be here, I won't bother the reverend with my idea. I'll wait and talk to Clara."

Her hands adjusted the fur collar, positioning the tails, stroking the pointed ears.

Matt suddenly looked up at Wilma with tears of fright in his wide eyes. He snatched at her dress, making the fabric cut into her shoulders. Wilma pulled his fingers loose and patted his hand.

Miss Wilford's hand waved at the air. She rose and stopped to tug the clinging jersey dress back into place.

"I wanted to talk to Reverend Thayer about holding a literary tea. I've just discovered a darling lady who writes poetry. But Clara would be the one. Clara understands the need for refinement in our little corner of civilization."

Wilma clenched her teeth at the inference. She might not understand all of Miss Wilford's big words, but it was obvious Miss Wilford considered Clara Thayer a special individual. Whatever a literary tea was, it sounded boring. Wilma managed to utter a weak "Oh" and bit her lower lip when she heard the sound come out in a flat monotone.

Miss Wilford controlled a slight arch of one eyebrow and put one hand on the doorknob. Her mouth fell open in astonishment when the knob turned before she could close her fingers around it.

The door swung inward so sharply it forced Loretta Wilford to step back in a quick maneuver to keep from being struck in the face by the strength of the impact.

Cerise raced three steps into the room before she noticed the woman. The rubber soles of her tennis shoes squeaked. Her feet skidded on the floor. Pigtails whirled forward over her chin and bounced on her shoulders. She came to a complete stop and turned toward the visitor.

Loretta Wilford's hand clutched at the fox furs while Cerise's mouth went from gaping openness to a straight, appraising line. One hand flipped a braid back over her shoulder. Her eyes measured the distance between herself and Miss Wilford, then she backed toward the chair and slipped up onto the cushion beside Matt.

His arms caught Cerise's neck. With a last peek at the furs, he buried his face in his sister's shoulder.

"Is she always in such a hurry?" Miss Wilford patted her braids with fluttering fingertips. She watched Cerise with a wariness close to suspicion.

Wilma wondered if the woman thought Cerise would spring from the chair and attack her.

"I'm afraid Cerise runs more than she walks. I never seen such an active kid."

The delicate lift of Miss Wilford's chin made Wilma's cheeks burn. She knew better. Phil had told her often enough. Not *seen*. It should be *saw*. Oh, God, would she ever learn to talk right?

Well, she wasn't going to make Cerise apologize. It wasn't the child's fault. Cerise hadn't known Miss Wilford was behind the door. It served the woman right for taking so long to get her ass in action and get out.

Wilma kept her chin high in half-defiance and nodded only when Miss Wilford finally stepped out the door. No point in saying anything else to the woman and making another mistake.

"What did the animal lady want?" Cerise glared at the door through half-closed eyes.

"Cerise, her name is Miss Wilford. You can't keep calling her the animal lady."

"What if one of those foxes quits biting the other one and bites her?"

Wilma expelled a huge sigh. "They're dead, Cerise. They can't let go. Dead things can't bite."

Matt squirmed out of the chair and toddled across the floor toward the davenport. The forgotten cat had emerged and was curled in sleep on an orange velvet pillow— made for them by one of the gushy members of the Lady's Circle.

Wilma hoped the cat hair would ruin the hideous creation, with its rows of orange crocheted lace and gaudy green embroidered "God Bless This Home."

"Kitty," Matt gurgled.

"Matt, come on. I'll pull you in the wagon." Cerise hopped out of the chair and reached for Matt's hand.

"No!" Matt's brown curls shook. He crawled up onto the davenport and scrambled across the cushions toward the cat.

"Don't you want Sis to play with you?"

Cerise reached to grab his leg and was rewarded with a kick of his foot.

"No! Play with the kitty." His arms went out, and he gathered the cat up against his chest in a possessive hug. "My kitty."

Wilma groaned. "Cerise, leave him alone. He doesn't want to play with you. He wants to play with the cat."

Wilma felt miserable. First Miss Wilford—now the cat—and it was getting harder to move about. She didn't care what Phil thought, she wasn't going to be a blimp all her life. Before she came home from the hospital, she was going to have something done about it. If Phil didn't agree, she wouldn't come home. Let him argue with that. He wasn't the one who had to wear flat-heeled shoes and sack dresses all the time.

A furious squawl erupted from the cat, followed by Matt's scream—a shrill scream of rage. Wilma turned to see the cat streak across the living room floor and disappear into the front bedroom.

Tears spilled down Matt's cheeks while Cerise stood half-smiling, her lower lip caught behind her shining upper teeth. Her fingers were laced behind her back. She was partially turned away, and Wilma couldn't see the full expression on her daughter's face, but the stance of Cerise's body indicated she was pleasantly enjoying Matt's display of temper.

"She pulled Kitty's tail," Matt yelled.

"Cerise! Did you?" Wilma's voice floundered as she uttered the words. She already knew the answer, and Cerise wasn't going to confirm it. All Wilma could expect was a sober, unwavering stare. This time, Cerise didn't even turn her head in response to the question. Instead, she suddenly reached out and hugged Matt. His angry struggles to escape her embrace quieted after she whispered in his ear. A smile replaced the pouting lower lip, and Matt started to giggle.

Cerise turned and glanced up at Wilma with a flashing glitter of her green eyes.

"It's okay, Mommy. Matt wants me to play with him. I'm going to pull him in the wagon."

Wilma sighed. "Okay, but stay out of the street."

She lumbered into the kitchen, welcoming the slam of the door and the silence in the house. All the extra weight she carried began to push down against her pelvic bones. She inhaled slowly. It felt as if the baby was simply going to fall out onto the kitchen linoleum.

Thank goodness, Phil had never gotten around to oiling the rusty wheels on the hand-me-down wagon. She could keep track of the children by the squeak of the wheels and Matt's high-pitched peals of laughter.

A pain surged up her spine and disappeared. Wilma stood thoughtfully rubbing her back and wondered. When Matt had started his arrival into the world, she'd had pains in her back. Should she call Clara Thayer?

She massaged her back a little longer and then reached for the refrigerator handle. Not until after dinner. If she had any more pains during dinner, she'd have Phil call. She would put it off as long as possible.

If it was false labor, Wilma told herself, then she'd be stuck with Clara Thayer as a houseguest. Guest, hell — Clara would take over, acting as if she was being helpful when she was really just getting her own way. Like the Sunday Clara had used all the eggs for a potato salad when she knew Wilma was saving them for deviled eggs.

Wilma poured herself a glass of iced tea and slammed the refrigerator door. Everything was ready. She was going to sit down and put her feet up until Phil came home.

She struggled into the armchair, lifted her legs with agonizing slowness onto the stool, and listened for the sound of the wagon.

The second pain didn't start until they finished dinner. Phil was lifting Matt from the high chair when the twinge started in Wilma's back. It stabbed at her pelvic bones and moved to the small of her back. Her eyes flew open. Her breath caught in a loud gasp. The coffee cup clattered to its saucer before she could breathe normally and lean against the wooden back of the chair.

"I think you'd better call your mother, Phil." She could feel the perspiration beading her forehead.

Phil eased Matt to the floor and gave her a wide-eyed look of concern.

"It's a week early," he said. His hand gripped hers and shook. "Are you sure?"

She nodded. "Sometime tonight, Phil. It's beginning the same way Matt did, in my back."

She checked the clock while Phil went to the phone. How long would it be before the next contraction? She had to be certain the children's routine was as normal as possible.

Poor Cerise. Clara Thayer wasn't going to do anymore than necessary for "the girl," as she persisted in calling Cerise. She used Cerise's name reluctantly — usually only to snap orders.

Wilma heard the click of the phone. Dresser drawers slammed. Cerise must be hunting for her pajamas.

Phil stuck his head around the kitchen door, and she wiggled her little finger in an acknowledgment of his concern.

"I'll get the kids into bed before mother gets here." His smile was infectious, but Wilma could see the worried furrow between his eyebrows.

"I'm okay so far," she assured him. "Put Cerise in with Matt and let your mother have Cerise's bed."

Phil's eyes flashed with amusement to match his grin. "Cerise will love it. She might even be reasonable about mother being here if she can sleep with Matt."

Wilma choked back the giggle she felt rising nervously out of her chest. If she let herself laugh now, it was going to upset Phil. Why couldn't she laugh like some of Phil's church ladies? They sounded like polite bells, tinkling pleasantly among each other. Her laugh came out rasping and coarse. She sounded like a braying animal.

She never laughed around Phil's church people. She had learned to keep her mouth shut. Quiet little Mrs. Thayer. Except for her slip with Miss Wilford this afternoon, she hadn't made many mistakes. Mistakes that made people lift their eyebrows in that strange surprised look.

Her head turned toward the clock. A half hour since the last one . . . this was definitely labor. She waited until the pain completely subsided, then began to gather up the dishes, stacking plates and sorting the silver.

"Let them go, hon." Phil's hand reached across the table and took a glass out of her fingers. "I'll do them, and if I don't have time, Mother can do them. It'll make her feel useful."

Wilma dropped her fingertips to brush at the placemat.

103

She could feel her spine giving way. The solidness of the chair back was all that held her body in a sitting position. She thought about moving to the comfort of the bed, but the walk had all the appeal of a ten-mile hike. The dishes were too much. She wouldn't be here to listen to Clara Thayer clucking her tongue against her teeth.

Phil moved the last traces of the meal out of the room. She heard plates clatter on the countertop. The jarring sound of a glass shattering in the sink made her wince.

"Don't worry about mother." He rumpled the top of her head with his hand when he came back into the room. "If she has a little extra work to do, she won't have time to spoil Matt."

The corners of her mouth lifted, and she leaned her head against the firmness of his abdomen.

"Oh, Phil, don't let her pick on Cerise too much."

She could feel the rumble of his chuckle through her cheek as he held her against him.

"Don't worry about Cerise. I'll let her tag along with me during the day." He gave her hair a gentle pat. "Now, let me go make sure those two are ready for bed."

Wilma propped her elbows on the table and rested her chin on her hands. She closed her eyes and listened to the sounds of Matt giggling and then the deep resonant tones of Phil's voice. She couldn't hear the words, but it had what she called his praying sound. It was the sound of Phil's voice that kept her entranced during his prayers. She still didn't understand many of his words. After five years, she was ashamed to tell him so. *Hallowed*. What did *hallowed* mean? Phil didn't seem to think it was important for her to know.

Another contraction. Short, quick . . . but a contraction. Twenty minutes. They were getting closer together. What was keeping Clara Thayer?

"Phil, why don't you put my suitcase in the car?" she asked when he emerged from the bedroom.

She pressed both hands against the tabletop and pushed herself to her feet. "I think I'll get my purse."

Only a quick biting of his lips gave her any indication of Phil's nervousness. He moved with his long, easy steps into the bedroom and out the door with the suitcase.

Her own movements were a matter of slow, deliberate concentration. Think: where was her purse? Think again. Run a comb through your hair.

She looked down at her pudgy hands. No more. This was the last.

"Mom just drove in," Phil said as he came into the bedroom. His arms went around her from behind and caressed her swollen breasts.

Wilma nodded in reply and leaned against him. Dressed in her flat heels, her head rested in the center of his broad, muscular chest. The hardness of his body was as comforting as the wooden chair back.

"We'd better go," she said to his mirrored reflection.

The next contraction timed itself to Clara Thayer's entrance. Wilma stopped and dug her nails into Phil's arm while she counted to herself. This one was longer than the others.

The vision of Clara Thayer with her sandy hair mussed and her blouse misbuttoned sent an exhilarating burst of energy through Wilma's body. The contraction ebbed away, and she straightened with a deep breath.

"Thank you for coming, Mother Thayer," she said, amazed to find herself meaning the words for the first time.

"Come on, don't take time to gossip." Phil was tugging at her elbow with a compelling urgency.

The giggle came bursting out, and Wilma didn't try to

choke it back. It was worth having a baby just to see Clara Thayer clutching and twisting her handbag between her scrawny fingers. Even the great Clara had uncertainties. Wilma forced back the rest of the giggle and pushed herself forward. Walking took too much effort. Phil's hand tightened on her elbow and steered her across the grass to the driveway.

She sighed with relief and lowered herself onto the car seat. It was almost over.

Clara Thayer felt oddly out of place without Wilma in the house. She was alone with the strange furniture and the neatness. There wasn't any place for her among all the polished end tables and sparkling floors. Not even two children and a pregnancy diminished Wilma's ability as a homemaker. There was nothing for her to do. The children were asleep.

She wandered into the kitchen. Dishes: there were dishes to do. Phillip would be pleased when he came home and found the dishes done. Done and put away. She'd be certain things were neat. Wilma kept the house in such perfect order. She had to be sure it stayed that way.

It was true. A woman lost her son when he married. Nothing she could do would make her important to Phillip again.

She sloshed the plates through the hot sudsy water. Even the earthenware plates were not something she expected her son to have in his own home. He had been raised with fine, delicate china. All her efforts to teach him elegance, and he ate on earthenware plates. No matter how often she suggested to Wilma that a home needed fine china for entertaining, they still used these heavy things. Suitable for a common laborer—not a minister.

And mugs! She scowled at the two mugs. It was Wilma. Wilma had changed Phillip. Her big, blue eyes watching Phillip with those worshiping looks . . . how could a mother expect her son to talk to her anymore? She couldn't compete with Wilma's adoring, simpering gaze.

Not even her changing to Phillip's church, attending faithfully every Sunday, had brought him back to the closeness she had felt with him before his marriage.

She rinsed the mugs twice and moved mechanically through the rest of the dishes. Now she would have Phillip to herself for a few days. Maybe he would talk to her. Talk with the excited energy she used to see when he was home on his college vacations. He'd hardly spent any time with her since Mathew was born.

After the dishes were all put away, with a sniff at the orderliness of Wilma's cupboards, Clara prowled about the kitchen. A chocolate chip cookie from the whimsical gingerbread-man jar proved to be so soft and full of flavor, she helped herself to a couple more and flipped the kitchen light switch.

Phillip said she was to sleep in Cerise's bed. Where had they put the girl?

Clara gathered up her overnight case and tiptoed into the children's bedroom. With only the light from the window, she had to pause and let her eyes become accustomed to seeing in the semidarkness. A light would only wake up little Matt.

She eased her suitcase onto the bed and moved cautiously across the room to check on her grandson. When she bent over the bed, Cerise turned in her sleep. One foot pushed the covers off the sleeping form. Clara stiffened and took an angry step forward. Little Matt flinched in his sleep. The girl was disturbing him.

She took a sharp intake of breath. The girl was uncovering her grandson. He could catch cold. She snatched at the covers and pulled at them, yanking them from under Cerise's legs and tugging them up around Matt's shoulders.

Cerise rolled again. This time Clara was ready for her. She caught the girl's foot and held it. The girl rolled to a sitting position and rubbed at her eyes.

"Get up!" Clara snapped in a hoarse whisper.

Cerise only rubbed at her eyes again.

"Why?"

"I'm moving you to the couch."

Clara grabbed a folded blanket from the end of the bed and snatched Cerise's pillow.

"Come on. Don't argue."

The girl stumbled out of the bed and stood shaking her head.

"Daddy Phil told me to sleep with Matt."

"Shh. Don't talk. You'll wake him up." Clara continued to whisper. Cerise hung back against the bed, and Clara grabbed. Grabbed the girl's arm and yanked her away from the bed and across the floor. She pushed Cerise through the door and closed it behind her.

"Why do I have to sleep on the davenport?"

"Don't know what Phillip is thinking of," Clara grumbled.

"Why?" Cerise persisted.

"Because boys and girls aren't supposed to sleep together. It's not right. Not right at all."

Clara threw the pillow down on the davenport and shook the blanket out.

"Get up here, girl, and I'll cover you up."

"But Daddy Phil said . . ."

Clara reached out and clamped one hand on the girl's shoulder. Her fingers dug into the flesh, but Cerise didn't budge. Her bare feet were planted firmly apart in a defiant stance. Her eyes glared up into Clara's. The girl's chin tilted upward in an outright challenge of Clara's order.

"Phillip isn't here now." Clara snapped the words out. "I am. And you are going to do as I say."

The room was too dark for Clara to see the girl's eyes clearly, but she could see the glistening rebellion. The muscles of the girl's shoulder were tight under her hand. They stood and glared at each other until Cerise shook her shoulder free and climbed up on the davenport.

"And don't lie there crying, either. I don't want to hear it."

Cerise sat with her fists clenched and the eyelashes lifted. For a moment she looked directly into Clara Thayer's eyes.

"I don't cry. I never cry." The eyelashes lowered, and Cerise stretched out on the davenport. Her eyes remained focused on Clara from beneath the half-closed eyelids. Clara could feel the resentment, and for a second her hands shook with loathing.

At the other end of the davenport, a furry shape stirred. The cat stretched and meowed in confused protest against the movement on the cushions.

"A cat!" Clara tossed the blanket over Cerise and reached for the offensive creature. "You can't have a cat in the house."

Clara snatched the cat roughly in her hands, relieved at having something to take her attention from the colorless girl. She started to the door with the squirming creature, but Cerise's voice cut through the semi-lighted room.

"It's not my cat. It's Matt's."

Clara glanced down at the ball of multicolors and hesitated. Matt? What if the cat wandered off? Matt might cry. She pulled the animal against her body and

109

turned back toward the bedroom.

"If it belongs to Matt, it should be on his bed, not yours."

"Mommy doesn't let us have the cat in bed."

Clara halted at the bedroom door. Cerise's statement rang in her ears. The girl was telling her what to do.

"Your mommy's not here, either. I'm running things."

Clara stepped into the bedroom and shut the door before she dropped the cat distastefully on the floor. Let it find its own place to sleep in here. Away from the girl. They were all away from the hideous child. She had no respect for authority at all.

After Phillip get home, they'd settle things. Phillip would make the girl understand that obedience was important. The girl would straighten up. Phillip was always respectful to elders. He'd be shocked if he knew the girl had argued, and Clara meant to tell him.

Matt twisted and rolled over onto his back. Clara stood beside his bed and touched the soft curls with a gentle finger. For a few minutes she looked down at the sleeping boy and smiled. What a difference between the two children! It was obviously the result of having a decent father. She brushed the child's hair once more and turned to her suitcase.

Tomorrow she'd fix Phillip's breakfast. He'd loved hotcakes when he was a boy. She would fix hotcakes.

Tomorrow they could have a nice long talk after breakfast, and she would tell him—gently—about Cerise's attitude.

Phil braced one shoulder against the wooden pillar on the porch and tilted his head upward. An awning of drifting clouds shut off most of the visible stars. Low on the western horizon he could see an expanse of gray sky where a cluster of stars glistened above the mountain peaks. It must be clear at the Oregon coast.

In the warmness of the night air, he felt a wild excitement in his mind, an excitement like the first time he preached a sermon in a strange town. All the unknown faces turned up toward him, waiting for his words . . . the shining eyes . . . the thrill of seeing people inch forward in their seats . . . the electrical tingle in his spine when he transferred his own energy into their waiting bodies.

He had to get it back, had to get back to that kind of preaching. Back to the exhilarated faces, the shouted amens. It was applause. There was applause in the gospel tent. A man knew he'd touched souls. He could see it — feel it; he could hear it.

The church. The polite nods. Occasionally a mouth opened. Most often the heads bowed on cue and lifted on cue. The polite nods. They didn't feed a man's vitality. He could feel the tentacle of complacency reaching out from the pews, tentacles that would engulf him if he didn't make a move soon.

Wilma was right. Her big, pleading eyes looking up at him from the hospital bed. Her dark hair was damp with sweat, strands clinging to the white hospital sheets. "No more, Phil. No more kids."

More children would only force him into the trap of staying where it was secure. He turned toward the darkened windows of the parsonage. Odd, he had expected his mother to be up, waiting for news. He groped for the light switch and decided against waking her. If she wanted sleep, let her sleep.

The blond head lifted from the pillow and Cerise sat up, shaking her head back and forth at the sudden onslaught of light. One pigtail had come undone, and the soft tresses of her hair swirled with the movement of her head.

"Cerise, honey, what are you doing out here?" He bent and took her small face in his hands, looking into the sleep-induced blankness of her green eyes.

Her pale lashes squinched shut, recoiling against the light in the room. Her lower lip drew back under her upper teeth for a long, breathless second. He continued to sit holding her face in his hands.

She blurted the words out. *"She* made me sleep here."

"But why? Were you and Matt playing instead of sleeping?"

Cerise tried to shake her head but his hands kept her turned toward him. "We weren't playing. She woke me up and made me come out here. She said boys and girls weren't supposed to sleep together."

Phil took his hands away and sat back on his heels. The urge to laugh made him explode a long breath of air. He reached out and gathered Cerise into his arms.

"Why is it wrong, Daddy Phil?"

Phil hugged the girl against her chest and rubbed his chin in the whispery softness of her hair.

"There's nothing wrong, Cerise. Grandma Thayer has some old-fashioned ideas. I expect she forgets you and Matt are brother and sister."

"I told her you said I was to sleep with Matt. She made me move anyway."

She snuggled tightly against his chest and yawned. One hand twisted at a button on his shirt, the other fell limply into her lap. She tipped her head back to look up into his face.

"Why can't I sleep with Matt, Daddy Phil? The davenport is all lumpy."

"I'll say it is," Phil chuckled. One glance showed the uneven hollows and ridges. The scratchy mohair was reaching through his pant leg to scratch at his skin. One of the universal features of a furnished parsonage appeared to be davenports that defied all rules of comfort.

"I guess your Grandma Thayer thinks the bed is too narrow for two of you."

Cerise's head shook. "She's not my grandma, and she hates me."

Phil slid his hand around behind Cerise's neck and cradled the back of her head. He hugged her and tried to find some soothing words.

"She doesn't hate you, Cerise."

Her head twisted away from his chest, and she looked up into his eyes. Phil saw the flash of green and the squinting of her eyes. Her mouth twisted in one corner. Children knew . . . they had instincts. There was no way he could lie to Cerise. But how could he explain his mother's actions? He decided to change the subject.

"Cerise, don't worry. You have a new sister. You can sleep with her, and Grandma Thayer can't say a word about it being wrong."

He felt her body stiffen. The muscles steeled like a balloon expanding under his fingertips. When he glanced down, both of Cerise's hands were balled up into fists.

"I don't want a sister."

"Cerise, honey, you'll love her. She's going to look a lot like Matt. Lots of dark curly hair and the biggest eyes."

There was no relaxation in Cerise's body. Phil struggled to think of something to melt the girl's resentment.

"We named her Kathleen."

Her spine stiffened against his arm. When he looked down, her lower lip was protruding in an angry pout, and he sighed. It had been a long night. He was too tired to think about anything else. Cerise would adjust. She had accepted Matt—doted on Matt. It would be all right after

113

she saw the baby—and Wilma would be home. Wilma would handle Cerise.

An ache was building between his shoulder blades, and Phil pulled himself away from the davenport. It took the last of his strength to concentrate on getting to his feet with Cerise held in his arms.

"Come on, Cerise. You can sleep with me."

Her delicate frame relaxed instantly at his words, and she clung to his shoulders with a muffled giggle. Her cheek rubbed back and forth on his chest with a circular motion while he carried her into the bedroom.

"Daddy Phil." The words were whispered in the darkness, and he answered sleepily.

"What is it, Cerise?"

"*She* put the cat in Matt's room. Mommy doesn't want the cat in the bedroom."

"We'll take care of it in the morning."

He drifted into sleep, aware that Cerise had sidled over in the bed and was plastered up against him. Her hand slid up and down across his chest. Her fine hair had unbraided itself and caressed his arm. Cerise hummed softly to herself. She sounded contented, he thought, and said a silent prayer of thanks for the temporary moment of peace. Fatigue snatched the last traces of consciousness from him.

The peace was shattered by Matt's shriek. Phil's eyes flew open and then relaxed. Daylight. The shriek meant Matt was protesting against clothes. Phil smiled wryly. Matt's ordinary routine every morning was to spend a half hour running through the house in the nude. Clara Thayer might ordinarily forgive Matt any indiscretion, but her puritan soul would rebel against nudity, even in a two-year-old. Matt might have to suffer the indignities of being forcibly dressed.

The shriek was cut off by the slamming of a door. Phil rolled gingerly out of bed and resisted the impulse to stroke Cerise's forehead. Let her sleep. She needed her rest. The little girl would have enough troubles with Grandma Thayer.

If Matt was still fighting the confinement of clothing, the shower drowned out the sound effects. By the time Phil came into the dining room, the boy was perched in his high chair with a cherubic smile, cheerfully hammering an empty cup with his spoon.

One strand of Clara Thayer's hair had fallen over her forehead. She pushed it back in annoyance and then picked up a fork. She laid the silverware out in a precise line across the brown linen placemat.

"I couldn't find a tablecloth, Phillip." She looked up at him with a frown.

"We never use them," Phil answered. "Wilma says placemats are better. If the kids spill, she only has to wash one placemat. There are some plastic ones somewhere."

"I loathe plastic," his mother snapped. "Even for children. Children should be taught good manners—not to spill. Placemats are bad enough without being made of plastic."

Phil watched his mother rearranging the position of one fork, adjusting the placement of her coffee cup.

"Mother, aren't you curious about your new grandchild?"

Her head darted up. The corners of her mouth drooped with chagrin.

"Oh, Phillip, what came over me? I got so rattled . . . what . . . I mean, is it a boy or a girl?"

"A girl, Mother, and she's the prettiest baby I ever saw." In spite of his determination to act unconcerned, his grin spread. He felt a glowing warmth inside his chest. The tiny little girl had eyes that opened wider than any baby in the hospital nursery. He'd been amazed at his own pride.

"Wait until you see her."

"A girl?" Clara's mouth was still half opened. "A girl," she repeated. "What are you going to name her?"

"We've already chosen her name." He caught a spoon with an automatic reflex as Matt sent it sailing into the air. "Her name is Kathleen. Kathleen Wilma Thayer."

Clara's forehead wrinkled. She straightened and rose from the table. "What kind of name is Kathleen for a minister's daughter? Mathew was a good name. I expected Rachel or Mary; Kathleen sounds frivolous."

Phil handed the spoon back to Matt and smiled. "Not frivolous. Feminine."

"Strikes me there's too many fancy names for girls around here, Phillip. I admit it's not as bad as . . ." She glanced toward the living room and her eyes flew open with surprise.

She turned to Phil with her chin rigid. Her shoulders snapped upward. "I put the girl on the davenport. Where is she?"

Phil raised on hand to calm her. "Don't get excited, Mother. She's in my bed."

"Your bed?" The words came out in a shocked rush of air. "Well, I'll straighten her out. Spoiled brat. I told her to sleep on the davenport. I don't like sneaky kids. Sneaking off into your bed as soon as my back was turned."

"She didn't sneak off, Mother. I put her there."

The color faded from Clara Thayer's face. Her mouth snapped shut. She stared at him as if she didn't believe him.

"Phillip . . ." Her tongue slid across her lips. She paused, and finally her eyes moved from his to stare down at the table. "It's not right, Phillip. You're a man of God.

116

You should know it's not right. You're no relation."

Phil grabbed a cup and headed toward the kitchen. "There's nothing wrong with it, Mother. Cerise is my daughter, and she was unhappy. And uncomfortable, too, I might add—that davenport is a torture chamber. You can't make something sinful out of the normal need of a child to be loved."

He paused before he passed her chair and felt a wave of sympathy at the dejected slump of her shoulders.

"Mother," he said softly and put one hand on her shoulder. "Are you sure you aren't letting your bitterness about Dad affect your thinking? You can't see everything in the world as sinful when it's merely normal love."

He felt the quick tenseness in her shoulder before she sagged in the chair.

"I don't know what you're talking about, Phillip. Why should your father have anything to do with it?"

He gave her another pat. The tremor in her arm betrayed the indifference of her words.

"Forget it, Mom. I know you never said a word, but I heard all the gossip from the other kids in school. Now, let's have some breakfast."

In the few minutes it took him to fill his coffee cup, Clara managed to regain the color in her face. She bustled into the kitchen with her chin up and pushed him toward the door.

"The girl is up, Phillip," she snapped. "See that's she's dressed before breakfast. There'll be no sitting down to the table in pajamas while I'm here."

Phil smiled to himself and sampled his coffee. It was weak but drinkable. Not as hearty as Wilma usually made, but then his mother never could make a decent pot of coffee.

Cerise scampered from the bedroom to the bathroom

117

clutching an armful of clothes. She emerged from the bathroom dressed but holding a hair ribbon and a brush.

"Daddy Phil, can you fix my braids?"

Phil set his coffee cup down and groaned. Like it or not, he was stuck with the job. No hope of handing the task to his mother, not the way things were going between her and Cerise. His fingers twisted woodenly and then started to work the slithery strands up and over into a loose plaiting. It didn't resemble Wilma's handiwork at all. He brushed the strands out and started over, pulling more tightly, until this time it resulted in a halfway acceptable pair of pigtails.

"You've been very patient with your dad," he said and patted Cerise lightly on the backside when he finished tying the ribbon in place.

His mother's loud sniff indicated her disapproval of his action. She placed a plate of hotcakes in the center of the table and slowly eased herself into her chair.

"Say grace, Phillip."

He stifled an impulse to add a few words about humility and compassion and concluded with a simple "Amen." His mother echoed the word so loudly that Matt jerked and stared at her with a puzzled expression.

Clara raised her head. She gazed at him with an air of expectancy.

"Aren't you surprised, Phillip? Hotcakes."

"Juice," Matt demanded and held his cup out toward Phil.

"Okay, tiger, I'll get it."

He moved quickly into the kitchen and grabbed the pitcher of orange juice from the refrigerator. He hesitated, then reached into the bowl of boiled eggs and snatched one.

"What did I forget?" his mother asked. She looked at

Matt and shook her head. "I gave him a glass of milk."

"Mommy gives us orange juice every morning." Cerise announced the words into the air without a glance in Clara Thayer's direction.

"Every morning?" Clara's words were a confused echo. She watched Phil tapping the shell of his egg against his plate. "Phillip, aren't you going to have any hotcakes? It's your favorite breakfast. When you were a little boy you always wanted hotcakes."

Phil could detect the slight twang of a whine creeping into her voice, and he hit the egg even harder against the dish. Fragments of shell fell to the placemat.

"When I was a boy is right, Mother. Have to watch the waistline now. Usually only have toast and an egg for breakfast." He sprinkled salt across the shiny white of the egg and bit into it. "Don't worry, Matt will eat my share."

"Kitty wants some." Matt leaned over and dropped a sticky chunk of the hotcake onto the floor.

Phil groaned. "That's enough of that. Cerise!" He turned to Cerise, who was wiping her hands on a napkin. "You look like you're finished. Put the cat outside."

"Oh, but Phillip, it's Matt's pet. What if it gets lost?" Clara's voice was almost lost in Matt's yell of protest when Cerise carried the cat to the front door and dumped it on the porch. She leaned against the glass panes of the door and watched the cat while Matt subsided into a sniffling pout.

"It's a stray that wandered in here, Mother. It shouldn't be in the house so much."

"But Matt loves it."

"He forgets it the minute it's out of sight." Phil washed the last of the egg down with the weak coffee and added, "If you leave it outside, it might go back to where it belongs."

119

His mother began stirring at her coffee. Phil had the sensation of having seen her do this often. A ritual. The stirring of the coffee, a few clearings of her throat. He could remember baseball games that were pushed aside. Times when he squirmed in his chair wanting to go to the bathroom. Whenever his mother started clearing her throat, it meant a forthcoming discussion. A discussion that wouldn't end until Clara Thayer ran out of complaints.

Phil hastily put his cup down and stood up before she could get her speech under way.

"Didn't realize it was so late, Mother. I'll have to leave the dishes to you."

"But Phillip," her voice stuck as if she'd been caught before she could clear her throat. "I thought we'd have some time. Time to talk. I hardly ever get to talk to you alone anymore." Her glance darted to Cerise and came back to focus on her plate. "I think there are some things we have to get straight."

"Not this morning, Mother. I have an appointment and some notes to go over before the man gets here."

He glanced at his watch and shook his head. "I'll be in my office when he gets here. Just send him back."

She began stacking the plates with over-elaborate care. "Of course, Phillip. Is it anyone I know, dear? One of the church board members?"

He grinned at her attempt to probe for information.

"No, it's no one from the church, Mother." He stopped, suddenly remembering it was Friday morning. The janitor would be waiting at the church.

"Cerise, will you do Daddy Phil a favor?"

She turned from her vigil at the front window, nodded, and walked to him. She stood waiting expectantly. The braids didn't look too bad. Tomorrow he'd do a better job.

120

"Take the keys up to the church and wait for Mr. Wilkins. Tell him to bring the keys here to the parsonage when he's through. You've done it before." She reached for the keys as he patted her on the head. "Thanks, Cerise. You're a big help."

"Can I play at the church for a while?"

He nodded. "Be home for lunch."

"What if she loses the keys, Phillip? Certainly Mr. Wilkins knows enough to come down here and get them if you don't show up." Clara was scowling at the door, watching Cerise close it behind her.

"Mother, you fret about the most unimportant things. Cerise won't lose the keys."

He bent and dropped a quick kiss on her forehead, surprised at the coarseness of her hair against his cheek. Not like the softness of Wilma's curls, but then, there was no softness anywhere in his mother's nature. Even her hand was bony and hard when she patted his arm.

"Would you like me to make some more coffee? Perhaps your visitor would like some."

"No. It's strictly a business matter, Mother." He squeezed her hand and realized from the disappointed droop of her chin that she was trying hard to be helpful. "I'm counting on you to keep Matt out of my hair," he said and watched her face blossom at the mention of her grandson.

"Of course I will. We'll have lots of fun, won't we, Mathew? Would you like Grandma to read you a story?"

Matt shook his head. "No."

Phil laughed at the look of dismay on his mother's face. "Thought it would be easy, didn't you?"

He retreated to his office and chuckled at the coaxing tones of his mother's voice while she attempted to find an appealing entertainment for the headstrong two-year-old.

121

It was hardly fifteen minutes later when Clara Thayer opened his office door, but already a second strand of hair was dangling over her forehead.

"Mr. Gower is here. I guess he's the man you were waiting for." Phil detected a note of disapproval in her voice before she gave a long sigh. "Does Mathew have another pair of shoes? He threw one of his in the sink—right into the dishwater."

"I think so, but if you can't find them, let him go barefoot." He looked over her shoulder and motioned to the man waiting behind her. "Come on in, Ted."

"Hope you've come to a favorable decision, Reverend."

"Oh, I have a couple questions, but on the whole, it sounds good. Come on in and let's hash it over."

Clara Thayer stepped aside to let the man enter. Phil watched her eyes sweeping over the man's gabardine suit, evaluating the silk of his shirt and resting on the gold cross cuff links. She hovered in the doorway, her glance going from one man to the other. Her head thrust forward, chin tilted up, she was straining to hear every word of the conversation.

"Mother, you'd better check on Matt."

Her head pulled back. Her mouth clamped itself into an offended pursing of her lips.

"Of course, Phillip. I do know my responsibilities," she said and stiffened her shoulders before she turned and left the doorway.

"She said she was your mother," Ted Gower commented. "Guess it means you're a father again."

"Last night," Phil smiled. "Cutest little girl on earth." He picked up a stack of papers and tapped them with his index finger. "You have an interesting idea here, Ted. The percentages interest me."

The man leaned forward on the edge of his chair. "I

122

thought they would. I do all the promotion and setup work. You do the preaching. All you have to do is go in and conduct the gospel meetings. Everything will be set up of you."

"For fifty percent of the collection?"

Ted Gower nodded. "That's right. You get half."

Phil rubbed the back of his neck while he considered the situation. It had tempted him ever since Ted Gower appeared in the vestibule after church a month ago.

"How can you be sure I'm the one you want for this, Ted?"

"I told you, Reverend, I've been studying most of the good gospel-style preachers, and you've got promise." Ted struck the edge of Phil's desk with an open palm. "You have the personality, the ability. All you need is for someone to take charge of arranging the meetings, and you can reach more people in one week than you will all year here in this dinky farming community."

Phil stroked his cheek and took a long deep breath. "But I have a contract here for another year. I don't feel right about leaving them high and dry. They're good folks."

Ted shrugged and leaned back in his chair. "Don't think it's a problem. We want to start out slow anyhow. I can set up meetings for weekdays in other towns. You can be back here for the Sunday service. It'll take awhile to build up your demand to the point where you'll be having services every week. There are going to be a lot of dead weeks in the beginning."

"You sound like a theatrical agent," Phil murmured.

"In a way, I am," he admitted with an embarrassed grin. "Don't mean to offend you, Reverend, but the ability to preach wasn't all that made me come to you. You've got youth and good looks. Run a snappy photograph of you in the local papers a week or so ahead of the gospel meetings and there'll be a crowd of women out there for every meeting. Some of them might even drag their husbands along."

He leaned forward and patted the desk again. "Twenty-five percent of the collection goes to every church that invites us in—that keeps them happy. All they have to furnish is the meeting place and a pianist. I get twenty-five percent for my setup work, and you get all the rest."

Phil leaned back in his chair and fingered the contract with one hand. "How can you be sure there'll be enough to divide?"

Ted Gower grinned so broadly there was a flash of metallic fillings. "Reverend, I'm counting on your preaching and my advertising genius to make it worthwhile."

Phil let the contract fall back to the desk top and sat looking at the dotted lines that waited for his signature. He closed his eyes and thought about the proposition. Last night he had been so sure this was what he wanted, a series of evangelistic meetings—only around the state to begin with—but Ted Gower was making it sound like a carnival circuit. He had to be sure he'd keep control.

When he opened his eyes, he met Ted's waiting gaze.

"You understand, I am not a faith healer. I'm not a messiah. No outlandish claims or publicity. If there's anything I object to in any ad, I cancel the agreement."

"Right! Right!" Gower leaned forward. "Dignity. I know. You have my word. I'll keep the standards up, Reverend. Count on it."

Phil began making notes across the neatly typed forms. "Just to be sure, Ted, I'll write these conditions in and sign it when you have it retyped."

"Sure, sure." Gower nodded so vigorously the chair legs squeaked with his movements. "It'll take a few weeks to get things lined up. We'll need to get a couple good photos, too."

He took the papers when Phil folded them and handed them across the desk. "This time next year, Reverend, we'll have meetings set up all over the state. People will be flocking to see you."

"I hope you mean flocking to *hear* me, Ted." Phil grasped the man's shoulder and felt the flabbiness give way under his fingers. Did he really need this man? He directed Ted Gower to the door and watched the man climb laboriously into a small economy car. Phil thought about the time it would require to make all the arrangements for the meetings and turned back into the house. If he wanted to accomplish anything, he had to admit he did need a Ted Gower.

Matt crawled out from behind the davenport and grabbed one of Phil's ankles.

"Kitty's gone," he announced and looked up at Phil with his wide, pleading eyes.

"I've looked all over the yard, Phillip," his mother said. "the cat is nowhere around."

Phil tossed Matt lightly in the air. "It probably found another place for a free meal, Mother, or else it'll come back when it gets hungry."

He set Matt back on his feet and headed to the privacy of his office. The whereabouts of a stray cat was hardly an important problem. He had some serious thinking to do.

The cat was waiting on the front steps when Cerise came out the door. She jangled the keys and stuck her tongue out when the cat meowed in a plaintive plea for attention.

She bounced down the front steps one at a time and stopped when she landed on the sidewalk. The cat stretched and followed her. It walked around and around, rubbing against her legs, purring enticingly for affection.

Cerise caught the cat under its soft belly and held it to her chest. She clutched it tightly while she ambled up the street to the church. Even after she settled down on the front steps of the church to wait for Mr. Wilkins, she continued to hold the cat. It squirmed and twisted, but after a pat on the head and a scratch behind the ears, the cat relaxed into a purr and closed its eyes.

"Are you waiting for me, Cerise?"

She raised her head and nodded to the ruddy-faced janitor. The question was a part of their game. He knew she was waiting for him, but he always asked.

"Got a friend with you today?"

Cerise followed his glance down to the cat and shook her head. "No. Daddy Phil said it was a stray."

"Your dad must be busy again."

"He had a man coming to see him."

Mr. Wilkins coughed and dug into the pocket of his coveralls for a package of gum. It was part of the ritual. Cerise watched soberly. Mr. Wilkins took out a stick of gum and chewed slowly. After a few minutes he would say, "Mmm, that's good," and smack his lips. Then he would offer her a stick of gum too. She kept her face emotionless and watched him without saying a word. Another part of the game. She waited.

"Mmm, that's good." Mr. Wilkins finally smacked his lips, smiled and handed her a stick of gum. She handed him the keys and the game was over. Mr. Wilkins would start cleaning the floors and dusting the pews.

She shifted the gum from side to side in her mouth while she decided where she would play. Sometimes Daddy Phil let her play the piano in the basement, but Mr. Wilkins didn't like her getting in his way. She was in the cemetery yesterday, and the bell tower wasn't fun unless there were

126

people to watch in the churchyard.

The cat slipped and dug its claws into her leg to regain its balance. Cerise flinched, grabbed the animal with both hands, and stood up.

She'd go through the cemetery to the creek. Her arm tightened around the wiggling cat as she walked through the graveyard and crawled under the fence. She hadn't been to the creek for a long time. The weeds in the field were as high as her head in some places, and there were thistles. She had to watch out for them.

The cat meowed, and Cerise looked into the animal's yellow eyes. Only a faint sliver of black showed in the center of them. The cat blinked up at her, and she squinted in an attempt to imitate the cat.

They stared at each other until a soft smile appeared on Cerise's face. She stomped the weeds down, making a path ahead of her, and headed for the creek.

Every bone in Clara Thayer's spine ached, but she wasn't going to admit it. Not as long as there was an aspirin left in the house. Either she was getting old, or Mathew was the most active little boy she had ever seen. After only three days, she was exhausted. Thank goodness Phillip would be bringing Wilma and the new baby home tomorrow. She was ready to go back to her own house.

Clara sank onto the dining room chair and leaned both elbows on the table. Mathew was tucked into bed and asleep. At least he'd quit asking about the cat. She hated to admit Phillip was right. It must have found another home. She had time to rest.

Phillip had taken the girl with him to the hospital. Tonight Clara intended to wait for him to come home. If she was going to have a talk with Phillip, it would have to be tonight. There were too many things wrong in this house.

Too lax . . . things were too lax. Phillip should know better. First the girl—sleeping in the same bed with Mathew. Phillip letting her sleep with him. They were no relation. He even put the two children in the bathtub together.

She wasn't raised that way. She hadn't raised Phillip like this. The private parts of the body should be covered. The casual way Phillip treated Mathew's nakedness was unthinkable. It must be Wilma's influence.

And that fancy-shirted man. Phillip hadn't given her one hint about his business with the man. He certainly wasn't a local man. No farmer around this area wore gold cuff links.

If Phillip was planning to move to another parish, she had a right to be told. She wasn't going to drive this far to attend church if Phillip wasn't planning on staying here.

Headlights flashed at the windows. Two car doors slammed shut, and Clara pulled her shoulders up into an erect, waiting alertness. She fixed a welcoming smile on her face, determined to look happy even if the girl spoke to her.

The girl was strangely subdued. She glanced once at Clara, then turned and ducked into Phillip's bedroom without saying a word.

Clara almost sighed with relief. At last she was going to have a few minutes alone with her son. She cleared her throat and pointed to the chair beside her. "Phillip, come here and talk."

"Are you sure you want to, Mother? You look tired." He hesitated, but after a second he shrugged his shoulders and moved across the living room toward her. She almost weakened when he flashed a radiant smile at her and dropped into the chair. Phillip's smiles always made her feel warm — proud to be his mother — but things had to be said. She couldn't let his charm divert her.

"I am tired, I admit," she said, "but if we don't talk tonight, there won't be another chance. There are things I must say to you, Phillip."

"Sounds serious." He leaned back in the chair with a suspicious twinkle in his eyes.

"Don't laugh at me, Phillip. I'm older than you are and I know when things are wrong." She folded her hands together and cleared her throat. "Now, I know you're a minister, but that doesn't give you the right to excuse sin."

Phillip's mouth dropped in a moment's surprise and the twinkle came back into his eyes. Well, he could treat it as a joke if he wanted, but she was going to have her say . . . even if it made him mad.

"Don't scoff at me, young man. I'm your mother. You know better than to condone nudity and lust. These things start early. You can't go on letting Mathew run around here without clothes in front of a young girl. Putting them together in the bathtub . . . it's going to lead to trouble."

"Now, Mother, they're only children. If you don't put ideas in their heads, they won't think anything is wrong. After all, our bodies are created by God."

"Not the girl's. She's no creation of the Lord's. And you let her sleep in the same bed with you."

Clara brought her hand up to her mouth and glanced away. Phillip's eyes had lost their merriment. Good. He could be mad if he wanted to. She was his mother. She had a right to straighten things out.

"Cerise is my daughter. I legally adopted her, and if she sleeps with me, it's only because she needs some affection. With Wilma in the hospital, she doesn't have anyone to turn to except me."

"She's not really your daughter," Clara retorted. The steely tone of Phillip's words stung in her ears. "And don't take that preachy attitude with me. I'm your mother. I have a right—a duty—to speak up when you're doing something wrong. It *is* wrong, Phillip. Wrong!"

He shook his head and then closed his eyes. She heard him take a long, slow, deep breath and hold it. She clenched her hands so tightly she could feel her knuckles ache under the pressure. This wasn't the way she had expected the talk to go. Phillip had never argued with her before. She suspected he didn't always agree, but he never argued. She had taught him to respect her, and here he was implying she was wrong.

Phillip slowly expelled the breath he had been holding and opened his eyes. The smile had vanished, and Clara looked quickly away when he spoke.

"As far as Cerise is concerned, I am her father, and I want you to treat her as my child. You can't shower all your attention on Matt without Cerise knowing you don't like her. You're not even trying to treat her like a grandchild. You don't even treat her like a member of the family."

Clara could only shake her head over and over. He was asking too much of her.

"I can't treat her like a grandchild, Phillip. I won't. Why, I don't know anything about her . . . who her father was. You've never told me a thing. I don't know if Wilma is a widow or divorced. I'm assuming she's a widow, since no decent man would marry a divorced woman. At least a minister wouldn't. I do know the girl is not your blood, and who knows what she is? She's evil. I know evil when I see it."

"Mother . . ."

"Don't interrupt me." She struggled to keep her voice

130

under control. The anger was making her sound whiny.

"She's insolent. She stares at me as if she hated me. Sometimes she won't even answer me. When I tell her to do something, she just stands there looking at me."

"Perhaps if you tried asking her, Mother, instead of always telling her—and it might help if you called her by name instead of referring to her as 'girl.' She might respond better."

"I refuse to use that ridiculous name. Cerise. What kind of Christian name is that?"

He put his hands on the table and pushed his chair back. "If you're not tired, Mother, I am. I'm going to bed."

Clara raised her chin. "I'm not through, Phillip."

"Later, Mother." He stretched and bent toward her, but she pulled her head away. She wasn't going to let him end this with a swift kiss on her forehead. She was going to get some answers. If Phillip thought she was going to be pushed aside easily, he was underestimating her.

"Not later, Phillip . . . tonight. I want to know what's going on. Who was that man with the fancy clothes? Are you thinking of changing churches?"

He patted the top of her head and laughed lightly. "I think the kids have tired you out. Good night."

"Phillip!" She slapped the top of the table with her hand, but he continued to walk away. "I said I wasn't through. Come back here."

His only answer was a shake of his head and another laughing, "Good night, Mother."

She watched the bedroom door close behind him, and a tear rolled down her cheek. He might be a minister, but it was a sin. God would punish him. It was the girl's fault. The girl had twisted his mind. Well, he'd have his own daughter now. He'd see how strange the colorless girl was.

131

Clara rose to her feet and sagged with weariness. She hadn't talked to her son at all. This was more than fatigue ... it was defeat. Phillip had avoided answering her questions. Laughed at her opinions.

She turned out the light and knelt, drawing strength from the firmness of the bed. She prayed silently in the darkness.

Chapter Four

The last note from a vibrating piano string hovered in the air when Cerise escaped. She turned her head, took one swift glance about the church, then inched toward the side door. No one noticed her slip through the opening and up the stairs to the tower room. They were all busy lining up, waiting to shake hands with Daddy Phil before they went out of the church.

She tiptoed across the tower room trying not to look at the ugly peeling brown enamel on the floor. Daddy Phil always stood in the hallway, and the people in the hallway below could hear footsteps in the tower room. She could hear Mr. Wilkins when he cleaned up here. Not only could she hear him walk, but she could hear the swish of his broom on the uneven floor.

The skinny door made to look like a wall panel creaked when she opened it. She swung it outward just wide enough to slide through and then climb the narrow, rough boards into the bell tower.

She had learned the only way to escape the flower-smelling ladies with their head-patting hands was to keep out of sight until everyone left the church. The head-patting was bad enough—now they asked her if she wasn't proud of her little sister. Especially Miss Wilford, with her stinky breath and the dead animal skins around her neck.

Miss Wilford kept pinching Kathleen's cheeks, and Mommy never said a word. It wasn't fair. She'd pinched Kathleen and been spanked. Why did everyone think she was supposed to like Kathleen's curly hair and her big, dark eyes? It was bad enough when Kathleen was a little baby. Now she was walking. Everyone expected her to hold on to her baby sister. To watch her and listen to them making a fuss over Kathleen. Who cared if Kathleen looked like Daddy Phil? She didn't want to watch Kathleen. Watching Kathleen was worse than being patted on the head. Kathleen wasn't like Matt. Kathleen pulled and tugged to get away, and worst of all, she screamed and bit.

Cerise knelt on the floor of the bell tower and looked out through the louvered opening. From this position she could watch the people standing around the lawn or getting into their cars. Some cars jiggled when the fat ladies got into them. Some cars belched out funny blue smoke when the motor started. Mr. Wilkins had to slam his car door three times before it stayed shut.

Mommy stood at the bottom of the steps, smiling and holding Kathleen. Today, *she* was standing beside Mommy and holding Matt's hand, but Matt never cared who held onto him.

She was worse than ever. Bringing Kathleen new toys— even some Kathleen couldn't play with yet. Like the dishes. Not plastic ones. Real china dishes with blue flowers. Mommy had put them in the closet until Kathleen got older. *She* kept calling Kathleen a "real Thayer" and bragging about how pretty Kathleen was.

Cerise glared at Clara Thayer through the louvers. She stuck her thumbs in her ears and waggled her fingers, first at Clara and then at Miss Wilford.

Miss Wilford pinched Kathleen, and even though

134

Mommy took a step backward, Kathleen opened her mouth and screamed. When Clara Thayer whirled and shook her finger up and down under the tip of Miss Wilford's nose, Cerise giggled. She leaned closer to the opening. She was too far away to hear whatever Clara Thayer was saying. *She* looked mad.

Cerise scrambled to her feet and bounced down the bell tower steps. She scurried across the tower room, not caring if anyone heard her. If Miss Wilford and Clara Thayer were going to have a fight, she wanted to hear it.

She thumped down the last flight of stairs, opened the door, and peeked around the church. The fat lady was putting her music away into a folder. Cerise tiptoed toward the vestibule doors before the lady could turn around and start fussing over her, then she slipped into the hall.

Daddy Phil was busy talking to some strange man with a funny baggy suit, and neither of them noticed her. She ducked around them and edged down the church steps in time to hear Clara Thayer's loud accusation.

"Loretta Wilford!" Clara's face was as red as Matt's when he held his breath. "You don't have to be so rough. How would you like it if I pinched your cheeks?"

Clara Thayer's hand darted out. The scrawny fingers clamped down on the fleshy jowls of the woman in front of her.

Cerise heard the long intake of breath. Miss Wilford jerked back. Her cheeks puffed full of air, and her nose twitched. But as Miss Wilford opened her mouth, Daddy Phil brushed past Cerise and hurried down the steps. He caught Miss Wilford's arm with one hand and leaned forward. Cerise saw the flash of his smile before the other arm went around Miss Wilford's shoulder.

She worked her way to the bottom of the steps, staying close to the railing. No one noticed her moving closer to the group. She inched her way nearer and nearer, trying to hear every word.

"Loretta," Daddy Phil's voice sounded coaxing, like when he tried to make Kathleen eat her peas. She risked a swift glance at Clara Thayer's face, and her own eyes glistened. Clara's face was even redder than before, only now she was hanging her head and not looking at anyone. She clung to Matt with one hand, but the other one was holding her mouth and trembling.

"I didn't pinch her hard enough to hurt her, Reverend Thayer." Miss Wilford's voice was so faint that Cerise had to slide up against her mother's skirt before she could hear the words clearly.

"I know. I know." Daddy Phil patted the fox skins and bent close to Miss Wilford. "Kathleen has recently learned to scream. Believe me, Wilma and I understand. She screams over everything."

Wilma lowered Kathleen to the grass, but Cerise tried not to pay any attention. She waited, hoping Daddy Phil was going to make his mother tell Miss Wilford she was sorry.

Instead, Daddy Phil kept patting Miss Wilford's shoulder and talking—his mouth smiling, but not his eyes; his eyes were sober and didn't laugh at all.

"I'm sorry, Loretta. The truth is Kathleen is slow in talking. I'm afraid she gets her way by screaming. We know you didn't hurt her."

Miss Wilford nodded. Her head bobbed up and down, but she didn't smile back at Daddy Phil. Cerise sneaked another look at Clara Thayer, then turned her head away when she discovered Clara glaring back at her.

"Daddy." Kathleen pushed her body in front of Cerise and looked up at Phil with a wide smile.

Cerise bit her lip. Daddy Phil smiled back at Kathleen. Not just his mouth—his eyes smiled too. Her hand darted out and rested on Kathleen's head. Kathleen held her arms up, begging to be picked up, and Cerise waited.

When Daddy Phil bent to lift Kathleen, Cerise was ready. A lock of Kathleen's hair was wedged firmly between Cerise's fingers, and Daddy Phil was the one who made it pull. Kathleen screamed again and shook her head with an angry pout.

Miss Wilford's chin shot up into the air. She glared at Clara Thayer. "It's obvious some people simply don't understand children," she said.

"At least I've been a mother," Clara Thayer retorted. "Some people act as if they know what being a mother is like when they've had no experience."

"You were a mother only once, Clara. It doesn't make you an expert." Miss Wilford stroked the fur around her neck with short, nervous pats. "Wait until the church picnic next Sunday. Some people are going to find out what work it is to watch more than one child." She straightened her shoulders, patted the crown of braids, and marched down the sidewalk to her car.

Phil juggled Kathleen into a firmer grip against his shoulder. "I think it's time Kathleen had her dinner and a nap." He looked down at Cerise and frowned. "How on earth did you get your dress so dirty?"

Cerise shrugged and reached for Matt's hand. She lowered her eyes and inspected the streak of dust across the front of her dress.

"She's probably been out in the cemetery again," Clara Thayer sniffed. She took a firmer grip on Matt's other hand. "I can't understand why anyone would want to hang around a bunch of tombstones. It's hardly a normal place for a child to play."

Cerise wrinkled her nose and dropped Matt's hand. She moved back to her mother's side. This time she received an affectionate hug. Wilma put an arm around

Cerise's shoulders and pulled her close.

"Let's go home," Cerise said and tugged at Wilma's arm.

She waited, looking from her mother to Daddy Phil. Neither of them asked Clara Thayer if she was coming to dinner. Cerise caught her breath and closed her eyes.

Maybe Daddy Phil was right. Maybe she should pray more. Cerise tried saying over and over inside, "Please, God, make her go home. Please, God."

"Cerise, take Matt and walk ahead of us."

She heard Daddy Phil's voice and opened her eyes. At his next words, she grabbed Matt's hand and clamped her mouth together with a triumphant look at Clara Thayer.

"We'll see you at the picnic next Sunday, Mother."

Matt hesitated, pulled by Cerise and held by his grandmother. He shifted awkwardly to keep his balance. When Clara released his hand, he accepted the switch without expression. Cerise started down the sidewalk before Daddy Phil could change his mind.

"Are we going to a picnic?" Matt asked.

"Next Sunday," Cerise answered. She knew all about the church picnic. Daddy Phil had been planning it for weeks. They were going to have the church services outdoors in a park, with a picnic afterward. And ice cream. Daddy Phil had promised they'd have ice cream. Lots of ice cream and hot dogs.

And Daddy Phil would be home all week. He wasn't going to have any revival meetings anywhere. Daddy Phil would be home all week, and school was out. She skipped with excitement until Matt had to break into a trot to keep up with her.

Daddy Phil said the picnic was an appeasement to the church board. 'Cause they were upset about his being gone so much.

138

If she had time before dinner, Cerise decided to look up the word *appeasement* in the dictionary. If Mommy hadn't taken it again. Mommy used the dictionary a lot lately. But Mommy hadn't known what *appeasement* meant either.

When they reached the house, she let go of Matt's hand and let him run ahead of her. An angleworm had crawled out on the concrete walk and was wriggling desperately, trying to find its way back to the grass.

Her foot went out. She pressed down hard. The ends of the worm twitched and wiggled on both sides of her shoe. She ground her foot around and around until the worm ends collapsed into limp, contracting bits of pink skin. A kick sent the remains off into the lawn. She scraped her foot against the concrete and ran to the steps.

At least *she* wasn't going to be there for dinner. If she prayed real hard, maybe Clara wouldn't come to the church picnic either.

She sat down on the steps, brushed the dirt off her skirt, and squinched her eyes shut. The world was shut out.

"Cerise, stop it." Wilma heard the scratchy tone in her voice and tried to get her temper back under control. "Don't put your hand over Kathleen's nose and mouth that way. You'll smother her."

"But she keeps screaming."

"I know," Wilma sighed. "But she'll get over it. She's only trying to get her own way."

"It hurts my ears."

"It hurts everyone's ears, but you're a lot bigger than she is. If you don't watch it, you could make her stop breathing."

"Then make her quit screaming."

Cerise stared back at her with a determined tilt of her chin. Wilma inhaled a deep breath. Cerise's eyes were like cold hunks of jade, as if she was defying her, daring Wilma to do better. Challenging Wilma to punish Kathleen.

Wilma let her breath ease out and groped in the cookie jar for the guaranteed distraction. She handed the cookie to Kathleen and swung the toddler up into the high chair before she turned back to Cerise.

"Go play outside," she said, "then you won't have to listen to her."

"I'm waiting for Daddy Phil."

Cerise walked to the cookie jar and fished out three cookies for herself. Wilma avoided the girl's accusing glance. She had slighted Cerise. For once she didn't feel guilty. She was tired of always being fair. Cerise couldn't expect her to measure out every mouthful of food. Cerise was old enough to help herself — Kathleen couldn't.

"Phil's having a meeting in his office with the church board, Cerise. He might be a long time."

Wilma stared out the window at the driveway. It was crowded with cars. As crowded as Phil's office. Would the sober-faced men and women force Phil to choose between the evangelist meetings and the local church? She knew Phil's absences had made some of the members unhappy, but not all of them. Phil could smile his way out of almost anything. Would he be able to do it this time? She didn't want to move.

Her fingertips stroked the softness of her new velour shirt. She didn't want to give up all the new clothes. For the first time in her life, she was buying with nothing but desire. "You want it — you buy it" was what Phil told her. If he had to give up the gospel meetings, there wouldn't be enough money.

Worse . . . she'd have to give up the books. Phil objected to the books. He hadn't said she couldn't buy them, but he'd scoffed at the waste. The kids could get library books, and she didn't need them, he said. But she did. She needed them worse than the kids . . . *Heidi*, *Black Beauty*, and the fairy tales. She had to catch up. If there wasn't enough money, Phil would say no books.

The lid of the cookie jar rattled, and Wilma turned her head to see Cerise reaching into its depths once more.

"No more cookies. You've had enough."

The girl's hand hovered and withdrew with two more cookies.

"I'm getting these for Matt." There was no expression in Cerise's face, only a bland innocence. The pale lashes were veiling her eyes. She stood motionless, her body tense and alert, waiting for Wilma to relent.

"Okay, take them outside to Matt and play with him for a while."

She watched Cerise amble toward the front door. What a strange walk for a nine-year-old . . . not the quick awkwardness nor the frantic hurry of the other girls in Cerise's grade at school.

Cerise appeared to tuck her backside in. She flowed from step to step . . . like a cat, Wilma thought. She walks like a woman—not a little girl. Her hips were almost swaying . . . almost but not quite like a woman's.

Would she be able to keep Cerise from making her mistake? So far Cerise hadn't asked any questions about sex.

Wilma slipped into a chair and chewed at her thumbnail. Perhaps Cerise didn't think she knew enough to answer the questions. She always went to Phil with her queries. Had she asked Phil about sex?

Cerise hesitated at the door. The eyelashes lifted, and

141

her eyes sparkled.

"The ice cream at the picnic," she asked, "will it be strawberry?"

Wilma's breath almost whistled with relief. It was a kid's question. She worried too much about Cerise.

"I don't know," Wilma answered. "I think Miss Wilford is in charge of getting the ice cream."

"She'd pick vanilla." Cerise wrinkled her nose and flipped her braids over her shoulder before she stepped out onto the porch.

Wilma listened to Cerise calling for Matt and then turned to her youngest daughter.

Kathleen's eyes were alert and appealed to her from above an angelic smile. Wilma bent toward Kathleen, and the tiny hand patted her face. Wilma reached and scooped Kathleen into her lap.

She hugged the girl against her and caressed the silken curls. It was so hard to keep her hands off this one. She wanted to hug Kathleen each time the child's smile appeared, but there were always Cerise's accusing eyes.

Only when Cerise was out of sight, only when she was alone with Kathleen, could she give in and hug the miniature edition of Phil.

"But you have my curls," she murmured into Kathleen's hair. "Why couldn't Cerise have had your hair?"

Her thoughts made her glance guiltily toward the window, but Cerise was teaching Matt to turn cartwheels. Cerise couldn't see her holding Kathleen and rubbing her cheek against Kathleen's clean-scented hair. She didn't want to worry about making Cerise's mouth pucker up or turn into an angry line.

Wilma's arms tightened around the little girl. She whispered into the wisps of Kathleen's curls, "When you're old enough, I'll be able to answer your questions.

I'm learning, Kathleen. I'm learning."

Kathleen's form became heavy. The delicate head drooped lower and lower on Wilma's breast. One chubby hand fell with the limpness of sleep into the girl's lap. A chunk of soggy cookie rolled to the floor.

She carried Kathleen in to her crib and tucked the pink teddy-bear blanket under the dimpled chin. As she started out of the room, she paused and picked up a library book Cerise had dropped beside the bed. *The Polka Dot Dragon*. Wilma hadn't read this one. She flopped down on Cerise's bed and opened the book.

There was so much to learn. At least the books Cerise was reading were easy, but they got harder all the time. Already she had found words in Cerise's schoolbooks that she hadn't understood, but she had learned to look them up in the dictionary.

She leaned back against the pillows on Cerise's bed, propped the book against a floppy-eared, stuffed rabbit, and began reading. When Kathleen was as old as Cerise, she wouldn't be giving her mother rolling-eyed looks of disgust. Kathleen wouldn't hear her make mistakes like saying "I seen" for "I saw." She'd learned to correct that mistake already, and she was going to learn more. Even Clara Thayer would quit lifting her eyebrows and giving out those disgusted sighs.

Phil eyed the faces of the church board members while they filed out of the office. At least the smiles outnumbered the frowns.

Each of them shook his hand, and Phil noted with relief most were firm handshakes of assurance. Grips of affirmation. Only ancient Mr. Becker and Mrs. Foley gave him the dishrag fingers. Mr. Becker was so infirm he had difficulty holding his cane, and Mrs. Foley shuddered away from everyone's touch. Perhaps they weren't important. Since the board hadn't presented him with an ultimatum, the crisis was temporarily averted. They'd only expressed concern. As long as the church attendance remained high, the church board would be satisfied.

Only Loretta Wilford hung back. She stepped away from the door, letting the others pass, and kneaded her fingers together. She hung her head instead of meeting Phil's eyes.

After the last of the board members left, Loretta remained with her chin sagging against her chest. One hand gripped the back of a chair for support. When she lifted her head, her chin quivered. Her nose had acquired a raspberry tinge.

"Reverend Thayer, I want you to know I think you should be here—in the parish—full time. I'm not happy with having a part-time minister. Not happy at all."

Phil bit his tongue between his teeth as he flexed his shoulders and thought. So *this* was the agitator. Was it his evangelism that upset Loretta Wilford, or was it antagonism toward his mother?

He eased himself back into his chair and nodded his head before he spoke. Better choose the words carefully.

"Loretta, you flatter me. I didn't think I was so important."

The woman's chin came up. She pushed the chair aside and straightened her shoulders as if called to attention.

"Important? Of course you are." She took a deep breath before she plunged into her speech. "You've made some of us a part of the church. This—well, you have to admit—it's not a sophisticated crowd . . . all farmers." She leaned forward with her hands spread out on the desk. Her eyes gleamed with a feverish zeal. "Until you came, Reverend Thayer, we never had a real choir. We never had flowers on the altar. Why we never had decent hymnals."

She leaned farther across the desk and peered into Phil's face. He held his breath at the blast of air. Cerise was right. The woman had the breath of a scavenging dog. He tried not to inhale while her words continued to belch out.

"The church needs you. Without you we'd be nothing but a backwoods congregation."

Phil forced his swivel chair to tilt back as far as it would go but held her gaze with his eyes. The niceties of life meant a lot to Loretta. She flaunted the outdated fur, the diamond ring on her right hand, the pearl-framed cameo—all remnants of a mother buried years before.

"Loretta, you restore my faith in my work," he said and leaned forward to cup his hand over one of hers. The warm softness of her flesh didn't hide the slight tremor of the woman's emotions.

"If it weren't for people like you, Loretta, good-hearted folks keeping the desire for an active church alive, I wouldn't be able to continue my work."

He saw a faint rose tinge returning to her cheeks and continued to hold his hand over hers. She was no longer trembling.

"There are so many nonbelievers out there, Loretta. So many people who will never hear the word of God and never be brought into the fold. I feel the whole world can be my parish as long as there are people like you to keep this one alive."

The color in her cheeks darkened to a deeper pink. The eyes lost their fire and softened. The corners of her mouth crept upward.

"But Reverend Thayer," she swallowed hard, "we need you here."

"I am here. I'm only trying to expand our circle of God's love." He gave her hand a gentle pat. "If it weren't for you taking charge of things like the picnic, I couldn't do my work nearly so well. You're one of my mainstays in the church, Loretta. I hope I can count on you to continue helping me get on with my work."

She placed her free hand over his. Her eyes glistened. A proud smile lit up her face as she clung to him.

"Oh, I will, Reverend Thayer, I will. You wait. Everyone's going to enjoy next Sunday. Why, I haven't been on a real old-fashioned picnic since I was a young girl."

"That's not so long ago." Phil grinned and was amused to see Loretta wiggle and preen like one of his mother's hens adjusting her feathers.

She released his hand and put one plump index finger up to her lips as if attempting to hush the slight giggle. A gushing, "Oh, Reverend Thayer," was accompanied by the rolling of her eyes, which Phil supposed was her generation's equivalent of flirting. He pulled his hand back, holding his amusement in check, and stood up. There was only one way to bring Loretta's visit to an end.

"Shall we have a word of prayer before you go, Loretta?"

Her head bent eagerly. Phil closed his eyes and prayed aloud for Loretta. The cultured mainstay of the church. The dedicated loyal servant of the Lord. The patient, understanding woman — the Martha among many Marys. As he finished his Amen, he lifted his hand, placed it on her head, and urged the Lord's blessing on this special woman. He felt confident. Loretta's eyes had the glazed and dazzled expression of a totally captivated woman. She would cooperate — at least for a while.

"Go in peace, Loretta. We'll see you on Sunday." He smiled very gently and moved to open the door before she could gather any more words together. Her fingers fluttered a coy good-bye and her eyes rolled up at him with adoration. She minced out the door, the sound of a delicate giggle trailing behind her.

He leaned against the door frame. The church would let him stay . . . for a while. Loretta was placated—for a while. Be sure his mother didn't get into any more disagreements with Loretta. Give Ted Gower the go-ahead. Line up as many places as possible. Six months. Maybe. By then they could afford a house of their own. They wouldn't be caught without a roof over their heads if the church board demanded his resignation.

He moved to the phone and dialed.

"Ted? Phil Thayer."

"Rev! I've been waiting for your call." Ted's voice boomed in Phil's ear. "How'd it go? I mean, did they say quit the meetings or get out? What happened?"

"Not much, really," Phil answered. "A few expressed concern about my not being available for visiting the sick. A couple worried about attendance going down, but they've decided to leave me alone. As long as the Sunday attendance stays high, I'm free to go on with the gospel meetings."

"So I go ahead and keep scheduling?"

"Yes, of course."

Phil twisted a pencil between his fingers and flipped the pages of his calendar. "About this fall, I think, we should step up the number of meetings. The coast circuit we talked about—maybe by then I can manage to find a replacement and go to full-time evangelism."

"Well, now you're talking." Ted's voice took on a surge of enthusiasm. "I've lined up some possibilities for November and December. Astoria, Newport—been waiting on your situation before I tied the ends together."

"What about September?"

"Naw," Ted replied. "Tourist season not over. Local people are all too busy. We hit 'em after the tourists go.

147

Nothing doing in the towns. People still have money. We wait too long—like January or February—and they're broke again."

Phil tapped at the paper with the end of his pencil. "You're making it sound mercenary, Ted. The idea is to spread the word of God."

"Yeah, I know, Rev," was the reply. "But the local churches need a decent return for their time and space. If we don't make good collections, they get discouraged. We have to work this into your being asked back. A well-filled collection plate will get us a return invitation."

"I know. Crass but realistic," Phil sighed.

"That's why I'm important to you, Rev," Ted laughed. "You keep your ideals. I'll make the deals. The nuts and bolts all put together. We're getting lots of inquiries from all over. Whenever you decide to go out full time, there'll be enough places eager to get you."

Phil settled back in his chair and began making notes. He listened to Ted's voice rumbling on with dates and figures. Ted Gower was busy.

"Roseburg?" Phil interrupted. "That's new."

"Yeah. A Reverend Thatcher contacted me. Remember him? Says he talked to you at Scappoose."

Phil nodded to himself. Thatcher with the buck teeth and one missing ear lobe. An odd man, but sincere.

"Thatcher bought up an old church," Ted continued. "Wants to have gospel meetings every night, but thinks he needs visiting preachers. Change of pace, you know. He thinks you'd attract a different crowd. Get new faces into the meetings."

"I hope so," Phil laughed. He saw Cerise and Matt dart across the backyard and disappear behind the garage. His family was complete. Time to concentrate on his own life. Thatcher's dream was a small scale of his own.

148

He opened the bottom drawer of his desk and pulled out the sketches. His dream: an interdenominational retreat, a chapel, guest houses. The drawings were beginning to curl at the edges from his constant handling.

First they'd have to have a home, their own house. Not be at the mercy of a church board. The family needed a solid, comfortable base.

He started figuring the average collection. He ought to be able to save enough by October . . . sooner, if they went into a few of the larger towns. Roseburg was bigger than any place they'd held meetings so far.

"Work on the Roseburg angle, Ted."

"I was hoping you'd okay it. There's money in Roseburg. Lots of timber money."

Phil smiled to himself. Good and practical Ted. "We'll have to see what happens. Go ahead and step up the scheduling. I think you're right. Full time is the way to go."

"Now you're talking. When?"

"By the first of the year. I'm afraid I wasn't cut out to be a country church pastor."

"Not with your talent. You can really work up a crowd."

"It's hard to feel talented when you have to spend your time appeasing contributors and soothing the ruffled feathers of little old ladies."

"Had a bad morning?"

"Oh, it turned out all right, but I could have been doing so much more."

"We will be doing more, Rev. I'll get ahold of Thatcher."

"Great. You coming out to our picnic this Sunday?"

The groan vibrated in the earpiece, and Phil winced at the phone.

"Rev, I'll do most anything, but not the outdoor life.

149

My idea of roughing it is a Big Mac."

"You won't settle for a hot dog?"

He hung up the phone and chuckled to himself. Ted Gower had a knack of handling his own affairs. No placating the attention-starved old ladies for Ted. He avoided all contact with the congregations with the agility of a ballet dancer. In and make the deal — out and on to the next movement.

The drawings went back into the bottom drawer. Hidden away. Even Wilma had never seen them, didn't know they existed. No use starting a lot of speculation. The drawings were his secret until the right time, the right place . . . and the money. It would take a lot of money, a lot of collections. Or at least one big donation. One person would be the financial backer of his dream. Somewhere on one of his crusades, he would find the potential backer. Then he would dig out the plans.

Then he would tell Wilma . . . but not his mother. She would never understand why he wasn't content at this church. He smiled to himself over the difference between the two women. Neither one would understand his visions, but Wilma wouldn't argue about it.

He gazed out the window and saw Cerise turn a cartwheel, her pigtails flying. Cerise would probably understand his dreams better than his mother or Wilma. Sometimes Cerise looked at him with those calculating green eyes and a shiver would run down his spine. It felt as if she was seeing into his mind.

Matt sauntered around the corner of the garage and grinned up at the window. Phil waved and turned the key in the desk drawer. He should take time to spend a few minutes with his children.

The phone rang before he reached the door, and he paused. No . . . it could wait. Whoever was calling would go on for hours over something as petty as a

150

drinking neighbor or a husband who wouldn't attend church. Some women seemed to expect him to bodily carry the man to the services.

He stepped out onto the lawn and swung Matt up into the air, letting the phone continue to screech for attention.

Clara Thayer pursed her lips together and picked up her purse. She would go to services in her old church this morning. If Phillip thought she was going to attend any picnic where Loretta Wilford was on the food committee, he was in for a shock.

The nerve of the woman! Saying she didn't understand children . . . it was her grandchild Loretta had pinched. And Phillip! Phillip had put his arm around Loretta and buttered up the old maid. What did an old maid know about children?

Well, let Phillip have his picnic without her. Let Wilma keep track of those two little ones by herself. Phillip would be too busy to help watch the children. Wilma had the girl to help her. Do the girl good to work once in a while. Never saw the girl around when she could be useful.

Phillip knew she detested picnics. Awful paper plates and paper cups. No way a civilized person could eat properly on those flimsy things. Bugs getting in your food. Dust on everything. But what did Phillip care? He hadn't even asked her to come to dinner Sunday as he usually did.

Patting the old biddy's shoulder. Well, it must have felt like patting one of her laying hens. That's the way Loretta's cheek had felt—exactly like squeezing one of the old hens, one that had gone too fat for laying and was ready for the stew pot.

151

She opened her purse and checked the contents of her billfold. No. She'd give the church a check. Make sure they knew she hadn't deserted them. She might be back here attending church if Phillip had to leave the Pleasant Home church. She'd heard some of the women whispering about him being away so much.

For a second she hesitated. Should she apologize to Loretta? Loretta Wilford was on the board of Phillip's church. If Phillip left Pleasant Home, he might leave the state. The man, the one with the gold cuff links—he looked like a city man.

She reached for the pen and wrote out the check in a firm hand. No apologizing. It was Loretta who was wrong. Phillip would sweet-talk Loretta. He always could charm his way around any sort of trouble. She'd done nothing to apologize for, and the Lord knew it. The Lord would keep Phillip in Pleasant Home.

She clawed her keys out of the bottom of her purse and checked her hair in the mirror. She'd go back to Phillip's church next Sunday. When they had real services in the church. But she wasn't going to apologize to Loretta Wilford. Not for Phillip or anyone. Not ever.

Cerise crossed her legs and bowed her head when Daddy Phil started his closing prayer. Church outside was different. Only the old people sat on the benches. Even Mommy was sitting on the grass. Sitting and holding Kathleen.

The smell of hot dogs made Cerise so hungry. She quit listening to Daddy Phil and squinted at an ant crawling up a blade of grass in front of her. The green leaf swayed and drooped until the ant toppled into her lap. She pinched the insect between her fingers and wiped her hand across the back of Matt's shirt.

". . . while we are absent one from the other."

Cerise lifted her head before Daddy Phil reached the Amen. Sunlight gleamed through the trees and surrounded his head. When he raised his arms at the word *Amen*, he looked like one of the pictures in the Sunday School paper. He wasn't Daddy Phil . . . he was an angel. She caught her breath and held it until he smiled. He was Daddy Phil again. Angel pictures never had smiles.

Kathleen emitted an excited squeal. In the act of getting to her feet, Wilma had released her grip. The small girl tottered across the grass and grabbed Phil's leg with a jabbering stream of nonsense syllables.

"Cerise, go get your sister."

Cerise frowned at her mother. The picnic wouldn't be any fun if she had to watch Kathleen.

"Daddy Phil has her," Cerise answered. She grabbed Matt's hand and scrambled to her feet. "I'll watch Matt."

She heard her mother's disgusted groan before she headed for Kathleen, but Cerise didn't care. Mommy knew how hard it was to keep hold of Kathleen. She wiggled all the time and ran away the minute you let go of her. Matt was easy to watch.

"Come on, Matt." She tugged at his hand. "Let's get in line for a hot dog."

The line was already jammed with pushing and jostling kids. Cerise held Matt back and waited. They had to go last. Daddy Phil said it was polite, but it didn't matter. The church ladies always put extra food on her plate at the potluck dinners. They treated her nice because they hoped she would tell Daddy Phil.

"Be sure and tell your Dad we fed you plenty," the lady said. She put an extra pickle on Cerise's plate and tucked another olive on the edge of the potato salad.

"Come back for seconds, now," the piano-playing lady

urged.

Cerise moved her head enough to make the patting hand miss the target. It wavered in the air and brushed lightly against her shoulder. She shoved Matt ahead of her and started toward an empty table.

"Where's Mommy?" Matt asked. He crawled up on the bench across from her and picked a stalk of celery out of his baked beans.

"She's coming," Cerise muttered.

"Look, Kathleen sees us."

Cerise bit her lip and held her hand up to her mouth. Kathleen was running across the grass a few steps ahead of Wilma.

"Sissy!" she shrieked. Her foot caught on a clump of grass, and she tumbled forward. A scream of rage erupted when Wilma caught the back of her dress and swung her up into the air.

Cerise turned her head away. If she pretended not to see Kathleen, maybe Mommy wouldn't notice them at the table.

It didn't work. Mommy put Kathleen on the bench beside Cerise. A hand yanked on one of Cerise's braids.

"Watch her while I get some food," Wilma ordered.

"Do I have to?" She tugged the pigtail out of her sister's hand and pushed the hair back over her shoulder out of Kathleen's reach.

"Yes, you have to," Wilma snapped. "Give her something to chew on until I get back."

Cerise picked a deviled egg out of her plate and handed it to Kathleen. It wasn't a good one anyway. Mommy put red stuff on top of hers.

"Well, Cerise, you do have your hands full, don't you?"

She stared up at the women and wrinkled her nose. Miss Wilford looked different without her animal skins.

154

She smiled down at Cerise and leaned over Kathleen.

"Your poor mother. Trying to keep track of both these little ones by herself. The one day when she could use Clara's help, and Clara doesn't show up."

Cerise nodded and took a big bite from her hot dog. Miss Wilford had plunked down on the bench beside Kathleen. If she was going to sit there, Kathleen could be Miss Wilford's problem.

She peered from under her eyelashes at Miss Wilford's face. Her voice sounded almost happy about Clara Thayer's absence. Maybe Miss Wilford had prayed that *she* wouldn't be there too. Why did Miss Wilford think Mommy needed any help? Mommy didn't need any help. Mommy only had to watch Kathleen. Anyone could watch Matt. All they had to do was pick up his bread crusts. Cerise reached across the table and took his discarded hot-dog bun.

"Oh, my, such a waste." Miss Wilford clucked her tongue against her teeth at the sight of Matt's rejected food.

Cerise shrugged. "I'll feed it to the ducks."

"How sweet." Miss Wilford's voice sounded like a cat purring. Cerise lowered her eyelashes again and peeked at the woman from the side of her eyes.

Kathleen grabbed for a pickle and held it toward Miss Wilford with a giggle.

"She's certainly a cutie."

The voices resounded from behind Cerise, but she kept her attention on the plate in front of her. No reason to turn around. It was only a bunch of the church ladies. They could fuss over Kathleen if they wanted to — as long as they didn't start the head-patting stuff.

"Doesn't she look like a perfect little doll?" another voice babbled from somewhere over her left shoulder.

"How does Mrs. Thayer keep her so clean?"

"All in white, too . . . like a little angel."

"Isn't it nice she's so dark . . . blondes look so washed out in white."

"Look at those big brown eyes."

Cerise scraped up the last of the baked beans and wiped her mouth with the back of her hand. Wilma had reached the table with two plates heaped into food mountains.

"Can I go feed the ducks?" Cerise gathered up the remnants of the hot dog buns and waved them at her mother.

"Can't you wait? I need you to watch Kathleen."

Cerise's groan was lost in the clamor of women's voices behind her.

"Oh, let her go, Wilma. We'll help with the little one."

"Of course we will."

"Be sure you stay near the swimming area."

"Don't go wandering up the lake."

"If you get away from the beach area, it's awfully muddy."

Cerise kept her eyes on her mother and tried not to listen to all the different voices. At last, Wilma nodded her head in agreement.

"Yes, go feed the ducks. But follow the walkway, and don't go off on any of the trails."

Cerise bobbed her head up and down while she crumbled the bread into a paper napkin.

"Be sure you get back for the races."

"Oh, yes, the races. We're going to have the ice cream after the races." Miss Wilford's voice cut through the babbling. "The winners each get an extra ice cream bar."

"Ice cream bars?" Cerise's eyes flew open. "With chocolate on them?"

"With chocolate," were Miss Wilford's reassuring words. She stopped and removed Kathleen's hand from

156

her arm, wiping at a spot of mayonnaise and trying to get a napkin across the tiny hand.

Cerise gulped the last bite of dill pickle and hurried up the walkway. She stopped and retrieved a half-slice of bread from beside the walk and added it to the napkin-wrapped bundle. A paved walk led up the hill and down toward the swimming beach. Beside her a dirt path beckoned. It curved around the edge of the trees and past clumps of sword ferns.

She stood still and looked back at the table. No one was watching. They were all talking at once. She narrowed her eyes into slits and thought: if she was careful she would stay on the path. It was shady and secret. The trees made creaking noises above her head, and the bushes whispered to her.

With one last glance at the cluster of women, Cerise darted around the tree and down the packed dirt trail. The trail branched, one side going toward the swimming area and the other down to the left. The sword ferns towered as high as her shoulders. The firs shut out most of the sunlight, and the picnic sounds faded away.

She turned down the hill. Dried needles ground into the dirt made the going silent as she moved. The path arched around tree trunks and beside rotting logs and stopped at the lake's edge, beside a forest of cattails. The cove was all hers.

Her eyes scanned the rippling surface and spotted the six ducks. The white-feathered birds bobbed up and down on the water. A yellow bill dipped. All but the twitching tail of the bird vanished below the water. The head resurfaced, shaking a bunch of twisted greenery that dangled from its mouth.

Cerise looked down at her feet. The water came right up and lapped at the edge of the path, but the ground was solid. Below the surface of the lake she could see the thick, sticky-looking mud. As long as she stayed on the path, she wouldn't get her shoes dirty.

She began tossing bread out across the water until the ducks started paddling toward her. They started squawking as they neared the cattails, and she stepped back, throwing the bread out as far as she could.

"Sissy!"

Cerise whirled around at the sound. Kathleen . . . Kathleen had followed her. She would scare the ducks away. And even worse, Cerise knew she would have to take Kathleen back to the picnic grounds. She hurled the last crumb of bread into the water and scurried off the path, crouching behind a huge growth of ferns.

"Please, God, make Kathleen go away. Please make her go away."

She squinched her eyes shut and said the words over and over to herself. It had worked with Clara Thayer. She had prayed that *she* wouldn't be at the picnic—and it worked. Maybe God would find a way to make Kathleen disappear.

"Sissy?" Kathleen was beginning to whine.

Cerise peeked through the ferns and watched Kathleen toddle up to the edge of the water and look out toward the ducks.

"Birdie."

She could see Kathleen's back. The little girl stood at the rim of the path. She was clapping her hands together and jabbering at the ducks.

"Time for the races."

The faraway call echoed through the rustling sounds of the trees. Cerise squinched her eyes together again. If Kathleen didn't go away, she'd be late for the races. She might not get any ice cream.

"Please, God, make her go away," she repeated silently. "Birdie."

158

Cerise rose up and saw Kathleen step off the path into the water. Mud bubbled up around the top of Kathleen's shoes.

She darted forward. It took only one movement. One good shove with her hand and Cerise was racing up the trail toward the swimming area. Get away before Kathleen started screaming. Boy, would she scream!

Cerise ran. Ran out onto the walkway and across the picnic grounds to the game area. She knew she could win the race. She could run faster than any of the other kids, and that meant two bars of ice cream — with chocolate on them.

She tucked her braids behind her head and got into line where Daddy Phil was busy handing out ice cream. The ice cream bar she won tasted even better than the first one. She bit through the chocolate and into the vanilla insides. Mommy hadn't been there to see her win the race, but Daddy Phil had given her an extra big hug.

She moved the ice cream around in her mouth. Mommy was running toward the game area. She was running to Daddy Phil and her nose was all red. Mommy's face was streaked with black around her eyes, and she was shaking Daddy Phil's arm. Pulling at him and yanking on his shirt.

"We can't find her, Phil. We can't find her anywhere."

The chocolate melted across Cerise's tongue. She listened to the shrill squeak in her mother's voice. Mommy wouldn't be so glad to find Kathleen when she found out how muddy she was.

"All those women." Mommy's voice was high and squeaky. "I only went for a cup of coffee, Phil. No one even knows which way she went."

Daddy Phil was holding Mommy, but his eyes were searching the picnic grounds.

"Cerise, stay with your mother."

159

She swallowed the last of the ice cream and licked the stick.

"Phil?"

"We'll find her, Wilma." He pushed Wilma's hand into Cerise's and bent to look right into her eyes.

"Your sister Kathleen is lost, Cerise. Now you stay close to your mother. Don't leave her—even for a minute. Understand?"

He had the serious look in his eyes. It meant he wanted a promise. Cerise nodded.

"Take your mother back to the picnic table, Cerise. We're going to spread out and hunt."

Other men moved behind Phil. A long line began to fan out, stretching down the beach and pushing bushes aside.

Cerise chewed on the end of one braid. Daddy Phil said she was to stay with Mommy. She couldn't go back down the trail. Why hadn't Kathleen come back? She was too little to get spanked for being in the mud. She couldn't talk enough to tell. Anyhow, her back was turned. She hadn't seen who'd pushed her in the mud.

Better stay with Mommy. The men would find Kathleen. Nobody would think Kathleen was pretty with all that mud on her. She was probably sitting in the mud and playing. She wouldn't be all white and looking like any angel.

The strength in her mother's hand made her wince. Mommy was clinging so hard it hurt her fingers.

"She was there when you left, wasn't she, Cerise?" Mommy's voice sounded funny. "Wasn't she?"

"Um-hmm." Cerise started down the walk, tugging at her mother to make her move. Mommy didn't even notice the shrubbery and walked into a tree before Cerise could pull her back to the center of the path.

"She was there. All those women. They were supposed

160

to watch her."

Wilma huddled on the bench, holding her arms around her chest and shivering. Cerise listened to the sniffing sounds and felt her mother's arm shaking. Suddenly Wilma's fingers dug into her shoulder.

"Cerise! Do you have any idea where she went?"

Cerise only turned her head and looked into Wilma's eyes. Mommy didn't really think she was going to answer the question, did she? She stared up at Wilma. The fingers dug harder. It felt as if the fingernails were reaching through her skin and poking into her bones.

"Answer me!"

The swiftness of Wilma's open hand caught Cerise by surprise. She jerked backward, and the force of Wilma's slap combined with her own movement sent her hurtling off the bench onto the grass. One hip stung with needles of pain from the hardness of the ground. She rolled up and squinted at Wilma.

Her mother began crying. Cerise had never seen anyone cry so hard. Mommy's shoulders shook. The air whistled when she gulped in big breaths. Her mother's eyes started to swell until Cerise could hardly tell if Wilma was looking at her or not.

She picked herself up off the ground and stood twisting a braid in one hand. Should she leave Mommy and go get Kathleen?

Daddy Phil's hand caught her shoulder before she could make up her mind.

"Help me get your mother to the car, Cerise."

"Kathleen? You found . . ." Wilma's voice stopped and a low moan came out of the back of her throat. Daddy Phil shook his head and he only said one word.

"Wilma . . ."

Cerise looked up and tugged even harder at her braid. Daddy Phil's face was pale. Why was he so upset because

Kathleen got all muddy?

He held Wilma against his chest, leaning forward until his chin was in the curls of her mother's head. Tears ran down his cheeks. Daddy Phil was crying.

"She fell in the lake. Wilma, honey . . ." His voice stopped and he made funny choking sounds. "She got into the mud and couldn't get out."

"She's . . ."

Wilma's mouth was open. Sounds gurgled in the back of her throat. Red blotches began to show on her cheeks. Her lips moved but no words came out.

Cerise felt the bones in her own body go stiff. Someone was holding her around the shoulders.

Mr. Wilkins carried a blanket-wrapped bundle up the path from the lake. He stopped at the edge of the trees and laid it down gently. Mr. Wilkins' head was bent, his shoulders jolting up and down.

A man with a tan uniform directed people away, pointing toward the parking lot with one hand, waving with the other.

Cerise closed her eyes. God must have been listening. She had asked God to take Kathleen away. God must have made Kathleen drown because she asked him to. First God kept Clara Thayer away from the picnic, then he got rid of Kathleen. God had listened to her. She hadn't really meant God to take Kathleen away forever, but it would be nicer without Kathleen. Daddy Phil said God knew best.

Cerise opened her eyes when she heard the wailing siren. The men moved quietly between the whispering groups of people.

She kept hearing the word *tragic* over and over as the ambulance moved away. It moved slowly. This time the siren was quiet.

She squeezed against the back door of the car. Someone's hands steered them into the backseat. She reached out and hugged Matt against her like Daddy Phil was holding Mommy. She wanted to tell Daddy Phil it was God who made Kathleen go away. Maybe he would stop crying. Maybe when Mommy stopped crying she would tell them not to cry anymore. They still had a daughter.

Matt's eyelids drooped and his thumb went into his mouth. He wriggled against the tightness of her arms and asked, "Where's Kathleen?"

A long wail like the moaning of a faraway horn rose from Wilma's mouth. Her lips gaped open, and the sound emerged in one long continuous tone of anguish. The wail wound on and on until Phil's shaking hands caught her shoulders. The wail turned into another burst of sobs.

"God took Kathleen," Cerise half-whispered to Matt.

"You mean to heaven?" His face was twisted in confusion.

"Where else?" She felt the engine start and tightened her grip around Matt.

Cerise could see two lines between Daddy Phil's eyes when he glanced over the seat. His mouth contorted as if something hurt. She felt her own breath catch and stop inside her chest. There were tears in Daddy Phil's eyes. She turned her head away and looked out the car window. Why did Daddy Phil have to cry?

She chewed on the end of her braid. When Mommy and Daddy Phil quit crying, they'd see how nice and quiet it was without Kathleen. Maybe *she* wouldn't come around so much now.

Would Mommy let her have Kathleen's dishes? She bit into her braid again. Better pray about it. God would let her have them.

Trees slid past the window. The car started to move. One by one, staring faces peered through the glass. Miss

163

Wilford's face, puffy and red; Mr. Wilkins, all shaky, with a big red handkerchief held to his nose. The car eased over the bumps and out of the park.

Cerise stared up at the tree branches. They moved back and forth, sending arrows of sunlight down onto the car window.

She'd have to pray again. If she prayed, God would make Daddy Phil love her. Daddy Phil would quit crying for Kathleen, and the church ladies would start calling *her* Daddy Phil's girl.

Her head fell back against the seat. She'd have to be careful what she said when she prayed. What if God made Daddy Phil quit loving Matt and Mommy?

She stared at the curl twisted behind Daddy Phil's ear and thought about the blanket-wrapped bundle. Was Kathleen all muddy inside the blanket? Or did God clean her up after she died?

They'd have a funeral. Her eyes narrowed thoughtfully. Would Daddy Phil preach a sermon? Would they let her and Matt go to the funeral?

She closed her eyes and tried to remember the one funeral she had seen. Would they have a great big coffin for someone as little as Kathleen? Were coffins always so big, or did they make them to fit the person?

She would be at the funeral.

The corners of Cerise's mouth twisted. Wait until the next time *she* came to the house. *She* wouldn't have anyone to bring presents to now. Cerise hoped *she* cried even harder than Mommy.

Clara Thayer slumped into the chair beside the phone. Her body felt as if all the bones had been plucked out and discarded. Nothing seemed to be holding her skin in position. She was melting, dissolving into a lump.

164

The ache in her chest was building to an explosion, but the tears all stopped up behind her eyes. She wanted to cry, but nothing worked.

In the silence of the empty house, she heard a rhythmic rasping. Her own breathing. Desperate, painful gulps of air.

Like the sound of Phillip's voice, gasping out words. "Kathleen's gone. Wandered away . . . no one . . . saw her. Found in the lake."

She closed her eyes and pictured the tiny girl. The small curly-haired bit of laughter. Gone. Her granddaughter. Her only granddaughter. Phillip's image. *Gone.*

The little girl she had never had. If she had been given a daughter, her own daughter, she would have looked exactly like Kathleen.

It was a punishment. God was punishing her for her pride. She should have been at the picnic, should have been there to help watch Kathleen.

Probably all Loretta's fault. The picnic. All Loretta's planning. She should have known lakes were dangerous. They should have had the picnic somewhere else. They could have had it right outside the church.

Clara pushed herself up from the chair and stared around the room. The knitting bag. Move. Do something.

The room was too large. She didn't need such a big house. It was growing dark outside. The room was decidedly gray, but the idea of turning on a light was repugnant. She could knit in the dark.

She sat down on the davenport and groped in the bag for her knitting needles.

The soft pink yarn slid soothingly across the stiffness of her hands. She stared down at the rows of stitching. It was the knitting that broke the dam and let the tears flow out of her eyes. The knitting. The soft pink sweater,

165

the sweater she had started for Kathleen.

As the tears came flowing forth, she slowly unraveled the sweater and cried. She rolled the yarn into a ball and cried for the granddaughter who would never need the sweater.

She wound the thread and cried soundlessly in the empty house. She wound until the darkness kept her from seeing the color of the yarn. She tucked the fraying end under another thread to secure the ball and sat in the darkness. Tears dripped from her chin and saturated the ball of yarn.

It was the high chair, Kathleen's gleaming white, enameled highchair, that started it. Pushed back against the dining room wall, the red bib folded on the tray. The highchair and Cerise. Cerise putting the floppy-eared rabbit into the highchair—as if the rabbit could replace Kathleen. A rabbit in Kathleen's chair!

The scream started then. It started in the dining room and traveled across the living room and into the bedroom. It drew the muscles in her cheeks into taut bands that pulled at the corners of her eyes.

Wilma could hear it, her own scream echoing inside her head, bouncing around her brain and crashing into her eardrums. Even the force of Phil's hands shaking her shoulders, whipping her head back and forth, couldn't stop the sound. It was rising out of the bottom of her lungs, surging up from the sick, sore pit of her stomach.

"Wilma!"

She heard him. Through the sound of her scream, she could hear. Hear the desperation in his voice. The pleading and the frustration as he continued to shake her free from her scream. At last the scream died for lack of air and strength. She sank to the edge of the bed and sucked the sobs into herself, quick, inward sobs that ached when the air expanded her ribs, ached like the knot in her stomach. As if something had been wrenched out of her womb and flushed down the drain.

The pressure of Phil's hands on her shoulders eased. The shaking had stopped with her scream, and his arm slid around her.

It was a human arm, but she felt no warmth. Only the weight. The pressure of him trying to pull her close to him.

Her shoulders tightened and she twisted away.

"Wilma, honey . . ." His voice was hoarse. He dropped his hands and looked at her with his wide dark eyes.

She turned her head. Phil's eyes. Like Kathleen's wide eyes. Could she ever look at him again without being reminded of Kathleen?

The women! Damn those do-gooding women. All their helpful offers and they couldn't watch Kathleen long enough for her to get a cup of coffee.

She fell back onto the bed and burrowed into the softness of the pillow.

"Wilma . . ."

She felt the bed move as he shifted position. The springs jolted, then recoiled when he rose. She lifted her head at the sound of his voice, faint and mumbling. Phil was praying. On his knees, by the bed, face buried in his hands and praying. As if God could help.

How could he pray to a God who let children die?

She rolled herself up and leaned over him.

"What good is that doing, Phil?" She spat the words at him. "What good? It won't bring Kathleen back. Ask God why? *Why?* How could He let her die?"

Phil's head remained in his hands. She couldn't hear any words, but in the dim light she could see his lips

167

moving silently. His hair glistened in a shaft of light as he continued his silent prayer.

She grabbed and caught his hair in one hand, pulling furiously.

"Stop it!" she screamed at him. "It won't do any good."

His head snapped back. Strands of his hair were left in her fingers when he tore himself free. Kathleen's eyes were looking at her again. Accusing eyes.

"How can a God who lets children die help you?"

"Wilma, I'm praying for strength. I don't understand the why any more than you do, but praying helps." He paused. The light in the room was fading. Now she could hardly see his eyes. Only his voice penetrated into her existence.

"Then go to your church to pray. Don't do it around me."

She watched him straighten and stand up. For a few seconds she held her breath, but he didn't leave. Instead she heard him say, "Maybe it would help if we prayed together."

"No! Never again, Phil. I can't."

She pushed the words out painfully. She was too exhausted to talk. Instead she leaned back against the pillow, staring up at the blackness where the ceiling should be. Her jaw hurt from the tenseness. Her body hurt. Even her skin felt stretched and ready to split—like an overripe melon. All of her insides would splatter on the bedspread.

Phil was only a shadow above her. A silent, unmoving shadow. She closed her eyes and heard Matt crying, a cry that was too far away to be important.

It was the motion of the bed that brought her back into the room. The absolute darkness and the stillness meant she must have been asleep. But a sleep hadn't eased any of the aches.

Phil stirred beside her and rolled in her direction. She felt the softness of his curls brush her cheek, the warmth of his breath on her neck. His nearness only made the ache in her chest increase.

"Wilma?"

He must know she was awake. She felt his hand slide across her waist and under her breast. Felt the warmness of his flesh against hers, but nothing else. It was only physical knowledge. The ache inside her chest continued to be more important.

The gentleness of his kiss on her forehead was easy to ignore. It was only a touch of dampness—not a kiss. Nothing inside of her responded.

"Wilma, we need to talk."

She lay without moving. Let him talk.

"Wilma, Matt was crying."

"I heard him."

"He was crying because he was afraid God was going to take him too."

Matt too? The thought made her muscles stiffen. She felt her nails digging into the palms of her hands, but she remained silent. She wouldn't talk about it. He couldn't make her talk about it. Talking only made the pain worse.

Phil's hand moved gently across her skin as his voice continued. "Matt thought you didn't kiss him good night because God was coming after him."

The pressure swelled inside her chest. This time she was certain. Her ribs were going to split apart. She would bleed to death all over the sheets. Poor little Matt . . . he never asked for attention like the girls.

"I told Matt you'd give him an extra kiss in the morning."

He was quiet again. His hand slid in caressing circles

across her skin until she reached down and pushed it away.

"Is Matt asleep?"

"Yes."

She could hear Phil's steady breathing in the darkness, could feel the tenseness of his body. He was waiting, waiting for her to make some motion, some indication of affection. She wanted to roll over and bury her face against his shoulder, but she didn't want to hear any more about God's will. No more prayers. What good would prayers do Kathleen?

"Wilma," Phil's voice broke the silence. "We have two other children, and they need you."

He was trying to make her feel guilty. She took a deep breath and discovered it eased the pain in her ribs. She held it and released it slowly, repeating it over and over until she alleviated the soreness enough to turn on her side and put her head on Phil's chest.

His arm moved and wrapped around her shoulders. She choked out the words. "I have two children, Phil. You only have one left."

"Shh." His arm stiffened. "Cerise doesn't think that way." The muscles flexed as he tightened his embrace. "She looked up at me and said, 'You still have me, Daddy Phil.' " His voice sounded congested, as if he was struggling for breath.

She felt the dampness seeping out from under her lashes. "Cerise is such an odd child, Phil." Part of the ache seemed to ebb away when she finally managed to say the words. "She never cried about Kathleen at all. Never even acted upset. I can't understand her."

"Cerise never cries about anything."

His hand began stroking her arm, and she relaxed against him.

"She's not normal, Phil."

170

"Honey, Cerise will be all right. She simply accepted God's control over his creatures. In her mind, there isn't any fear of death."

Wilma shuddered in the darkness. "She's not a warm, loving child. She looks at me sometimes as if I'm dumb and she's right. I am dumb."

"Now, honey, you're upset. What you need is some sleep."

"I need to learn. I wanted to learn for Kathleen."

He pulled her tightly against him. "You know enough to take care of the house and me. It's sufficient."

She tensed against his arm. Why did he have to use words like sufficient? He didn't care. Phil didn't understand how hopelessly lost she felt every time Cerise said, "Oh, never mind," and wandered off to question him.

His breathing became deeper. His arm grew heavy across her shoulders. The limpness of his sleep added to the weight. Now it was trapping her instead of comforting her.

She turned and rolled over to her side of the bed without reaction from Phil. His hand fell to the sheet. A gentle snore mingled with the sounds of his breathing.

Wilma stared into the blackness and felt the warm tears dripping from her cheeks. This time she cried without sound.

Chapter Five

Wilma yanked the straight pin out of the hem and bit her lower lip. The wispy chiffon had to be adjusted again. She had lost her touch at handling materials. It had been so long. She hadn't done any sewing since Kathleen . . . well, since Kathleen.

She pushed the thought back into the recesses of her mind. Don't think about Kathleen. Think about Cerise's costume. Thinking about Kathleen often made tears well up in her eyes, and she knew Cerise would ask questions.

Questions she wasn't going to answer. She was sick of Cerise's eye-rolling, disgusted expressions. Sick of her "God took her" comments. God didn't take Kathleen. The church women killed her. Church people! She was sick of them too. Sick of Cerise and Phil both, with their "God's will" explanations. They might think she was dumb, but she wasn't dumb enough to believe God took Kathleen.

The pin twisted, piercing her finger with a sharp thrust of pain that made her jerk and emit a loud "Ow!" She jammed her finger into her mouth to keep the blood from staining Cerise's costume. An angel had to be immaculate.

"Stand still, Cerise," Wilma snapped.

"I am, but you're taking so long."

"This material isn't easy to work with," Wilma grumbled.

"But the program is Friday night. It's only two days away."

"I'll have it done by then. Now turn."

Wilma sat back on her heels and eyed the hemline while Cerise turned slowly in a circle.

"Is it okay this time?"

Wilma sucked on her throbbing finger and nodded. "It looks a little odd with sneakers, but it'll be okay with your white sandals."

Cerise revolved, this time in a quick spin that sent the fabric swirling around her ankles.

"Don't do that!" Wilma spat out the words in sharp annoyance. "You'll make the pins fall out."

"Miss Ryan said I should wear makeup for the program."

Cerise had caught a glimpse of herself in the mirror and was tilting her head from side to side. Her shoulders wiggled, and she raised her arms to let the full sleeves fall into a winglike cascade of white chiffon.

"You're only ten, Cerise. That's far too young to wear makeup."

"She said I'm too fair. No one can tell if I have eyes or a mouth if she doesn't put makeup on me."

Cerise dropped her arms and twirled one long blond pigtail around the end of her finger.

"She picked me for the angel because of my hair, Mother. We're going to take the braids out and let it hang. She says it will look more like an angel." She stopped abruptly and turned her head to look down at Wilma. "I'm not ten, Mother. I'm ten and a half."

"I know how old you are." Wilma leaned back and looked up at her daughter. The snug fit of the bodice over the emerging breasts predicted a rapid end to Cerise's childhood. Wilma looked at Cerise's half-closed eyes as the girl preened before the mirror. Was Cerise ever a real little girl? Wilma had never been able to cuddle Cerise like she had Kathleen. She chewed her lip at the thought and stared at Cerise's eyes.

They were greener than ever—like chunks of malachite. The expression was so cold—as if the girl was weighing and judging her own appearance with some plan in mind. They weren't the eyes of a ten-year-old child.

"Mommy, can we try the makeup?"

Cerise tilted her chin and tossed her braids back over her shoulders. "I mean, can we see what I'll look like? You have lots of makeup."

Wilma's breath made a slight rushing sound as it escaped. Why was she worrying about Cerise? Wanting to try on makeup was natural for a ten-year-old.

"Please, Mother?"

Wilma uncoiled her legs and rose. "All right, but I'll put it on you, and you'll have to wash your face after you see what it looks like."

Cerise trailed behind her into the bedroom. She made wide sweeping circles with her arms to send the chiffon swirling and drifting about her.

"Are you going to come to the program, Mother?"

Wilma reached for the eyebrow pencil and frowned before answering. She hadn't been in the church since the picnic. She hadn't wanted to see any of the women. After the first few weeks of bringing cakes and peace offerings to the house, the women had left her alone. Now when they wanted to see Phil, they went to the back door, directly to his office.

Cerise was watching her hesitation. Wilma rolled the eyebrow pencil back and forth between her fingers. She felt the insistence in Cerise's voice.

"Please, Mother. I've never been picked for anything

before."

"Yes, Cerise. I'll be at the program." She nodded with a tired smile and reached for Cerise's chin. "Now hold still while I see what I can do."

She stroked the pencil lightly across the colorless brows, then reached for the mascara and brushed the tips of Cerise's pale lashes into dark fringes. The transformation made Wilma catch her breath. Colorless Cerise would be stunning when she was old enough to use makeup.

The thought made Wilma hesitate. Was this a mistake? Cerise was too intelligent. One look in the mirror and it was going to be a fight to keep the girl out of her makeup. Cerise would badger her every day—or beg Phil. There was too much begging to Phil lately and too many times when it worked.

"Cerise, you understand this is only for the program, don't you?"

The gemstone eyes looked back at her, cool and glistening from under the newly defined lashes. Wilma straightened her shoulders and tried to reach every bit of her own height. Only ten and a half and Cerise was almost looking her directly in the eye. The gap between them was narrowing fast.

Cerise swung her head toward the mirror and a smile flitted around the corners of her mouth.

"Mother, I'm beautiful." She leaned forward and eyed herself intently in the mirror. "I have a face like other people. Eyebrows. I have eyebrows!" She fluttered her eyelashes up and down at her own reflection. "Billy Carter can't say I look like a lizard anymore."

"I don't want to hear about Billy Carter," Wilma said. "Ever since the Carters moved in, you've paid too much attention to what Billy Carter says. He's thirteen, and thirteen-year-old boys say dumb things. Especially to

176

little — I mean younger — girls."

She reached out and touched Cerise's shoulder, only to withdraw her hand quickly when she felt the sudden tensing of the muscles in Cerise's back.

"He's right," Cerise answered. "Lizards don't have eyelashes. I do look like a lizard."

"You're a nice-looking girl. When you're old enough, you can wear makeup. By then you won't care what Billy Carter says."

"More of your mother talk. Who says I care now? I just want to show him how stupid he is."

She wiggled her eyebrows at her own image and lowered her eyelashes again. For a brief second, the glance was cold and speculating. Then the lashes lifted and the eyes sparkled with excitement.

"Remember, it's only for the program," Wilma repeated.

Cerise gave no indication she was listening. She only leaned forward and reexamined her reflection in the dresser mirror.

"Let's go show Daddy Phil." She turned with her chiffon sleeves flowing and grabbed Wilma's wrist.

"He's in his office," Wilma protested. "He might not want to be bothered if he's busy."

Cerise tugged harder. The strength of the girl's hands amazed Wilma. There was no escaping that grip. The fingers felt as if they were pressing through Wilma's flesh and mashing the veins against her bones.

"He's not busy, Mother. Matt's with him. He never lets Matt stay in the office when he's busy."

They were moving across the living room. Wilma felt snatched up by a whirling wind as Cerise swept ahead, through the dining room and the hall, swirling clouds of white chiffon. Cerise's grasp was relentless.

"Look, Daddy Phil, look!" Cerise started bubbling as

177

soon as her hand swung the door open. "Look at my angel costume and my eyebrows." She dropped Wilma's hand and darted to Phil's side. She stood over his chair and leaned forward to put her face close to his. Her eyelashes flickered for attention.

"I'm going to be the angel in the Christmas program, and I'm going to have eyebrows like you do."

Wilma rubbed at her wrist and caught her breath. The look in Cerise's eyes. It was more than excitement. She was . . . Wilma shivered and hated herself for the thought. It was a stupid idea. Cerise was too young. She couldn't know how much it looked as if she was flirting. Anyhow, Phil was — well, almost her father. She couldn't be flirting with him.

She put her hand up and rubbed at her throat while she watched. Matt took one glance at Cerise, shrugged, and turned back to drawing pictures on the back of a discarded calendar. None of Cerise's enthusiasm touched his world.

Phil, however, was different. Wilma saw him raise his head and watched him inhale a long, slow, soundless whistle. Cerise straightened, put her hands on her waist, and drew her shoulders back. The forming breasts bulged at the soft fabric of the tight bodice, showing the erect nipples through the cloth.

Cerise is doing it deliberately, Wilma thought. Better take a few darts out of the dress and let the material hang loose. She would have to fix that problem before the program.

"The makeup is only for the stage effect, Phil." Wilma heard herself speaking and wondered, why was she explaining it to Phil? He hadn't objected.

Phil continued to stare at Cerise with a furrow between his eyes. The corners of his mouth softened. Cerise raised her arms, letting the sleeves of the costume unfold

178

ever so dramatically while she poised and closed her eyes. The chiffon clung and pushed against her small breasts.

A gentle smile crossed Phil's face. His eyes were intent, following Cerise's every move. Wilma saw his eyes begin to shine, and his smile spread into a grin.

"Phil . . ." Wilma stopped. Phil wasn't even aware she was in the room. He was staring at Cerise as if she were a genuine angel. It was the look he directed toward the ceiling during one of his evangelical meetings, a worshiping intenseness that made women get up out of their seats and flock to the altar. A shiver ran down the length of her spine. She felt out of place, as if she didn't belong in the room.

"Cerise!" Her voice sounded scratchy, and she drew a deep breath before starting again, this time speaking slowly. "Cerise, you'll have to take the costume off so I can finish hemming it."

The words had the right effect. The eerie tenseness in the air broke, and Phil's expression returned to normal.

"Your mother's right. Can't have you getting your angel costume dirty before the program."

Wilma gave a small sigh. The smile on Phil's face was now only a fatherly smile.

"Take it off carefully so you don't lose any pins, and put the dress on my bed," she said. "I'll start hemming it this afternoon."

Cerise twirled her arms once more and turned to Phil. "Mother's coming to the program."

Phil lifted his head, and Wilma met the question in his eyes with a nod.

"I'm glad." Phil's voice was as tender as the expression in his eyes. She smiled gratefully at him for not making an issue of her nonattendance at church and was rewarded with an answering smile. She dropped her face away from his glance and wondered why she no longer

179

felt any warmth inside her toward Phil. She ran her tongue across her lips, feeling the tense dryness creep into her mouth, but Phil's attention had swung back to Cerise.

"Even your Grandmother Thayer is planning on coming to see you be an angel."

"*She's* coming?" Cerise's voice held a sharp edge. Wilma looked up quickly, but the girl's face was a stoic mask.

Phil nodded. "And to see you."

Cerise shrugged. "She won't like it."

Phil's laugh was explosively loud in the small office. Matt stopped his drawing and scratched at his head before turning back to the paper.

"Probably not," Phil admitted, "but she is coming to see you, and that's a step in the right direction."

Cerise flipped her braids back and forth. "Can we take the pigtails out and see what I look like?" She turned with a bland sweetness in her expression.

"No," Wilma answered. "If you want the costume finished by Friday, you have to get it off so I can start hemming it. It's miles around the skirt."

Cerise pushed her lower lip out and scowled.

"And after you take the dress off, wash your face," Wilma added.

Cerise dropped her mouth open and looked at Wilma with the wide, mascara-defined eyes. She swiveled toward Phil and put her hands together under her chin. "Please, Daddy Phil, can't I keep my eyebrows? At least until I can show Billy that I don't look like a lizard. Please?"

"Cerise!"

"Oh, Wilma, let her," Phil laughed. "It's not really obvious. You managed to make it look natural."

"Ooh, thank you, Daddy Phil." Cerise bubbled and bounced forward, clinging to Phil and rubbing her cheek against his. When she broke free and darted past Wilma, there was a quick flash of the green glistening in her eyes. She gathered up the wide skirt of the gown in both hands and went sweeping out of the room.

Wilma watched her disappear and frowned when she turned toward Phil. "I don't think you should encourage her. She's too young to wear makeup."

Phil leaned back in his chair and fingered a pencil thoughtfully.

"I suppose," he answered, "but a lot of girls her age are far worse. You have to admit Cerise feels self-conscious about not having eyebrows."

"But she's not even eleven." Wilma shook her head. She was feeling an unreasonable sense of things going wrong. Cerise had maneuvered around her, gotten Phil's approval without even a discussion.

"I'm not saying Cerise should start wearing lipstick and a lot of the other stuff," Phil murmured, "but what's so wrong about letting her feel human and having eyebrows?"

He let the pencil fall to the desk top and looked up at her. His eyes, wide and brown — Wilma turned away. The memories of Kathleen began to surge into her mind. Damn Phil's eyes. She still couldn't look at him when he was appealing to her — not without thinking of Kathleen. Wouldn't it ever go away?

"Wilma, can't you see? It isn't makeup for Cerise. It's the chance to look like other people."

"I never knew it bothered her," Wilma choked. "I thought it was only the Carter boy's teasing."

"It could be he's not the only one who teases her."

"Maybe," Wilma replied in a dull voice. "But she pays too much attention to the things Billy says." She turned back toward him. "Phil, she's growing up too fast. I'm scared she'll be like me. She's too mature for her age."

181

"You're worrying too much, Wilma. After all, Cerise has been raised in the church. You weren't."

"What does that have to do with it? You sound as if churchgoing cures a need for sex." She snorted as she took in a deep breath. "It never slowed you down any."

Phil leaned forward and put both elbows on the desk. For a long time he sat rubbing both hands across his curls and staring at the papers on the desk before him. The only sound in the room was the paper crackling under the pressure of Matt's crayons.

Wilma leaned against the wall and waited, wondering if he was going to find some magical prayer to make everything all right. As if prayer was going to stop the glint in Cerise's eyes.

"You're right, Wilma." Phil raised his head and gazed at the wall above her. He nodded and straightened in his chair. "Have you talked to her about it? Sex, I mean."

Wilma shook her head. "Every time I try to talk to Cerise, she acts as if I don't know anything. She only says she'll ask Daddy Phil."

Phil leaned on one hand and sighed. "I guess she's my gosling. It's up to me to talk to her."

"I wish you would. She's hanging around the Carter boy too much."

"He's not the problem, Wilma. I'm sure he thinks she's a pest." He chuckled quietly. "All the time my mother had hopes for Ginny, I was convinced she was a first-class annoyance. Girls next door are usually pests."

"What about a year from now? He won't think she's a pest, and we'll be grandparents." She slumped, feeling suddenly tired, and reached for a straight-backed chair to sag into. "Oh, I know I'm overreacting, but I'm scared. I know how girls get flattered whenever an older boy looks at them. Especially the first boy."

"Let me show you something." He spread the papers

across his desk. "I want you to look at these and then you'll see why we won't have to worry about Billy Carter a year from now."

She got up and walked to the edge of the desk. He spread the huge sheets of paper out flat across the surface.

"What are they?"

"Plans. Plans I've had for a long time and didn't want to talk about until there was a possibility of them coming true. It's a dream of mine. To have a gospel center, a chapel, an auditorium. Even a school. Now it looks as if it's really going to happen."

She stared at the drawings but they were only lines that meant nothing to her, lines drawn on paper. "What does it have to do with Cerise?"

"We'll be moving. After the first of the year."

"Moving?" She felt her mouth fall open and knew she was gaping like an idiot, but the words weren't making any sense. Moving? Where?

"We've saved enough to buy a house near Eugene. A home of our own."

"Eugene?"

"Wilma, you sound like a parrot. Eugene, Oregon. It's in the center of the state." He waved one hand as if to dismiss the explanation. "Ted's found a backer who's willing to help us, a retired lumberman who heard me speak in Roseburg."

She started to repeat the word *backer* and snapped her mouth shut before it came out. After a minute she said, "I don't understand any of this, Phil."

He gave a slow breath outward and tapped the drawings with his index finger. "We're going to move to Eugene. This man owns a lot of property in the area, including an old unused dance hall. We're going to start by holding regular gospel meetings in the building. Then the backer will match every dollar we take in, and the Thayer Gospel Center will be built. He's even promised to donate the land."

She shook her head again. "But what does this have to do with Cerise?"

"We'll be away from here, Wilma. We'll be away from Pleasant Home and Eddie Carter and all the bad memories this house has for you."

She walked back to the chair, sank onto the solidness of the wood, and tried to absorb the words he had been pouring at her.

"There'll be other boys, Phil. There will be boys in Eugene, too. It doesn't solve the problem."

"But I'll be home more. I won't be traveling all over the state. I can have more time to talk to Cerise and watch her." He stopped and leaned back in his chair, rubbing his hands together.

"That angel costume, Wilma, think how great Cerise would look opening the meetings in that costume. Lighting the candles while the organ plays. Just having her up there on the stage . . ." His face began to glow with enthusiasm. "What a theatrical touch—and I'd be able to keep track of her every night."

"Phil, she has to go to school. You can't keep her up every night, not at her age." She shook her head again. "I don't like her getting so much attention so young. She's too headstrong now."

He gave a short laugh. "Oh, don't worry. I'm getting carried away with my own dreams again." Then he grinned and added with a mischievous gleam in his eye, "Well, how about Friday nights?"

She rose, feeling drained and lifeless. "I still want you to talk to Cerise."

"All right, honey, I will. But the plans are to be out of here by March first. I think we can keep the Carter situation under control until then."

"So soon?" She looked at him, bewildered by the impact of the sudden changes he was proposing. "Phil, how long have you been thinking about this move? This gospel center idea?"

He looked up at her with a fiery intensity in his eyes. His finger was gently stroking the inked outlines on the paper in front of him, up the roofline and across the outline of the cross.

"Since I started high school, I suppose. The whole concept, I mean. But the Eugene plans—well, Ted's been trying to find a site and a backer for months."

His eyes drifted to the window, and his voice was subdued, almost as if he were talking to himself.

"If Ted can find a few more backers, we'll start building before another year is out. The chapel first, then the auditorium."

He smiled and turned back to the papers on the desk, smoothing them out with the palm of his hand. He started rolling the papers with a carefulness she had never seen before, lovingly, as if the papers were sacred to him.

"Phil." She waited until he glanced up at her before continuing. "It sounds good. I think I'll like Eugene."

His hands continued to work the papers into a tight roll. He slipped a rubber band over the end, working it meticulously toward the center of the roll.

"You'll love the city. The Blaylocks—he's the backer I mentioned—are anxious to meet the whole family. The house we're buying is close to the gospel center site and the community college. When Cerise is old enough, she won't even have to go away to school."

"Community college?" Wilma's eyes flew open. "They have adult courses, don't they? I mean, anyone can go there, can't they?"

185

"I suppose, but why is it important?"

"I want to take some courses. I could take those classes that help you get a high school diploma." She felt a sudden eagerness and started planning things in her mind. Typing courses . . . business courses . . . she could learn to do things. Pack . . . they would have to pack everything. She could get rid of some of the old furniture. It meant they could leave the church-donated stuff behind. The frayed and lumpy davenport would be gone.

"When are we going to move?" The words came tumbling out. "How close are we going to be to the college? I want to get started as soon as we move."

Phil dropped the papers into the center drawer of his desk and shoved it close with a violent slam.

"Wilma, there's no reason for you to take any classes. You know everything you need to for running the house."

"Oh, Phil, it's not to run the house." She straightened her shoulders and took a deep breath. "It's for me. So I don't feel so dumb around other women."

"There's no reason you should feel dumb. It's all in your mind."

"I even feel dumb around Cerise." She bit at her thumbnail, wondering how to make Phil understand. She couldn't find the right words to explain how she felt — the uncertainty every time she opened her mouth.

"Your mother, Phil, she's smart. She knows when I use the wrong words. Sometimes she gets a look on her face as if I had pinched her. Phil, don't you see? I don't want to be such a dummy. I want . . ."

"Wilma, stop it! You're babbling." His hand struck the top of the desk, startling Matt into dropping his crayon and looking up from his sketching.

"My mother may be educated, Wilma, but she doesn't know half as much about being a woman as you do." He swung himself out of the chair and hit the desk top again. He leaned forward and glared fiercely into her eyes.

"All my life I've heard her brag about how educated she was. How she had been a schoolteacher." His voice dragged out the word *teacher* with a venomous twist of his mouth. "She kept saying she was so much better than the other farm wives—and do you know what a lousy wife she was?

"My father died while he was out with another woman. So don't tell me how education is going to improve you. You're all woman, and I like you the way you are. You know everything I want you to know."

He braced himself against the desk. His breathing became heavy and rasping. The cramped space of the office made it sound even louder.

Wilma felt as if someone had been removing her spine bone by bone. Any minute now she would sink to the floor like a jellyfish. The words stuck in her tonsils. Her mouth opened and closed soundlessly until the tears came to the surface of her eyes and began to swim over the edge and run down her cheeks.

"Don't do that, Daddy!" Matt stood with his feet braced. He clenched his small fists and glared up at Phil. "Don't make Mommy cry."

Phil's chin sank. He dropped back into his desk chair and held his head in both hands.

"I'm sorry." He didn't meet her eyes but kept repeating, "I'm sorry, honey," over and over.

She glanced down at the floor and sniffled, trying to stop the deluge of tears.

Phil's voice broke the silence. "We'll talk about it later. I have to have time to think." His head came up, and he looked into her wide brown eyes. "Okay?"

She nodded, knowing her vocal cords wouldn't work

and felt Matt's small sturdy arms clutch her legs.

"Here, Mommy, you can have my picture." He held up the flopping sheet of paper and waited for her to take it.

The tears were still trickling down her cheeks, but she forced the edges of her mouth upward and reached for Matt's offered gift.

"That's Daddy in the church." Matt poked one finger at the largest of the figures in the drawing. "And that's you—and that's Sister in her angel dress."

"It's nice, Matt." She rubbed at the tears with the back of her hand. "But where are you?"

"There." Matt poked his chubby finger at a green colored blob in the lower corner of the drawing.

"You? Why are you green?"

"Cause I'm a frog."

"A frog?"

"Uh-huhh. Cerise got mad at me and turned me into a frog."

In spite of the tears, Wilma felt a giggle erupt in her throat, and she shook her head. "Matt, you've been listening to too many fairy tales."

She bent and kissed him on the forehead, brushing a lock of her hair back and stroking it into place.

"I like it, and I love you for giving it to me," she said softly.

Matt threw his arms around her neck with a fierce hug. "Will you love me if Cerise turns me into a frog?"

Wilma couldn't hold the laugh back. "Yes, I will, but don't worry. Cerise can't turn you into a frog, and if she could, I wouldn't let her do it."

Matt squeezed her about the neck and darted back to his papers. He settled back on the floor with a thud, picked up his crayon, and gave Phil a long, silent appraisal before returning to his drawing.

Phil slumped in his chair, and his eyes turned to meet

Wilma's, silently appealing to her.

She folded Matt's drawing between her fingers before she turned away and started out of the room. She had to hem the dress. Think about the dress. Give Phil time to change his mind.

And if he didn't change his mind?

One way or another she was going to learn. Phil wasn't going to stop her. He couldn't stop her. Even if she had to sneak off during the day and take the courses, she was going to learn.

She walked into the bedroom, stared down at the yards of chiffon spread across the deep royal blue spread, and lifted her chin.

Okay, if he wanted an angel to light the candles, he'd get his angel. But if Phil thought a few more prayers were going to be the answer to Cerise, he was dumber than she was. The girl had been deliberately trying to attract his attention — and not as a daughter.

She picked up the fabric and tossed it back on the bed. Better dry the tears first. It wouldn't do to have tears on an angel costume. She dabbed at her eyes, wiped at her nose, and flopped down on the edge of the bed.

An angel lighting the candles? It was hardly going to be enough to keep Cerise in line, no matter what Phil thought. Wilma reached for the needle and thread and looked down at the white chiffon. He'd be lucky if his precious angel didn't burn down the church while she was flirting with some boy.

The chiffon slithered to the floor. Cerise stepped carefully over the filmy material and lifted the costume gingerly. It didn't look as if she'd lost a single pin. Her hands stroked the fabric and smoothed the dress out across her mother's bed, then she wriggled her shoulders in one last moment of delight before reaching for her T-shirt and jeans.

It was going to be the greatest Christmas ever. An angel! No one had ever picked her for anything before. Now she was going to be the angel in the Christmas play. It was the best part, even better than Mary. The girl who played Mary had to keep her head down all the time, and her face was all covered with a crummy hood. The angel was the best. Everyone could see the angel.

She pulled the T-shirt down and cinched it into her jeans, frowned, and pulled it a little tighter. With a scowl, she looked down at the front of her T-shirt. Why were her breasts taking so long to get bigger? Were they ever going to look like Mother's?

One quick tug pulled the top loose, and she looked at herself in the mirror. Would they look bigger if she left it loose? She turned sideways. It didn't fit tight enough. Eddie Carter wouldn't notice anything if she let it hang. She jammed the shirt back in as tightly as she could.

She hesitated, fingering her mother's tube of lipstick, and dropped it. Better not. Daddy Phil was going to let her keep the eyebrow pencil. If he caught her with lipstick, he might change his mind.

As she crossed the street she remembered a story she had read in a library book. She started biting at her lips. In the story the lady had made her lips look redder by rubbing her teeth against them. Cerise took one last hard bite before she slipped into the Carters' side door.

"Well, Cerise, you're looking pretty today." Eddie's mother stood at the sink, sloshing plates through a panful of suds. Her glance had been only a quick one, and Cerise knew she hadn't paid any more attention than usual. She always said exactly the same words.

"If you're looking for Eddie, he's in the basement

wrapping his dad's Christmas present."

Cerise stared coldly at the woman's back and said, "Thank you, Mrs. Carter," with an emphasis on the words *Mrs. Carter.* It always helped her get away from Daddy Phil's church ladies. If you acted real polite, they didn't try to make you stand around and listen to them. Mrs. Carter didn't go to Daddy Phil's church, but she was exactly like the church ladies—ready to ignore her as soon as they heard a polite response.

She walked down the basement steps, sauntering as if it wasn't really important. She hooked her thumbs into the back pockets of her jeans and even managed to yawn when she walked into the Carters' family room. With an effort, she kept her voice bored and toneless as she said, "Hi."

Eddie wadded up a newspaper, crammed it into a huge cardboard box, grabbed another newspaper, and began crumpling it into a ball. His rumpled red hair stood up wildly in all directions from his head as he continued to pad the carton without turning his head to acknowledge her presence.

Cerise ambled toward the pool table and leaned against it, still keeping her hands tucked behind her and straightening her shoulders.

"What are you doing?"

"I'm wrapping a present, dummy," he said without looking up. "Don't be so stupid."

"How can I tell?" she droned. "Looks more like you're making a mess out of a lot of paper."

She waited, but he went on filling the inside of the box without paying any attention to her.

"Must be a big present."

"Nope."

"Then why is the box so big?"

"Because he'd know what it is if I put it in a small

box." This time Eddie turned and glared at her, but it was only a disgusted sneer. There was no sign that he noticed anything different about her.

"Well, what is it?" she insisted.

"A Manlicher."

"A what?" She wrinkled up her nose at the strange word.

"A deer rifle, dummy." He straightened, stomped toward the pool table, and snatched up a gun. His hands patted the wood as he held it, turning it back and forth to the light. "See? Isn't it a beauty?"

Cerise shrugged her shoulders. "It's only a gun. Guns aren't pretty."

"It's not *just* a gun, lizard. It's the best deer rifle there is. Dad's wanted one for years, and Mom and I finally managed to save enough to get it for him." He whistled between his teeth, then he held the rifle up to his shoulder and aimed at a Playboy calendar on the far wall. "Wait'll he sees this baby. Boy, is he going to swallow his back teeth. Some jerk swiped his old one."

He squinted at a wall light, pretended to take aim, and squeezed the trigger. "Pow!"

Cerise sniffed. "You're not supposed to do that. It might go off."

"Dummy, it's not loaded." He lowered the gun tenderly and laid it back on the table. "It doesn't even have the clip in it. I'm not stupid."

"What's a clip?"

Eddie snorted. "You don't know nothing, do you? It's this part." He reached for a sack and dumped the contents on the top of the pool table. "This clip. It has to be in the gun or the gun won't shoot." He held up a small metal piece in front of her face.

"That little thing is a clip? It doesn't look important." She leaned forward and peered at the piece in Eddie's hand, then lifted her head to look up at him, lowering her eyelashes seductively when she met his gaze.

"Yeh, it works like this." Eddie grabbed at a box of shells and shook a bunch of them out onto the green felt tabletop. With a quick movement, he placed three shells inside the clip.

"See? First you put the shells in the clip, then you put the clip right here in the gun and it's ready to shoot."

He pulled the shells out of the magazine and dropped both shells and clip on the tabletop.

Cerise continued to frown. "How do the shells get into the gun?"

Eddie sighed and pulled the bolt back on the gun. "You really are stupid. Here. You slide the bolt back. It pops a shell from the clip up into here. When you shoot, you pull the bolt back and it pops out the casing."

She looked into the inner workings of the gun as Billy placed it in front of her face and pointed to the parts.

"Right here—when the bullet gets into this space, it's ready to shoot." He put the gun back down on the pool table and emitted another disgusted grunt.

"What a dummy!" He grunted and mumbled, "I gotta get some more newspaper. Don't monkey with nothing, lizard. Put the shells back in the box while I'm gone—and the clip, too."

"Why don't you put it in the gun?"

"You want me to get my ass chewed out? My Dad don't never let anyone leave a clip in a rifle. He'd rake me over the coals but good. Put it in with the shells. That's the way he wants things."

Cerise tossed the small piece of metal from hand to hand while he scrounged through the bookshelves looking for more newspapers. He hadn't even looked at her if he could still call her "lizard." She should have put on some lipstick, too . . . even if she had to wipe it off

193

before she went home.

"Eddie, hurry up with your wrapping," Mrs. Carter's voice echoed down from upstairs. "Your dad's driving in."

"Oh, jeeze!" He snatched up a stack of magazines and began ripping the pages in a furious pace. "Hey, lizard, help me. I gotta get this in the box."

Her eyes narrowed thoughtfully, and she reached for the rifle. She picked up a shell from the open box. With one quick push, she fit it into the gun. Eddie was right. A shell would fit into the space. She pushed the bolt back into position and lifted the gun from the table. Her face twisted. It was much heavier than it looked. It made her arms ache to hold it. She panted and raised it over the edge of the box, letting it slip down into the bed of newspaper.

"Grab the bag with the shells and clip. Hurry!" Eddie was tearing out pages faster and faster. "He always comes downstairs to get a beer when he gets home. I gotta have it all covered up."

His hands worked feverishly, wadding the papers into huge balls, whirling them into the box. Cerise dropped the bag into the mound of paper and went back to leaning on the pool table.

"You coming to the program at the church?" she asked.

Eddie never looked up from his work. "Nope."

"I'm going to be an angel in the program." She waited, hoping he would at least turn his head and look at her.

"So who cares?" Eddie muttered. "We open our presents Christmas Eve. Who'd want to go to a dumb program and miss opening their presents?"

"You could open them Christmas day, like we do." She scuffed at the carpet with the toe of her shoe. For a minute she considered punching Eddie in the back. Then

194

maybe he'd look at her, but she heard the door slam. Billy grabbed the last of the papers, shoving them all inside the box. He snatched up a huge roll of masking tape and started frantically taping the top of the box shut.

"Get outta my way," he ordered. He shoved her aside with one hand and circled the huge box.

Cerise doubled up one fist, but the sound of Mr. Carter's footsteps on the stairway made her drop her hand to her side. She didn't like Eddie's dad. Mr. Carter always smelled sweaty and belched too much.

"I have to go." She started to the stairs and stepped aside. Mr. Carter reached the bottom of the steps and walked past her with only a brief nod.

All the way up the stairs and across the yard, she kept wishing she had at least given Eddie one good punch. But it would be all right. Mr. Carter would chew him out. Wait till he opened the package and found the shell in the gun. Boy, Eddie would wish he'd paid more attention to her.

She pushed the front door open and leaned against it to close it. For a minute, she pushed her back hard against the wood and shut her eyes.

"Please, God, make Eddie sorry he called me a lizard."

"Cerise?"

The sound of her mother's voice made Cerise's eyes fly open, and she paused, tense and waiting.

"Is that you, Cerise?"

"Yes." She took a deep breath and eased her fists open before Wilma emerged from the bedroom. She forced herself to look up and smile before she met her mother's glance.

"Boy, that Eddie is really stupid," she said and tossed her braids back with one hand. "All he looked at was that dumb gun they bought his dad for Christmas. He never even noticed I look different. He still called me 'lizard.' "

It was a quick movement. Wilma's hand flew up to cover her mouth, and Cerise took a deep breath. Mother's hand was hiding the expression of her lips, but the lines at the corners of her eyes gave her away. Mother was laughing. Laughing at her.

"It isn't funny!" She hurled the words out and reached to snatch Wilma's hand down—away from her mouth, exposing the hidden smile. "It's not funny. Nobody's ever called *you* a lizard."

She released Wilma's hand and hurled it away from her. She gulped in a deep breath and tried to get her temper back under control. Mustn't shout. Daddy Phil never shouted.

She couldn't stop the furious anger. Mothers weren't supposed to laugh at their children. Mothers were supposed to understand. She forced her mouth closed and glared steadily into Wilma's eyes, then turned and walked toward her room, her back straight and her chin up, pretending nothing was wrong. Mother was being as stupid as Eddie Carter.

"Cerise, I'm sorry."

She heard Wilma's words but didn't stop. Mother shouldn't have laughed at her.

"Cerise, I said I was sorry." This time there was a harsh edge to the tone, and Cerise hesitated at the door to her room.

"Be mad if you want, but what Eddie Carter calls you doesn't make any difference. Everyone gets called names—especially by older boys."

Cerise took a deep breath. "But they don't get laughed at by their own mother." She lowered her eyelashes and glanced out of the corner of her eye before bolting into her room and shutting the door.

196

The look on mother's face. The open mouth. The wide eyes. She'd really been sorry. Well, she should be.

Cerise crawled up onto her bed and crossed her legs underneath her. She closed her eyes and squeezed them together as she concentrated on praying.

Eddie Carter would be sorry. She would pray hard, and God would fix things. God always fixed things if she prayed hard enough.

The room was completely dark when the knock on the door made her open her eyes.

"Cerise, it's Daddy Phil."

The sudden light made her blink when the door opened and she stared up trying to see his face in the semi-lighted room. He didn't look mad. His eyes were lined, like they were when he was writing a sermon. Like he had been thinking hard.

"It's time for dinner, Cerise, and your mother is worried about you."

"Why?"

He moved across the room and stood beside her bed. She bent her head, and his hand stroked the top of it.

"She says you're mad at her."

"She laughed at me." Cerise stared down at the rows of chenille on the bedspread and whispered the words.

"I know." Daddy Phil murmured the words so softly she had to strain to hear him. "She's sorry. We all say some things we're sorry for, Cerise."

"You don't."

There was a soft laugh, and his hand slid down to her shoulder. "Oh, I do. Ask your mother. She's the one who hears most of them."

He kept on patting her shoulder, and Cerise relaxed. She liked the firmness of his hands and the solid feeling they gave her.

"Your mother's been sitting in the living room waiting

for you to come out. She felt so bad, she didn't even feel like getting dinner. I did the cooking, and I'll feel insulted if you don't come out to eat."

Cerise stiffened. "She didn't sew either?"

"No. She's really feeling sorry, Cerise. You should be kind and forgiving." His hand stopped, slid around and lifted her chin. "God would want you to be forgiving, Cerise."

She could see the light shining on his cheek and the soft look in his eyes when he gazed down into her face.

"I will, Daddy Phil. I will." She reached out and clasped his legs. Her head struck the metal of his belt buckle and she put one hand to her forehead. She felt the sudden jerk of his body—the hardening lump under the fabric where her cheek rested.

His backward step was hasty and awkward. He stammered, "Ah, well, come eat."

With a few quick steps, he was out of the room. Cerise stared after him and fought the urge to smile. Instead, she stretched herself slowly off the bed. She tucked her T-shirt down into her jeans and ran her tongue across her lips before leaving the room.

As she crossed the floor, she glanced at the kitchen, but Daddy Phil was being too careful about not looking in her direction. The smile flitted across her face before she bent to give her mother a swift hug.

"It's okay, I'm not mad anymore." She watched her mother's face carefully as she talked. "We can eat now." She relaxed her grip and stepped back, waiting for Wilma's reaction.

"I'll swear, you'll give me gray hair yet," Wilma said. "The way you change moods—one minute you look like you hate me, and then you're all ready to feed your face."

Cerise wrinkled her nose. "I'm impetuous."

"Don't use words I don't understand," Wilma snapped, but her eyes were gentle. Cerise only smiled and used her most polite church-lady voice to answer, "Yes, Mother."

Wilma's sigh made Cerise relax. When Mother sighed with the deep "ah," it meant she was going to forget the argument. They could eat, then Mother would go back to hemming the angel dress.

Cerise concentrated hard on being as polite as she could. She said "please" and "thank you" and didn't make faces at Matt. The dress had to be finished by Friday, and Mother said it was miles of hemming. After Friday no one would call her "lizard," and God would fix Eddie Carter.

She said her prayers over and over when she went to bed. God only worked if you prayed really hard, and God had to fix Eddie Carter. Eddie had to be sorry.

As the Christmas pageant unfolded, Wilma found herself waiting breathlessly for the appearance of the angel. Matt had stopped squirming and was staring in rapt attention at the figures on the stage.

She found a strange comfort in the soft music of "Silent Night." For the first time she felt no resentment toward the people around her. The warmth of sentiment in the music made her turn to smile at Clara Thayer, who sat rigidly beside Matt.

Her smile changed to open-mouthed amazement. Clara Thayer smiled back, then bent her head and looked down at her lap. The averting of the older woman's glance hadn't quite hidden the tears.

Wilma reached across Matt to squeeze her mother-in-law's hand. She hadn't been fair to Clara. If anyone doted on Kathleen, it had been Clara. How empty her life must be now.

The spotlight came on, illuminating Cerise. They both turned toward the stage when the intake of breathing from the audience indicated approval. In the harsh glare, Cerise's blonde hair hung loose and shimmered with dancing highlights. The girl's arms lifted gradually upward and hovered above the heads of three burlap-robed shepherds. The soloist began a hesitant and faltering, "While shepherds watched their flocks by night . . ."

Wilma held her breath. The singer wavered precariously on. A childish voice squeaked into a high note, but Cerise remained motionless, steady in angelic perfection. It was worth every minute of hemming the chiffon. The dress fell in soft folds. The sleeves moved airily in the slight breeze from a hidden fan. Cerise's eyes appeared closed, and the light glowed across her cheekbones, making her porcelain skin glisten.

Someone had fashioned her a pair of wings edged in a silver trim that reflected darts of lights into the air. The wings were attached with a gold sash that crisscrossed Cerise's chest. Wilma's hand tightened over the clasp of her purse. The effect of the costume was exactly what she didn't want. It made Cerise look busty. Too busty. Was there padding under all the chiffon?

She twisted her head and peered at the faces around her. Only gaping attention. Pleasant smiles. She turned back and leaned against the solid wooden pew. No one else would notice, she thought. No one else would know Cerise wasn't that well developed.

Cerise's timing was perfect. Before the reedy sound of the soloist's voice died away, Cerise's eyes flew open and one arm moved in a dramatic sweep of the stage. Her words came through clear and unwavering in the silence of the church.

"Ye will find him in Bethlehem . . ."

Wilma clutched her purse even harder. Cerise dominated the stage. Phil would insist on having her at the services. Before, it had been only an idea, but after this, Phil would be eager and insistent. Cerise was too young.

The choir voices rose in volume, bringing the program to a finale. Wilma watched Cerise make a low, sweeping bow and swallowed hard at the gleam of triumph in the girl's eyes.

Where was Phil? She took a quick look around the church, but the movements of the crowd made it impossible to see him. Parents were gathering up coats, and hands began to grasp her arm.

"My goodness, how your girl has grown up."

"The best program we've ever had."

"Good to see you out again, Mrs. Thayer."

"How old is she now? She must be at least thirteen."

The voices came at Wilma from every wide, and she could only nod politely. She wanted to scream at them. She's not grown up, she's not even eleven yet. But the voices moved on, and she was left clutching her purse tighter and tighter, following Matt and Clara Thayer out of the church.

"Where's Cerise?" Matt craned his head and looked at his mother. "Aren't we going to wait for Cerise?"

"She'll meet us out in front as soon as she takes off her wings," Wilma answered.

"Why doesn't she keep her wings?"

"They aren't her wings, Matt. She borrowed them."

She could see Matt screwing his face into puzzled contortions and groaned to herself. They were almost at the door. If Matt asked any more questions, she was going to leave him with Phil. Let Phil explain how angels could borrow wings.

Her knee banged into Matt when the line came to a halt. Clara Thayer held her son's hand with a grasp that made the knuckles white. Her chin quivered, and once again Wilma caught a glimpse of the dampness in Clara's eyes.

Phil leaned close to his mother's ear, and Clara nodded, then moved on.

"I asked Mother to stay for hot chocolate," Phil said. "Her car is at our house anyway."

He touched Wilma's shoulder lightly with his fingertips. He sounded hesitant, as if he was asking her approval, and Wilma nodded.

"Why can't she spend the night, Phil?" She saw his eyebrows lift and added, "It's silly for her to go home and come back for dinner tomorrow."

His hand rested lightly on her head, ruffling her curls with an affectionate pat.

"You ask her, honey. She'd feel more welcome," he said. His glistening brown eyes were wide and pleading. She turned away before she lost her self-control. No wonder Clara Thayer couldn't let go of Phil. His eyes must haunt her as much as Kathleen's. Wilma elbowed and nudged her way through a collected mass of overweight women to reach Clara and Matt.

"Are you sure I won't be in the way?"

Clara's face lit up the invitation, but there were lines of doubt across her forehead, lines that disappeared into a beaming happiness when Matt uttered a loud, "Oh, boy, do I get to sleep in my sleeping bag?"

Clara's laughter was unusual: a short, quick catch in the back of her throat, followed by a slight gurgling sound. She looked down at Matt and then turned to Wilma with a sober earnestness and said, "We'd better enjoy this one, Wilma. He's the only little one left."

Clara shifted her feet and looked away, leaving Wilma feeling oddly embarrassed . . . not for herself, but for Clara Thayer's discomfort.

"Okay, the star is ready. Shall we walk home?"

Wilma tilted her head and met Phil's question with a nod. Cerise stood beside him, one hand clasping her coat, which was draped around her shoulders like a cape. She glanced from one parent to the other, then shrugged and swept dramatically ahead of them. One hand gathered the folds of the skirt up away from the ground. She walked confidently, as if she had been wearing long skirts all her life.

Phil's arm went around Wilma's shoulder. "She really made a perfect angel."

He started humming softly to himself, and Wilma felt a queasy twist in her stomach. Phil was too elated about the evening. He was already planning on taking Cerise to the gospel meetings. She could feel it. The way Cerise was prancing—swinging her shoulders, holding her chin up, and tossing her head—it was going to be a losing battle. They were lining up against her.

"Look, Daddy. Look at the lights." Matt's voice was a shrill intrusion into her thoughts. Her head jerked up, and her eyes followed his excited pointing.

Two revolving lights sent shafts of blue sweeping into the night, lighting and relighting the roadside in an eerie imitation of daylight. Lights from the Carters' kitchen were crossed by the silhouetted figure of a uniformed man and recrossed by another shadow.

Wilma's hand went to her throat. She watched the red lights blinking on and off in an unremitting pattern. The ambulance crouched at the back door like a giant beetle waiting for its prey. Hurrying figures moved through the alien illumination. The door opened and closed, opened and closed. Shadowy figures moved from car to house and back again. The crackling of a radio broke the ominous silence.

"Police cars!" Cerise stopped so suddenly she lost her grip on the white chiffon. The wispy material caught in the chilly winter air current and swirled up around the edges of her coat.

"They're at the Carters'." Phil's arm dropped away from Wilma, and he hurried forward. "I'd better see if there's anything I can do."

"There's an ambulance, too!" Cerise's voice had an excited pitch. She snatched frantically to regain control of her skirts. When she looked at Wilma, her eyes were wide and glistening. "Hurry up, Mother. Something must have happened."

She gathered up the chiffon and started after Phil. Her blond hair swirled around her face and shimmered in the flashing blue lights.

"Cerise! Stop!" Wilma screeched the command out, halting Cerise in the middle of her spring. "You aren't going. You stay with us."

"But Daddy Phil's going to be there. I'm going with him." She turned toward Wilma, her feet still braced and ready to continue the dash.

"You can't go everywhere Phil goes." Wilma beat at the air with one fist. "You are going in the house. And don't argue."

"Mother!" The word was dragging out in a defiant, half-protesting wail.

Wilma's queasy feeling disappeared and was replaced by a knot of rage that began pushing itself up from the pit of her stomach. A pressure built inside of her until she looked into Cerise's eyes and took a long, deep breath. This time the words came out loud and slowly but shaking with an inner fury.

"One more word and I'll rip that angel costume apart." She jerked her chin up and glared down into the suddenly side green eyes. Cerise's lips parted, hesitated a brief moment, and closed. Her eyes fell away from Wilma's intense glare. She paused, then flipped her hair

204

back, straightened, and walked toward the house with her own chin up and jutted forward.

The rigidness of her shoulders, the rhythmic evenness of her steps . . . Wilma clenched her teeth. Cerise was making a defiant march instead of an obedient retreat.

The touch on her arm was gentle, a reminder. Wilma turned and looked up at Clara Thayer. In her rage at Cerise, she had forgotten both Matt and her mother-in-law.

"Maybe I shouldn't stay," Clara's voice was faint and troubled. "I put the presents in the house already. Maybe I'll be in the way."

In the spectral flashes of blue light, Clara's face showed tiny, hairlike wrinkles around her mouth. The tautness of her skin over the bones of her face made her seem thinner than ever. The woman looked as if she was losing her body juices and turning into old leather.

"No," Wilma said and found herself meaning it. "I don't want to wait for Phil alone. Please stay." She drew her collar tightly against her throat and shivered. It was more than cold. It was dread. Fear. She was afraid to know what was happening at the Carter house.

She moved more rapidly, anxious to get inside her house. As if the walls could keep the blue lights away. Her teeth had started a rapid vibration. Her fingers shook. Her feet began moving faster and faster toward the door.

She turned away from the cars. Now she could see only the flickering blue lights darting their presence on the white siding of the house.

The sounds. The electronic vibrations. Static and another voice. Inside. She could shut the sounds out when they were inside.

Matt dawdled in the doorway, turning back to look at the police cars. She put the palm of her hand against his back and shoved. She pushed him into the room and stepped back, almost propelling Clara across the threshold with the firmness of her grasp on the woman's elbow.

She slammed the door shut and leaned against it, trying to slow her rapid breathing. To gather up the security of her own living room and hold it around her like another coat.

"Cerise, get away from the window." She found enough air in her lungs to rasp out the order when she saw the girl, leaning on the windowsill, staring out the window with an excited eagerness. Cerise was becoming impossible.

"Did you hear me?" she screamed at the unmoving figure. "Mind!"

Cerise only continued to stare. "The ambulance is going away."

Wilma heard the words in a half-fog of fury. There was no siren. No siren at all.

Her eyes moved toward Clara Thayer, who was standing behind Cerise. Clara could see what was happening.

The flat dullness of Clara's eyes . . . an imperceptible shake of the head—like the ambulance at the picnic, the one that took Kathleen. No need to hurry. No siren.

Wilma pushed herself away from the door and snatched for the drapery cord. With one swift yank, she shut the view of the Carter house out of her living room. She leaned against the wall, holding the cord in her hand, and shook with anger.

"How can you stand there and stare at other people's misery?"

She choked and tried to understand the expression on Cerise's face. The girl had frozen in her watchful position. Her head turned toward her mother. The eyes were half-closed. Accented by her mascara, they held a firmness, an animal glitter. A hardness that disappeared when

Cerise relaxed her shoulders and opened her eyes wider. The muscles in her cheeks softened. She shrugged as if the closed curtains were no longer important.

"I wasn't staring. I was interested," she announced in a cool voice. "Something happened to Eddie Carter, and I want to know what."

Wilma stared at her, trying to believe what she heard. Cerise was stating it as if she was positive.

"How can you tell? All you saw was an ambulance. Mr. Carter could have had a heart attack. Mrs. Carter could have gotten sick. What makes you think it was Eddie?"

Cerise straightened and flipped her hair back. "Because Eddie is horrid, and God is going to punish him." Her eyes narrowed, but the gaze was unwavering and steady. She looked at Wilma as if challenging her to argue. There was a positive and unshakable sound in Cerise's voice.

Wilma sagged against the arm of the davenport and began unbuttoning her coat. It was an automatic reaction. She felt neither cold nor warm. Everything inside her had ceased to function. All the blood had stopped pumping. The nerves were dead in her skin. Nothing in her body seemed real.

"Want to see the tree, Grandma?"

Matt's voice penetrating her dulled senses was a welcome relief. He scrambled around the carpet at the foot of the tree. Presents tumbled, and the tree lights flared into full color.

Wilma felt her lungs expand when the glowing lights cascaded warmth into the room.

"Look, there's presents from Mommy and Daddy." Matt picked up packages, shook them, and tilted his head, listening to the sounds of the contents.

"There are some from me too," Clara said. She bent

207

toward a stack of plain tissue wrappings. "Didn't have any fancy paper, but I hope everyone likes what I brought."

"Everyone?" Cerise had turned her head. The penciled brows arched upward.

"Yes, everyone," Clara repeated. "Yours is the biggest one. The bottom one."

She reached over Matt's shoulder and pointed a skinny finger at the tag. "See? 'To Cerise from . . .'" There was a slight pause before Clara Thayer cleared her throat. "From Grandma Thayer."

Cerise gazed at the package and stooped to pick it up. She shook it gently and squeezed the tissue paper before glancing at her grandmother. She met Clara's eyes in a long, appraising stare. It was Cerise who turned away murmuring a polite "Thank you."

She tucked the present back under the tree and stood up, shaking the folds of her skirt. Then she lifted her head and added, "Thank you, Grandma Thayer." Her tongue slid across her lips, and Wilma sighed with satisfaction at seeing the lipstick gradually disappearing.

Wilma forced herself to move toward the kitchen, but stopped to say, "Cerise, you and Matt get your pajamas on. Cerise, be sure to wash your face." Action helped her keep her mind from the lights at the Carter house. "I'm going to fix the hot chocolate."

It was an effort, acting as if this was going to be a normal Christmas Eve. Normal? What was normal? Sirens that weren't used. Silent ambulances?

Her hand shook. Milk spilled across the countertop. She reached for a sponge and found herself wiping and rewiping the same spot, wondering when Phil was going to come home.

* * *

It was a silent crowd—unusually silent. Not even a whisper stirred among the neighbors huddled in small groups around the lawn. The downturned faces of two women, hiding their mouths with work-reddened hands, indicated the seriousness of the tragedy.

"I'm Reverend Thayer. The Carters' neighbor."

One uniformed man turned his head and nodded. Light from a yellow bug light on the back porch gave the deputy's face a greenish cast—or was it the green of the Multnomah County Sheriff's uniform reflecting on the youthfulness of the man's skin?

"Go on in. Maybe they can use you." The man waved a brown-gloved hand toward the door, and in an afterthought admonished, "Don't get in the way."

"I'm Reverend Thayer . . ." The same explanation, repeated again, moved him through the back hall, past two ambulance attendants who stood with their backs braced against the wall, waiting for a signal.

One of them jerked his head toward the kitchen with a terse "Check in there," and returned to the task of paring his nails with a jackknife.

Again the explanation, this time to a deputy with tired lines worn into his cheeks. He listened without comment and pushed his hat to the back of his head, exposing graying temples below a sparsely covered scalp.

"Wait a minute. Gotta make a phone call. Besides, the doc has to get outta the way."

Phil shoved his hands into his coat pockets and waited. The officer's voice was low. His back was turned. What happened? He should have asked the ambulance attendants. Phil shifted uneasily and waited for the men to finish.

The receiver clicked into place, and the officer turned. His eyes showed a dull fatigue as his glance traveled up and down, evaluating Phil before squinting in a question.

"You their preacher?"

"No." Phil shook his head. "Don't think they went to any church. I'm only a neighbor."

The officer rubbed at the tip of his nose for a few minutes before he made a decision. "Guess that's enough. God knows they'll need somebody.

"Christ, I get tired of these damn accidents." His mouth twisted. "Sorry, preacher. The language goes with the job."

"I understand." Phil waved a hand as if to brush the words away. He'd heard the words before, but he wondered if the police officer would believe it.

When the deputy's face relaxed, Phil asked, "You said accident. What happened?"

"Another of these stupid unloaded gun things. God, because some dumb shit gets a new gun for Christmas, the first thing he does is shoot his own damned kid. For Chrissake—sorry, preacher, can't help it."

The deputy shook his head once more and jammed his cap forward, putting the tired eyes in shadow.

"The boy—Eddie—was shot?" Phil felt a twinge hit his stomach at the thought. "Billy Carter? How bad is it?"

The deputy's cap moved from side to side.

"Dead, preacher. Out-and-out dead. Old man cocked the rifle. One shot right through the kid's neck snapped the spinal column. Kid didn't stand a chance.

"Can you imagine, the kid sitting there all hyped up, waiting to see the old man's reaction. Next thing—pow! No kid."

He tilted his head back, and Phil sensed the eyes measuring him once more.

"If you're going to get sick, preacher, will you use the john? My partner's already hit the sink. He cleaned it up, but it stinks. Damned rookie."

Phil shook his head and swallowed the warm saliva

that was surging up into his throat. "I'll be okay."

The kitchen was too small, too hot. He swallowed again and wished he was outside in the cold air. He should have gone home with Wilma and the kids. Anywhere but here. Pray . . . he should pray. He closed his eyes and inhaled. Breathe slow. Breathe deep. Ask for strength.

"Are you sure you're okay, preacher? You don't look so hot."

Phil smiled weakly and opened his eyes. "I'll make it," he murmured, but he was grateful to see the deputy turn away and start into the living room.

"Gotta check with the doc, preacher. You wait here."

He was alone. Only for a few minutes, but alone. He had time to compose himself. Time to think of something to say to the Carters. There were no answers coming into his mind. He stood questioning himself. What good could he do here?

What made him think he could comfort the Carters? He couldn't even ease his own wife's agony. How was he going to find words to say to the Carters when he had never found the right ones for Wilma?

Whatever he said, he knew the Carters couldn't accept it as God's will. Wilma only turned away from him when he tried to explain. Cerise was young enough. She accepted it, but the older ones felt death as a pain. What was Cerise going to say? Would she accept Eddie's death as an act of God?

It wasn't an act of God. This was the act of a careless man, and Phil bent his head, praying for compassion.

"Okay, preacher." The deputy's voice cut into his prayers. "Doc's signed the death certificate. Says if you're in there when they take the body out, it might help."

The deputy stood nodding his head as if agreeing with himself. "Guess he's right. Some folks go all to hell when

211

they see the body going. First time they really believe it, I guess."

He motioned toward the door and hesitated. "Ah, I wonder if you could do me a favor?"

"If it's possible," Phil answered.

"Mrs. Carter has a sister. I called her. She's agreed to come out, but it may take her an hour to get here. Will you stay with them until she shows up?"

"You're leaving?"

The man nodded. "Nothing more for us here. Accident, plain and simple. Body goes — we go." He stepped aside as Phil started into the living room and muttered, "Good luck, preacher."

Phil was forced to peer around the room before he could spot the Carters. He turned his head away to avoid watching the ambulance attendants bend over the dark shape to his right. He looked past another deputy who snapped his notebook closed and jammed his hat back on his head. Past the deputy and past the Christmas tree with its blinking apparatus still turning the rainbow of lights off and on, off and on. Why didn't someone unplug the lights?

Nell Carter huddled in the depths of an armchair that was parting at several seams, the cotton stuffing trying to erupt and spill out of the dark brown tapestry covering. She huddled in the chair, hugging herself and staring into the fireplace. She stared at the flames shooting up and sending flashes of light across her face. Her eyes were unmoving, unseeing. If it weren't for the steady rocking back and forth of her body, she could have been carved from granite.

Mr. Carter sat on the hearth, head down, clutching an unstoppered decanter in his hands. The biting scent of whiskey hovered in the room. Long, low moans came from Carter's open mouth. He paused, tilted the bottle, and after the sound of gurgling liquid, began moaning once more.

It was the moaning that made goose bumps run down Phil's back. What was Carter's first name? He could remember her name—Nell—but what was his? He groped through the blackness of his mind with a growing sense of panic. He couldn't remember Carter's first name. He couldn't call the man Mr. Carter—they borrowed tools from each other. Carter had helped him put the partition up in the children's bedroom. Worked with him shoulder to elbow, holding sheetrock, pounding nails—and he couldn't think of the man's first name.

To Phil's right, men moved the plastic-covered shape onto the stretcher, lifting the lumpy weight in a quick swing, as if it were only a large garbage bag. The clicking of a fastener, the whirr of wheels. Only a dark spot on the carpet was left.

Blood. Such a small spot of blood.

He moved forward, hesitating, still fumbling in his mind for Carter's first name.

The deputy's voice rumbled as if far in the distance. "We're going now. Reverend Thayer is here. He'll stay until your sister gets here."

The woman's face turned away from the flames. The eyes remained blank. She stared at Phil with the same unseeing expression, then turned back to watch the fire.

"Ned, it's Phil Thayer." Her laconic, disinterested voice drifted off into a whisper. She continued to clutch her arms and rock her body back and forth in silent self-comfort.

Phil squatted in front of the man and rested one hand on his shoulder. "Ned . . ."

Ned Carter raised his head and stared into Phil's eyes. The sharp stench of whiskey stung Phil's nostrils as he looked into the man's red, tear-filled eyes.

"If you came to preach, Phil, we don't need it." The man moaned in the back of his throat. "Too late for preaching. Don't need no preaching. Don't need no praying."

"I'm here as a neighbor, Ned." Phil lowered himself to the floor and sat looking up at the soundless tears running down Ned Carter's face. The tree lights kept their steady flashes, sending colored reflections of red and yellow back from Ned Carter's eyes. The bottle of whiskey clutched in Ned's hands reflected back the same array of hues. Red—blue—green. Off and on. Off and on.

Ned Carter looked down at the bottle in his hand. His shoulders heaved and shook. He gripped the narrow neck of the decanter with both hands, lifted it, and took a long pull at the contents.

"Can't understand it. Just can't." The man's voice rasped. Another long moan emerged from his throat. "Taught the boy—since he was big enough to walk—taught him about guns. He knew better. Only a damned fool would put a shell in a gun and then wrap it. He knew better."

He choked. Tears began to spill over the edge of his chin, dripping onto his sleeves in a pattern of wet dots that gleamed in the flashing of the tree lights.

"I was going to get the feel of it. Trying it out. How was I to know the . . ." He stopped again and took a firmer grip on the bottle. "Why would he put a shell in the gun? Why would he do anything so dumb? *Why?*"

Phil could only shake his head. He couldn't find any words. He looked up at Billy's mother, but she was still silently rocking herself as if she didn't hear her husband's voice.

Ned Carter turned his head and followed Phil's glance. This time the moan became a howl of pain. He got to his feet and stumbled. His hand flailed through a mass of wrapping paper and sent the papers flying into the air. Gaudy patterns of Santa Claus and candy-caned boxes swirled about the room. A red ribbon fell and clung to his shoe. He hurled a gold-foiled package at the wall. A choking gurgle echoed in his chest.

He lurched toward the davenport and swept the rifle up from the cushions with one hand. The bottle fell at his feet, whiskey splashing out across the carpet, and Ned Carter began to scream.

With the scream of rage that sounded as if it were rising from his testicles, Ned Carter dashed the butt of the rifle against the rocks of the fireplace. Then, grasping the barrel, he began swinging it over his head and down—smashing the wooden stock against the gray boulders again and again, raising the rifle and pounding the wood into splintered fragments.

All Phil could do was to watch helplessly, watch until Ned Carter's arms tired, the swing of the rifle not quite so wide. The breath became heavier between each swing until the man stood, panting, each breath a broken sob. Spit ran from the side of his mouth and dripped off his chin. Phil stood waiting. When Ned Carter slumped to his knees, Phil caught the falling rifle and watched Carter collapse, folding into a lump on the floor.

Carter beat the floor with one fist, crying out in heavy sobs and muttering, "He knew better. Eddie knew better." Still mumbling a string of incoherent words, Ned Carter closed his eyes and passed out.

The static sound of the blinker buzzed off and on. The Christmas tree lights continued to dance. Splotches of yellow and green appeared and disappeared on Ned Carter's sleeping face.

Phil reached over, righted the fallen decanter of whiskey, and placed it on the hearth. He tossed another log

215

on the dying flames and watched the lights playing their reflections on the glass of the almost empty decanter.

The lights were too much. He had to stop the lights, had to find the cord. A scarlet glass ball crashed to the floor and disintegrated into bits of crimson. A package crunched under his knee. He found the wall outlet and yanked at the plug.

The buzzing ceased. The tree was dark. Only the light from the fire illuminated the room.

Ned Carter's breathing had become deep and regular. Phil looked at the big man with the tousled red hair and envied him the release he had found in the alcohol. At least Ned Carter had found a way to sleep.

But Ellie Carter . . . she didn't look as if she would sleep for days, not until exhaustion forced her eyes closed. And he still couldn't find any words.

"Nell, is there anything I can say?" He moved to the side of her chair and put his hand on her arm. "I didn't come except as a neighbor, but I'll say a prayer if you like."

She stopped rocking and looked blankly in his direction, then shook her head and began rocking her body with her arms once more.

He stared down at the floor and bit his lower lip. What was he doing here? They were not even his parishioners. He wasn't good at this sort of thing. In fact, he hated sick calls. Hated burials. He wanted to be with the living. What could he do for Nell Carter?

Ned's hand twitched, and he groaned in his stupor.

"I'll get Ned into the bedroom for you," he said and patted her shoulder.

"Let him be."

She startled him when she spoke—even more when she stopped rocking back and forth. She lifted her head and looked up into his eyes. There was a drawn tightness in the skin of her face. The twist of her mouth was like the anguish of someone in physical pain.

"He'll wake up soon enough, Phil. A soft bed isn't going to make his sleep any more healing."

"I feel helpless, Nell. I'm supposed to bring people comfort, and I can't find any words."

"Not your fault. We're not churchgoing folks."

She reached out with one hand and patted his arm, a gentle, consoling pat. Phil felt as if his lungs had turned into blocks of ice. He was supposed to be helping her. He was doing it all wrong. These things didn't happen at gospel meetings. He knew how to get people fired up about living, but he knew nothing about this. He was an evangelist, not a minister.

"Nell . . ." The words were jammed up in his throat. All he could manage to do was repeat, "Is there anything I can do?"

She nodded her head, and the firelight reflected the dampness on her cheeks. "One thing."

"Name it."

Her head turned toward her sleeping husband and then back to Phil. "In the desk drawer. Top left. There's a pistol. Take it."

"Take it?"

"I don't want to see another gun. Ever. Especially in this house." She clutched at her arms once more. "Get rid of it for me. I don't care what you do with it. I want it gone."

Her chin quivered, but each word was slow, distinct, and final. "I want it out of this house."

"All right."

What was he going to do with it? What on earth could he do? Throw it away? Better not. The wrong person might find it. Ned might want it back. Why was he fretting about a gun? Why was he having so much

217

trouble making a simple decision? Get it out of the house. Make Nell happy and figure it out later.

"Anything else?" he asked.

She bobbed her head. "After you do it, you can go. You don't need to stay. It was nice of you, but I'd rather sit here alone."

He felt the ice melt and flow out of his lungs at the freedom from his duty. "What else can I do?"

She began to rock back and forth again, bending forward more and more, like a person with bad stomach cramps.

"There's a scatter rug in the hall," she said. "Will you put it over—over . . ." Her voice stopped. She looked up at him with her eyes wide. Wide and pleading.

"I understand," Phil said and patted her shoulder.

She sighed and curled her feet up underneath her on the chair. She collapsed into a corner of the chair with the firelight's reflection flickering across her face, no longer rocking back and forth, but still hugging herself tightly against the chilling events of the night.

Phil moved across the darkened room and opened the desk drawer. The gun was holstered, wrapped in a cartridge belt. It was bulky, but he managed to wedge it into his overcoat pocket. It hung there, heavy and threatening, while he tossed the hand-hooked rug over the stained carpet and smoothed out the wrinkles. He felt it thudding against his hip when he straightened and stared down at the floor.

Such a small spot of blood. So easily hidden.

He paused at the hallway and looked back. Ellic Carter never lifted her head nor glanced in his direction. At least she had leaned back against the chair and was sitting quietly. Not moving. Only staring at the tongues of fire, and aging minute by minute. The fire snapped, and a long, turbulent snore rose from the sleeping shape at her feet.

Phil shifted the weight of the pistol and stepped out into the empty yard.

The ambulance, the police cars, the bystanders were all gone. Gray shadows of frost sprinkled the lawn. The blades of grass snapped and crunched in protest. He pulled his coat tightly around his body, and the gun jarred his hip, a grim reminder of its presence. Better not take it in the house. Wilma would be upset enough. If she saw the gun, she'd never calm down.

He was relieved to see the drapes in the living room had been drawn. No one was watching out the window and waiting for him. He swerved and crunched across the frozen grass to the back of the house toward his office entrance.

He opened the door quietly. He quickly unlocked the desk and shoved the pistol back behind his drawings. The desk was relocked and secure.

He stood in the dark office and leaned against the desk, waiting for his strength to return. He felt as if he'd been traveling all day. He was back with his family, back in his own home—but hollow inside. He had failed again. He wasn't a minister. He wasn't able to be soothing and comforting. Let some other minister handle the grief. He wasn't going to do it again. A man had to face his own failings. Another two months and this sort of thing wouldn't happen.

Eugene was a big enough city. No one would pay any attention if he avoided a neighbor in trouble. Pleasant Home was too small. No more small communities.

He pulled off his coat and ran his fingers through his hair before he looked at his watch. The children must be in bed. The only ones he had to face tonight with the tragic story would be Wilma and his mother.

Phil walked down the hall and said a quick prayer

before he entered the house. It was Wilma he dreaded facing. Wilma, who still got tears in her eyes when Kathleen's name was mentioned. He had not only failed her, but he had alienated her from the church. He stepped into the house and took a deep breath.

It wasn't until after Matt went to bed that Clara started feeling the first fingers of apprehension chilling her spinal column. Phillip was certainly staying at the Carters' for a long time . . . too long for it to be a simple heart attack. Could the girl be right? An accident? The boy?

The girl—not the girl—Cerise. She must stop thinking of her as "the girl." She had to accept it and live with it, like it or not. She didn't like it. Didn't like the look on the—Cerise's face, so positive that God was punishing Eddie Carter. The girl's eyes. They were . . . like the dead goslings. The same look. Cat's eyes seeking out the prey. The tomcat defying her. The same eyes.

How did Wilma cope with the girl? Cerise. She had to remember to use her name. Phillip was right. She had to quit being so stubborn. But Wilma was doing a good job, she had to admit it. Fixing the hot chocolate, all covered with whipped cream and a dusting of nutmeg. Sending the children off to bed. She wasn't letting Cerise buffalo her either. Stood right up and ordered her to bed, no matter how sweetly she begged to wait up for Phillip. Odd child.

Wilma had finally snapped, "Maybe nothing happened. Maybe the ambulance left because it wasn't needed."

It was at that moment that Clara first remembered the goslings. The defiant look in the girl's eyes. The mouth almost but not quite a sneer. Nothing you could put your

220

finger on to correct the child about. You couldn't correct her for a taunting derision you felt. Cerise had given them both that one last look and disappeared behind her bedroom door.

She snapped out of her woolgathering with a startled jerk of her shoulders. Phillip was standing beside the table. How long had he been there? He hadn't said a word.

"Phillip?" She found herself staring and waited with her hands folded before her. She had tried to read but the words all blurred. Wilma had dragged out a stack of Matt's shirts for mending. She noticed Wilma was still on the same shirt, looking at the same sleeve over and over.

"Phil, the ambulance, it . . ." Wilma floundered, dropped the shirt back on the stack of mending, and waited with her lips parted. Her face had acquired a chalky color, making her eyes look wider, bluer and more frightened.

"It was Eddie." Phillip's voice was flat, tired sounding. He dragged a chair out from the dining room table and almost folded into it. "Stupid accident."

"What . . ." Wilma's hand went to her mouth. Her teeth closed over the flesh of her thumb while she waited for Phillip to continue.

He leaned forward with his elbows on his knees and stared down at the carpet.

"Carter—Ned—got a new hunting rifle. Eddie wrapped it himself. Evidently he tried loading it—forgot to take the shell out again." Phil's shoulders shook. The room was so quiet Clara could hear the sound of his jaw snapping when he swallowed hard. "Anyhow, it went off and Eddie was killed."

Clara leaned back in her chair and laced her fingers together. "You're right, Phillip. It was stupid."

"Most accidents are," Wilma snapped with a fury that made Clara open her eyes and stare at her daughter-in-law.

Wilma's eyes were wide, flashing pools of blue. Both fists were clenched, but she wasn't looking at either Clara or her husband. "The poor parents. Oh, God, what a hell that's made of Christmas for them."

Clara stiffened in shock at Wilma's words, and her glance flew toward Phillip. Surely he wasn't going to allow his wife to use language like that—but Phillip only nodded, and his head slumped further forward. His hands went up to hold his head, and he continued to stare at the floor.

She took a deep breath and sniffed. Well, it was Phillip's house. Phillip's wife. No wonder he didn't want her to help him in his ministry.

"Phil, what about the Carters? Should I go over?" The fire had gone out of Wilma's eyes. Color began to ebb back into her cheeks.

"No, there's no need for you to go." His voice sounded flat. "Mrs. Carter has a sister who's on her way now. Ned drank himself to sleep." Phillip chewed nervously at his lip. "He sat there with a bottle of whiskey—maybe his second one, for all I know—sat there and drank until he passed out on the living room floor. Poor guy."

This was too much. Sympathy for a drunkard? First Wilma using profanity, and now Phillip sympathizing with an alcoholic. Clara slapped the table with one hand. "Poor guy, indeed! Drinking is a sin, and you sit there feeling sorry for him. You should have taken the whiskey away! Thrown it out! You were supposed to pray for those poor people, not sit there and allow sin to go on right in front of you. What kind of minister are you, Phillip?"

He straightened in the chair and stretched his long legs

out in front of him. For a second he looked at his feet as if seeing them for the first time, then he glanced up at her. His eyes looked as tired as his voice sounded.

"That's the problem, Mother . . . I'm not a minister, I'm an evangelist." He raised one hand to stop her from interrupting. "If the poor man can find some relief for his misery in drinking himself to sleep, who am I to stop him?"

His eyes were fixed on Wilma's face while he talked. Clara choked back her protest as he continued to explain.

"When it comes to words of comfort and easing someone's grief, I simply don't have the ability. I'm a failure at it. I can't do it."

Wilma's expression puzzled Clara. She was looking at Phillip and nodding her head. Her eyes had softened as if she understood and was supporting him. Well, she probably would. A woman who used the word *hell* and took the Lord's name in vain. She might be a good mother, but Wilma certainly wasn't a good minister's wife. She had warned Phillip, and now he was getting weak. Weakness didn't belong in a minister.

Clara turned back to Phillip and tapped one finger on the table to emphasize each word. "You're talking nonsense, Phillip. A minister can always pray. If he can't find the words himself, he can always pray for God's help. He can't condone drinking , , ," She shot a quick glance at Wilma, "or profanity. You're not a failure, Phillip, but you're weak. It was your duty to stop Mr. Carter from drinking and pray for those people. It's part of a minister's duty."

She pushed herself back in the chair and lifted her chin defiantly. Phillip's eyes had lost the softness. He only shook his head once more.

"You weren't listening, Mother. I admitted I'm not a

223

minister. I can't comfort people. I can rouse their eagerness, make them excited, but I can't ease their suffering.

"Ned Carter didn't want my prayers, Mother. He specifically asked me not to pray for them, so I didn't. I'm only glad he could find his own way out of the guilt he was feeling. Ned Carter didn't want or need my prayers."

"Well, he's certainly not a Christian," Clara exploded. She pushed herself up from the chair and started to the bedroom. She stopped with her hand on the doorknob and added, "Why you wasted your time, Phillip, I don't understand. If you weren't going to make Christians out of them, you shouldn't have gone over there."

She stepped into the bedroom before Phillip could answer and stood with her back against the door. The dimness of the room, with only the faint night-light in the wall socket, was a comfort after the harsh lights of the dining room. She would undress, and she would pray. Silently. Mustn't wake little Matt in his sleeping bag beside the bed. But she would pray. Pray hard for Phillip. He was going to need her prayers, she could see that. She wasn't going to pray for Wilma or the girl, but Phillip needed her prayers.

Cerise heard the door to Matt's room close and tiptoed back to her bed. If *she* was going to bed, Mommy and Daddy Phil would go to bed too, and she wouldn't hear anything more.

Eddie Carter had been punished. Oh, boy!

She sat cross-legged on the bed and smiled. It was more than she had asked God to do, but God must know best. If God had only made Mr. Carter mad at Eddie, Eddie might have figured out who put the shell in the gun. Eddie wasn't always dumb. God really knew how to fix things.

She stretched out on the bed and pulled the sheet up first, then one blanket at a time, and lay open-eyed in the darkness.

It wasn't right for *her* to bawl out Daddy Phil. Daddy Phil wasn't her little boy anymore. Maybe she should ask God to make Clara Thayer sorry.

Better not. She remembered how much Daddy Phil smiled whenever *she* gave him a check. *She* always said, "Remember it's for the church," but it made Daddy Phil happy. Better wait and see. See what was in the big box under the tree.

The box would be the first present she opened. It was the biggest present *she* had ever brought. Usually *she* only gave Cerise a Bible. Matt got good presents. Matt got a whole toy farm from Grandma Thayer last year. This package was too big to be a Bible, and anyway, she had enough Bibles. She didn't need another one.

It was nice to know God listened to her. Daddy Phil was right. If you prayed hard enough, you did get your prayers answered. The secret was how to pray hard enough. She knew she had to close her eyes so hard she could hear funny noises in her ears—and then she had to say the prayer over and over.

Her hair fell over her face when she rolled over on her side, and she pulled her fingers through the long strands. She didn't want pigtails anymore. They were too babyish.

She yawned. Tomorrow she would ask Mother to let her have it cut. Maybe a ponytail. It wouldn't be as bad as the braids.

If Mother didn't agree, she'd talk to Daddy Phil. If she coaxed hard enough, Daddy Phil would let her get rid of the pigtails. Especially if she sat in his lap. She smiled to herself. Daddy Phil always got red in the face when she sat in his lap and wiggled against him. That's when he would say yes, she could get her hair cut.

She yawned again and closed her eyes, remembered she hadn't said her prayers, and decided it wasn't necessary. God was there. When she prayed hard enough, he listened.

"Mommy, it's morning. Get up."

The sound of Matt's excitement shook Wilma awake. He was hopping up and down beside the bed as frantically as if he had to go to the bathroom. Why did kids have to get up so early on Christmas morning?

"Okay, son. We're getting up." Phil grumbled an answer from his side of the bed. His face was still buried in the depths of the pillow, and the sounds were muffled, but Matt grinned in understanding and scurried out the door.

"Phil, are you going to tell the children about Eddie Carter?"

Phil rolled himself to a sitting position and rubbed at the back of his neck. Finally he reached for his robe and shook his head. "Not unless they ask. I'll have to tell them eventually, but why spoil their Christmas?" He adjusted the belt and flipped one end over, pulling it tight. "Come on, the kids are probably sitting under the tree waiting."

The tree lights glistened on Cerise's blonde hair. It cascaded over her shoulders and reflected pinpoints of green, darts of blue. When she moved, the hair shimmered softly and swirled about her face.

"We're all here," Cerise said and looked up at Phil with a question in her eyes. "Can we start opening the packages now?"

At his nod, Cerise reached under the tree and grabbed the box from Clara Thayer. She handed Matt his white tissue-wrapped gift and proceeded to ignore everyone, tearing at the paper with determination.

Wilma caught her breath. The girl's hands reached into the middle of the tissue paper. Cerise's eyes had narrowed into slits. The mouth . . . Cerise wasn't smiling. What on earth had Clara Thayer given her?

"Let us all see, Cerise." She leaned forward trying to see over Cerise's shoulders. The girl's back was too stiff. Whatever Clara had chosen, it wasn't right.

"Thank you." Cerise's voice sounded polite, but not enthusiastic. It was the same polite voice she used when she talked to the women at church. Wilma glanced at Clara Thayer, hoping Clara wasn't offended. Clara was smiling proudly, sitting with her chin tilted upward, viewing the scene before her as if she was going to lift her hand and bless the subjects. Thank God, Wilma thought, Clara was unaware of the disgust in Cerise's manner or the distaste shown in the rigid set of Cerise's jaw.

"I thought the doll's hair looked like yours." Clara nodded. Her gaze swept over Cerise and went to Phil. "Don't you think so, Phillip?"

"Let's see it." He shifted in his chair and stifled a yawn.

Cerise held the doll up in the air. It was true. The doll's long blond hair hung in the same delicate straightness, catching the tree lights with the identical reflections. But a doll for Cerise? Clara couldn't understand much about girls if she bought a doll for a girl who was already begging to wear makeup. Wilma chewed at her thumb, hoping Cerise would at least continue to be polite about it.

Cerise's glance swung from the doll to her mother with an exasperated glint in her green eyes, then she laid the doll back in the box and shoved the tissue paper over the top of it.

227

"Open mine, Cerise." Matt grabbed a lumpy, misshapen package from the stack and pushed it into her hands. "I wrapped it myself," he said proudly. There were almost more stickers than paper. Matt's attempts to tie a bow had resulted in long streamers of red ribbon dangling from both ends of the package. To Wilma's relief, Cerise giggled. The doll was forgotten. The rest of the packages were doled out. The pile of wrappings, hastily torn from the boxes, grew into a ragged mountain of paper.

By the time they progressed from a quick breakfast of orange juice and toast through the turkey-and-trimmings dinner, Wilma's tension headache had built into a pulsating throb in both temples. This was the worst Christmas of her life—at least since she had married Phil. She couldn't count her childhood in foster homes with nothing but welfare castoffs.

And most of the problems had been created by Clara Thayer.

Wilma scraped the leftover sweet potatoes into a plastic bowl and wished she could shove one right down Clara's throat. Clara had insisted on adding her own words of prayer after Phil said grace. She managed to bring up Kathleen with "a word of prayer for the absent member of the Thayer family." That's when the headache started. It began as a dull feeling behind her eyes.

By the time Clara progressed to "comforting the Carters on the loss of their son," Wilma felt tears running down her cheeks. If Phil hadn't reached for her hand, she would have broken into sobs. Instead the ache spread to her temples.

Matt was the first to lift his head with the question, "What happened to the Carter's son? Does she mean Eddie?"

Phil nodded and frowned at his mother. "Yes, son.

228

There was an accident last night." He cleared his throat and after a deep breath said, "It's not exactly the time to talk about it, but Eddie was, ah, killed." He ran out of words and breath at the same time.

"You mean before he opened his presents?" Matt's voice trembled. He looked from Phil to his mother, eyes wide, expecting an answer.

Phil swallowed and finally nodded silently.

"Who opened his presents?" Matt asked.

"I don't know," Phil sighed. "We'll figure that out later, son. Shall we eat?" His gaze moved from Matt to Cerise.

Cerise looked across the table at Matt. She shrugged, and her eyebrows went up. Wilma bit her lower lip. Cerise must have sneaked an eyebrow pencil into her room and applied it herself.

"I'm sorry, Cerise," Phil said. "I was going to tell you later, after we'd had our own Christmas."

The indifference in Cerise's eyes amazed Wilma. The girl calmly reached for the cranberries and scooped a huge helping out onto her plate.

"It's okay, Daddy Phil," she said coolly. "God does things His own way."

Wilma passed the dish on to Phil and clutched at the napkin in her lap. Not more of that "God's will" stuff. The headache was beginning to make her nauseated, and Clara Thayer's smirking approval of Cerise's comment wasn't helping any.

From Cerise's nonchalant comment on, the entire dinner became a fog, and now Wilma scraped at the roaster pan, taking out her frustrations on the singed dressing stuck to the edges. At least Clara Thayer was getting into her car. Maybe the headache would go away.

"Mother, why did she get me a doll?" Cerise wandered into the kitchen and plucked a slice of turkey from the

229

platter. "I'm not a little girl anymore."

"You're not grown up either," Wilma snapped. "And do something with your hair. If you come in here with it dangling, we'll have hair in all the food."

"But Mother, braids are for babies."

"Then put it in a ponytail, but do something."

"Can I get it cut?"

"You heard Phil. He wants it long, although it sounds dangerous to me. Lighting candles with that long hair—you might catch it on fire."

Cerise stuck one finger into the dressing and scooped up a quick taste. "But I don't want pigtails anymore."

Wilma looked at the fixed set of Cerise's jaw and groaned. She'd listened to enough arguments for one day.

First it was Clara being upset over the plans for Eugene. She was positive Phil belonged in a small church. Then Cerise wanted her hair cut and Phil opposed the idea. The dinner had turned into a disaster, and Cerise wasn't going to give up.

"Cerise, no more munching." Wilma grabbed the platter of sliced turkey and reached for the roll of aluminum foil. "Maybe we can taper the sides of your hair."

"Taper it?" Cerise's eyes opened with excitement. "You mean short on the sides and long in the back?"

"I'll talk to Phil." She stopped and rubbed at her forehead. "In the meantime, tie it back or something."

She listened to the sounds of Clara Thayer's car starting, the motor idling. Cerise's footsteps retreated. The headache was getting worse. The nausea was coming back. Wilma's eyes felt as if they were about to pop out of their sockets.

It wasn't only the arguments . . . part of it was her reluctant admission that Clara Thayer might be right. Moving to Eugene *might* be a mistake.

She reached for the cold water tap and splashed water

on her temples. This man, this backer . . . Phil said the man had—how did he put it? Old-fashioned values. Family and home. They were important. Phil's family . . . he wanted to meet Phil's family.

She turned the water off and daubed at her forehead with a towel. Fear—that was the feeling in her stomach. It wasn't the headache making her feel nausea approaching. It was fear of Eugene.

Chapter Six

A bank of clouds hovered above the mountains bordering Eugene. The customary greenness of the hills was gone. The fir-covered mountains appeared almost black in the increasing shadows as the clouds grew darker and more threatening. The valley was surrounded by clouds. *The valley of the shadow of death.* Wilma shivered and wondered why she'd thought of those words.

The air felt moist on her face, as if the rain might start at any second. She hurried down the sidewalk, ignoring the maple leaves that tore loose from their branches and assaulted her face. A crumpled paper bag rattled past her on the sidewalk and came to rest in a bed of heather.

She dodged a slow-moving, bearded young man dressed in a pair of cut-off jeans and wondered how he kept warm. The mere threat of the first September storm had chilled her into wearing a ski jacket. She darted across the street, clutching the jacket collar around her throat, hurrying to get home before Cerise and Matt arrived from school.

The wind swept ahead of her, clearing the long, circular drive of brown-tipped lawn clippings. It tore at

233

her skirt all the way up the brick walk to the massive front door. It dominated the front of the house, all mahogany panels and wrought iron hardware. Like entering a castle. After the parsonages, the large colonial house was too spacious. It didn't feel like a home. It was Phil's entertainment center.

Let Phil enjoy his toy. She was going to do something, not just open doors and usher people to Phil's office.

Even before she took off her jacket, she pulled the sheaf of papers out of her purse, held them for a minute, and then tucked then into her dresser drawer under the bras. It wasn't sneaky—at least, not yet.

First she would tell Phil about the courses—adult courses—to get a high school diploma. There were lots of people like her. Already the class on remedial reading had twenty people enrolled. Twenty-one, counting herself, and the adviser had taken so much time to explain everything.

She was going to take the classes—with Phil's permission or without it. She'd already wasted too much time. By the time they had finished moving, school was out and both children were at home. Now, with both of them back in school, she had lots of extra time. The morning classes wouldn't interfere with anything. Phil was too busy to notice whether she was home or not. Too busy? Some days Cerise saw more of Phil than she did.

She hurried toward the kitchen and glanced at the new dining room drapes. Maybe they were too long, but after three hemmings, they were going to stay that length. She wasn't going to do them over. Cerise and Phil could hem the darn things themselves if they wanted them above the windowsill instead of covering it.

Cerise and Phil! Cerise would probably laugh at the idea of her mother going to school. She couldn't argue with both of them at once. She'd talk to Phil before Cerise came home, settle it with Phil first—Cerise's opinion didn't matter.

Why was she building this resentment of her own daughter? Was she losing control over the girl? She shook the feeling aside and went downstairs.

She hardly ever went down to Phil's office. Until the plans for Phil's center became a reality, the daylight basement was converted to his office. He called it an office, but a meeting room was more like it. It was seldom she could talk to Phil alone. Too often he was with someone. Mr. Blaylock, his backer, with his pompous references to Phil's "little woman." Ted Gower, loud and boorish. Or Cerise, pestering Phil with her homework.

For once he was alone—on the phone—but no one else was in the large room. The burgundy velour carpet was as plush as the carpeting upstairs in the living room, and Phil didn't even hear her. She walked across the room to the window and stood looking out into the .backyard. He was tilted back in his chair, papers strewn across the desk.

Wilma only half listened. From Phil's comments, he was evidently making plans, discussing a television program. His plans were moving too fast. She couldn't keep up with them. First, the radio programs—he taped those ahead. Now the television. Ted Gower had found a sponsor, and Phil was going to carry his sermons to every home in the Eugene area. Ted was already talking about getting it on a network station. Too many things were happening.

She looked out at the fading hydrangea bushes and wondered if they should get some chicken manure from Clara Thayer—but Phil probably wouldn't have time. He hadn't even been up to visit his mother since the move to Eugene.

The receiver clicked and she heard the squeak of Phil's swivel chair.

"Did you hear that, honey?"

She turned as he leaned back in his chair and stretched both arms above his head, clasping and shaking his hands in a victory salute. "The television program is set. Ted signed all the contracts this morning. Every Sunday morning, we have our own half hour."

"That's nice, Phil," she said, but she couldn't find any real enthusiasm. Phil seemed to have ideas as often as he used the telephone. All he talked about since they moved to Eugene was his latest idea, his latest project. Ideas or Mr. Blaylock.

"Nice?" He swung forward in the chair and started assembling his papers into neat stacks. "Nice? It's a gigantic step. Can you imagine how many people we'll reach with television? Ted thinks we may be able to syndicate the show."

"Syndicate?" She looked at him with confusion.

"Syndicate it—sell it to independent stations all over the country. And you know, Ted came up with a great idea for opening the show." He began setting the stacks of papers into neat rows. "We'll open with candelabra. Cerise will be behind the candles, lighting them one by one. What a dramatic effect. Cerise in white . . . white candles."

"Phil, no. Don't use Cerise."

He looked at her with a puzzled frown. "Why not?"

"She's getting too much attention now. It's not good

236

for her at her age."

Phil settled back into his chair and his face sobered. For a few minutes he gazed at Wilma as if seriously considering her objection. Then he shrugged.

"It's hardly going to make a lot of difference. Ted plans on using the same opening every week. We only have to take the shot one time. They'll reuse the same film clip."

Wilma braced her back against the window. The coldness of the glass against her spine had a steeling effect.

"But she'll be seen by all those viewers every week. People are bound to make a fuss about her."

"Wilma, it's not as if she's going to be a television star. One short action shot, no more." He swung the chair back and forth as he talked, his foot nudging the desk with every swing. "It won't hurt anything."

"Yes, it can." Wilma pushed herself away from the glass and dropped into the large leather-upholstered chair facing Phil's desk. Even the chair had been purchased especially for Phil's important visitors. The ones with money. She'd never sat in it before. Odd, Phil hadn't bought a new desk. The desk had looked so big in the Pleasant Home parsonage. Now in this huge room, it was too small. He needed a new desk.

"Cerise is letting this go to her head," she said.

"All she's done is the candle lighting at the services. She doesn't even stay for the service. You know that. She lights the candles and scurries home after the first hymn."

"Scurries home with some boy tagging along beside her. She's too young for all this, Phil."

"It's hardly *some* boy, Wilma." Phil's mouth pulled back at the corners, and his teeth clenched for a second

237

before he relaxed. The calm, poised smile was back. "I make certain not just anyone walks her home. I asked Bobby Blaylock, and he walks her home every night. Not just anyone, Wilma . . . Harry Blaylock's son."

"He's fifteen years old, Phil, and Cerise . . ." She stopped and squirmed. How could she explain the look she saw in Cerise's eyes? Phil would only say it was her imagination. The quick flicker of her eyelashes when she looked at Bobby Blaylock. "Cerise prances like she just starred in a movie. She doesn't act like a girl who merely went in and lit the candles for a church service."

"She's only a child, Wilma, and for that matter, so is Bobby."

"He's fifteen, Phil. Fifteen is old enough to think about sex. Believe me, I know."

Phil flashed his most persuasive grin. Damn him, he was buttering her up. Smiling at her the same way he smiled at Harry Blaylock.

"Honey, Cerise probably does put too much emphasis on herself. It's sort of a childish fairy tale. She imagines it to be a lot more important than it is. It's her first touch of glamor. She's feeling like Cinderella."

"Who's Cinderella?" Wilma frowned when Phil chuckled at her question.

"Sorry, honey. I forgot your parents weren't the sort who read you the classic fairy tales. A scullery maid who became a princess and won the handsome prince."

Wilma continued to frown. "You also forget, I never had parents at all, Phil. At least not real ones." She looked up at him, and the worry kept gnawing at her stomach. "She acts as if Bobby Blaylock were the prince, all right."

Phil's smile became softer. "Don't worry. Bobby Blaylock is a good Christian boy. He'd never do anything

238

Harry Blaylock would disapprove of. Believe me, Harry is a strict father, and I trust Bobby." He swung back and forth in the swivel chair again, and the smile became more gentle. "Anyhow, Cerise is still a baby."

"A baby? Phil, in case you haven't noticed, I had to remake her white dress. She burst out of the seams in the bustline, and then I had to lengthen it by three inches. She's taller than I am now."

Phil only lifted his shoulders in an unconcerned gesture. "She's one of those girls who develop early. It doesn't mean she's an adult. She's only a schoolgirl."

"So are the girls at the community college, and a lot of those schoolgirls are carrying babies around the campus."

"I haven't been watching the local coeds, Wilma."

"I have. I was over there this afternoon."

He looked across the desk at her with his eyebrows drawn together. Two lines pulled across his forehead. "Why? It will be a long time before Cerise is ready for college. She's only in junior high."

"I wasn't thinking about Cerise. I went over there for myself."

"For yourself?" he repeated. His forehead creased even deeper. "What do you mean, for yourself? You never even finished high school."

"You don't need to rub it in, Phil." The tone of his words scratched at her resolve. She took a deep breath and braced herself in the chair. "I spent the time with an adviser. She says I can take continuing education courses for adults." Wilma said the words slowly, exactly as the adviser had said them to her. "I can take a test. A GED test. And get a high school diploma, or something like it."

"Don't be silly. You don't need a high school di-

239

ploma. You won't be any smarter."

"It's not that I need one, Phillip. I *want* one."

"Don't call me Phillip. You sound like my mother."

She stared at him without wavering. He wasn't going to make her back down. Maybe he was right . . . she might not become any smarter. But she'd feel smarter. Smart enough not to sneer at anyone who wanted to learn.

"The next thing you know, you'll start acting like my mother," he said.

"That's not fair, Phil. I'm nothing like your mother, and you know it."

Phil crumpled a piece of paper in one hand, rolled it back and forth between his fingers, and started tearing at the edges.

"I don't know anything of the kind. All my life it was 'don't argue, Phillip. I know more than you, Phillip. I was a school teacher.' "

He sent the wad of paper flying into the wastebasket. "I don't want a wife who brags about how much she knows. I want to make the rules, not listen to them."

"Well, I certainly can't brag, now can I?" She stifled a nervous laugh. "All I want is a high school diploma—not a whole college education."

"It's out of the question. You have a home to run, children to take care of. You can't do it."

"Lots of students have children. Lots of the people in the adult education courses are older. Some of them are older than me."

Phil shook his head, paused, then shook it again. "You have too much to do at home."

"I do not. I can go mornings, while the kids are in school."

He got up and leaned against the desk, then began

240

to walk slowly back and forth — always behind the desk — pacing as he often did during his sermons. Tight, wired movements, the corners of his mouth flexing while he thought.

He stopped, put both hands on the desk, and lifted his chin. When he looked into her eyes, his face had a perplexed lift to the eyebrows.

"I don't know. I don't think Blaylock would approve."

"Who cares?"

The eyes were dull. No sparkle in them now. Phil shook his head again.

"Honey, Harry Blaylock is the entire key to succeeding. He won't approve of my wife going to school."

"You always said I wasn't the minister — you were. You said I didn't have to go to the church stuff. Why should what I do make any difference to Harry Blaylock?"

"Blaylock is as old-fashioned as my mother. He decided to back my ventures because of our family."

"Our family?" Wilma's eyebrows lifted, and she caught the edge of the chair, digging her fingernails into the leather padding.

Phil flopped back into his chair and propped his elbows on the desk. For a long time he rubbed his temples with the tips of his fingers and stared down at the stacks of papers in front of him. Wilma caught the flash of his gold cuff links and scowled. They were exactly like Ted Gower's. Phil never used to wear cuff links.

"Blaylock believes in a solid family. A dedicated mother taking care of the house. He believes working women are ruining the traditional family."

"I'm not going to work, Phil. School, that's all.

School—and I'm doing it while the children are gone."
A fingernail cracked under the pressure of her hand,
and she winced. "What does Mr. Blaylock's wife do
while their kids are gone? Gossip on the phone? I
suppose that's okay with Mr. Blaylock?"

She snorted, examined the cracked nail, and pushed it
back into position. It was split to the quick, and it
hurt. Funny . . . Mr. Blaylock hadn't griped about her
long nails. Would Phil tell her to cut them if he did?
She had a growing suspicion that Phil would make the
request. He would make the whole family into vegetari-
ans if it would please Harry Blaylock.

"I think his wife does tole painting." Phil's head
lifted with a gleam in his eyes. "Why don't you take
one of the courses in cake decorating or tailoring?
Something domestic. Blaylock would approve. He'd still
consider us the ideal family." He leaned back in his
chair and gave her a long, appraising look. "He really
thinks we have an ideal marriage, Wilma. I can't have
him doubt it."

"The ideal family doesn't have a dummy for a
mother," she snapped. It really came down to Blaylock's
money. Phil was so damned afraid of losing the money,
he didn't care about her feelings . . . only Blaylock's
opinion. To hell with both of them. She was going to
get her diploma.

"Wilma, I've never called you a dummy."

She jerked her head up and glared at him. "You
might as well. Telling Cerise to bring her homework to
you . . . telling me not to talk too much. Cerise acts as
if I don't know anything. I can't help her with her
homework. All I'm good for is sewing her clothes and
fixing the meals."

She looked away, sensing her tears getting close to

the surface. She wasn't going to cry. Phil wouldn't understand; he'd never understand the tears were from anger.

He moved so quickly across the carpet that she jerked with surprise when his hands caught her shoulders. He slid one hand under her chin and forced him to look at her through the blur.

"Honey, those things—cooking and sewing—they're important. You can teach Cerise how to cook."

"Who says Cerise is interested?"

The haze of tears started to clear. She stared back into his wide, pleading eyes.

"She's a girl. All girls are interested in housework."

She shook his hands off her shoulders in one swift move and pushed herself out of the chair. There weren't any tears left, only a surging anger. An anger that made her clench her fists as she spun away from him and started toward the stairs.

"Sometimes, Phil, you're a damned fool."

"Wilma!"

Let him be shocked over her language. Too bad old Blaylock wasn't around. Cake decorating!

He caught up with her when she started up the stairs, catching her and whirling her around to face him. Face him from the second step and stare directly into his eyes. Funny how much more human Phil looked when she wasn't staring up at him. She kept her eyes on his without blinking. The damned fool was right. He might not like the language but it fit. Cake decorating, when she wanted to learn important things!

"Wilma."

She continued to stare at him until his hands slowly loosened. She waited, watching the red anger of his face gradually fade.

243

"I'm sorry, Wilma. I know I can't see your side of it, but everything—everything hinges on Harry Blaylock. If he even suspected you used the word *damn*, he'd wash his hands of me and the whole project."

She clamped her lips together and glared. He wasn't getting an apology . . . not ever.

"Wilma, Harry Blaylock thinks you're a quiet homemaker, one who reads the Bible to her youngsters. He comments on how comfortable you've made our home. How you're always here when he comes by. How can I explain why you're not here? Especially when he thinks the colleges are full of degenerates and drug addicts."

She smiled and lifted her chin. It was so much easier when she didn't have to look up. She was on his level now, and it made her feel a surge of willpower.

"Tell him the truth, Phil. Tell him I'm learning to read. I can hardly sit around reading the Bible when I can't read well enough to understand it."

She pushed his hands away gently, but with a firmness he must understand.

"Tell Mr. Blaylock whatever you like." Her voice was cracking at the high notes. She hated the unsteady sound of her words. "I am going to take the courses."

She looked into his eyes, turned, and braced her shoulders as she went up the stairs. There was nothing but quiet behind her. The argument was over, whether Phil understood it or not. She had made up her mind. She still had her fists clenched with determination when she stepped into the kitchen.

The refrigerator door was open, and Cerise groped among the contents. She turned her head and smiled through a wisp of long blonde hair.

"Hey, Mom, what's for snacks?"

Wilma flexed her fingers and opened her hands. Was

244

Cerise's blouse too low cut or was it only her half-bent position?

"Matt took the last of the cookies," Cerise grumbled. "I can't find anything else."

"Fix yourself a peanut butter sandwich, or learn to cook," Wilma snapped. She walked on through the kitchen. Damned if she was going to worry about snacks now. "And wipe the lipstick off," she ordered as she reached the kitchen doorway.

"Daddy Phil said I could wear lipstick when I started junior high." Cerise's head shot up over the refrigerator door, her eyes wide and startled.

"He didn't say you could put it on like house paint. You look like a clown," Wilma retorted. "Blot it off so it looks natural, or you'll shock your Daddy Phil's precious Harry Blaylock."

She sent Cerise one last angry look and went on through the house. Matt barely glanced at her when she passed him. He stayed curled in a chair with his reader and a handful of cookies. He gave her only a quick smile before she went into her bedroom and headed for the dresser.

The enrollment papers ... she took them out and looked at them with a gush of elation. She was going to school. Phil might not like it, but she would stick to her decision. Nothing could make her back down now.

She pushed them into the far corner of the drawer and shoved all her bras over them before she leaned against the dresser and trembled.

The trembling developed into a complete case of the shakes. What was happening to their marriage? Was it Clara Thayer's iron rule or Harry Blaylock's money that made Phil so stubborn? She sat down on the edge of the bed and waited until the trembling stopped. Phil would find some story for Blaylock, she knew that much, but would Phil forgive her for standing up and deciding something for herself?

He had to. She wasn't going to give him any choice. He'd learn. After she was in school, he'd see it wouldn't affect their family, except for the best. She would read to Matt like she'd wanted to read to Kathleen.

Phil watched Wilma ascend the stairs and felt the bottom of his stomach disintegrate. It was the square set of her shoulders even more than her defiant stare. Wilma had never argued with him. He had the bewildering sensation of being in the middle of a maze. Which way was his desk?

He found his way across the room by instinct and dropped into his chair. Wilma. Pain started to spread through his stomach. Was this what an ulcer felt like?

The chair was a haven. A smooth, wooden-armed cave. He leaned against the cushion, letting his hands fall limply over the sides.

None of it was true or more than only partially true. It wasn't Blaylock, or Clara—it was Wilma. He didn't want her to change. It was the childlike Wilma he wanted. The wide eyes, so often frightened. The child who hung on him, needed him. She couldn't balance a checkbook, couldn't support herself. She needed him. She never demanded anything, only asked. Asked with those innocent blue eyes that looked as if everything depended on his answer.

The look was gone, and she hadn't even attended school yet. Once she got the diploma, it would never come back. She'd keep on trying new things for herself.

246

The little girl—the vulnerable Wilma—all he wanted was to shelter her from the world. She didn't need anything else. Why did she want to change?

It was his own fault. The pain began to spread up into his chest. He shouldn't have been so soft-hearted. It was the tubal ligation. He shouldn't have agreed to it. Those big, pleading eyes. He'd signed the papers without thinking.

Wilma was such a perfect mother. He should have expected this. They should have had more children. She needed children. If they could have another baby, she wouldn't be considering this nonsense. His head drooped against his chest.

She'd been different since Kathleen's death. Not going to church. She hardly ever went. Only here in Eugene, and only because he'd told her how important it was for appearances. She went, but there wasn't any joy in it. She never smiled, never sang. Said she couldn't read all the words in the hymnals.

He bent his head and tried to find some comfort in praying, but nothing came. His head was filled with nothing.

He didn't hear Cerise, didn't sense her approach. He felt the movement of his chair first and then the weight of her body as she sat on the arm of the chair and leaned against his shoulder.

"What's Mom so crabby about? She's a real bear."

A strand of her hair tickled his ear when she wiggled into a better position.

"She's mad at me—not you." He stared out the window and said the words almost automatically. As mad as Wilma was, there wasn't any way to keep this argument hidden from the kids. Especially Cerise with her inquisitive mind.

247

Cerise popped the last of a sandwich into her mouth and licked at her fingers. He caught the heavy scent of peanut butter.

"You'll ruin your dinner eating sandwiches so late in the afternoon."

"Matt took the last of the cookies." She took one final lick of her index finger and rested her head on his shoulder.

"Just as well. You'll ruin your complexion if you keep eating so many cookies."

She giggled against his ear. "Whatever I do, something will get ruined."

Her body slid off the arm of the chair and into his lap. As she twisted her head around to fit into the hollow of his shoulder, Phil looked down. The front of Cerise's blouse gaped open, and he saw the soft swell of her breasts. Pink. Or was it a reflection of the red material? The flesh was as full and soft as Wilma's.

She twisted again, swinging her legs across his. Her hip rubbed against him and sent a surge of excitement rising up from his scrotum. He felt the tingling, then the erection.

Cerise giggled and wiggled a little harder. "Matt's silly."

Phil felt beads of perspiration rising on his forehead. He'd try to ignore what was happening. He clenched one hand on the arm of the chair. If he pushed her away, she'd wonder why. He decided to control it . . . act normal.

"He asked me if I was going to marry Bobby Blaylock."

Phil took a long, slow breath. It might have been funny if he wasn't feeling such a strong physical attraction. What was wrong with him?

"You're too young to be thinking about marriage, Cerise. Too young even to talk about it."

"Not too young to think about it, Daddy Phil."

He thought he detected a faint tone of amusement in her voice. He must be imagining it. This conversation wasn't funny at all.

"I'm only too young to do anything about it," she added and rubbed her head against his chest.

"You're only a baby, Cerise, and so is Bobby Blaylock. I don't want to hear any more talk about marriage. Not at your age."

Age? He wondered if age had anything to do with the way he was growing this fury in his groin. Wilma was right: the girl was growing up too fast. He wasn't going to have her get married before she finished school. Cerise could be—she already was—a great asset to his evangelism. Sometimes he thought she might follow him into the ministry. Marriage? He wanted to grab her and hold her, but the sensuality of her body held him rigid against the back of the chair. He hadn't felt like this since the first time he had seen Wilma. This must be a reaction. The fight with Wilma . . . it was only a reaction. It was Wilma he wanted, and his body was reacting to Cerise. It had to be the solution. A man didn't lust after his own daughter.

Cerise brushed her cheek against his chest and patted him with one hand. "Don't worry, Daddy Phil. I'd never marry Bobby Blaylock. He's too dumb." Her fingers twisted at a button on his shirt until he reached up and moved her hand away. She giggled softly and tossed her head back, looking up at him from under the darkened lashes.

"Do you know Bobby Blaylock didn't even know what the word *fuck* meant?" She tossed her head again, and the blonde hair swirled around her shoulders.

Phil let his mouth fall open and choked as he forced the shock back into his throat. His voice started to crack. He'd be sounding like Wilma if he didn't get himself under control. He cleared his throat and tried to act as if Cerise hadn't startled him at all.

"I'm surprised you know an obscenity like that, Cerise. I'm even more shocked to hear you use the word."

She shifted her weight and stretched her legs. Phil fought an urge to dump her on the floor. He'd have to stop this. She was getting too old to sit in his lap.

"I don't use the word, Daddy Phil, but it's on all the bathroom walls at school. A person has to be really dumb if they don't ask what it means."

Phil looked down at her, wondering how she knew Bobby Blaylock hadn't understood the meaning. The sight of her curved breasts flashed in front of him, and he decided not to ask. At least, not now. He was afraid to know the answer.

"Mr. Blaylock is right," Phil said. He'd already made Wilma mad. Now he was forced to be the stern parent. "The schools are corrupting our children. The sooner we start a church-oriented school, the better. I don't want you associating with anyone who uses that word, and I don't want you using it."

He slid one arm around her and shook her shoulder until she turned her head up toward him.

"Don't be mad, Daddy Phil." She lowered her eyelashes and smiled. "I'm not going to marry any of those dumb guys. When I grow up, I'm going to marry you."

Phil let his hand fall back to the arm of the chair and tried not to laugh. Poor little daydreamer.

"Cerise, you can't marry me. I'm your father."

She shrugged and the mouth drew together at the corners. "You're not really my father. We're not really related at all, so I can too marry you."

"Cerise." This time he couldn't hold back a small chuckle. "I'm an old man compared to you, and a married man at that."

"People don't stay married. One of the girls in my class has had four different fathers." She tightened her arm around him as if she was trying to crush herself against him.

"I intend to stay married, Cerise. Divorce is a sin— one more thing these public schools don't teach."

She was silent, and Phil began to feel the renewed stirring of his erection. He was losing control of the situation. He pushed her way from his chest and turned his eyes quickly toward the window. Her blouse! No wonder he could see so much of her breasts.

"Cerise, your blouse is coming undone. Button it up."

She peered up at him from one corner of her eye. The smile was so fleeting, Phil wasn't positive he had seen it.

"You must have homework to do." He gave her a slight push, afraid to touch her with more than a hand on her back. "And I have to work on a sermon."

She lingered beside his chair, swinging her hips from side to side. He pulled one of the stacks of paper toward him to avoid meeting her eyes. The printed words made no sense. The fire in his gut was taking command. The throbbing penis! He stared at the paper and felt nauseated. It was wrong!

Cerise leaned forward. Her fingers rested on his shoulder, and she kissed him on the forehead. Her breasts pushed against his arm, and he could feel the hard nipples through the cloth. She moved, and her breasts slid across his arm. Her hair swept across his cheek, sending an electrical tingle shooting down into his shoulder.

His hand tightened on the papers.

"Cerise . . ." He caught himself before he started shouting, but Cerise was moving across the room toward the stair.

He leaned back in the chair and took a long, slow breath. The papers shook in his hand. He dropped them as if they had come to life. The walk . . . even her walk had a provocativeness. He hadn't noticed how fluid her movements were. No wonder Wilma worried about Cerise. Why hadn't he noticed?

He shoved the chair away from the desk and stared down at the shadows on the carpet. His day was like the swirling streaks in the pile, twisting endlessly in different directions. Why? Why this physical attraction for Cerise? It was sick. He must be sick.

Did this happen to other men? For the first time he wished he had known his father. Had had someone to ask. How did men react?

"Oh, Lord, forgive me." The words ripped up out of his chest and with them the erection. The guilt. He hung his head and prayed for forgiveness.

What he felt for Cerise, his reaction to her body—it was sinful. He couldn't let it happen again. He put his hands over his face and prayed. He was weak. It was a weakness in his nature. It wasn't Cerise. She was only an innocent child, too young to know what she was doing. He was the one who needed help.

Cerise stopped at the top of the stairs and looked at

her reflection in the window. Daddy Phil was right: too many cookies could give her pimples. Or even worse, she might get fat like her homeroom teacher or like Miss Wilford back in Pleasant Home.

Matt could have the cookies. She'd fix another peanut butter sandwich. The kitchen was empty, and mother hadn't even started fixing dinner. One more peanut butter sandwich wouldn't hurt.

She walked into the living room and leaned over Matt's chair. With her mouth against his ear, she smacked her lips and blew her breath into his face.

"See, smarty, I found something better than cookies."

He pushed her face away with one hand and shook some crumbs off his book. "Make me one."

"Make it yourself, like I did."

Matt looked up at her, and Cerise grinned. He could look so sad. Served him right for taking all the cookies.

"I can't reach the shelf. It's easier for you."

"Nope." She took a small bite and chewed it as loudly as she could.

"Mommy won't like you eating sandwiches before dinner."

"She told me I could, since you ate all the cookies," Cerise retorted and flopped on the davenport. She chucked the last of the sandwich in her mouth and dug under the cushion for the candy bar she had hidden there. The crackling of the paper made Matt turn and stare. His eyes popped open so wide he looked as if she'd stuck him with a pin. She giggled at the thought.

"Where'd you get the candy?" He raised up in his chair and the book fell to the floor.

"God gave it to me." Cerise took a bite and closed her eyes.

"You're not supposed to tell lies," Matt glared. "God doesn't give people candy bars."

She continued to chew on the caramel-filled treat. "I'm special. God does things for me."

"You're telling lies. Daddy won't like it."

"I'm not telling lies." She peeled the wrapper back farther. "Well, maybe about the candy bar. But not about God doing things just for me."

She broke off one end of the candy bar, held it out, and then hesitated. "I'll give you some, but you better not tell Daddy Phil, or I'll have God fix you good."

Matt grabbed at the piece of candy and sank back into his chair. "You can't. It'll be you that gets fixed. Daddy will fix you for telling lies."

"But I'll have God fix you even worse." Cerise wadded the candy wrapper up into a small ball and tossed it up into the air. She lowered her eyelashes and squinted at Matt as she caught the wad of paper.

"You're telling more lies." Matt reached for his book and turned his head away.

"Okay, smarty," she answered. "You wait and see. I know how to pray better than other people, and when I pray really hard, God will do what I ask him to. If you aren't careful, I'll have God fix you."

"You're lying." Matt picked up the book and clamped his mouth into a stubborn line.

"Yeah, well, Eddie Carter got fixed when I asked God to fix him, didn't he?"

Matt looked over the edge of his book and began to wiggle down into a coiled lump. His eyes were wide, and his mouth drew up into a scared pucker. Cerise tossed the candy wrapper into the fireplace. He was about to cry, and if he cried, Mother would be asking questions.

"I won't do it to you, Matt, unless you make me mad."

His lower lip trembled. "Promise?"

She got up and stretched. "Well . . ." She looked at him without smiling and watched him carefully. He looked as he believed her. "Okay, I promise, but don't tell about the candy bar."

Matt shook his head and scrunched back into his chair. "I won't tell, Cerise, honest . . . I won't."

"Okay," she yawned. "I'm going to do my homework. Call me when Mom has supper ready."

She picked up her books and carried them into her room, where she dumped them on the end of her bed. She didn't have very much homework. She could read her history in about twenty minutes. What she wanted to do was think. She didn't want to bother with Matt.

Daddy Phil thought it was funny, but she really did want to marry him. She'd be a lot better than Mother. Mother didn't like going to the meetings.

She crossed her legs and sat on the bed, staring at the wall. Should she pray about it or not? If Mother died, then Daddy Phil wouldn't be married anymore. It wasn't the same as divorce at all. Still, Mother hadn't done anything really wrong. Would God answer her prayers? Eddie Carter had called her a lizard. *She* had been bossy and mean. Kathleen screamed. They deserved being punished. But Mother hadn't done anything except be crabby.

Daddy Phil said God wouldn't answer prayers if they were selfish prayers or bad prayers. He only answered prayers when they should be answered. If Mother was supposed to go to heaven, then God would answer the prayer.

Then there would be only Daddy Phil and herself.

She could go to all the services with Daddy Phil. She could sleep in the bed with Daddy Phil and smell his shaving lotion and feel his strong arm around her.

There'd be only Daddy Phil and—and Matt. Who would take care of Matt? She didn't want to be stuck taking care of Matt. He still had to be watched in the bathtub or he wouldn't rinse the soap out of his hair. Or scrub his neck.

Maybe Daddy Phil would hire someone to take care of Matt. But maybe Daddy Phil would marry someone else before she was old enough to marry him. Better wait.

How old did she have to be to get married? Mother didn't usually know anything, but she had gotten married. She must know something about it.

She opened her eyes and uncoiled from her cross-legged position. It would be better to wait and pray about Mother later. If she did it too soon, Daddy Phil wouldn't marry her. How old did she have to be?

When she went into the living room, Matt was still scrunched up in the large chair. His eyelids flickered, and then he turned back to his book, as if he didn't want to see her. There were clanging noises coming from the kitchen.

"Get busy and set the table," Wilma snapped when Cerise came into the kitchen. The spoon banged against the saucepan in a furious circling of the contents. The kitchen was heavy with the aroma of corn muffins and ham.

She was still crabby. Cerise opened the drawer without arguing and started picking out the silverware.

"Mother, how old do you have to be to get married?" She gathered up the last of four spoons and took four placemats from the next drawer.

"A lot older than you are," Wilma grumbled.

"I know that, Mother, but how old?" Cerise insisted.

"Sixteen, if your parents okay it. Eighteen if they don't." The spoon banged even harder, and Wilma slammed the lid on the pan with a resounding clatter.

"That's old," Cerise groaned.

"It's not old." Wilma reached for a potholder and opened the oven door. The scent of ham mushroomed out in a cloud of steam and filled the room. "It's too young, and you're too young even to ask about it. Get those things on the table."

Cerise stopped in the doorway. "What if your parents are dead? Who gives permission?"

"Who knows?" Wilma answered. She grabbed another potholder and lifted the pan out onto the stove top. "Anyhow, you have to finish school and . . ." she paused, glaring at the roaster pan as if it were an unwelcome bug, ". . . and you'd better learn to cook."

Cerise lifted her eyebrows. Mother was mad at everything. She had her fist doubled up as if she was ready to fight with the ham. Maybe Mother was getting sick.

"Anybody can cook, Mother. If they can read a cookbook, it's simple. A dummy could do it."

The potholder missed her head and bounced off the wall.

"Set the table! Now!"

"Okay, okay, I'm going." Cerise frowned. Mother looked as if she was going to cry.

She put the silverware on the mats and bit her lip. Either Mother was getting real sick or the fight with Daddy Phil was serious.

Her lips parted and the corners of her mouth turned up. Maybe she wouldn't have to ask God for help at all. Mother didn't act as if she was going to get over being mad at Daddy Phil for a long time.

She went after the plates and was careful to avoid getting in her mother's path. God would work things out. She wouldn't pray unless it was absolutely necessary. Not for a couple years at least.

Her hands stroked the placemat, and she readjusted the silverware beside Daddy Phil's plate.

Why did they keep telling her she was too young? Too young to stay late at Daddy Phil's services. Too young to think about boys, or sex, or marriage. She was old enough for a lot of things. Old enough to make Daddy Phil get a hard-on. Daddy Phil could see how old she was getting. She hummed to herself as she went back for the glasses.

It was going to be a long mad, Cerise decided. No one said anything all during supper. Daddy Phil had even mumbled the words when he said grace, and Mother had only closed her eyes. She didn't bow her head at all.

And they hadn't looked at each other either. But Daddy Phil hadn't looked at anyone.

Cerise finished stacking the dishes and started scraping the plates. Sixteen. She would have to wait a long time. It was too long. Maybe a couple years. Daddy Phil could make love to her even if she wasn't old enough to get married. He wanted to; she could tell. He looked down her blouse the same way Bobby Blaylock did.

She'd have to find some way to show Daddy Phil she was old enough to think about marriage and making love.

He couldn't sleep. The sick feeling in his stomach,

258

the ache in his chest . . . he tried to pray, but the guilt kept blocking his words. Even in the dark, he could still feel Cerise's nipples sliding across his arm, see the breasts bulging under her blouse, and he couldn't stop the erection. It kept coming back. Nor could he relieve it. Worse yet, he couldn't excuse it—not to himself, nor to God.

Wilma lay motionless beside him. Too motionless. No sounds of her regular breathing. She was awake, too. Awake, with her back to him, rigid.

Phil stared up into the darkness, started to reach for her, and then put his hand back under the covers and squeezed at the stiffness of his penis. She would only pull away if he touched her. He couldn't talk to God. He had to talk to Wilma.

"Wilma, I'm sorry."

She shifted uneasily. The room remained silent.

"Wilma, at least let me talk to you."

"Why?"

"So I can admit I was wrong." He released a long breath and paused. "I was wrong about a lot of things."

No movement, but he could feel the rigidness of her body ease in the springs of the bed. She was listening. Choose the words cautiously. No blunders now.

"I was wrong about what you're trying to do, and mostly about Cerise."

The mattress moved. She had shifted position. He waited until she moved again and turned onto her back. She hadn't moved toward him, but she had softened enough to listen.

"She is acting too adult. I'm going to quit having her light the candles at the weeknight services. I'll have one of the older girls. More participation will be better for

259

the congregation."

He found himself amazed at his own thoughts. It was a good idea. Cerise wouldn't be walking home with the Blaylock boy. What if the Blaylock boy wasn't as innocent as he looked? If Cerise had the same effect on young Blaylock. . . . He didn't want anyone to . . . Cerise was his.

He caught his breath. Jealous . . . he was jealous of the Blaylock boy!

"What about school? I'm going to go, Phil." Her voice sounded flat and toneless in the darkness.

"All right. I'll get used to the idea."

He turned and reached for her. She had to understand.

"Wilma, I can't help it. I'm afraid you'll change." The words broke loose as he buried his face between her soft, warm breasts. "I don't want you to change. Don't want you to be different."

Her arm was warm and comforting around his shoulder. So gentle. The tears came into his eyes. "I love you the way you are, Wilma."

Her fingers twisted in his hair and slid down to the back of his neck. She stroked his earlobe, circling behind his ear with the tip of her index finger. Her lips murmured into his hair until he raised his head and closed his mouth over hers. She rolled her hips upward against him.

The ache in his stomach was gone. There was only a fire left burning in his groin. He reached one hand under the soft fleshiness of her bottom and pulled her against him, rubbing himself into her pubic hair.

Was Cerise blonde? The idea flitted through his mind, and he groaned with a surge of desire. Groaned and pushed Wilma's thighs apart with a sudden frenzy.

"Phil!"

Wilma's voice caught in his ear. He couldn't hold it back any longer. He plunged into the openness of Wilma and felt the desire, the lust for Cerise, shoot out. It left him in one long burst, and he fell drained and panting against Wilma's shoulder.

She continued to stroke his hair and hold him as he clung to her.

"Wilma, forgive me?" He whispered the words, but would it be enough? She didn't know. Oh, God, she mustn't know how much she was forgiving. The kiss on his forehead was an answer, but it wasn't an absolution. What was he going to do about Cerise? He couldn't avoid her.

"What are you going to do about Cerise?"

Wilma's words sent a chill across his shoulders. Did she know what turmoil was going on in his mind? He lay stiff and tense, trying to figure out what she meant. What was he going to do?

"I mean about the television program. Are you still going to use her?"

His shoulder muscles relaxed. Odd, he had already forgotten that part of the argument.

"I think so, but we'll shoot it here at the house."

"Here?" Wilma's hand stopped stroking him.

He rolled away from her and let his body melt into the comfort of relaxation. He could think now. Think of the possibilities.

"In the family room. Set up the candles, then shoot the sermon. By the fireplace. We want to make them informal chats. Better place for the filming anyhow."

Wilma rolled over against him. "I still think it's too much attention."

"It will make up for her not going to the weeknight

261

services. She'll fuss about it, but at least she won't be walked home by a fifteen-year-old boy. Weekends, she can do it. She comes home with me on weekends."

His arm tightened about Wilma's shoulders. "You're right about Cerise, honey. She's not a little girl anymore."

"Was she ever?" Wilma yawned.

Her breathing started into a deep, rhythmic pattern of sleep. Phil lay in solitude and tried to pray. The words still wouldn't come. He had to find strength somewhere.

It wasn't strength; it was evasion he found. He shut himself off, writing sermons, planning the television programs. Scheduling his conferences with Ted Gower for late afternoon. Pushing his chair so tightly against the desk that Cerise couldn't climb into his lap. She had to be content with rubbing her head against his shoulder, and he buried his head in his hands after she left the room.

She accepted the no weeknight services ultimatum with only a shrug of her shoulder and a long, penetrating stare. A stare that make him bend his head and try to pray away the guilt, without success.

He redoubled his conferences and crammed his daily schedule until the first videotaping of the television program was set. The basement room was packed with cameras, lighting equipment, sound equipment, and cables crisscrossing the floor. The candelabra were set in one corner, with the shot to be taken before they started taping the four fifteen-minute segments of Phil's talks.

Phil checked his reflection in the mirror and took a long, exhilarating breath. This was it. The charged excitement.

He surveyed the room from the stairs and grinned. Ted Gower, the sponsor, the sponsor's wife, the Blaylocks—they were all his family. Even Wilma was holding Matt and waiting for the taping to begin. She smiled at him across the room, and he felt warmly encouraged. Maybe school was good for her. It felt good having her there.

The cameramen were finishing with Cerise, and the lights were being positioned around his desk. Ted Gower was serving as a stand-in. The table was set up for the after-filming party. Wilma had laid out a buffet that would have them all dieting for a week. Mrs. Blaylock had asked Wilma to help out at her next dinner party. There were at least seven people from the film crew. The room was jammed. It was another innovation. He was making progress faster than he expected.

It would succeed. The final-fifteen-minute segment was an appeal for funds to start a school. Blaylock would be proud. Cerise would have a decent school to attend. She'd be a normal child.

He glanced across the room. Behind the candles, she was only a small girl in white. Nothing stirred. He had worked himself out of his personal crisis.

On top of it. In control again.

He moved through the crowded room toward the fireplace. This would make the state wake up. What altar calls he would have after this program started on the air!

"Okay, Reverend Thayer, we're almost ready."

He settled into the chair and turned toward the camera.

* * *

"It's good, kid. You can go."

The lights swung away from Cerise and went out. She blew out the lighting taper and blinked to readjust her vision to the room light.

The lights were being set and adjusted around Daddy Phil's desk. The cameramen checking through viewfinders, cables being moved. Ted Gower stepped away from the desk, and Daddy Phil moved into place behind his chair. He shook Ted Gower's hand, turned, smiled, and spoke to one of the men adjusting cables. The man laughed, bent over, and disappeared behind the desk.

Cerise tried to catch Daddy Phil's attention, but there were too many people. The room was getting hot. The lights had been hot. The log in the fireplace crackled, and a man moved Harry Blaylock's chair to make room for another light.

She looked at the cheese tray on the table and gathered up the skirt of her dress. There was lots more food in the kitchen. Daddy Phil said she could change after they finished with her.

She snatched a piece of cheese and glanced over her shoulder. No one was paying any attention to her anyhow. Everyone was watching Daddy Phil. She ambled up the stairs, watching the crowd as she went, but no one even looked up.

The refrigerator was crammed, and she peered through the cans of soda trying to find a Dr. Pepper.

"They through with you?"

She grabbed a can and straightened to look over the door into Bobby Blaylock's eyes.

"Um-hmm." She held the can out toward him and snatched another.

"How come you're not downstairs?" she asked. She shut the refrigerator door and leaned back against it as she pried open the tab.

"It's boring." The can hissed when he opened it, and the liquid gurgled in a noisy swallow.

Cerise flattened her shoulders against the refrigerator, lowered her eyelashes, and looked at Bobby. He was looking at the front of her dress, and she pushed her chest forward. She arched her back to make her breasts push out even farther.

Bobby took another swallow and tried to stifle a burp.

"Are those real?" He pointed at her breasts. "Some girls are all rubber."

"They're real," she answered and wiggled back and forth against the coolness of the appliance.

"I'll bet they're not. They're probably fake." He leaned against the refrigerator beside her and whispered in her ear. "Let me feel and see whether they're real or not."

She glanced up at him from one corner of her eye and smiled as his hand moved hesitantly toward her, touching her lightly, then squeezing.

All the times she had rubbed her own breasts, it had never felt like this. It was exciting. She felt the nipples hardening and a tingle run down her body.

"Now do you believe they're real?"

Redness covered his cheeks at her words, but he kept his hand cupped around her breast and squeezed once more.

"Maybe. Feels real, but there's too much material." He dropped his hand away and moved his gaze to the can of soda in his hand.

"Come on." She grabbed his hand. "I'll show you."

He faltered once as they crossed the living room. "What if someone comes upstairs?"

"Come on," she tugged at him. "They'll be at least an hour. More if they have to reshoot anything."

When she dropped his hand at her bedroom door, he hung back, first leaning on the door, then moving a few steps into the room. One strand of hair fell across his forehead. He brushed it back, nervously rubbing his ear and shifting from one foot to the other.

She undid the zipper and bent forward, whisking clouds of chiffon over her head and letting it drift to the floor. Her hands went to her hips as she stepped across the dress and stood facing him. Her eyelashes fell and flickered while she waited for his reaction.

"Don't you wear a bra?" Bobby's eyes bulged. His voice fell almost to a whisper—slow and so hushed that Cerise had to strain to hear him.

"Sometimes," she giggled and moved closer to stand in front of him. "Now do you believe they're real?"

His head bobbed up and down. He gulped the last of the soda without taking his eyes from her and stood squeezing the can between his fingers. His gaze slid down to her underpants, and he swallowed hard.

"You blonde down there, too?" he asked.

Cerise gave him an evaluating look and reached down with one hand to expose her pubic hair.

"Have you ever done it?"

He blinked at her question as if he didn't understand and then moved his head from side to side.

"Want to try?"

She moved closer, letting her breasts rub against his fingers, and she smiled to herself at the growing redness in his face.

"Someone might come upstairs," he choked and squirmed back and forth.

"I told you—they have a whole hour of stuff to film.

No one's going to come up."

She twisted her head and looked up at him. The blonde hair swirled about her shoulders. When Bobby reached for the zipper on his pants, she slid her hand down, pushed the panties to her feet, and sent them into the pile of chiffon with one swift kick.

It wasn't fun at all, Cerise decided. Bobby wasn't as big as she thought boys were. He jabbed at her without effect until she had to guide him into her with one hand, and it didn't feel good at all. She bit her lip when he pushed into her. He looked odd. His eyes had a funny glazed look, and his mouth was hanging open.

She put both of her hands on his chest and pushed. Pushed hard until he stopped and stared at her with a puzzled look.

"We'd better quit." She pushed again and forced him away until he backed from the bed and stood up.

"I thought you wanted to." He sounded whining, but he was hastily shoving his wilted penis back inside his pants.

"I changed my mind," Cerise shrugged. "I keep hearing noises like someone coming upstairs."

He yanked the zipper up and darted out the door. Cerise grinned to herself and rolled lazily off the bed. He was such a poop. It didn't take much to scare him.

She took her time dressing, buttoning and unbuttoning the top button on her blouse until she scowled and unbuttoned the top two buttons.

Bobby was waiting in the kitchen, pacing around the floor and looking anxiously at the stairway.

"Cerise." He paused, cleared his throat, and then stared at the refrigerator. "You're going to be my girl now, aren't you?"

She nibbled at her lower lip and the corners of her

mouth twitched. He looked so serious with his hair falling in his face.

"How can I be your girl?" she giggled. "You never kissed me."

"But I . . ." Bobby stammered and reached for her. His hand tightened on her waist as his lips closed upon hers in an overly moist kiss.

"Cerise, what's going on?"

At the sound of Phil's voice, Bobby jerked away from her and backed across the kitchen. Phil walked toward Cerise, not even glancing in Bobby's direction. His stare was fixed directly on the front of her blouse.

She looked down and hastily buttoned the top two buttons. From one corner of her eye, she saw Bobby sidling along the wall, inching his way behind Phil and bolting down the stairs.

"Are you through already?" she asked. She peered up at him, but kept her head bowed and waited for the answer.

"I'm changing jackets." He clenched and unclenched one hand while he glared at her. "What's been going on up here?"

She shrugged her shoulders and opened her eyes wide. "Nothing, Daddy Phil."

"You call that nothing?"

"It was only a kiss, Daddy Phil." She lifted her chin and smiled at him. It was the first time she had been alone with him for a week. He had been too busy for her. She hadn't been able to sit on his lap or talk to him at all.

She darted forward and leaned against him, hugging him around the waist and rubbing her cheek against his chest. His hands gripped her arms. They dug into the flesh and shook her until her hair swung around her face. Shook and then shoved her with a violence that sent her hurtling back against the kitchen cabinets.

The wrenching twist of her body thudding against the wood sent a spasm of pain down her back. Her mouth flew open, and she gasped for air. Her hand went up to her face and pushed the strands of hair away from her eyes.

Her mouth closed and her eyes narrowed as she watched him—alert, ready for another blow. He was standing with his feet apart, facing her with his hands shaking. She kept her eyes on him without wavering and braced herself, ready to duck if he made another move.

The pain in her back stung as if she'd been burned. It kept going on and on without easing. Daddy Phil had never been so furious before. He had no right to be mad. He had no right to push her around. All he saw was Bobby kissing her. She kept her eyes steady and glared at him until he looked down at his hands.

"I won't have you kissing boys at your age." He raised his head and took a deep breath. "And quit looking at me like that. I'm not a monster. I'm your father."

She watched him without saying a word. Waited for him to apologize. He'd hurt her. He should be sorry.

Phil turned his head away. "Go to your room, Cerise, and stay there until everyone is gone. Maybe if you aren't allowed to talk to Bobby, this will blow over."

He started out of the room, and Cerise rubbed at her arms.

"Daddy Phil, you hurt me!"

He paused at the doorway and shook his head. "Not as much as you deserve," he said and continued to walk away from her.

She dug her fingernails into the palms of her hands and glared at his back. He'd seen Bobby kiss her and he still thought she was a little girl. But you weren't supposed to hurt people. He shouldn't have shoved her so hard.

Her entire back hurt when she straightened and walked slowly to her bedroom. She kicked the white angel dress under the bed and flopped on the bedspread. The pain was going away, but she was seething inside.

She didn't love Daddy Phil at all. Not anymore. He was mean and he wasn't even sorry. He should be sorry. He *would* be. She rolled up to a sitting position and crossed her legs. She squinched her eyes shut as tightly as she could. She prayed harder than she ever had and prayed over and over.

She prayed until the bedroom door opened and Matt stuck his head through the crack.

"Daddy says you can come out now. There's still lots of food."

"I'm not hungry." She closed her eyes again and clamped her mouth shut.

"What are you doing?"

"Praying." She opened her eyes and glared at Matt. "Go away and leave me alone."

He frowned and his eyes grew wide. "Are you mad at me, Cerise?"

"No, dummy. I'm mad at someone else, and God will fix him. Now go away."

"Who are you mad at?"

"Will you go away?"

"If you tell me." His voice quivered. "If it's me, I'm sorry."

"It's not you. It's Daddy Phil. Now get out!"

270

She closed her eyes again and heard the door close. If he didn't leave her alone, she'd take care of him next.

"Make Daddy Phil sorry he hurt me." She rocked back and forth and repeated the words over and over in a rising fury. Her ears rang and her jaw muscles hurt. God would fix Daddy Phil. God fixed everything.

Matt darted into the kitchen and snatched a ripe olive from the bowl, drawing a frown and a tap on his fingers from Wilma.

"Enough, young man. Leave some for your sister."

"She's not going to eat," Matt announced and stepped out of Wilma's way when she reached for a roll of plastic wrap.

"Not going to eat?" Wilma looked at him with disbelief. "Is she sick? Cerise always eats."

"She's not sick," Matt answered. "She's mad."

Wilma wrapped the last of the celery sticks and pushed the plate aside to make room on the drainboard as Phil carried more food up from the basement.

"Maybe I should talk to her," she said and glanced at Phil. "It's not like Cerise to refuse food, even when she's mad."

"She's pouting," Phil said. He set the plates down and wiped a glob of dressing from his thumb. "I sent her to her room."

"She said she was mad," Matt argued.

"I suppose she is," Phil answered, "but she's mad at me and pouting." He looked at Wilma and sighed, "I don't think I handled it too well, but she'll get over her pouting when she gets hungry."

"She's not pouting. Daddy, she's praying."

Phil rubbed Matt's curls with one hand and smiled, "She needs to do a lot of praying."

271

Matt grabbed Phil's leg and looked up with his lower lip trembling. "But she's praying for God to fix you."

"Fix me?" Phil started to chuckle, but Matt's eyes filled with tears.

His small head bobbed up and down. "Cerise says God makes people sorry when she prays real hard. She'll make something bad happen to you, like she did to Eddie Carter."

Phil's face sobered and he bent to pick Matt up in his arms and hold him against his chest. He patted the boy's shoulder and kissed him gently on the forehead.

Wilma stood frozen and disgusted. She dropped an empty plate into the sink with a furious urge to break the thing. "What's wrong with her, telling you a story like that? I'll give her something to pout about."

She grabbed at a towel and twisted it between her hands before she started out of the room. Matt's wail halted her at the doorway.

"No, Mommy. Don't make her mad. Please, don't make her mad at you, too."

Phil hugged Matt closer to him. "Son, your sister can't make bad things happen. She's only telling you that to scare you."

"But she said she prayed for God to fix Eddie Carter, and he died." Huge tears ran down Matt's cheeks. He buried his face against Phil's chest and his shoulders shook with muffled sobs.

"This has gone too far, Phil," Wilma exploded. "I'm going to talk to her. Right now."

Phil shook his head. "There's a better way, honey." He tilted Matt's head upward and held the boy's chin gently in his hand. "Son, God doesn't do things like kill people. Your sister can pray all she wants to, but she can't make bad things happen to people. What

272

happened to Eddie was an accident, and it would have happened whether Cerise prayed or not. God doesn't punish anyone who doesn't deserve it." He patted Matt's back. "You wait and see. Nothing will happen, no matter how hard your sister prays. That should prove Cerise can't make anything happen."

Matt wiped his nose with the back of his hand and sniffed. "Are you sure?"

Phil gave him another squeeze about the shoulders. "I'm sure, Matt. You watch. Nothing is going to happen to me."

Matt sniffled once more, and Phil let him slide to the floor. Matt looked up in a struggling attempt to smile, and Phil gently wiggled the boy's ear with his index finger. "Son, who taught your sister and you how to pray?"

Matt's face was sober as he answered, "You did."

"Well, then remember, I can pray even better than your sister. Now don't worry."

Matt's face cleared up, and a wide smile appeared. Phil gave him one last pat on the head and said, "There's one more plate of rolls on the table downstairs. Why don't you bring them up for me?"

Matt grinned and darted down the stairs, leaving Phil rubbing thoughtfully at the back of his neck.

Wilma tossed the towel on the cupboard and bit at her thumb. "I still think I should talk to her," she said. "I don't like her scaring Matt like this. What kind of crazy ideas does she have, anyway?"

"The best way for Matt to quit believing that nonsense is to see that nothing happens. What worries me is the odd ideas she's getting about herself. Blaylock is right. The public schools aren't good for children."

Wilma turned her head to stare at the cupboard. "I

273

don't think the schools are to blame for Cerise. She's different, Phil. Sometimes she frightens me."

Phil chuckled softly. "She gets her way by backing everyone down. The way she glared at me was hair-raising, but she found out I don't scare easily. I can see how she scares a small boy."

"I don't think she was trying to scare you," Wilma said thoughtfully. "She's never been mad at you before."

"First time for everything." He flashed a smile at her. "You look as worried as Matt. Don't tell me you believe she's going to do me in with a prayer?"

Wilma continued to frown. "What Matt said—about Eddie Carter . . ."

"Nonsense. It was coincidence. A rotten coincidence, and Cerise believed she made it happen." He put his arms around her, and she snuggled against him. It did seem silly to worry, but Cerise had been so sure. The night of the accident, it was as if she knew something had happened to Eddie even before Phil had come home with the news. She shivered in spite of the warmth of Phil's body against hers.

"Once Cerise sees nothing happens to me, she'll get over the ridiculous idea that she can make anything occur."

Wilma clung to him and nodded as he spoke. He was right. Talking to Cerise wouldn't help. Cerise had to see that she wasn't capable of making things happen to people. She couldn't make anything happen to Phil. Wilma pushed her body closer to Phil's and wondered why she felt so cold.

Cerise stopped in front of the school bulletin board and stared at the yellow sign with its bold black letters.

274

She'd seen it before. Today she read it more carefully. *"Child Abuse. You don't have to take it."* She had bruises. There were bruises on her back and the imprint of Daddy Phil's hands on both arms. Bruises should be reported.

The jarring sound of the bell scattered clusters of students down the halls and through classroom doors. Cerise stood reading the sign, twisting a strand of hair between her fingers.

If the school counselor knew about her bruises, they'd call and make Daddy Phil say he was sorry. They'd tell him he couldn't push her around.

She walked toward the nurse's office. The sign said she should report any physical abuse.

The nurse scowled at Cerise, but the expression faded when Cerise rolled up her sleeves and the bruises stood out blue and ugly against her white skin. The woman's breath sucked inward in loud disapproval and came out in a loud "Oh!" when Cerise pulled her blouse up and exhibited the bruises on her back.

"How did you get those, child?" The woman clucked her tongue against her teeth and pulled Cerise's blouse higher, examining the skin carefully.

"My stepfather." Cerise let her blouse drop into place as the woman backed away and reached for a note pad.

Cerise settled into a chair and studied a cabinet full of medicine bottles and racks of thermometers. The woman kept rattling off questions, scribbling Cerise's answers and clucking to herself. She left Cerise alone for a few minutes and came back with a file card in her hand.

She frowned at the card and eased herself into the chair behind her desk. Her lips worked back and forth, finally blurting out, "According to the records, your father is a minister."

"Stepfather," Cerise corrected and wondered what made the lady frown so hard.

"It's difficult to . . ." The woman laid the card down on the desk and reached for her pen once more.

Cerise stretched her legs and waited. When was the woman going to stop asking questions and call Daddy Phil?

"Why did your stepfather do this, Cerise?"

She stared at the woman. What difference did it make, why Daddy Phil did it? She had bruises, and he shouldn't have done it.

"I mean," The woman seemed to be floundering. "Is there anything else you want to tell me?"

Cerise kept her attention on the woman's face. What else did she want to know?

"Did he touch you in any other way, Cerise?"

Cerise glanced at the clock and bit her lip. What was she trying to find out? She stared into the woman's eyes until the nurse glanced down at the papers on her desk and sighed.

"Cerise, if there has been any other form of abuse, you should tell me. If this has happened before you shouldn't be afraid to tell me. If there have been sexual abuses, you should tell me. Do you understand?" She paused and added, "Don't be afraid, Cerise. I'm here to help you."

Cerise nodded and half-closed her eyes. "He wants to . . ." she answered in a low voice.

"Wants to what?" The pen was suspended in the air, pointing like an arrow at the paper.

"Well, you know. He looks down my blouse and he gets . . ." She didn't want to say it, but the woman was waiting for something. More answers to put down on the paper. "He wants to fuck me." She watched the pen scratching across the paper. It must be what the woman wanted her to say. She leaned back in the chair and stared at the floor.

The woman got up from her desk and walked to the window, staring out at the courtyard. Was she going to call Daddy Phil now? Cerise looked back down at the floor and waited.

"This isn't really my field, Cerise. I'm going to call in Miss Donahue. She's with the children's protective division. I have to report these cases to her." She turned away from the window. As she passed Cerise, she took the girl's hand and patted Cerise's head.

Cerise jerked her head away and gritted her teeth together. She wasn't a little girl anymore. And the woman wasn't one of Daddy Phil's church women. She was too old to have her head patted.

Why didn't the lady just call Daddy Phil and get it over with? She didn't want to talk to any Miss Donahue. All she wanted was for Daddy Phil to be sorry.

Chapter Seven

Officer Virginia Donahue motioned Cerise to a seat. She scanned the notes handed to her by the junior high school nurse and whistled softly under her breath. The city's newest Bible thumper, no less! Another of the self-righteous hypocrites. The child abuse division dragged in all sorts of unbelievable offenders.

She raised her head and studied the girl. An odd one. Makeup. They wore makeup so damned young. This one appeared older than eleven and a half. She would have guessed Cerise to be at least thirteen or fourteen.

Strangely stoic girl. Not a word out of her during the ride from the school to the office. Some of these kids were difficult. Hiding the truth. Some ashamed to talk. Some frightened. This one didn't seem to fit any pattern. But she had bruises. She had asked for help.

"Cerise . . ."

The girl gazed out the windows that lined Virginia's office. She appeared calm and unconcerned. Her attention was focused on a group of six green-and-yellow-clad runners heading toward the Prefontaine Trail. Her hands lay folded in her lap. At the sound of Virginia's voice, she turned her head. Her eyes narrowed. Her chin lifted only a fraction before she tilted her head in an attentive position.

For a flashing second, Virginia Donahue was reminded of her Siamese cat. The same watchfulness. Alert and waiting. She turned back to the paper on her desk. The girl hadn't actually accused the stepfather of incest. Only said he *wanted* to fuck her. Even a minister's kid used the street language for it.

Better ask more questions. See if she could define the situation. If this went to court, she had to be positive. Did he lay the kid or didn't he?

"You told Nurse . . ." What the devil was the woman's name? Her fingers flipped through sheets of paper. "Nurse Jordan. You told her your stepfather was responsible for your bruises." She hesitated, waiting for a comment, but Cerise only stared back.

"Is that correct?"

Cerise nodded her head once. The hands were still calm and in place. Not even a twitch of the fingers.

"You said he wanted to have sexual intercourse. Did he have actual sexual relations with you?"

The eyelashes flickered once. The girl's face remained expressionless.

"Do you understand what I'm asking you, Cerise?"

"Yes."

No tremor in the girl's voice, but no answer. The girl was old enough. She wasn't an infant. According to the records, Cerise had completed a sex education course. She didn't show any sign of embarrassment. No reason not to be direct in her questions.

"Did your stepfather ever penetrate your vagina? Either with his hand or with his penis?"

Cerise dropped her chin. Her eyes narrowed and her mouth closed into a firmly set line. Nothing. Again, no answer.

"I know it's a personal question, Cerise, but I'm not asking it to embarrass you . . . only to help you."

She waited. Let Cerise think for a few minutes. Don't pressure her. Get the girl's confidence. This one didn't act frightened. She acted totally devoid of feeling. The silence could be simply distrust.

A truck rumbled and grated through gears in the street outside. Cerise turned her head toward the windows.

Virginia Donahue fingered the soft silken scarf at her neck and ran her tongue across her top teeth. Try another approach. Deal with the beating. Get to the sexual abuse problem later.

"Cerise, do you want me to help you?"

"Yes."

"What kind of help do you want?"

The head turned, and Cerise looked at her with cool poise. "I want you to make him say he's sorry and promise not to hurt me anymore."

"Did your mother try to stop him?"

Cerise's nose wrinkled. Her eyes rolled toward the ceiling in an expression of disgust. "She wasn't there."

"What did she say about it?"

"She doesn't know." The nose wrinkled again, and Cerise leaned back in her chair, kicking idly at the floor with one foot.

"Why didn't you tell her about it?" Virginia made a rapid series of notes. It added up to more question

281

marks than answers. These cases were never simple. This one could become a dilly—if she ever got any answers. At least the girl wasn't sobbing.

"Don't you think your mother would know what to do?"

Cerise shrugged her shoulders. "She's kinda dumb. She never knows what to do. Daddy Phil's smart."

Submissive mother? Was it the girl's problem too?

Virginia added a notation to have some psychological evaluations made of the girl. She flipped through the Rolodex, wondering what tests. Who should she request to administer them?

"Are you going to call Daddy Phil?"

Cerise's unexpected question startled her. Her finger slipped, and she lost her place in the cards.

"No, Cerise. I'm going to have a doctor check you over. We're going to take some photographs of the marks on your body, and we'll have the doctor check you for sexual damage."

"Then will you call him?"

"Why should I?"

"To make him sorry he hurt me." Cerise stiffened her shoulders, and her hands went up to clutch the arms of the chair.

"It's not up to me," Virginia said. "It will be up to the court."

For the first time, Cerise was showing some reaction. She twisted in the chair and chewed at her lower lip.

"You mean a judge and stuff like that?"

"Possibly. First we have to have the doctor look at you."

The girl's left hand twisted at a lock of hair. Her eyes no longer met Virginia's. Instead, Cerise stared at

282

the tip of one pink running shoe and wiggled her foot up and down.

"What happens after the examination? Then do we see the judge?"

Virginia leaned back in her chair and found her fingers back at the Rolodex, flipping cards without looking at them.

"It doesn't happen that quickly, Cerise. You'll be made a ward of the court—placed in protective custody—until we get this matter straightened out. It means you'll be in a foster home for a while. Tonight you'll be at the children's shelter—but it's temporary."

"You mean I can't go home?"

Cerise leaned forward on the edge of the chair with such a puzzled expression that Virginia drew a few more question marks on the margin of her paper.

"No, but don't worry. I'll call your mother and talk to her after the doctor's exam."

When the assurance failed to alter Cerise's expression, Virginia decided to try a gentler approach. Perhaps Cerise was more frightened than she was showing on the surface.

"We're going to keep you at the foster home, Cerise, so your stepfather can't hurt you. It takes time to set up the legal work so we can protect you. We don't like to have children hurt, Cerise. We care about what happens to you."

God, the girl had the oddest green eyes. Her gaze was fixed on a remote point above Virginia's head. Her eyes were steady, half-squinting—glistening like waters in a deep mountain pool.

"What about clothes?" Cerise frowned.

Virginia felt an odd snap in her spinal column.

Girls! You looked for all the complex reasons, and they were only worried about what to wear. She should have guessed. The makeup should have tipped her off. Cerise would be the type to be worried about her appearance.

"When I call your mother, I'll see about picking up some of your clothes. I'm sure she'll want you to stay with us."

Virginia smiled for the first time since Cerise had become her case. Give it a little time, Donahue, she said to herself. You're trying to make it too complex. You'll figure it out.

"We'll get things fixed for you, Cerise," she said calmly and reached for the phone. "First the examination."

The paper gown dropped to the white tiled floor. Cerise stood in the examination room and reached for her clothes. This wasn't going the way she thought it would. No one was going to call Daddy Phil—at least not for a while.

She was sore. No one told her doctors poked their fingers up inside and pushed on your stomach until they made you want to go to the bathroom.

What was going to happen? Court? A judge? They couldn't make her say anything. Not if she didn't want to. What were incest charges? She wanted to ask Miss Donahue, but she hadn't come back into the room. Not since the doctor finished examining her.

"That does it! We file incest charges on the bastard." Miss Donahue's voice had been so loud that Cerise had heard it through the door, but still Miss Donahue hadn't come back.

She didn't want to stay in a foster home. She wanted to go home. Go home and have Daddy Phil hug her and say he was sorry.

She finished buttoning her blouse and dug her hairbrush out of her purse.

They shouldn't put those signs up in schools. The signs didn't tell you about staying in a foster home.

She stopped brushing her hair and listened. It was awfully quiet. No one was walking around the halls. A car horn bleated outside the window. A motor revved. Then silence.

Her fingers darted into the bottom of her purse. Lunch money. She had a whole week's lunch money. Enough for a cab.

She pulled the door open, checked the hall, and grabbed up her shoes in one hand before she darted across the gleaming tiles and through the front door. Miss Donahue couldn't keep her here if she didn't want to stay.

She pushed her feet into the shoes and surveyed the street. A bicycle brushed past her and turned up the curb into the alley, passing a small sign. "Emerald Hotel. Employee Entrance." She smiled and followed the bicyclist. Hotels had cabs. She was going home.

Phil returned to his desk, slightly puzzled at having to call upstairs for Wilma to take the phone. She never received phone calls. Perhaps it was someone she met at her classes. He should tell her how wrong he had been. The classes were good for Wilma. Her eyes sparkled with excitement when she came home. If anything, she was putting extra effort into the housework. The buffet dinner she put together had made Ted Gower encourage her to start a catering business and Harry Blaylock threaten to diet.

Magnificent move, inviting Harry Blaylock to watch the filming.

The prospects of a television program impressed Blaylock. He followed every move of the cameraman. The last segment, the appeal for the Christian school, had Harry Blaylock lifting his backside off the chair and grinning like a miser watching gold coins drop into his palm. Phil had touched Harry Blaylock. Who cared about the viewers?

Phil reached for the financial reports from Ted Gower. The percentage Ted received for his promoting efforts was well earned. The radio broadcasts produced a steady river of checks from all over the Willamette Valley. Now Ted had placed the spots in California. The coverage was growing faster than he believed possible. Even with Ted collecting ten percent for handling the correspondence, the bank account was multiplying every week.

They had enough. With matching funds from Blaylock, the chapel would be built now. Set up a meeting with Blaylock . . . get the building permits. They were on the way. The Thayer Gospel Center! His dream!

He glanced at Ted's attached note. Ted needed more autographed pictures.

Phil pulled the desk drawer open, estimated at fifty, and tossed the snapshots out onto the desk. As he opened the center drawer and groped for a pen, the photographs were snatched up, hurled across the floor. He jerked his head up and stared into Wilma's flushed face.

Even under the makeup, her skin was pale. Two angry red blotches stood out on her cheekbones. She began beating on the desk with both fists. Beating on the desk and screaming.

"Damn you! Damn you!"

The burst of violence stunned him. He couldn't move. His throat was numb. His mouth opened, but nothing came out.

"You, you . . ." she sputtered—grabbed the pen out of his hand and flung it after the pictures. "What have you been up to with Cerise?"

His mouth formed the name *Cerise*, but the word wouldn't come out. What was she screaming about? She was screaming at him. Wilma? Screaming? Cerise? What about Cerise?

"You and your fancy preaching. All the big talk about protecting her . . . protecting her from what? So you could screw her yourself?"

She slapped both hands down on the desk and screamed the words into his face, spitting the words out with a spray of saliva that turned into a drooling stream from the corner of her mouth.

"Shut up!" He slammed the desk drawer shut and came up out of his chair with such force that the chair spun backward and fell to the carpet.

"It's bad enough to have you swearing and cursing like some ungodly heathen. You have some nerve, to accuse me of . . ." His voice froze. He couldn't say the word. How could she? How could she accuse him of intercourse with Cerise? *Why* would she accuse him?

She swung. Her open hand hit his face with a force that jarred his hair down over his forehead. He lifted his hand, rubbed at his cheek, and stared at her. The physical attack released the tension in her shoulders and sent her into a burst of tears.

Words came floundering out, and Phil reached back, groping blindly for his chair. She was serious. His hand grasped the arm of the chair and tugged it upright. His knees buckled, and he fell back into the security. Something had to hold him up. His legs wouldn't.

"The woman—on the phone—they're holding Cerise at a foster home, because—" She wiped at her mouth at last. The saliva washed away a streak of her makeup. "Because you beat her. And they said she had—the doctor said someone had—there was proof she'd been sexually . . ." She faltered for a second and finally forced the words out in a gust of air. "She'd had sexual intercourse."

"What woman? Who's holding Cerise?"

"The police. She's at the children's protec—oh, I can't remember the name for it. Where they take abused kids."

"But why? Why think *I* had anything to do with it?" Phil heard his own voice and couldn't believe it had gone so high. He was squeaking. He fought himself trying to get some control.

"Cerise said the reason you beat her was because you wanted to fuck her."

He was going to vomit. He knew it was only seconds away from spewing out onto the desk. Take a deep breath.

"I didn't beat her. I didn't . . . I never touched her sexually."

"Someone did. She has bruises, and they had a

doctor check her over. They said they have proof she was fucked. Proof, Phil."

Phil put his head down between his knees. Stop the dizziness.

"How did she get the bruises?" Wilma demanded. "The woman said Cerise had bruises like finger marks on both arms, and a bad bruise across her back. Cerise told the school nurse you did it."

The Blaylock boy! Phil inhaled a long breath and raised his head. The kiss . . . it wasn't a first kiss he'd interrupted. It was an aftermath of sex.

"Explain it, Phil!"

There was an edge to Wilma's voice. A keen edge. And he didn't want to look into her face.

"I might have bruised her." He tried to think. Maybe he had pushed her harder than necessary. He'd been too mad. Furious at having her try to plaster her body against him. "I caught her kissing Bobby Blaylock. I was mad. I didn't think I hurt her—at least not badly."

"What about the rest of it?"

He looked up at her, feeling as if he was looking at a stranger. The helpless blue eyes were cold. Didn't she believe him?

"It must have been—it had to be—Bobby," he said bitterly. "They must have already had their bedroom adventure."

"Why would Cerise say you wanted to . . ."

Phil groaned. Wasn't she going to leave him anything? Her questions tore into his flesh, scratched into his conscience and raked open the confession.

"I suppose because lately she's been giving me such a come-on. I couldn't take it. She got some romantic idea she was going to marry me when she grew up. I've tried to avoid her as much as I could."

"She's been giving you a come-on?" Wilma's voice rang with skepticism. "Are you sure you didn't encourage it?"

"Wilma . . ." He struggled to find the right words. He couldn't tell her. Couldn't admit how much he'd been physically attracted to Cerise. Things were bad enough. "I couldn't take the way she kept rubbing up against me, but I didn't—I never encouraged her ideas. If she's been sleeping around, it was Bobby Blaylock. It had to be."

He put his head between his hands and leaned over the desk. Cerise would ruin him. He had to talk to Cerise. Find out why. Why was she doing this?

"Call up Bobby Blaylock. Let's see what he says." Wilma's voice sawed into his thoughts, harsh and demanding.

"He wouldn't admit it." Phil felt a rush of despair. He must talk to Cerise. Bobby was too afraid of his father. Bobby wouldn't admit a thing. But Cerise—he would get the truth out of Cerise. He'd shake it out of her.

"Then get Bobby's parents on the phone. I want the truth, Phil."

All he could do was shake his head. "Wilma, if Harry Blaylock hears about this, I'm finished. He wouldn't let one of his family come near the church or me."

"To hell with Harry Blaylock."

"Wilma! Stop using profanity. I've heard all I want to hear. I won't have it."

She backed away from the desk and braced both

290

hands on her hips. "You're not telling me what to do or say, Phil. This whole thing is your fault."

"My fault? She's your daughter. Evidently she takes after her mother. Can't resist getting into bed with anything handy."

The shaking started as soon as he said the words. His hands were sweating. The palms stuck to the desk when he put them down on the wood to stop the shaking.

"You should know," Wilma snapped.

"I'm sorry." He barely whispered the words. "It wasn't called for, Wilma. I'm sorry."

"A little late, Phil." She stood and watched him as his shoulders began to shake.

Why couldn't he get control of himself? Would calling Bobby Blaylock do any good? He glanced at the phone—almost reached, then stopped and hung his head.

"Bobby wouldn't admit it. He's too scared," he murmured aloud. He raised his head and looked at Wilma. "We have to talk to Cerise. *We have to*. She's trying to get even. Matt said she was mad, remember?"

Wilma's eyes changed expression. She quit glaring at him and became thoughtful.

"The woman, Wilma, the one who called you . . . call her and see if we can talk to Cerise. You and I together."

She walked toward the window and gazed out across the lawn. Phil wiped his hands on his pant legs and began to breathe slowly. If they could talk to Cerise, she wouldn't try to appeal to him using her body. *Not* with Wilma present. She couldn't face him and accuse him—or could she?

Wilma turned away from the windows and walked slowly toward him. Her head was down, and she was chewing on her thumb.

"I don't think they'll let us talk to her, Phil."

"But we have to!" He felt his voice drifting up into a dangerous note of panic. "Try, Wilma. Call her and ask."

She stood and thought, then shook her head. "I asked her when she called if I could talk to Cerise. She said, maybe after they run some psycho—oh, some sort of mental tests—and only if Cerise wants to talk to me."

"If Cerise wants to talk? Don't we have any rights?"

Wilma shrugged her shoulders. "The woman—Donahue—said they were to protect the rights of the child, not the parent. She's coming by to pick up some clothes for Cerise later. I can ask her then, but I don't think they will let us talk to her, at least not until after the hearing."

"Hearing? What hearing?" Phil rose up in his chair and clutched at the desk.

"They're going to charge you with child abuse. There will be a hearing, but I don't know when."

"Oh, God!" Phil felt the words blurt out and couldn't believe he had taken the Lord's name in vain. It wasn't in vain . . . it was a prayer. God was all the hope he had. "Charge me? Are they going to arrest me?"

Wilma nodded. "She said they couldn't prove the incest charges in court until they investigate more, but they can charge you with beating Cerise."

"Isn't there anything I can do to stop it?"

"I don't know. You're supposed to be the smart one,

remember? I'm only supposed to run the house."

She turned and started walking toward the stair. Phil let his mouth fall open as he stared at her back.

"Where are you going?"

She looked back at him from the stairs with a flat, disinterested dullness to her face. "I'm packing some of Cerise's things," she said and continued on up the stairs out of sight.

He sank back into the chair, feeling like a lump of melting snow. Cold. He was cold.

Arrested? This was a nightmare, and he was living it. There must be some way to stop it.

The phone. He tried to think. Call Ted Gower . . . No, Ted was too close. Something might slip to Blaylock. A lawyer . . . he needed a lawyer, but the only lawyers he knew were the ones who handled the legal contracts with his television sponsor.

He groped for the phone book. How much time did he have? Would he get a summons? Would he be arrested and have to post bail? Did it make any difference?

The phone book tumbled to the floor. What difference did it make? If they couldn't talk to Cerise until the hearing, there wasn't any hope. He'd be on record as being charged with abuse. He would have a police record. Blaylock would drop him.

He picked up the financial report. Could he make it without Blaylock? The report dropped back onto the desk. Who'd believe him now? How many people would turn out for services led by a man charged with beating his child? He wouldn't even have a place to hold services without Blaylock.

The television show would never be broadcast. Phil

293

cringed in his chair. The sponsor had the right to pull his support if Phil was charged with or convicted of a crime. He had thought it an amusing clause. Now there was nothing to smile about. Cerise had fixed him, all right. It wasn't her prayers that did the damage. It was Cerise. He shouldn't have pushed her so hard.

The look in her eyes. She'd looked at him with such a strange expression. What had his mother said? Hatred. The girl that followed him around like a gosling was ruining everything.

The goslings. The look in her eyes when she complained that he had hurt her. The afternoon when she stomped the goslings to death. The same eyes: cold, defiant. Hard, cold, green eyes, without a waver in her stare.

He shivered and moved his chair closer to the fireplace.

What hope did he have? He was guilty of the bruises. The sex charge would always be hanging over his head. If Wilma didn't believe him, how could he expect anyone else to? Only Cerise or Bobby Blaylock could clear him. If Bobby told the truth, he would still be ruined with Harry Blaylock. Harry wouldn't part with a penny—not if he knew Cerise had seduced his son.

Start over. Could he start over? He dropped his head in his hands. With a police record of child abuse? Someone would talk about it. Cerise would find other ways to make him sorry. Every time he opposed her, he would be the victim. She would never believe her prayers hadn't caused his grief.

The Thayer Chapel would never be built.

He put his head down and tried to pray for strength. Would praying stop the summons? Would it stop the police from coming?

The plans . . . all the plans. Now they were only so much paper.

He pulled the drawer open and drew out the roll of papers. He rolled the rubber band back and forth under his fingertips. Tears rolled down his cheeks and splashed onto the paper until he hurled the plans into the fireplace. The flames snatched at the corner and flared.

He stared at the fire and then pulled the extra photographs from the desk. Slowly he fed them one by one into the destructive blaze. When they were gone, he groped in the drawer. Might as well forget the dream. Cerise had smashed it. Go home and run his mother's farm.

His mother? She wouldn't believe him either. Like his father. She wouldn't forgive the scandal.

His fingers touched leather, and he wiped at his tears. The gun . . . Ned Carter's pistol was still tucked away in the bottom drawer. He had forgotten it was there. Forgotten all about the Carters.

What kind of person had he become? Forgetting the Carters and the boy Cerise hated.

The gun came out of the holster so easily. Funny, it didn't feel so heavy now.

He laid it out on the desk and watched the firelight reflecting on the metal barrel.

The financial report. He picked up a pen and scribbled a note across the top. If Wilma had enough sense, she wouldn't starve. At the thought of Wilma, he slumped in his chair.

She wasn't the same anymore. She hadn't cried and asked him what to do. She had believed the story. Maybe she still did. He didn't even know what Wilma thought anymore.

At the sound of the doorbell, he lifted his head. He couldn't hear voices. The basement was too far away. Only the bell sounded here. Was it the Donahue woman, or a process server?

He reached for Carter's gun and removed a cartridge from the belt, then let it drop, rolling across the top of the desk.

Matt's voice, high-pitched and squeaking, echoed down the stairs. As he pushed the chair away from the desk, Matt pounded across the carpet.

"Daddy, there's a deer in the backyard. Look!"

Matt made a lunge around the edge of the desk, dodged the candelabra, and skidded to a stop with his nose pressed against the sliding glass doors.

"Look," he whispered hoarsely.

Phil blinked away the dampness in his eyes and bent his head. He'd forgotten Matt.

His fingers trembled, then clenched around the note and tore the paper into shreds. Matt needed him. Needed to grow up knowing a man could be human.

He crossed the carpet and knelt to put his arm around Matt's shoulders.

"Daddy, it's going away." Matt looked up into Phil's eyes with disappointment.

"Let's slip out and see if we can find it." Phil reached for the handle and slid the door open. He caught Matt's hand tightly in his and held on, holding the one last moment of peace with his son.

* * *

"What's a kid like you doing downtown?" the cab driver asked.

Cerise looked up at the sound of his voice and met his eyes in the rearview mirror. She laced her fingers together and leaned back against the seat before answering. The cushions reeked of stale cigar smoke that made her nose itch.

"I mean, aren't you supposed to be in school?"

She stared at a mole on the back of his neck and wondered if it got in the way when he had a haircut.

"Holiday or something," the man persisted.

"I'm going to be on television," she said and pulled her hair forward away from the smelly upholstery.

"On television? You're an actress?" The cab swerved right, dodging a street-repair barrier, and swung down the maple-lined avenue.

Cerise spotted the white car with the Lane County insignia on the door. Miss Donahue must be here, looking for her. She leaned forward and tapped the man's shoulder.

"Could you stop in front? I mean right here."

"It's okay. I'll take you to the door."

"No," she blurted out, then took a long breath. "I mean, I want to surprise them. They don't know I got the part."

"Okay." He braked and pulled the car alongside the curb.

Cerise dropped the money into his hand and looked toward the windows of the house. No one appeared. The drapes hung without moving. Miss Donahue must be inside, talking to Mother. She didn't want to talk to Miss Donahue anymore. If Mother thought she should

297

stay at the shelter, then she didn't want to talk to Mother either. Daddy Phil . . . she had to talk to Daddy Phil.

She darted across the lawn and around to the side of the house, slipping through the garage to the back door. She put her head against the wood and listened, then turned the knob and listened again. The back part of the house was quiet. Her hand gripped the knob as the door closed, holding it until she could let it turn and latch without a sound.

A murmur of voices came from the living room. Women's voices . . . Mother and Miss Donahue. She moved quickly toward the stairs and descended into the daylight basement. The room was empty, but the glass door stood open.

She moved across the room and flopped into the chair behind Daddy Phil's desk. When he came back, he would say he was sorry. As soon as he saw the bruises on her arms, he would hug her and everything would be all right.

The gun caught her eye, and she tilted her head to one side, looking at the leather grips on the handle. Where did Daddy Phil get a gun?

She picked it up and turned it over and over in her hands, then picked up the bullet and scowled. The bullet must go into the round part, but how? She pushed at it, turned it, and shook it in her hand. What good was a gun if you couldn't get the bullets into it?

From the top of the stairs, she heard Miss Donahue's voice.

"I'm sure the police will find her, Mrs. Thayer. After all, there can't be too many missing girls with flaxen

298

hair like Cerise's."

She couldn't hear Mother's answer, only a blurring of sounds. They were coming downstairs. She hurled the bullet into the fireplace and leaned back against the chair.

Let Miss Donahue try to take her back to the shelter. She would pray hard, and God would keep it from happening. She put the palms of her hands together and squeezed her eyes shut.

Virginia Donahue stopped in mid-step. Her foot hovered in the air, then slowly came down to the next tread of the stair. The girl was here, sitting calmly behind the desk as if nothing had happened. The sharp intake of breath from Wilma Thayer convinced Virginia that Cerise's presence was equally surprising to the girl's mother.

"Cerise, where have you been?" Wilma darted down the rest of the stairway, leaving Virginia staring at the girl.

Odd. Why didn't she open her eyes and answer her mother? Wilma reached the front of the desk, and still Cerise ignored her presence.

Virginia pushed herself into action to bounce down the last of the steps and cross the room to the desk.

"Cerise, answer me." Wilma's voice was sharp, but Cerise's eyes remained closed.

Virginia moved around behind the desk. "Please, Mrs. Thayer, let me talk to her." She touched Cerise's shoulder with her fingertips. "Cerise, you came to me for help. I'm here."

Cerise jerked her shoulder away before she swiveled

the chair around and opened her eyes. When she looked up, Virginia caught her breath and yanked her hand back when faced by the intensity and hatred in Cerise's eyes.

"You don't want to help," Cerise said. "You weren't going to let me come home."

Virginia knelt in front of Cerise. "Cerise, we're only trying to protect you. We can't let you come home if there's a chance you'll be beaten." She reached out and placed her hand over the girl's, only to have it shoved aside.

"Daddy Phil didn't beat me."

Virginia stared into the girl's eyes. Was she changing her story to protect her father? Some children did, yet this one was calm—too calm. There seemed to be no emotion at all in Cerise's face.

"Cerise," Virginia tried to sound soothing, "you showed me the bruises. You told me your father did it."

"Stepfather," Cerise corrected primly. "I didn't say he beat me. I said he hurt me."

"But the sexual abuse," Virginia said. "You said he hurt you because he wanted sex. We can't let you stay here if he's going to do that to you."

Cerise sighed. For a second, Virginia felt as if she was the child and Cerise was the adult. The girl acted bored. She was bending here, making her knees ache, and the girl didn't give a damn about being helped. "Cerise," she tried touching the girl's hand again, but this time it was pushed away with force.

"He didn't do it," Cerise said. "I said he wanted to, and you made the rest of it up."

Virginia gasped and looked across Cerise's shoulder

at Wilma Thayer. "The examination. Mrs. Thayer, the doctor said Cerise had intercourse. I can't ignore the doctor's report."

Wilma stared at Cerise and only nodded at Virginia's statement. She looked down at the desk, frowned when her glance rested on the handgun, then lifted her chin and studied Cerise's face. "I think there's another answer, Miss Donahue."

She walked around the desk and spun the swivel chair around, forcing Cerise to face her. "Now, young lady," she snapped, "who really got in your pants? Phil or Bobby Blaylock?"

Virginia caught the edge of the desk and pulled herself erect. She edged around the chair, waiting for Cerise's answer. The corners of Cerise's mouth moved as if she was fighting a smile.

"I want an answer," Wilma said.

Cerise giggled. "Bobby looked so dumb."

Virginia gasped. "And I've already started the arrest proceedings. My God!" She felt her rib cage crushing her lungs. False arrest charges . . . she had to stop the warrant. But the bruises—there were still the marks on the girl's body. But she said he hadn't beaten her.

The sharp crack of a bullet exploding reverberated through the room. The metallic twang of metal striking stone and the whine swelling up out of the fireplace. Virginia found herself face down on the carpet as her reflex reactions took possession of her body.

She lifted her head and stared up at Cerise. The damn girl had her eyes closed again. Her eyes were closed and Cerise was smiling.

* * *

Phil's head jerked around at the sound. Gunfire? His fingers tightened on Matt's shoulder. The gun. He'd left it lying on the desk. Wilma? She didn't know anything about guns.

"Daddy, what was that?" Matt's face was curious but not frightened.

"You stay here," Phil said. "I'll check."

"It was loud."

"I know," Phil said over his shoulder. "You watch for the deer, son. They might come back." He tried to keep the panic out of his voice. What if Wilma had loaded the gun? He broke into a run across the lawn and hit the patio, almost slipping on the flagstones, caught his balance with one hand, and stepped through the door.

Wilma's face was a white blur in front of him. She was standing. She wasn't hurt. The air was laden with the scent of gunpowder, but Wilma was turning toward him.

"What happened?" He forced the words out as he crossed the room, caught her in his arms, and looked down at the desk. The gun was still on the desk top. No one seemed to move except the woman brushing off her skirt.

"Cerise, did you . . ."

"It came from the fireplace, Mr. Thayer," the woman spoke up. She tugged her jacket into place and straightened to face him.

"But how did it get there?" Phil asked. He stared down at the gun and then glanced across the top of the desk. The bullet. He'd laid it down on the desk top, and it was gone.

"I'm sorry, Mr. Thayer. I don't know," she replied

and added, "By the way, I'm Virginia Donahue."

"She's from the children's protective division," Wilma murmured.

Phil groaned and let his arms fall away from his wife. He put one hand on the desk top and looked at Cerise. "Open your eyes, Cerise. I think it's time you answered some questions." He turned toward Virginia. "If it's allowed."

She rubbed one hand across her forehead. "It's not, according to the rules, but nothing about this case seems to be going right. She's already admitted you didn't sexually abuse her." She exhaled and nodded her head. "As long as I'm here to listen . . . there are still the bruises to explain."

He felt Wilma's hand on his arm, but there was no other feeling in his body. The child abuse charges still hung over him like a ceiling ready to cave in, and Cerise sat there with her eyes closed.

"Cerise, open your eyes and look at me," he demanded. "What's going on?"

"I'm praying, Daddy Phil." She opened her eyes and smiled up at him.

He forced his hand open, surprised to find he'd doubled it into a fist while he waited for her answer. "What are you praying for?" he asked.

"I was praying God would make Miss Donahue go away," she said. "And He almost did."

He heard the intake of air as Virginia Donahue faltered backward and eased into a chair.

"It wasn't God, Cerise. Someone threw a bullet in the fireplace." He watched her face closely, but there was only the serene smile. "Why?"

"It was God. God always fixes things. I can't help it

303

if God makes things happen differently. I pray, and he fixes things. He always does. He sure scared her."

Cerise smiled. "I prayed God would make Eddie sorry and He did. If Eddie was so smart, he'd have seen me put the clip in the gun. God doesn't answer bad prayers. You said so, Daddy Phil." She got up and stretched both arms. "God always answers my prayers. I have a special way of praying."

She glanced at Virginia Donahue and then turned back to look up into Phil's eyes. "I'm hungry," she said. "Can I go get a sandwich?"

"No." Wilma's hand fell away from his arm. "What do you mean, God answers your prayers? What other prayers has he answered?"

"Lots of them," Cerise sniffed.

"It wasn't an answer to a prayer, Cerise," Phil said. "God wouldn't make someone die because you prayed for it."

"I didn't ask for him to die," Cerise said. "I just asked God to fix Eddie for calling me a lizard. God does things. Like Kathleen."

"Kathleen?" Wilma choked the name out. "What about Kathleen?"

Cerise moved around the end of the desk, stopped, and drew circles with her finger on the desk top. The lashes fluttered and the eyebrows lifted.

"What about Kathleen?" Phil repeated softly. Even the lining of his stomach felt cold as he waited for the reply.

"God took her," she said. "You know that."

"Did you pray for God to take her?" Phil leaned toward her.

"No, I only prayed God would make her go away."

She let her finger trail off the end of the desk. "I'm awfully hungry. Can I go now?"

"Phil," Wilma's voice crackled in a worried whisper, "she told Matt she could make things happen. She believes it."

Phil nodded without taking his eyes from Cerise's face. "God didn't put the bullet in the fire. It was here on the desk and it's gone. You must have done it, but why?"

"There's no way to put it in the gun," Cerise answered, then her nose wrinkled. "It's a stupid gun. Eddie Carter's gun had a thing you pushed in. What good is a gun if there's no way to put a bullet in it?"

"Eddie Carter's?" Wilma's voice slipped up into a shrill note of confusion.

"How did you know about the Carters' gun?" Phil felt Wilma's fingers digging into the flesh of his arm. From the corner of his eye, he could see Virginia Donahue stiffen. Her mouth opened and closed as if to interrupt, then she sank back in her chair. "You mean the rifle Mr. Carter got for Christmas?"

Cerise nodded and giggled. "Eddie showed me how it worked. How you put the bullets in the clip and push the clip into the gun."

"Who put the clip in the rifle?" Phil put his hand over Wilma's and squeezed. Her fingers were cold and rigid under his.

"I did," she shrugged.

"Cerise," Phil felt his throat growing dry. "That's what caused the accident. If you hadn't put the clip in, Eddie would still be alive."

She opened her eyes wider, then the mascara-darkened lashes lowered. "Oh, no. God did it."

305

"How can you say that?" Wilma squeaked. "You made it happen."

"Where were you when Kathleen died?" He felt Wilma shaking his sleeve, but he had to know the answer. "I'd like to believe you, Cerise," he said, and fought to keep the emotion out of his voice. "Tell me how it happened."

Cerise took both hands and placed them on the back of her neck. She fanned her long hair out and let it fall over her shoulders. "She followed me to feed the ducks and I hid. I didn't want her to see me so I prayed hard for God to make her go away."

"How did she get in the water?" Wilma's voice was faint and far away, even though she was still close to his elbow.

"She stepped in. She got mud all over her shoes." Cerise giggled. "She didn't pay any attention. Just stood there in the mud."

"Then what happened, Cerise? Why didn't you get her out of the mud?"

"They called me for the races and I didn't want to miss them."

"Did she try to follow you to the races?"

Cerise giggled again. "No. She couldn't. I pushed her. She was too busy trying to get out of the water. I ran before she could start screaming. She always screamed." She looked up at Phil. "I won the race, too, and then God decided to take Kathleen."

She twisted back and forth, then looked past Phil to her mother. "Can I eat now?"

"Not just yet," Phil said. "What makes you think God answered your prayer?" He waited until she turned, and his gaze focused on hers, looking into the

306

deep green, emotionless depths.

"Because if God hadn't answered my prayer, she'd have gotten out of the mud after I pushed her. It wasn't deep."

She moved forward and flung her arms around his waist, clutching him against her and rubbing her body against his.

He grabbed at her arms, pushing her away from him, seeing Virginia Donahue's eyes widen, feeling Cerise stiffen under his grip.

"See, Daddy Phil. You're hurting me again." Her head whirled about. "See, Miss Donahue, that's how he hurt me. And you didn't make him say he was sorry."

Phil dropped his hands away from her. "All this, because I pushed you away?" He hesitated, then leaned against his desk, feeling a bone-deep fatigue. "Go get a sandwich," he said hoarsely, "and go to your room for a while."

None of them spoke as Cerise strolled placidly up the stairway. Phil's gaze met Virginia Donahue's and saw only a wide-eyed stare of dismay. Wilma turned and walked to the fireplace, looking down into the smoldering embers. Light reflected from a streak of moisture on her cheek.

Phil put both hands down on the desk top and hung his head. He couldn't pray. For the first time, he couldn't find any words to help him. Only a huge aching throbbed inside his chest, and a numbness covered his mind.

"Mr. Thayer." Virginia Donahue used both hands to push herself up out of the chair. "I'm sorry." She stood looking from Phil to Wilma, her hands went to her face, pushed against her temples, and ran through her hair before she found her voice again.

"I should have had her tested, I mean psychologically," she said. "I don't understand half of what I've heard. I don't know who Kathleen or Eddie were, but I do know the girl is sick. Mentally sick. She needs help."

"Kathleen was Cerise's sister," Phil replied automatically. Wilma's shoulders were shaking, but he couldn't find the strength to go to her. All he could do was hold onto the desk and keep trying to find words in his mind.

Virginia groped through her pockets, then bent and reached for her purse. Phil watched her leaf through a stack of business cards until she stopped and pulled one out. She laid it on the desk and shoved the rest back in her purse.

"I don't know what you want to do," she said. Her fingers trembled as she fastened the snap on the purse. "But I'd recommend this man. He runs a private hospital for disturbed children. It's expensive, but he's the best in the area."

"You mean put her away?" Phil said. "That's what you're saying, isn't it?"

"No. I mean good psychiatric care for her."

"Phil, for God's sake, listen to her." The words gushed out of Wilma's mouth. She half-stumbled toward a chair, grasped the back with one hand, and stood, running her fingers over the fabric. "Matt's afraid of her. What are we going to do if she decides she doesn't want Matt around?" Her voice caught, and she began to sob before she collapsed into the chair and put her head against the cushions. "I'm afraid of her, Phil. I'm afraid of my own daughter."

"I'll call him myself as soon as I get back to the office," Virginia Donahue said. "It might make it easier for you if I explain the situation to him."

Phil lifted his head and gazed out the open door to the lawn. Matt was still sitting at the edge of the grass, intent on watching the bushes. He found his eyesight blurring. They couldn't lose Matt. He looked at Virginia and nodded his permission.

"What about the rest of it," he asked. "Am I still considered a child beater?"

"No. I'll have the charges dropped," she answered, and for a moment, Phil thought she paled. She pushed the strap of her bag over her shoulder before she met his eyes. "I try to do a good job, Mr. Thayer, but Cerise made it all sound so different." Her glance fell to the carpet. "I'm sorry," she said again. "I only hope none of it gets into the newspapers. You've been hurt enough."

"I wonder if it makes any difference," Phil replied. He felt frozen to the desk. The whole room felt cold. It wasn't the open door . . . it was his soul. His soul had crawled off and died somewhere. He couldn't find the energy to see the woman to the door. He clutched the edge of the desk and forced himself to move inch by inch around the piece of furniture, step after step, until he dropped into the swivel chair and sat holding his chin with one hand.

Was it his fault? Did Cerise get her ideas from him? Eddie Carter and Kathleen . . . A chill ran down his spine as he remembered Kathleen's body in his arms, so little and all covered with mud. Because of Cerise. Or was it because of him?

He lifted his head, looked at the card lying on the desk, and groped across the desk top. A beige card with brown letters. "Dr. Robert Benton. Goose Valley Home." Benton's logo in the corner was a brown, line-drawn goose.

Phil stared at the drawing of the goose. Like his mother's geese. Like the goslings Cerise had stomped to death. The look on her face. Defiant. Had it started then? He turned and looked at Wilma.

She was huddled into a ball in the chair. Her knees were drawn up to her chin, her arms wrapped around her legs as if she was trying to hold her body together.

He slipped out of the chair and bent in front of her. "Wilma?" He choked when he saw the puffy swelling around her eyes and the streaks of mascara running down from the corners.

"Don't tell me to pray, Phil." She kept her teeth clenched as she said the words. "Don't ever tell me to pray again."

He put his hands over hers, and the skin was cold against his. Even colder than before. "I can't. Can't pray either." Then he lowered his head against her hands and felt dampness. Tears. They were his own tears. Wilma stirred, pulled one hand away, and laid it on his head.

"Daddy." Matt's voice made him lift his head and turn. "Daddy, the deer hasn't come back. Do you think it's gone?"

Phil grabbed the edge of Wilma's skirt and rubbed at his eyes, then pushed himself to his feet and looked toward the door. Matt stood with both feet apart, waiting for an answer.

"Probably," he said and looked down at Wilma.

"Honey, we've got Matt. He needs us."

"What's wrong with Mommy?" Matt moved into the room and stopped, looking at Wilma with a puzzled frown. "Is she sick?"

"She'll be okay, son." Phil reached for the boy's hand and then swept him up into his arms instead, hugging him with the need for something solid and real in his grasp.

Cerise licked one finger and wiped it across the plate to pick up the last of the cracker crumbs. Miss Donahue had left a long time ago, and still no one had called her for dinner. Her peanut butter sandwich was gone, and so was the milk. How long did Daddy Phil expect her to stay in her room?

She pulled her legs underneath her and sat crosslegged, inspecting her fingernails. They let her wear makeup. Why couldn't she wear nail polish? She tilted her hand to one side and tried to imagine bright red nails. Long and decorated with one tiny star.

At least now they knew she could make things happen by praying, but why were they still treating her like a child? And Daddy Phil still hadn't said he was sorry.

They had come upstairs. She'd heard talking, and the phone rang lots of times. Maybe they'd forgotten her.

She opened the bedroom door and walked out into the aroma of spaghetti sauce and garlic. Garlic bread? But there were only three places set at the table . . . weren't they going to call her?

Matt came through the door carrying a bowl of salad, holding it dangerously by the very rim. He let it

311

thump onto the table and wiped his hands on his pant legs.

"Mommy's sick," he said. "Daddy cooked supper."

"Sick?" Cerise poked at the salad with one finger. It looked like nothing but a lot of lettuce. "What's wrong with her?"

"Don't know," Matt answered. His eyes squinched together at the corners. "Daddy carried her up to bed, but he said she'd be okay."

"Sit down, Cerise." Daddy Phil placed a platter of spaghetti on the table, motioned Matt into a chair, then sat down and reached for a fork.

"Aren't we going to say grace?" Matt asked.

"Not tonight."

Cerise grabbed a large piece of garlic bread and tore off a huge bite. Daddy Phil wasn't even looking at her. Mother must be awfully sick. He was still wearing his sweatshirt, and it was almost eight o'clock.

"Aren't you going to church?" she asked.

"No."

"But who's going to have services?" Mother must be really sick. Daddy Phil never missed going to church. She laid the bread down and rolled her fork around in the spaghetti, catching the loose strands in her mouth and slurping them in.

"There aren't going to be any more services," Daddy Phil said.

"But . . ." She wiped at her mouth and lowered the fork. "But the candle lighting. I won't get to light the candles any more?"

"No, and don't ask any more questions. It's final." He pushed his plate away and reached for a cup, frowned at the emptiness, and went to the kitchen.

Cerise swabbed up some spaghetti sauce with her bread and dumped more spaghetti on her plate. When he came back from the kitchen, she waited until he sat down and stared into the steaming cup of coffee. Mother must be going to die. Then maybe Daddy Phil would see how grownup she was.

"Don't worry, Daddy Phil," she said. "I'll pray for Mother."

The coffee cup came down on the table with a bang, slopping coffee over the side and making a dark brown spot across the orange placemat.

"No! Your mother will be fine. She doesn't need any of your prayers."

He flexed his fingers back and forth as if they hurt, then lowered his hand to the table and took a deep breath. "Finish your dinner, Cerise, and then go to bed."

"But it's too early. I never go to bed at eight."

"Then read in bed," he snapped. "Tonight I want this house quiet. No television." He bent forward and sipped at the coffee without even looking at her.

She shrugged and took a large swallow of milk, draining the last of the glass. "Okay. I'll say good night to Mother and go to bed."

"Leave your mother alone." Phil sagged against the table, and then his voice grew calmer. "She needs rest, Cerise. I don't want her bothered."

"It's okay, Daddy Phil." She smiled at him, but he still didn't look at her. She took her plate to the kitchen and grabbed a box of Triscuits before she went to her room.

Daddy Phil was still treating her like a baby. And he hadn't said he was sorry for hurting her. She listened to the sounds of the house. Mother's door opened and closed, then opened and closed again. Matt was saying good night. He let Matt go in and not her. Daddy Phil wasn't fair.

She crunched the last Triscuit and tossed the box on the floor. They were all stupid. No more church. No more lighting the candles and seeing all the people watch her. She could never wear the angel dress again.

She got up and took the angel dress from the hanger, pressing her cheek against the soft chiffon. Everyone said she looked like a real angel.

It took her a few minutes to get rid of her school clothes and slip into the dress. She stood and raised her arms, letting the folds of the sleeves fall into place.

The door to mother's room opened and closed again. Why did Daddy Phil keep going in there if he wanted Mother to be left alone?

She looked at her reflection in the mirror. Maybe she should have stayed at the shelter. Or gone to a foster home. Maybe someone else would see how special she was. How important it was to be able to pray and make things happen.

Pray. She would pray and make them all go away. Mother and Matt and even Daddy Phil. The candelabra was still downstairs. They hadn't taken it back to the church after the television filming. She would wear her angel dress, light the candles, and pray harder than ever.

She slipped out and tiptoed through the kitchen to the stairs. The fireplace matches were downstairs. She would pray until they all went away. If she prayed hard enough, God would take care of things.

314

The candles flared under the touch of the match, and she stood watching them flicker. Daddy Phil wasn't going to let her light the candles again. First he made her quit lighting the candles on school nights, and now he was going to quit having church. It was wrong to close the church.

She reached for one of the candles and stared into the flame. The glass door was slightly ajar. That's why the candles kept flickering. She moved across to the door, hesitated, and looked at the drapes. They were ugly. She told Mother they should be blue, but Mother picked out the ugly tan things.

She clamped her lips together and held the candle against the drapes. The fabric blackened. A wisp of smoke rose. The fabric smoldered, and then a tongue of flame flickered and caught. Fire opened a round hole which widened until the flames began to crawl up the folds of the drapes toward the ceiling. She smiled, dropped the candle on the floor, and backed across the room, watching the fire gulp up more and more of the ugly tan fabric.

When she reached the stairs, she backed up the steps and sat down at the top to watch the flames.

Now she would pray. She would close her eyes and pray hard. If she squeezed them really tight and prayed really hard, no one could make her stop. She would pray until God took care of things.

She laced her fingers together, pushed the palms of her hands together as tightly as she could, and prayed.

Somewhere above her, the whine of a smoke detector began, and still she kept her eyes shut.

Daddy Phil was yelling, but she wasn't going to stop praying. Hands caught her elbows. Someone was lifting

315

her, but she wasn't going to stop.

She squeezed her hands tighter and tighter, holding her breath when she felt her body dropped onto the grass. God would fix them. God always answered her prayers.

Phil held Wilma tightly against him and watched the beige car with the brown goose painted on the side pull away from the driveway. The doctor's hand waved in a consoling gesture, and the car eased over the curb and into the street.

Cerise sat in the backseat looking like a carved statue from an ancient cathedral. She still hadn't opened her eyes. The fire engines had come and gone, and still she kept her fingers twined together and her eyes squeezed shut.

He felt Wilma shiver and led her back inside where the odor of charred wood and smoke had taken possession.

"Phil," she said and looked up into his eyes, "what went wrong?"

He shook his head and hugged her closer to him. "It may have always been wrong. Maybe we should have seen it when she stomped the goslings."

"Your mother! Oh, God, Phil. What's she going to say when she hears you've closed the church?"

"Probably a lot, but it won't make any difference."

"Are you sure?"

He put one hand under her chin and lifted it toward him. "The decision's final." He watched Matt poking through the rubble scattered across the front yard and nodded to himself. "When a man gets to the point where he thinks of ending his life, it's time to change what's important."

Her eyes were wider than he'd ever seen them. She murmured, "Is that the reason for the gun?" but she didn't wait for a reply. Instead, she bent and began picking up leaves that had been trampled across the carpet.

"What are we going to do now?" she asked.

"I don't know," he admitted. "Except you're going to get your diploma." He turned at the sound of Matt's steps running across the porch.

"Maybe I'll try selling cars," he grinned. "I've had a lot of experience selling religion."

"Look, Daddy!" Matt held a white cat in his arms. "Can I keep it?"

The cat looked up and blinked. The eyes were a deep green, and the stare fixed steadily on Phil's face. For a second, Phil thought he was staring into Cerise's eyes.

"Please, Daddy. We haven't had a cat for a long time."

Phil met the cat's stare and shuddered. "Maybe, if we don't find the owner," he said, but he drew back when Matt held the cat up to him. It was just a cat, but damned if he was ever going to pet the thing.

WILLIAM W. JOHNSTONE
IS ZEBRA'S BESTSELLING
MASTER OF THE MACABRE!

THE UNINVITED (2258, $3.95)

The creeping, crawling horror had come to the small town of Lapeer Parish, Louisiana. Restless, unstoppable creatures, they descended upon the unsuspecting Southern community in droves, searching for grisly nourishment — in need of human flesh!

THE DEVIL'S CAT (2091, $3.95)

They were everywhere. Thousands and thousands of cats in every shape and size. Watching . . . and waiting. Becancour was ripe with evil. And Sam, Nydia, and Little Sam had to stand alone against the forces of darkness, facing the ultimate predator!

SWEET DREAMS (1553, $3.50)

Only ten-year-old Heather could see the eerie spectral glow that was enveloping the town — the lights of Hell itself! But no one had listened to her terrified screams. And now it was Heather's turn to feed the hungry, devouring spirit with her very soul!

THE NURSERY (2072, $3.95)

Sixty-six unborn fetuses, they had been taken from their human mothers by force. Through their veins flowed the blood of evil; in their hearts sounded Satan's song. Now they would live forever under the rule of darkness . . . and terror!

Available wherever paperbacks are sold, or order direct from the Publisher. Send cover price plus 50¢ per copy for mailing and handling to Zebra Books, Dept. 2841, 475 Park Avenue South, New York, N.Y. 10016. Residents of New York, New Jersey and Pennsylvania must include sales tax. DO NOT SEND CASH.

MASTERWORKS OF MYSTERY
BY MARY ROBERTS RINEHART!

THE YELLOW ROOM (2262, $3.50)

The somewhat charred corpse unceremoniously stored in the linen closet of Carol Spencer's Maine summer home set the plucky amateur sleuth on the trail of a killer. But each step closer to a solution led Carol closer to her own imminent demise!

THE CASE OF JENNIE BRICE (2193, $2.95)

The bloodstained rope, the broken knife—plus the disappearance of lovely Jennie Brice—were enough to convince Mrs. Pittman that murder had been committed in her boarding house. And if the police couldn't see what was in front of their noses, then the inquisitive landlady would just have to take matters into her own hands!

THE GREAT MISTAKE (2122, $3.50)

Patricia Abbott never planned to fall in love with wealthy Tony Wainwright, especially after she found out about the wife he'd never bothered to mention. But suddenly she was trapped in an extra-marital affair that was shadowed by unspoken fear and shrouded in cold, calculating murder!

THE RED LAMP (2017, $3.50)

The ghost of Uncle Horace was getting frisky—turning on lamps, putting in shadowy appearances in photographs. But the mysterious nightly slaughter of local sheep seemed to indicate that either Uncle Horace had developed a bizarre taste for lamb chops . . . or someone was manipulating appearances with a deadly sinister purpose!

A LIGHT IN THE WINDOW (1952, $3.50)

Ricky Wayne felt uncomfortable about moving in with her new husband's well-heeled family while he was overseas fighting the Germans. But she never imagined the depths of her in-laws' hatred—or the murderous lengths to which they would go to break up her marriage!

Available wherever paperbacks are sold, or order direct from the Publisher. Send cover price plus 50¢ per copy for mailing and handling to Zebra Books, Dept. 2841, 475 Park Avenue South, New York, N.Y. 10016. Residents of New York, New Jersey and Pennsylvania must include sales tax. DO NOT SEND CASH.